NDING CASEY

FINDING CASEY

Jo-Ann Mapson

BLOOMSBURY

LONDON • NEW DELHI • NEW YORK • SYDNEY

First published in Great Britain 2012

Copyright © 2012 by Jo-Ann Mapson

The moral right of the author has been asserted

Bloomsbury Publishing, London, New Delhi, New York and Sydney

50 Bedford Square, London WC1B 3DP

A CIP catalogue record for this book is available from the British Library

ISBN 978 1 4088 2926 4
10 9 8 7 6 5 4 3 2 1

Typeset by Westchester Book Group

Printed and bound by CPI Group (UK) Ltd., Croydon CR0 4YY

www.bloomsbury.com/jo-annmapson

To Sheryl Ann Simpson,
best friend ever

There are only two ways to live your life.
One is as though nothing is a miracle.
The other is as though everything is a miracle.
—ALBERT EINSTEIN

Chapter 1

SANTA FE, NOVEMBER 2005

EVERY HOUSE HAS a story to tell and, over time, will make whoever lives there a character. What happens inside the walls eventually finds its way into the plaster, hardening into the marrow of time. Paint it, remodel it, or set it on fire, but no one can take away its history. At night when the house creaks, tell yourself that's "settling." When the wind blows hard, and the house shudders like an earthquake, say, "Foundations shift." It all comes down to earth and straw, and in time of drought or deluge, a dwelling will crumble. With it go a few stories.

In 1690, the space this realtor woman is calling "the master bedroom" was a field where Indians grew corn. A century later, the "great room" was a stable for horses. One night, a Spaniard drank too much mezcal, stole one of those horses, and rode it up the dirt road that is now paved and lined with art galleries. It is said that mezcal came about when a bolt of lightning struck a maguey plant, and as such is called "the nectar of the gods." It's also called *aguadiente*, firewater, and responsible for many a deed that seemed brave at the time and stupid the next morning.

The horse thief galloped that gelding up the steps into what is now called El Farol, the bar the *New York Times* now rates as one of the best in the world. The oldest bar in Santa Fe, they call it, and he demanded more drink.

They know nothing of age.

I watch this woman with the realtor by her side, going from room to room, heedless of the mouse that scurries across the kitchen floor into the cabinet where its babies wait. I pop open a cabinet, but do they notice? They see what they want to see, a room to fill with material treasures, loved ones, and ample food. They don't see a nursery for the baby that will surprise them, or expect the grief that arrives over time, or sometimes in a single moment. They smell piñon fires in the kiva fireplace, not the burning of the bird's nest in its flue. Underneath the foundation sherds of bone china tell the story of my life, and so many others, but will likely remain untouched.

Just look at her face. She's imagining new glass in the windows will make everything clear, and that homemade curtains will shut out the unpleasant. A silk pillow for her head, new dishes on a shelf, touches that change things just enough to make it hers. Already she's in love, and what I know of love is this: It can fill a house, and change it into a home. A home can make people happy, for a while. But love has its betrayal and misunderstandings and eventual ends, and they're just as potent.

This house has been sold over and over again, yet never truly owned by anyone but me. People come and go, parting with massive amounts of money for their name on a paper deed. In no time they are on the move again, wanting more, or different, enough never being enough, or perhaps wanting less, having bitten off more than they can chew.

Ah, well. Who knows what might happen when they move in?

Outside, the wintry wind blusters through the cottonwood trees. Beneath the clay soil the forsythia is hard at work, because in a few months' time, its nature is to bloom a furious yellow, promising spring. The wisteria that came all the way from China hangs on to the trellis, hoping for sun and nitrogen and its roots to be tenderly attended. Last spring the hollyhocks flourished, and the albino hummingbird gorged herself on red flowers, raising twins, also white.

The truth is, there is no time here. There is only this moment, which becomes history the second it passes, and leads to the next moment, which is both a miracle and a curse, when you're a ghost.

Glory Vigil knew that she had fallen in love with the crumbling hundred-year-old Pueblo-style adobe on a tree-lined street across from the Santa Fe River the moment she laid eyes on it. The picture window was cracked. A dead peach tree stood in the courtyard like a forgotten scarecrow. What little yard that wasn't covered by snow needed attention.

When Glory lost her husband Dan after twenty years of marriage, she thought life was over for her, especially in the love department. She was too busy paying the bills to think about the future. Yet here she was now, married to Joseph Vigil, mother to their adopted daughter, Juniper, and moved from her native California to New Mexico. After three months at Joseph's parents' farm, not to mention ten pounds courtesy of Mama Vigil's meals, they needed their own place. The moment Jenny the realtor turned the key into the *clavos*-studded mesquite door of 103 Colibri Road, she began to use words like *charming* and *quaint* and *near-historical*. Code, Glory knew, for a major fixer-upper. Yet the viga ceilings and arched doorways leading from room to room called to her.

"Who used to live here?" she asked the realtor, whose family had lived in Santa Fe for twelve generations.

"It's been a rental for years. The current owners live in L.A. They're no longer interested in being landlords."

Glory ran her hand across a plaster wall and watched flakes rain down.

"Wiggle room on the asking price," Jenny said, "unless you think it's too much. I have two other houses to show you."

Glory thought of Joseph's bad back. Her husband was a proud Spanish-Indian man and liked repairing things, even though he couldn't really manage alone. "I'd like to see the rest of it."

The first closet she opened was painted a coral pink and turned into a library. Wooden shelves were just wide enough for some old Donald Hamilton paperbacks, their lurid covers chipped and coming loose from the binding. Cowboys and outlaws and Cold War spies—a way of life long gone and never as romantic as portrayed, but people kept reading them. The first bedroom was on the small side, big enough for a twin bed, though a little stuffy. Jenny cranked open the window and a faint, flowery scent Glory couldn't name drifted in.

It was a soggy November day, with temperatures in the thirties, but the thick adobe walls kept the interior at a comfortable seventy degrees. In the second bedroom, not as large as the first, Glory felt a chill and pulled her scarf up her neck.

"North facing," Jenny the realtor explained, pointing out the kiva fireplace, assuring her that winter nights would be cozy with a fire burning.

"My daughter might like this."

"Or it would make a good office."

The hall bathroom was big enough for a claw-foot tub, but the bathroom attached to the master bedroom was tiny, with a narrow shower stall. The chipped sink was rust stained and the faucet was dripping. How much time did a person spend in a bathroom, really? Glory pictured the king-sized bed facing the old window, leaving plenty of room for a dresser, reading chair, and dog beds. The kitchen was so old it reminded Glory of the pink metal toy stove she and her sister Halle had played with as children. "This might be a deal breaker," Glory said. "My husband loves to cook, and he makes quite a mess while he does it. I don't think this kitchen is big enough for all his copper pots."

Jenny the realtor smiled. "Knock out this non-load-bearing wall and you can fit state-of-the-art appliances in here." Behind her, the cupboard door popped open, seemingly all on its own.

"What caused that?" Glory asked.

Jenny laughed and pushed it closed. "Any house this old has a ghost or two," she joked. When Glory turned the kitchen faucet on and then off, the plumbing let out a creaky groan. Jenny said, "Probably just a matter of replacing a washer." She opened the French door that led outside onto the portal, Spanish for patio. "I saved the best for last. What do you think?"

Glory thought she had stepped back in time to an era when water was raised from a well by a bucket. Above her, wisteria vines wove so thickly through the vigas that they made a roof. Here and there a dried blue or purple plume remained, giving off a faint scent of rain-drenched violets, even in winter. She recognized the smell from the first bedroom's window and imagined the place in summer, when everything was in bloom. The portal's supporting posts were hand-carved in a spiral design. Corbels blended seamlessly into the lattice roof. Against the wall of the house was an authentic outdoor Spanish kitchen, with open shelves for storing cooking pots and hooks from which to hang spoons, ladles, and whisks. There was a wood-fired stove with iron doors that looked hand-forged. Next to the stove was a sink chiseled out of a single piece of granite that probably weighed a thousand pounds. Its rough edges had rounded with use over time.

Glory imagined an old woman standing there, adding well water to masa, patting out tortillas in short order. But the part of the kitchen Joseph would fall in love with was the beehive oven. The exterior had been covered with mosaic tiles of gold, blue, and red, making it look Moorish. Since they'd married, Joseph had begun writing a cookbook, re-creating his *madre's* recipes so that Glory and Juniper could learn authentic New Mexican cuisine. He would fall in love with this oven just the way she'd fallen in love with the house. Glory happily shivered in the cold. "You were right, Jenny," she said. "This is the one."

Jenny smiled. Since she represented both buyer and seller, she would make a killer commission on 103 Colibri Road, and thank goodness, because whether anyone else noticed or not, realtors could see that the bottom was beginning to fall out of the market. Already houses she might have sold in a weekend were sitting on the market for six to eight months.

"By law I'm required to point out that the roof will need replacing within the next five years. The master-bath toilet runs, and wasting water in Santa Fe is practically a felony. The fridge and the two-burner stove aren't Energy Star rated. They'll run you a thousand or so each to replace."

All her life Glory had worried about money. When she lived in California, she'd sold eggs to the cooperative market, baked cakes to sell, and catered weddings; she'd even worked at Target for minimum wage and maximum sore feet. When she and Joseph decided to marry, she'd leased her California ranch, Solomon's Oak, to Gary Smith, one of her former foster sons, on a lease-to-buy option. Though she'd formally adopted Juniper, Glory had no children to inherit the property, and Juniper had no plans to farm. It needed a family. When Gary converted the lease to a sale, it gave her the money to put down on the Santa Fe house, so it would belong to both Joseph and her equally, and that was important to her. And she had fallen as madly in love with 103 Colibri Road as she had with her new husband. But longtime habits are hard to break, so her tendency to justify big purchases kicked in.

The house was a short walk from the historic Plaza, which hosted free concerts, Spanish and Indian Market, and museums she never grew tired of visiting.

There was room enough for Juniper, who was starting college, to come home on weekends, and there was a guest room for her mother to visit.

The run-down state of the house made it affordable. Well, almost affordable. She'd have to get a job, but she liked working.

"Is that a garage?" Glory said, pointing to yet another crumbling structure at the end of the garden.

"*Por supuesto*," Jenny said—of course—"but as is common with Santa Fe homes it's actually a carport. There's also a casita, a guesthouse. Follow me."

They made their way through the snowy yard on no discernable path. Skeletons of hollyhocks rattled their seedpods in the wind. Yellow-headed rabbit brush and sage lay dormant under snow, waiting for the sun to bring them back to life. She'd have to employ one of her father-in-law's goats to mow down the weeds, but beneath the icy crust, she just knew there was a garden waiting. She pictured rows of vegetables. Window boxes cascading with flowers she was still learning the names of. There was room for a few chickens. She could put in three dog kennels, and someday resume rescuing and rehabilitating death-row dogs as she had in California. Halfway across the yard they brushed snow away from a shapeless mass that turned out to be a fountain, clogged with leaves and muck. Now that Glory no longer lived near an ocean, any running water would be a comfort, plus it would attract birds. She particularly loved New Mexico's array of hummingbirds, and planned to hang several feeders.

"Let me call my husband," Glory said, taking her cell phone out of her handbag. "Then we can go back to your office to write up the offer."

Jenny Montoya smiled and reached into her shoulder tote. "No need. I brought the contract with me."

That very afternoon, Jenny the realtor, who was one of Joseph's cousins' wives' in-laws, presented the offer to the out-of-town sellers by fax and within an hour they accepted the offer without a single concession. There were Vigils in mortgage, lending, banking, and home inspection, and they closed escrow in nine short days. Jenny had done everything correctly, signed and filed and faxed and notarized, performed her "duty to disclose" by listing the defects in the house. Call it splitting hairs if you like, but she *had* mentioned the ghost.

Just not any details about the ghost.

Chapter 2

INDIAN MARKET, SUMMER 2008

G LORY AND JUNIPER had waited until Sunday to visit the two-day art event because on the last day prices were always more flexible. She'd heard longtime Santa Feans refer to it as "Indian Mark-up," but anyone who worked on their art all year and hoped to sell it to afford another year of making art had Glory's respect and support. She had been hoping to find the perfect micaceous bean pot for her husband so he could cook the Santa Maria pinquito beans her friend Lorna had sent them from Jolon. Because today was Glory's birthday, Joseph was making her a fancy dinner. There would be Vigil relatives everywhere laden with cakes, side dishes, and chiles her in-laws grew on their farm in Hatch. Birthdays were nice, but *tomorrow* was the day Glory was looking forward to. It was Glory and Joseph's third wedding anniversary, the year you were supposed to give leather (traditional) or glass (modern) to your beloved. Glory had bought Joseph a braided leather key chain with a silver concho shaped like the sun, surrounded by rays. Tradition said you were supposed to be married eight years to give pottery, but what could possibly happen if she gave him pottery five years early?

"You hungry?" Glory asked Juniper as they completed the

first lap of Spanish Market, having found no candidates for the micaceous pot.

"A little. I never had breakfast."

"Why?"

Juniper smiled. "I wanted to get my run in before it got too hot."

"That's no excuse for skipping meals. Should we go to the Plaza Bakery?"

"Are you kidding? Look how crowded it is. Let's try Pasqual's. I love their food and they have that community table so we shouldn't have to wait."

"Good idea." Glory was thinking of ordering a side dish, a quick bite to tide her over until dinner because her stomach was a little upset. She kept a careful watch on Juniper, who'd entered college at age sixteen due to acing entrance exams and Joseph's pull at the university. Stress was part of college, but was Juniper ready for it? Glory worried about eating disorders. The books said overexercising was one of the symptoms, and skipping meals, well, that was a no-brainer. Outside the restaurant, a line of hungry people snaked around the corner of Water Street and Don Gaspar. Glory excuse-me'd her way to the counter. "Is there any room at the community table? We just want a quick bite."

The waitperson pointed. "There are two spots you can have right now. Follow me."

When it came to sitting at the community table, your fellow diners might be strangers when you sat down, but not by the time you pushed your chair out to go. Glory had lived in Santa Fe long enough to resist making snap judgments about anyone. That crusty old cowpoke in the scuffed boots sitting next to you might own three hotels. The woman in the Chanel sunglasses and cowboy hat pulled low could be a movie star, because New Mexico catered to the industry for mutual benefit. The middle-aged balding guy scribbling notes on his napkin might be writing the next Pulitzer Prize–winning novel, because in this town you couldn't help but run into a writer, artist, or both. UPS had once accidentally delivered them a package addressed to George R. R. Martin, the famous science-fiction fantasy writer. Juniper squealed when she got to take it to his house, even though it turned out he wasn't home at the time. For a solid week the only words out of her mouth were: *How many people can say they live down the street from George R. R. Martin?* Until Joseph pointed out that their house was worth a quarter of what his was, Juniper got a lot of mileage out of being neighbors. "You think he's the only writer that ever lived in Santa Fe?" Joseph said. "Google that topic, and come back and tell me what you find."

"P. L. Travers, Donald Hamilton, D. H. Lawrence, Cormac McCarthy, Tony Hillerman, Judi Hendricks, Rudy Anaya, Gary Paulsen, John Nichols, Sharman Apt Russell, William deBuys, Lynn Stegner, Roger Zelazny . . ."

"Now you get the idea," Joseph said. "I'd tell you to search artists but you'd die at the keyboard of old age."

That was life in the oldest state capital in the nation. New Mexico had history and infamy in every corner, from train robbers to Spanish conquistadors to aliens. Visitors traveled from around the world to mix with the Wild West, explore the site of religious wars and the fabled Cities of Gold, petroglyphs, adobe architecture, and Georgia O'Keeffe—there was drama aplenty to fuel great books, breathtaking landscapes for film backgrounds, and here, ethnicity had clout. A twelfth-generation Santa Fean trumped the wealthiest retiree. Tourism was key to the economy, but also drove up housing prices. Longtime families who had occupied houses on Acequia Madre and Canyon Road now lived in Pojoaque, Española, Rio Rancho, or even farther out. Galleries were filled with art the majority of people could never afford, but relied on the few who could. Every Indian Market there would be a newspaper story about some art dealer waiting in line all night to buy the grand-prize-winning pot or straw crucifix or turquoise nugget nestled in sterling silver. Meanwhile, grimy musicians sang in the Plaza with their guitar cases gaping open for spare change. Indians sat in the shade of the Palace of the Governors with handcrafted jewelry spread out on black cloth as they had for hundreds of years. For some it was an easy place to live, but to Glory it was a little lonely, even though she quickly got to know her multitudes of cousins and in-laws that came along with her marriage. After four years in Santa Fe, she could almost remember their names. She called her sister in California twice a week, and exchanged e-mail with Lorna Candelaria, who kept her up to speed on the doings in Jolon, California.

Glory studied the menu. What tasted good when it was ninety degrees in the shade? A side of flour tortillas dripping with butter? Flan? A chile relleno did not appeal to her today. "Could I have the cheese omelet, hold the tomatoes and onions, please?" Glory asked their server, a lanky Latino guy who looked harried. He nodded. "How about you, Juniper?"

"I'm not all that hungry. I'll just have a Diet Coke."

"Blue Sky okay? We don't carry Coke products," the waiter said.

"Hold on," Glory interrupted. "You skipped breakfast to run and you were hungry ten minutes ago. Order something. We can take the leftovers home to your dad."

"We make half portions of everything," the waiter said, tapping his fingers against his order pad.

"Fine," Juniper huffed. "I'll have half a BLT, half a side of cole slaw, and a whole iced tea. You guys should start carrying Coke. Blue Sky soda tastes like vitamins."

Glory smiled at her adopted daughter's sass.

"*Bueno*," the waiter said. "Be about fifteen minutes. We're really slammed today."

When weren't they? If Glory had a choice for dinner out, Pasqual's was where she wanted to go. Whether you were sitting at a side table in candlelight, or in the bright sunshine with colorful Mexican *papel picado* banners hanging like laundry across the lofty ceiling, she loved this place. Maybe it wasn't always a good place to have a quiet talk, but once the food arrived, who cared? Lucky for the people lined up around the corner, a couple of shops had awnings, offering shade. Glory and Juniper had filled the last two seats at the community table. To her left a couple of seniors were going on about their recent weekend in Pagosa Springs. In the talkative air around her, Glory heard Spanish, German, and Japanese. She was getting better at Spanish, but the other two languages were beyond her reach.

Juniper was leaning on her hands, elbows on the table, a vacant expression on her face. "Hey," Glory said. "Are you tired of Indian Market? We can go home if you want."

"No," Juniper said. "You still have to find Daddy Joe's pot, and I lost one of my porcupine-quill beaded earrings. I want to see if I can find another just like it."

"I bet you can. Anything bothering you?"

"Not really. Just thinking about, you know, her," Juniper said.

"Tell me."

"When we were little kids, Casey always wanted to be the

Indian, never the cowboy. She would have loved Indian Market. She would have gone both days, even if it was a hundred and ten degrees out."

When Glory and Joe formally adopted Juniper, she had been convinced that moving out of state and changing her name would release her from the grief of Casey's disappearance. She thrived in the anonymity that came with their move from California, where her tragic family history would always define her as "the sister of Casey McGuire, the girl who never came home." That was one of the reasons she'd asked to take both Glory and Joseph's last names when they adopted her. "If I drop Tree"—her middle name—"and McGuire"—her father's surname—"I can start over brand-new," she said the day that the papers were filed. Glory and Joseph had looked at each other knowingly, but they agreed, it was her decision.

Directly across the table from Juniper sat the prototype Santa Fe dude, rail-skinny, craggy face, Levi's worn smooth over many launderings, leather vest with clay pipestone beads, a silver bracelet crawling with turquoise, and long hair tied back in a ponytail. He had taken off his cowboy hat, leaving that telltale dent of longtime wear. His face was lined from the sun, and he could have been anywhere from forty to sixty. He was staring at Juniper with a glint in his eye that Glory did not like.

"Something I can help you with?" she asked loudly.

He chuckled at her protectiveness. "Sorry, ma'am. I didn't mean to stare. I noticed the young lady's tattoo. A mountain bluebird, right? My favorite bird. That's all."

Immediately Juniper covered it with her hand and looked down at her napkin and silverware. Glory kept her gaze on the man, but he did not back down. "Thank you for the compliment," she said in a voice that conveyed exactly the opposite.

Like the porcupine, the mother in Glory sent the man a warning: Come any closer, and you'll have a mouthful of quills instead of that relleno. Joseph's grandmother, Penelope Manygoats, who had died years before Glory met Joseph, had told her grandson a story for every creature on the planet. The mountain bluebird was an "angry bird that thinks it's a hawk," but the porcupine was an "ingenious survivor." One day, the story went, Porcupine climbed a hawthorn tree to escape Bear, and discovered that the thorns on the tree discouraged the bear's pursuit. Porcupine called out to the Creator, who spread white clay on his back and attached the wonderful thorns. The thorns evolved to microscopically barbed quills, and Bear never bothered Porcupine again.

"I haven't seen you around here before," Glory said to the still staring man. "Are you local?" For such a spread-out town, Santa Fe had a small-town atmosphere. Eventually you'd run into someone with a familiar face at Trader Joe's or La Choza. You recognized the regulars, but this man was not one of them.

He smiled. "Not far. El Guique."

"That's right next to the Ohkay Owingeh Pueblo," Juniper said. "The Rio Grande runs through it, right?"

"Yes, it does," he said. "My fourteen-acre property has three hundred feet of riverfront."

That's a valuable piece of land, Glory thought. Another person you'd never guess as wealthy. "So you're here for Indian Market, collecting, I take it?" she asked, wishing Juniper had not entered into the conversation.

"Actually, ma'am, I'm here to show."

Ma'am. As if he thought that would make up for ogling a teenager? If he were the least bit Indian, she would eat his hat. "Oh. What tribe are you?"

"Cherokee."

They always said Cherokee. If he had any Indian blood in him, it had to be a microscopic drop. "What kind of artwork do you do?" she asked.

"A little pottery."

"Really? Well, we don't want to keep you from losing any sales," Glory said as their plates arrived. "You'd better hurry so you can get back to your booth. Best of luck."

Glory had fired a few warning quills; the man put his cowboy hat back on, pulling it down on his brow. He ate quickly, tossed money on the table, and walked away without pushing his chair back in. Glory felt a tinge of annoyance at his lack of manners, but in no time his place was wiped clean and a new diner sat down. The new fellow took out a Tony Hillerman paperback and started reading.

"How's your sandwich?" she asked Juniper.

"Good, but nowhere near as good as Dad's when he broils the bacon with brown sugar."

Such sweets on a hot day sounded nauseating to Glory, but she said, "Daddy Joe is our own top chef, isn't he?"

Juniper sipped at her iced tea. "Thank goodness for that. Otherwise we'd still be eating hot dogs and grilled cheese sandwiches."

Glory laughed. "Hey, don't knock my culinary skills. I can still make a better cake than he can."

"Pirate ship wedding cake, for sure," Juniper said, referring to the day they'd met, Juniper a foster child looking for somewhere safe to spend Thanksgiving, and Glory, newly widowed, hosting a pirate-themed wedding on her ranch to pay the bills. "Think you'll ever make another one?"

"For your wedding, if you want."

And then Juniper's lower lip was suddenly trembling. "She'll never have a wedding or a cake." Tears puddled in her eyes and she tried to blink them away.

"Oh, honey," she said. "I'm sorry I said that."

Juniper swiped at her eyes. "It's all right."

Between the creepy man and Juniper's sorrow, Glory's omelet wasn't sitting right in her stomach. "I'm full," she said, setting her fork down. She dug in her purse for money to pay the bill. "I need to use the ladies' room. Meet me outside, okay?"

"Sure, Mom. Thanks for lunch."

Mom—the word still felt monumental to her—never in her life would she have expected to be called that, and whenever Juniper said it, it was like hearing it for the first time. She smoothed back Juniper's hair and kissed her forehead. "Finish your sandwich and I'll meet you outside."

As Glory headed to the bathroom, she thought about how some memories could never be filed away. Her first husband, Dan, had been gone nearly six years now, but she could call his face to mind instantly. He would always hold the deed to half her heart.

Later, as they were about to traverse the last aisle of the market, her cell phone rang. Glory glanced at it and smiled. It was Joseph calling. "What's up?" she said when she answered.

"I have bad news."

"Oh, no. What happened?"

"It's Dolores. She fiddled with the oven temperature and your cake is ruined."

Dolores was the name Juniper had assigned to what she called the "house ghost"; what Glory suspected was the groaning of elderly plumbing on its last legs. "A likely excuse," Glory said. "Just admit that even you, the great chef, have occasional culinary mishaps. Plus you'll always be second to me in the baking department."

He laughed. "It's my life ambition to catch up. Hey, happy birthday to the most beautiful woman in Santa Fe."

She laughed. "You said that this morning."

"I was worried you might have forgotten."

"As if I ever could forget you. We're almost done here. Where are you?"

"Oh, that's top-secret information. I need to talk to my party-planner partner in crime."

She handed the phone over to Juniper and stepped away to give them privacy. Throngs of people attended Indian Market. Glory never tired of the Plaza. The tall cottonwood trees had witnessed so much history, she wished they could talk. For hundreds of years people had been gathering here to celebrate one thing or protest another. On days like today it truly was the heart of the city, pulsating with music, overflowing with Native art, blessed with sunshine. The population was made up of so many different ethnicities that the first thing Glory did when they moved here was buy a history book on the state and spend a month reading it. When she learned that New Mexico was the only officially bilingual state in the Union, she told Joseph, "Governor Schwarzenegger should try this in California."

A strolling all-girl mariachi band came down San Francisco Street from the direction of the cathedral. People stepped aside to let them pass, taking cell-phone pictures and videos. They were young girls, maybe fourteen years old, dressed in turquoise blouses and black skirts. Glory applauded as they passed. How could a person play a violin and walk at the same time?

Juniper was still talking to her dad. Seeing the girls in fancy dress reminded Glory of the celebration following Juniper's formal adoption. "Just a small gathering," Joseph had said, and then invited over a hundred guests. Under duress, Juniper agreed to wear the dress Joseph's mother made for her. It was snow white, three tiers of lace, and something Juniper could have worn to her own wedding, except for the fact that Joseph wasn't going to allow Juniper to date until she was oh, say, seventy-five or so.

After the call, Juniper and Glory walked down Washington Street. By now it was beginning to feel like overload—all these booths, jewelry, religious paintings, folk art, sculpture, pierced tinwork. Her eyes blurred from so much beauty. To top it off, she could tell she'd had too much sun because she felt a little faint. How hard could it be to find a decent cooking pot that didn't cost an arm and a leg?

She'd been careful not to admire her mother-in-law's clay pot too much, because if she did, the woman would insist she take it. Even though it had been in her family forever, she'd give it to Glory just like that, she was so thrilled Joseph had found his soul mate. Glory wanted a pot of their own, new, so that Joseph could cook without the ghosts of the cooks who came before him.

While Juniper looked through the beaded earrings, Glory spotted a micaceous pot big enough to roast a turkey inside. It was the color of adobe, with smoky black patches reflecting the sun, revealing a bronze shimmer. It was fitted with a no-nonsense lid and a finger-sized loop on top, but it was so beautifully crafted it could sit on a shelf. "How much are you asking?" she said to the man standing behind the table filled with similar pots.

"Six hundred, but if you have cash I could go five-seventy-five."

"It's lovely, thanks, but out of my price range," Glory said, returning it.

"Mom," Juniper said as they moved on, "that sounded like a good deal to me. How much do you want to spend?"

"No more than three hundred."

"Seriously? They charge fifty dollars an inch. You couldn't cook an egg inside a pot that small."

"And you know this how?"

"Hello? Anthropology major here. Aced art history last quarter, which covered contemporary Native American Indian pottery."

"I want to keep looking," Glory said, and soon they were down to the last half block of booths on Washington Street. The sun beat down on her head mercilessly the way it did just before the temperature was about to break. Her lunch was definitely not sitting right.

"Look!" Juniper said, holding up a black card with porcupine-quill beaded earrings attached. "I found them!"

"I knew you would," Glory said. "Wish I could say the same for my pot."

Juniper paid for her earrings, tucked them into her purse, and then they were in front of another booth featuring micaceous pots. It was a bad location, out in the sun, farthest from the Plaza, and she imagined the foot traffic was a lot less because of the heat. The pots for sale were set directly on an unadorned tabletop, no bright cloth beneath, no effort whatsoever to make things look nice. A girl about twenty-five with long dark hair stood behind the pots, smoking a cigarette. She kept shifting the pots this way and that, and her movements made Glory wonder if the girl was high on something. "What are your prices?" she asked.

"Two-fifty to four hundred. Buy two and I can make you an even better deal."

Juniper picked up a tall pot that flared outward from the bottom up to an opening large enough to fit a whole chicken through. Micaceous clay was perfect for slow cooking. After hours on the stovetop, meat fell off the bone and ended up a tender, mouthwatering stew to warm your stomach on winter nights when the temperature dropped below thirty. "I like this one," Juniper said.

Glory picked it up and felt the weight. Nice, not too heavy, but not so light she'd worry about breakage. "How much is this one?"

The girl looked down to her left for a second, the way liars and car salesmen do, and Glory nearly set it down. "Three-fifty cash."

"I'll give you three hundred," Juniper said, and Glory was momentarily flustered.

"Now listen, it was my plan to—"

"Mom, you have to let me do this," Juniper interrupted. "I saved a ton of money from my summer job, Grandma Smith gave me a savings bond, and Aunt Halle and Uncle Bart send me a check every month like I'm starving in a third-world country. You and Daddy Joe pay for tuition, the dorm, and my car insurance, I think the least I can do is buy you a nice anniversary present."

The girl was already wrapping the pot in newspaper.

"Thank you," Glory said, feeling guilty that maybe she wasn't paying enough.

The girl took Juniper's money and opened an old-fashioned cash box. She bent down to put the extra newspaper away.

"Come on," Juniper said. "I see two spots and the band is about to start."

"Okay, I'm coming," Glory said, and just as she turned to walk away, a movement in the shadows behind the girl caught her attention. Glory saw that it was the man from the restaurant. For a moment, it felt as if time had bumped out of rhythm, skipped a few beats, and Glory was overcome with the desire to rescind the sale, but Juniper held the bag and was dragging her to the cement bench that encircled the spire sculpture in the center of the Plaza. The bench was warm from the sun and felt comforting on her bones. There was enough shade from the trees to feel relief from the heat. Onstage in front of them the band broke into "El Porompompero," one of the most famous gypsy love songs ever written.

"What did your dad want?" Glory said when there was a break in the music.

"Nice try," Juniper answered. "You're not getting the surprise out of me. You'll find out tonight. By the way, in addition to your request for tri-tip, Daddy Joe's making me a great big vat of menudo to take back to school."

Glory groaned. Tripe soup. Joseph and Juniper couldn't get enough of it. The name alone was bad enough. Two parts cow's stomach, it was the color of the khaki slacks she'd worn when she worked at Target. The dish took all day to simmer in chicken broth, filling the house with the most awful smell, and filmy grease that coated the surface had to be skimmed away from time to time. "Please stop talking about it."

"Why?"

"I don't feel well. I wonder if the eggs in my omelet were bad."

"Mom?" Juniper said, inching closer, and then Glory smelled

her daughter's bubble-gum perfume. Combined with the goat fajitas from a nearby vendor cart and the baked-sugar smell of kettle corn, just the thought of menudo was too much. She got up, raced to the nearest trash can, and in one long heave, lost her lunch. She rinsed her mouth with the bottle of water she carried everywhere and chewed some gum to get rid of the taste. Juniper appeared and put her hand on her mother's back.

"Oh, my gosh, do you think you have food poisoning?" Juniper said.

The way only a woman's mind can work, Glory began adding up clues. The intermittent nausea, dizziness that came out of nowhere, and a mental picture of the calendar that hung inside the pantry door. When was the last time she had her period? April? May? I certainly hope it's food poisoning, she thought, because what kind of birthday present is turning forty-one only to discover you're pregnant?

Chapter 3

OCTOBER 2008

THE CLAY POT simmered on the stove burner, the scent filling the kitchen and drifting out into the great room. If pressed to name the ingredients, Glory would have said barnyard animals, vinegar, and a thousand heads of garlic. She had banned menudo entirely from the house during her first trimester of pregnancy. She wouldn't even let Joseph cook it outdoors. While the nausea had lifted in her fourth month, just as the obstetrician had promised, certain smells, like tripe, made her want to gag. Who in their right mind found a cow's stomach appetizing? Not just Joseph, but also Juniper, eighteen years old and a junior at UNM Albuquerque.

Glory, preoccupied with nausea and the overwhelming fact that in a few months she'd have a baby, hadn't thought of the micaceous pot in months. All summer Juniper worked at Jackalope, the Spanish mercado on Cerrillos, with outbuildings selling furniture, rugs, pottery, and jewelry, and a prairie dog habitat at its center. There tourists could watch the endangered squirrel cousins dig their burrows, raise their babies, and tip their heads back, yipping to each other like miniature coyotes.

Glory bent to open a kitchen window. "It smells like you're boiling socks in here."

"Sorry." Joseph turned down the burner and gave her a kiss. "Ready for the sonogram?"

Glory smiled. "Are you kidding? I've been chained to the bathroom for months. I'm more than ready."

Joseph covered the pot with its braided clay handle lid. He plucked his keys from the hanging rack and hollered to Juniper, who was studying in her room. "Back in an hour, arbolita," he called, his pet name for her in Spanish, little tree.

"Find out what sex it is!" came back from her room.

Glory had agreed to the amniocentesis for health reasons, but she clung to wanting to be surprised about the baby's sex. She felt in awe of one of the last few mysteries in pregnancy. Of course, such thinking was silly, because everything about this pregnancy was already a surprise—she'd never thought it would happen to her, especially at forty-one. It was a good lesson for Juniper. See what happens when you're careless with birth control? Glory had told her. She wasn't convinced Juniper was sexually active, but whenever the topic came up, they talked about birth control and safe sex. Juniper had only recently acquired her first real boyfriend.

"*Andalé*," Joseph said, and opened the door off the kitchen that led through the garden to their carport. He'd put in a flagstone path the first summer they moved in. Though they'd been in this house for nearly three years, it seemed to be in a constant state of renovation, thanks to Joseph's many relatives in the building trade. His extended family was like a small city, including fifth cousins, their in-laws, and friends of friends. The Vigil family tree was more like a vine that twisted and

turned through New Mexico's complicated history. When it
came to making the house their home, all Glory really cared
about was that the bathrooms worked and that the kitchen was
finally finished. The six-burner Blue Star gas stove they splurged
on allowed Joseph to cook every night. He was now 180 pages
into *Vigilia Libro de Cocina Familiar, The Vigil Family Cookbook*,
and every week he tried out a different recipe. Another woman
might have felt threatened by a man taking over her kitchen,
but it was fine with Glory. Otherwise, he and Juniper might
have starved to death the last few months, when all she could
stomach was 7-Up and saltines.

In the garden off the portal, her favorite place, summer had
hung on tight through fall. The wisteria was in the throes of its
final bloom before winter set in. An army of yellow columbines
had rampaged through the flowerbed, giving it the random
look of a meadow. The restored fountain spilled clear water
down three tiers. A cinnamon colored rufous hummingbird
zoomed by a black-chinned hummingbird battling for territory
of the feeders she had to fill several times a day. This summer
an albino hummer had appeared, visiting the feeders every
afternoon, and Glory tried in vain to get a picture of it. As she
stopped to watch the antics, she said, "Listen to you two. There's
enough to go around, so learn to share."

The moment she said the words they struck her oddly, as if
somehow they were more important than the simple message she
intended, and she hesitated there for a moment, wondering why.
Pregnancy had fundamentally changed her, and while she was
lying there ill all those months, she'd had time to think about
subjects she'd never before given a moment's consideration. She'd
ultimately come to the conclusion that she'd never been happier
in her life, and that having a baby was the best surprise ever.

"Glory!" Joseph called. He was holding open the door to the yellow Land Cruiser, and she forgot the birds entirely.

"Here we go." The sonogram technician named Katie squirted gel onto Glory's bare stomach. Her belly was only slightly rounded at five months, giving her the look of a garden Buddha. With the shades closed, the room felt dim enough to fall asleep in, but Glory was too excited to relax. This was the moment she'd get a glimpse of the baby that so far had only made her sick—including the amniocentesis to test for birth defects—and that would make everything real. She and Joseph had countless discussions when she discovered she was pregnant. Initially, she was stunned into silence, and Joseph had been the one to bring up options, as in, Did she want to terminate the pregnancy if it was determined something was wrong. *Of course not!* she'd answered, but deep down she worried she wasn't up to the challenge. The possibility of children had never entered her mind, but now that one was on the way, she would do whatever she had to in order to protect it. Did she have it in her to be a good mother when she'd never even been an aunt? All those years with Dan and nothing had happened, so she wasn't always careful. In Joseph's first marriage, he and his wife had tried and gotten nowhere, so he wasn't careful either. They loved each other when the urge overtook them, and interrupting their passion to use birth control rarely occurred to her. Here was why it should have: At age forty-one, she was considered an "elderly *primigravida*, high risk." The first time Dr. Montano mentioned the term, Glory got a mental picture of Baba Yaga with a baby bump. Every passing day she wondered if she'd have the courage to terminate if the baby was found to have Down syndrome or

spina bifida or something worse. She dreaded that amnio needle so much that she would have traded another trimester of
nausea for it rather than have something so sharp anywhere
near the baby.

Well, maybe not a whole trimester, but a week or two. She
was so often sick that she knew each individual bathroom tile.

She and Joseph both watched the monitor, trying to tell the
difference between what was baby and what was just the swoop-
ing white trace the ultrasound wand left behind. When the
technician turned up the volume, the room was filled with a
glub-glub noise that sounded like an underwater drumbeat. On
the screen, Katie pointed the cursor to a dark gray pulse. "That's
your baby's heart," she said, and Glory felt Joseph take her hand.
"Now look here. That's your baby's face. Do you see it?" she
asked, and Glory tried to follow the pale, drifting peanut on the
screen. "See the ribs? The spine?" the technician said, pointing
out flashes of white.

"Maybe I need glasses," Glory said, and just then Joseph
gasped.

"Aieee! Is that a hand?"

The technician laughed. "I can tell this is your first baby.
Yes, that right there," she clicked the transponder over yet another moving part, "is your baby's hand."

"Is he sucking his thumb?" Joseph said.

"Looks like it," the technician said. "Do you want to know
the baby's gender?"

Glory knew Joseph and Juniper were dying to find out, so
she said, "All right."

The technician clicked several more pictures and zoomed in
on three white lines that looked smaller than her pinky finger-

nail. "Congratulations. You have a little girl. Have you picked out a name yet?"

Over the past three months Joseph had come up with several boy names, including Cortez (his middle name), Montezuma (the street where they had their PO box), and Geronimo, just to make Glory laugh because she felt so rotten. But somehow they'd never considered a girl's name. Glory had assumed only a little snips-and-snails boy could make her feel so sick. But Joseph answered the technician without hesitation. "Yes. We're going to name her Casey."

Glory immediately burst into tears. "How," she said between hormone-induced sobs, "did I get so lucky?"

"*La mano poderosa*," Joseph said, and kissed her on the forehead, while Katie the technician enjoyed her first laugh of the day.

One of Joseph's favorite sayings, it translated loosely to "the powerful hand," and it meant that a greater force, call it God, the Creator, or fate, held the reins in your life. The moment he said that, Glory knew the amniocentesis was going to turn out just fine.

Chapter 4

ESPAÑOLA, THANKSGIVING EVE, 2008

INSIDE THE WORD *Emergency* there are other words, hiding. *Emerge* is the biggest; *merge* is one letter less. Subtract another letter and you find four-letter words like *mere* and *gene* and *grey*. Looking for three-letter words, all I could find was *cry*. I was trying not to. When I'm afraid, I look for whatever words are near me, and then I peek inside them. Sometimes they make a cloak, sometimes they tell a story.

"Your daughter's condition is grave," the doctor said to me the first day we were in the hospital.

Rave, gear, ear. "She just needs medicine," I said. "She'll get better."

"We're all certainly hoping for that," she said as the nurses fussed with tubes and wires, the smell of medicine thick in the airless alcove. "But right now Aspen is one very sick little girl. Let us telephone your family for you. Just give the nurse the number."

"We don't have a telephone," I said. Seth believed telephone lines let off radioactivity and gave you cancer.

"Would you like me to call a chaplain?"

A chap, or a pal? Why? To make a plan? I sat next to Aspen's gurney and held her hand. It was cool from the ice bath to lower her fever. "My husband is a minister," I said. "I'm sure he'll be here soon."

A nurse in blue pajamas came into the room. "Mrs. Smith, the hospital's going to need your ID and insurance card for the billing."

"Yes, ma'am," I said, though I didn't have either. "I'll have my husband bring my purse from home."

Whenever I asked about things like that, Seth always said, "You know who you are and so does the Creator. Who else needs to know?" I tried to think of what to tell the billing people when they asked again tomorrow. I left it at home; I'll call my husband; or I could give them a fake number and that would buy me time. Probably we wouldn't be here long enough to need anything more complicated. It was just a seizure and a high fever. Soon the medicine would work, and Aspen would open her eyes. That's what hospitals do. They make people better. No matter what Seth thinks.

The nurse had so many questions. "How old is Aspen?"

"Six."

"Has she had any other illnesses recently?"

"A cough."

"Did you give her anything for it?"

"Honey and echinacea."

The nurse looked at me funny. "You sound as if you have a bad cold yourself, or laryngitis."

"That's just my regular voice," I said, which was more of a truth than a lie. "Medicine can't fix it."

"Is she up to date on her immunizations?"

"I don't know what you mean."

"Inoculations. Vaccines. Injections. HepB, DTaP, Hib, PCV, MMR, Varicella, HepA? She'd have had them done before she could register for school."

She was a nice nurse but in such a hurry, tapping her stethoscope against her hand while she waited for me to say something. "We don't believe in that."

"But she must have had them, otherwise she wouldn't be allowed to enroll in school."

"We homeschool."

"I see," she said, but I could tell she was thinking bad thoughts, such as I was not a good mother, so no wonder Aspen was sick. Seth would say, "That woman's spiritual compass is off. She needs a sweat."

"She's healthy except for the seizures," I said. "She had a cold this week, that's all. Yesterday she had the seizure and this morning she was hot."

"I see," the nurse said, and finished writing on the papers. "A social worker will be around to speak with you shortly."

"Why a social worker?"

"It's protocol in cases such as your daughter's."

Cool, root, cop. What did protocol mean? Cases like Aspen's? "No, thank you," I said. I saw how that nurse looked at me in my clay-covered overalls. I had my turtleneck pulled up so no one could see the scar on my neck. My raspy voice I was stuck with. I forgot about how it freaked Outsiders to hear it, because I never went Outside unless I had to. Seth told everyone at the Farm that's how it is in the Outside World. Everywhere you turn, Judgment. *Ten, men, met, judge. Dug, jug, mud. Jude, gent.* "Really, that isn't necessary," I said. "Once my husband gets here he'll tell you whatever you need to know."

I honestly thought Seth would come, once he realized where I'd taken Aspen.

A man dressed in the same kind of blue pajamas pulled back the curtain that shut out the other people. Like the nurse, he wore a nametag on a chain. "Mrs. Smith," he said, "things are a little backed up in radiology. We'll be taking Aspen to CT as soon as there's an opening. You're welcome to come along."

So many terms and letters I didn't know the meaning of. It made me dizzy. But Aspen had to get well. I had walked here in the snow, and my tennis shoes were soaking wet. I would do it again, even barefoot. When Seth found out, he would be furious. "Thank you," I told that man. Then I asked the nurse, "Is it okay if I tell her a story until they get here?"

She looked at me like I'd said, "Let's all spread our wings and fly to the moon," or "Isn't that Jerusalem cricket adorable?" People say the crickets are ugly, but here in New Mexico they're called child of the earth, because they have a face, even if it's a face only a mother could love. I smiled at her, because smiles are the universal language everyone understands. "I doubt she'll hear you," she said, "but be my guest."

In the Outside World people say things like "be my guest," and I have to think hard to figure it out because I don't live there. Not much in *guest* except for *suet,* like we fed the birds. This nurse obviously didn't believe in miracles, which do happen, I know. "Thank you," I said. Always be polite. Remain calm. Smile. When the nurse left the room, I bent down close to Aspen's ear and brushed her thin blonde hair back. Her skin wasn't flaming like before, but it was still hot. "No more playing possum," I said. "Wake up." When she didn't, I said, "Keep trying to get better. Try your hardest. Please."

I counted the tubes they put into her. One went into her hand and another into her forearm. There was one down below, too, under her covers, to catch her pee. I jumped to my feet when they started to touch her there, and tried to make the nurse stop, but the man dressed in the blue pajamas put his arms around me and pinned my arms to my sides until I quit fighting. "Relax," he said, "I'll explain everything and why it's important."

"What is that?" I asked.

"Heart monitor."

"That?"

"Blood pressure cuff."

"That?"

"Oxygen tank."

"That?"

"Pulse oximeter."

"Does it pinch?"

"She can't even feel it."

Aspen had had seizures since she was three. Whenever they happened, Seth would say, "Laurel, is your mind on yourself instead of the Creator? Is your spirit chaste?" *Haste. Teach. Eat. Cheat. Chase.* "Maybe you need to pray harder," he'd say to me, as if the reason my little girl thrashed her limbs and made faces she couldn't control were proof that I had bad thoughts and a sinful nature. Bad thoughts caused bad things to happen, Seth said, and the only cure was an hour inside the sweat lodge and chanting prayers until your mind traveled outside your body and became one with the Creator. I didn't know what happened inside Aspen's brain when she had a seizure, but I imagined it was like a dream where she had to climb a mountain backwards or run really fast to escape the monster chasing her, but she could only run in slow motion. All I knew was that it took away all her energy. She fell asleep after it stopped. Nothing would wake her. Seth would say, "Sleep is free medicine." I would hold her and when she finally did wake up, it was slowly, and she was confused. But this morning she wouldn't wake up at all, and her skin was so hot it hurt to touch. I wet a rag and placed it on her forehead, but she didn't try to push it away or anything. Her breathing was funny, sort of ragged. I woke up Frances, who we share the yurt with.

Frances said, "There's a curandera in town. Maybe you should go see her."

But neither Frances nor I had a phone to call one, only Seth did, a cell phone for emergencies and we weren't allowed to use it. I put on my clay-covered overalls because I had to feed the animals, so I wore my dirty clothes for that. It was wash day, so after the animals were fed, I'd put the overalls into the laundry and dress in the skirt I'm supposed to wear. I went looking for Seth and found him in the main house, where he was eating breakfast, an egg burrito with cheese, bacon, and green chile. He was our Elder, so he had to eat flesh to keep up his strength. The rest of us got oatmeal and picked the bugs out before we cooked it. I waited until he was finished and then I begged him to please drive us to the curandera. "No," he said. "I have a group coming at ten for a drumming weekend and a sweat. The Farm needs the money."

"I'd drive if you let me learn how," I said under my breath and the minute I said it I knew I shouldn't have. He grabbed my arm hard and gave me one of those looks that meant after the group was gone I was in for it. "I'm sorry," I said. I shut my eyes and put the word *curandera* in my mind. It was filled up with secrets: *dread, read, run, curt, card, dare,* and lots of smaller words.

"She'll be fine," he said, and let my arm go. It throbbed hard before it hurt. "She always is. Go do your chores."

My chores were cleaning the kitchen and the bathrooms, taking care of the chickens and feeding Brown Horse. If there was a big mail order, I worked in the hoop house, helping Caleb and old St. John. In my leftover time, which was hardly ever, I'd take Aspen on walks to see nature. We'd collect rocks. There's quartz near the Farm, and rocks made smooth by the river. We'd watch spiders spin their delicate webs, and if we were quiet enough, sometimes we saw deer or a bobcat drinking at the river. Once we were riding double on Brown Horse and we met Louella Cata and her horse, Lil Sweetheart. They lived a mile down the road. Louella was digging in the mud and when I asked what for, she told me it wasn't mud, it was clay from Mother Earth. She made pottery from the clay. I wanted to see that, but I was afraid to go because Seth liked to know where I was at all times. I invited her to try the café we had that summer, but she never came. I worked in the café, too, but we only ran it that one summer because it didn't make enough money. In the winter it stayed locked up and empty, even though it would have been nice to sleep inside a place with real walls. Instead, Frances, Aspen, and I stayed in the yurt, which wasn't very warm. We pulled our sleeping bags close together, with Aspen in the middle. That helped, but Aspen got sick anyway.

But this morning all I did was feed the animals, and then I went back to the yurt to check on Aspen. She was still sleeping. Still hot. I shook her shoulder a little, but she didn't wake up. I counted twenty of her breaths in one minute and mine were only twelve. I tracked Frances down in the main house where she was making meals for the drummers. This was the only time when she cooked meat, and I could smell the roast in the oven and it made my mouth water. I begged her to drive me to the curandera, but she said no, Seth forbid it, but that she'd pray for Aspen. Then I went into the greenhouse where Caleb and old St. John were sorting seeds for mail orders. Caleb was twenty-seven years old and he had already done eight years in prison for hitting his son that he wasn't allowed to see anymore. He had a chain tattooed around his neck that made it look dirty.

"Would you drive us?" I asked, and he looked at old St. John who shook his head no.

"Try rubbing a hen's egg over her body," Caleb said.

"What for?"

"A freshly laid hen's egg will draw the illness out. It works, I swear. My grandma used it on me."

Old St. John didn't even wait for me to ask him. He said, "If you find the right stones and place them on her chakras that'll balance everything."

"All I need is a ride," I told them. "Seth doesn't have to know."

But neither of them would go against Seth even though there were cars with keys right there. If only I could drive. But Seth said there was no reason for me to learn. So I did what a mother should do, something I hadn't done for seven years. I waited until Seth was all involved with the group retreat and then I took Aspen in my arms and started walking toward town. It was so cold out that my face went numb, but I thought maybe the cold would help lower Aspen's fever.

When I came to Pueblo Pottery, a mile down the road, I was tired. I knocked on the door of the trailer home. The people at the Farm are my family, but only Louella is my friend. She never asked about my neck scar or why my voice sounds so aw-ful. She gave me coffee with condensed milk when I visited, food when she had some, and she showed me how to make pots from that clay she digs up. My hands couldn't do what hers did, pinching, pulling, making a cup shape, so she showed me another way, to put the clay on a potter's wheel and pull at it while it spins. While Aspen looked at the books in her bookcase, or had a lollipop leftover from Halloween candy Louella gave out, I learned to throw pots.

Any free time I had, I climbed over the fence to watch her. Clay is a holy gift from Mother Earth, she always said. You only dig for it in the spring or fall. The other seasons, Mother Earth gets to rest. You only take as much as you need, and before you work, you thank Mother Earth for giving you the clay. Louella let me use the potter's wheel whenever I wanted, which was why my overalls were always so dirty. I meant to wash them later, after the curandera fixed Aspen. But after I was done feeding the animals this morning I didn't think to change clothes, only to get Aspen into town. I stood on the steps to Louella's front door knocking for a long time, because Louella also worked nights at the casino, and slept for part of the day.

"Good morning, Louella," I said when she opened the door. "Can I use your phone?"

"Phone company shut it off," she said. "I didn't have enough money to pay the bill last month. You want to come in for coffee?"

"No, thanks. Aspen had a seizure yesterday, and today she has a fever and won't wake up. I was hoping to call a taxi to take me to the curandera."

"Why can't Seth give you a ride? It's not far."

"He's busy with the drummers."

"What a freak."

"No, Louella," I said. "He's our prophet. He knows so much."

She made a disgusted sound. "Prophet, my ass. What about Prune Face or the criminals? Can't one of them drive you?"

These were her names for Frances and the others. "They won't go against Seth."

"Those people are nuts, Laurel! Why don't you leave that place? You can stay here until you find somewhere else to live. They're always hiring cleaning crews at the casino."

I felt ashamed trying to explain to her that I loved my family, even when they told me no. "Louella, I took ten dollars from the kitchen jar. Is that enough for a taxi?"

"No, it'll probably cost more than that just to get the taxi to come out here." Then she called Seth a "bastard" and a "liar," and another name I wasn't allowed to say out loud.

I said, "Then I better start walking."

"Wait. Billy," she called, waking up her brother from his bed on the couch. "Drive Laurel to the *cura,* please."

"Yeah, okay. Give me a minute."

He stumbled off to the bathroom carrying his boots. Billy worked on road crews up and down the state, patching the holes that big trucks cause. They're bad for the environment in so many ways. Carbon footprint, smog, fossil fuels, ruining the roads, noise pollution. Inside the word *pollution* are a *poll* and *pill, lint* and *tin.* It weighs a ton. Sometimes I wouldn't see Billy for three months. But he was home today and that was luck, a simple word, nothing hiding inside.

Seth says Indians are lazy bums, but Louella and Billy worked as hard as anyone I knew. Billy's radio got stolen out of his truck so he sang while we drove. Billy's tribe does the Butterfly Dance in the Ohkay Owingeh Pueblo plaza on Feast Days. I'm not allowed to go, but once I climbed to the barn roof and I could see them from a distance. They paint their faces, wear headpieces with feathers, and on their arms they wear wings, not real butterfly wings, but when they lift their arms and dance you can see the butterfly spirit rise up in them. Aspen loves butter-flies, and butterflies sometimes would land on her hands. She can stand so still that the butterfly would stay there for the lon-gest while, like maybe it loved her.

Billy's voice was giving me shivers.

The curandera's place had a "Closed" sign in the window and that made me cry a little. Aspen was hot and heavy in my arms. Billy rubbed my shoulder until I stopped crying and then he drove me to a place called Urgent Care, just a little ways down the road from that big hospital.

"You got money to pay?"

"I have ten dollars."

"That might be enough for a co-pay," he said. "Be sure you tell them you don't have a job," he said, and yawned. "They give sliding-scale prices for the unemployed. Too bad you're not In-dian."

I didn't know what that meant, but I nodded. "Thanks, Billy," I said. "You go on home and get more sleep."

He grinned and flashed me one of those signs Frances says are gang signs, but Billy doesn't belong to any gang. He's just a nice guy.

At the desk where people asked for help, the woman typing on the computer took one look at Aspen and opened the door wide. "Come on in here," she said, and called for a doctor, and one came out of a brown painted door that read "Private." *Vat, vet, tear, trip, trap.* I laid Aspen down on the doctor table because I didn't care if it was a trap, I just wanted her to wake up. She'd never slept this long, ever. The doctor felt her neck and took her temperature with this thing that looked like a pen. He ran it across her forehead and said, "That can't be right." Then he used a different pen inside her ear and I could tell Aspen didn't like that because she whined like Brown Horse when she had to be separated from her baby. He talked to her, telling her to wake up, rubbing his knuckles on her chest, but she wouldn't.

"How long has she been like this?" he asked me.

"Since I woke up, around six."

"Are you aware her temperature is 104.8?" he said.

"We don't have a thermometer, but I could tell it was high."

He sighed. "I can't do anything for her here. Drive straight to the hospital ER. I'll call ahead so they know to expect you. What's your name?"

"Laurel Smith," I said, just the way Seth had taught me. *I am Laurel Smith who is married to Seth White Buffalo Smith and this is our daughter Aspen and I am fine, thank you, I do not need any help. Always be polite. Look for the exits. If someone starts asking too many questions, ask if they know Jesus. That will shut anyone up.*

Even though I didn't have a car, I made it to the brick hospital by walking fast. It wasn't that far, but by the time we got there my arms were hurting so bad. I'd never been inside a hospital before and I expected bad men to come out and snatch Aspen so they could perform terrible experiments like Seth said they did, things that took away your mind and implanted computer chips to send messages you had to obey. But when I walked through the glass doors I entered this room made entirely out of windows. It had the tallest ceiling ever. Like a church, but see-through. So tall I couldn't get my mind to measure it in the usual way, like twice the height of a horse, or five hands stacked, or two doorways wide or five trucks long or whatever. There were chairs all over the place and carpet and padded benches, even trees growing indoors, and rocking chairs I wished I had the time to sit in because Aspen would have liked that. On the walls were pictures of mountains and animals and this one long list of names under a word: *Benefactors.* There were too many words inside of it. *Been, beef, fact, bat, fort, free,* except I wasn't free, I was in fear, another word inside. I belonged at the Farm and to Seth and that would never change, though just being here, I wondered, what would it be like to live Outside? To see a different view through windows, or to meet people who didn't live on the Farm?

There were all these desks like at Urgent Care if it cloned itself. Cloning is not only wrong, it's what the Outside World is coming to, Seth said, and only bad can come of messing with the Creator's job, like Tsunami Waves, Ice Age, End Times, or a Repeat of Hiroshima, which I was surprised to learn did not contain the word *hero* at all. Ladies sat at the desks with microphones. "Calling number 485 to desk five," a loud voice said, and a woman stood up and pushed a man in a wheelchair to desk number five. I wondered where to get a number. The doctor at Urgent Care had said he'd call ahead, that they would know I was coming, so I asked a lady waiting on a bench, "Excuse me, where do you go when they know you are coming?"

"No *Ingles,*" she said, and pointed me to another desk I missed the first time, away from the clones where two older ladies sat under a sign that read "Information." *Informant* with an *i* and an *o* left over. They had on pink jumpers. That seemed funny, older ladies in the color of clothes meant for a child, but I didn't laugh because maybe they were poor. They told me I was in the wrong place, that I wanted to go to Emergency. Where is Emergency? I said, and one of them got up to show me. She walked with me all the way, even though I didn't know her. When we got to the

doors, she said, "Honey, I hope your daughter feels better soon."
"Me, too," I said. "She needs medicine."

Things at the Emergency were like Abel used to get when he
took drugs, all speeded up, rushing, and yelling. Children were
crying. A man with blood running down his arm sat there with
his eyes squeezed shut while the blood dripped on the floor, splat,
splat, splat. So red. His life dripping out. Another man threw up
in a bucket and I remembered the time we all got food poisoning
from Frances's tomato sauce. Seth made her do a three-day sweat
and fast, and when she came back to the yurt her skirt had to be
pinned at the waist or it would fall right off.

After lots of questions from a lady at another kind of counter, and me having I guess the right answers, pretty soon we
were in another doctor room with a shower curtain around us,
and tubes coming from the walls and machines called monitors.
Moon, main, rain, not. There was a rolling dresser, and a TV you
could switch on from this control thing which you could also
use to call for help. TV is Turning Us Into Zombies, so I left that
alone. Aspen was still asleep. Medicine that looked like a bag of
water dripped into her arm through the tiniest needle, though
you can never tell what's in water, like salmonella, which is
invisible. Some doctors came in and talked to each other, and
went out and came back in again. The nurses all wore blue
clothes. "Why is everyone wearing pajamas?" I asked and the
nurse said, "They're uniforms and we call them scrubs." *Curbs,
sub, curs,* a bad kind of dog.

She cleaned Aspen up with soap and a washcloth. "This is one
dirty little girl," she said, and I knew she meant I didn't wash her
right, but I did, just not last night when she felt so sick.

"You're a brave one," she said to Aspen while she and another nurse packed her in an ice bath for her fever. She didn't even moan now. Aspen is brave, but I don't want her to be brave because of bad things happening to her like they did to me, which was why I got upset at the pee tube. Things that happen to her like needles and seizures and throw-up, I can't help it, but nothing else, especially nothing down there where it's private.

Then an older woman dressed in Outside clothes—a brown jacket and matching pants, a necklace of very big pearls and a short silver haircut (the Bible says women should have long hair) came into the room and said, "Hello, Mrs. Smith. I'm Ardith Clemmons. I came to see how Aspen is doing."

I didn't know her, and her knowing my name seemed tricky, like she was there to do something bad. "Hello," I said. "Who are you?" I asked, remembering to smile at the last minute. Always smile.

"I'm Mrs. Clemmons, dear. I work here at the hospital helping families and children. The nurse told me you might need some help filling out forms."

"I can read," I said, angry they would look at me and think I was that stupid. "There are probably lots of other people who need you more."

"That's thoughtful of you," she said. "But as it happens, I have some free time right now. May I sit with you? Keep you company?"

Why? I wondered. I was going to have to pay careful attention. "I was just about to tell Aspen her favorite story," I said.

"I love stories. May I listen in?"

I didn't know what to do. I smiled, I was polite, I told everyone my name. All that I had left was to bring up Jesus, but was it time for that? Seth said talking about Jesus would make even the nosiest person give up. I didn't want to do that right now. I was tired and I had to pay attention to Aspen and I might mess up. I could say, "Be my guest," like the nurse did, but that sounded unkind, and we are Here in This World to Practice Loving Kindness. I guessed it was all right for her to listen. It was just a made-up story.

So because it wouldn't hurt, be my guest, and maybe she could hear me, I started to tell Aspen her favorite story, *The Princess of Leaves*. She loved this story better than any of the other ones I knew, probably because it didn't come from a book and I could tell it wherever we were, even in the dark, and I could make anything happen in it that I wanted to, and whatever question Aspen might ask me, I could make the story change and twist, just like a river.

"This is the story of the Princess of Leaves," I said.

Once upon a time, long ago . . .

How long? Aspen would always say.

Long enough that everyone has forgotten this story. There lived a princess in a castle near the woods with her parents, the king and queen. Now all princesses are beautiful, but what made her different from other princesses was that she could sing so beautifully that if any bird within one hundred miles of the castle heard her singing, they were compelled to fly near. If she sang long enough, eventually every person in the village would come to the castle. There they'd stand, by the castle's moat, holding their hats in their hands, looking up to the highest tower, where silver birds perched on the castle walls. They waited for the princess to come out to the balcony so they could catch a glimpse of her.

Every young man in the kingdom dreamed of asking the king for his daughter's hand in marriage once she became of age. Her blonde hair hung down nearly to her waist, curling on its own. Her eyes were hazel, which is the name of the Tree of Wisdom. Some days they were green and some days they were brown. Her smile caused even the saddest person to forget his troubles.

The townspeople called her the Princess of Leaves, because she liked to collect leaves from the many trees at the edge of the forest. This was especially true in late autumn, when every leaf reveals its true color. Often they would look up from their chores and see her pass by with the palace guard, keeping her safe.

Autumn was her favorite time of year because that's when the earth begins to prepare for winter. The leaves turn gold, orange, scarlet, and rarest of all, a deep burgundy. That means red, but with purple in it. Like a plum, or a bruise at its sorest.

Toward the forest Princess Leafy would go, always with the castle guard at her side to keep her safe. There are some people in the world so angry and unhappy that they stamp on flowers, mistreat animals, and want to make everyone as sad as they are. But you don't have to worry, I'll always protect you.

Her mother the queen often warned the princess, stay clear of the darkest part of the forest. Not a single person who has ventured into the darkness has come back to tell the story. Promise me. The princess promised her mother she would do as she said, but sometimes even the wisest of princesses forgets, accidentally, or on purpose.

The princess picked up only fallen leaves, because she never wanted to harm any living thing. In her heart, she believed every living thing deserved a lifetime, even spiders that weave webs to catch insects that might otherwise bite or pester you. Their webs are made of silk, and when it rains, drops catch on the web and they shine like diamonds. Beautiful things should be admired and then left alone.

The princess would lay each leaf on her palm and examine it carefully. Every leaf told a story: the season it didn't rain, the time a pair of secret lovers laid down on the leaves to say good-bye, the way a rabbit blended in with the leaves, hiding, to avoid hunters. The palace guard's job was to keep a lookout for danger, to fight if necessary, but he loved the princess as if she were his own daughter and it made his heart as soft as butter.

He'd fought in wars, kept soldiers from untimely ends, and though they usually traveled on foot, he was an accomplished horseman. All that was in the past, however, and his job was to accompany the princess and keep her safe. The leaves she loved best came from maple trees.

Leaves come in all shapes, but these maple leaves were shaped like hands, with five fingers, just like you have. Each finger had a vein that led to its stem so it could receive sap, which is like blood to trees. People say no two snowflakes are the same, and when it comes to leaves that's true, too.

Now a leaf collection is a delicate business. Each must be handled with care and preserved, or they'll turn brown and crumble. That's why the guard carried in his rucksack a heavy book. It had leather covers and was embroidered with silk. This book contained all the words ever spoken in the language of the kingdom. It was actually the keeper of language, so that no matter how much time went by, the book would always be there, to keep the language safe.

One word in the book was *Acer japonicum*. It means "full moon maple." Inside those three words there were secret words, like *mull*, *lamp*, and *moon*, and *ape*, *pear*, and *plea*. That is how trees talk to you. Secretly.

It was the guard's job to press the leaves between the pages of the heavy book as they went along. That way, whenever she wanted to, the princess could open the book and see each leaf, and using the words right there in the pages, she could make up a story.

Some storytellers write down their stories and an artist draws pictures to go with it. The princess had pencils, paint, and paper in her room at the castle. Once she collected all the colors, she intended to write down the story, using the words she kept locked inside her head. I'll bet you're wondering how did they get inside her head. The same way as a dream. When you sleep, the story arrives, a dream with talking dogs or a moon with the face of an owl, all mixed up to make something so beautiful you can't forget it. There were the five leaves she wanted and these are their names:

Green leaf with golden spots.

Golden leaf becoming orange.

Orange leaf turning scarlet.

Scarlet leaf turning to burgundy.

That's only four leaves, because I haven't got to the last one. The rarest leaf was called Nearly Black Leaf with misshapen lobe. The same shape as your little ear. Even misshapen and torn leaves have stories. Turning colors was the second-best part of the leaves' lives. First best was being collected by the princess. A lucky few were singled out for ironing. The guard knew how to heat up an iron and place the leaf between sheets of wax paper. Once pressed, they never lost their color, and they never dried out. This was the best fate of all, as far as the leaves were concerned. Ordinary people didn't realize the leaves had feelings. They raked them up, stuffed them into bags, and even made bonfires with them. A bonfire is a great big fire out in the open. A good place for one is on a beach by the ocean.

The more leaves the princess collected, the more pieces of

wax paper the guard used. Soon they were stacked up under her bed, spilling out of the dresser drawers, filling every closet. When you have too much, you go to the thrift store, but the princess was selfish. She loved every leaf, so she had a hard time giving any of them away. It's hard for some people to give up pretty things, because sometimes pretty things are the only reason to keep going.

The man nurse arrived with his gurney. "We're ready for Aspen now," he said.

"Okay." I stood up.

Mrs. Clemmons stood up, too. "You have quite an imagination, Laurel. I would love to hear more of that story."

But would she really? People from the Outside play tricks. "I don't feel like telling any more of it today," I said.

"Does talking hurt your throat?"

I looked at her, wondering if this was a trick. "I have to go to CT with Aspen."

"May I visit you later?"

"We'll probably be gone as soon as the medicine works."

"I hope it works quickly," she said. "If you're still here tomorrow, I'll stop by and say hello."

She waved, turned, and walked down a hallway, holding up her nametag to a box on the wall that caused a door to open. In a story, it would be magic, but in real life, it was a computer chip. I had to walk fast to keep up with the man pushing the gurney.

In the room for CT, the man nurse moved Aspen from the gurney bed to a white table that connected to a tall white plastic wall machine with an arm shaped like a big circle. In the middle it had a perfectly round opening. "Aspen," I said. "It looks like a great big doughnut." But she didn't wake up. The person who ran the scanner came out of a small office and arranged Aspen the way she wanted her. "Are you staying?" she asked, and I said, "Yes." She got me an apron that felt like it was filled with sand and told me to put it on over my overalls.

She went into the small office where I guessed the switches were. The thing made a clicking, pounding noise that hurt my ears. I was sure it would wake Aspen up. After a few minutes, she started to move her legs and arms, and at first I thought, Hurray, she's waking up, but then they began to jitter and writhe and I realized what it was. "Please, stop," I told the woman in the booth. "She's having a seizure."

She came rushing into the room and so did the man nurse waiting outside, and they hollered, "Aspen! Wake up!" and one rubbed her knuckles on her chest, while the other one felt for her pulse. Then he said, "Holy shit, she's crashing. Call a code!"

Sh, hit, it. Tis, his. More people came. Doctors, nurses, I don't know, but there was yelling and pushing and carts on wheels and machines. I was shoved to the wall right next to the CT doughnut. Maybe the machine caused the seizure and the crashing. They put wires on her chest. They yelled out "Charging!" and "Clear!" and I could have left and no one would have noticed, but my feet would not go. I put my hands against the wall to make sure I was standing up, because it didn't feel like that.

Then I prayed, the way Seth always complained I didn't. With my whole heart.

Chapter 5

SANTA FE, THANKSGIVING DAY, 2008

T HE VIGIL FAMILY'S Thanksgiving began like any other morning in the City Different. Juniper awoke to the smell of bacon frying, which meant her dad had been out walking the dogs and was now in the kitchen making breakfast. She heard the dogs barking outside, probably at a rabbit. In the summer, the rabbits' tan bodies blended into the high-desert landscape, but come winter they stood out against the snow like targets. The rabbits' whole reason for existence seemed to be tormenting the dogs by staying just out of reach. Juniper looked at her watch and scowled. It was early enough that she was going to have to go outdoors and haul them inside. She sat up, pulled on her Ugg boots, and wrapped her old Pendleton blanket around her shoulders.

"Caddy!" she called as she hurried through the great room and flung open the French doors. A blast of cold air smacked her in the face. "Dodge, Caddy, indoors *now*!"

Her border collie came to her right away, but Dodge was being his usual asshole self, barking as if a rabbit in his yard meant Armageddon. Juniper sighed and crunched her way across the snowdrifts to fetch him. She slept in an old T-shirt, boxers, and socks, and her bare thighs were freezing. She grabbed hold of

Dodge's collar and hauled the sixty-pound heeler–golden retriever toward the portal. "What the hell is wrong with you, Dodge? You know better than to bark like a maniac and wake Mom up."

Dodge wagged his tail as if she was congratulating him. Juniper watched as he trotted behind Caddy into the house and headed straight for the kitchen. It never ceased to amaze her what you could make a dog do if bacon was involved. The cafeteria at the University of New Mexico Albuquerque served "fakon," a mysterious meat product that tasted like firewood. Their other specialty was unrecognizable casseroles that tasted so weird that Juniper had basically been living on vending-machine burritos since September. Her suitemates—Lily and Bernadette—had both put on twenty pounds since school began. No way that was going to happen to Juniper. She monitored her carbs, ate very little sugar, and ran thirty miles a week rain or shine.

"Morning, Daddy Joe," she said and hugged her adoptive father as he flipped eggs in the frying pan and slipped the dogs a slice of bacon each.

"Chiquita, what are you doing up so early? I expected you'd sleep in."

She smiled. "I wanted to, but the dogs had other ideas. Didn't you hear them barking?"

"They're dogs. Their job is to bark, and they do it very well."

"I didn't want them to wake Mom up. Besides, now that I'm up, I think I'll go for a run. Where's Eddie?"

"Snuggled under the covers, I expect. Take a break from running today. Sit. I'll fix you a special breakfast."

She filled and drank a glass of water. "Save me a plate. I want to run while the traffic is light. See you later, Señor Alligator."

"In a while, Professor Crocodile." He reached out and touched her shoulder. "Hey, happy 'Gotcha' day."

Her heart soared. Four years earlier, as a surly fourteen-year-old, she'd been dropped off on Glory Solomon's doorstep and everything changed. Glory adopted her, Joe married Glory, and then he adopted her as well. Today was the anniversary, and it just killed her that Daddy Joe never forgot, that he treated this day as if it were a national holiday aside from Thanksgiving. "Best day of my life," she said, and kissed his cheek.

She pulled on her running tights and laced up her winter running shoes. After a brief stretch, she harnessed up Dodge, waved bye to her dad, and headed out the front door into the brisk winter day ahead. Daddy Joe had convinced her to take up running shortly after they met in California and he'd become her tutor. He promised that pushing her body physically would help her deal with the grief over losing her sister, Casey, a sorrow that never seemed to abate. By the time she got to thinking about Casey, gone nearly eight years now, she'd run five miles and soon everything fell back into place. She ran longer on the weekends, sometimes ten or twelve miles, which was how she'd met Topher.

Christopher Adams VI. Junior class, incredible musician, and so good-looking it was kind of criminal. He was her first real boyfriend, the kind who asked you out on dates instead of just showing up at your dorm room with a toothbrush in his pocket. Earlier this fall, at quarter to six one morning, before the heat index made running impossible, she was heading out for a few miles. Laguna de Vargas, the residence hall she lived in, was filled with girls sleeping off the previous night's party. Juniper didn't fit in with that crowd, and in fact hated dorm life, but

Daddy Joe insisted she stick out the term since he'd already paid for it.

Topher was just returning from a gig. He had a guitar slung over his back and was smoking a cigarette. He smiled and waved, then turned to watch her run off. She hated cigarettes, but with his turquoise eyes and spiky dark hair he looked so much like Jakob Dylan that people whispered maybe he was attending school under a fake name so the paparazzi would leave him alone. The next time she ran, there he was, in the same spot, sans guitar, waiting. "I'll meet you for coffee at the Standard," he'd said, as if he was sure she wouldn't say no. The Standard was an Albuquerque diner in a yellow building with a red neon sign, and it had really great coffee. Lots of students hung out there, but Juniper rarely did, since she was usually studying. When she showed up, showered, her honey-colored hair brushed, blow-dried, and curled, there he was in a booth by the window, writing in his notebook. He was the same height as she was, and rock-star skinny. He wrote his own music, and he thought Juniper—and even her tattoo—was beautiful. Thanksgiving was always special to her, but this year would be insanely great because he was coming to her house for dinner, and *staying the weekend.*

Her heart pounded at the thought of seeing him in just a few hours.

At her side, Dodge woofed at nothing she could see. He was being so bad lately, chewing up shoes, barking at the chickens, and not minding, that she'd decided to get him good and tired by making him run with her so that maybe they could enjoy dinner in peace. He liked to run and he had no trouble matching her pace. They ran past houses already decorated for Christmas. On the adobe walls, farolitos—little candles wedged in sand inside paper bags—waited for dusk. Tiny electric fairy lights were hung across painted gates. Down the road a kid was half-heartedly working on making a snowman out of the snow dump they'd gotten in late October. Juniper pulled Dodge's leash close so he wouldn't bark at the child. He didn't mean anything threatening, he was just an oaf who forgot his manners the minute you stopped working with him. He gravitated toward young kids. Juniper always imagined Dodge's dream life would be as the neighborhood dog in a pack of kids that hung around the cul-de-sac. He was always up for fetch or Frisbee.

There was a hefty evergreen garland splayed across the faded purple gate of the artist-compound studios. On Christmas Eve, people who lived on Canyon Road and Acequia Madre lit little bonfires in their driveways—luminarias—and everyone strolled the streets as neighbors handed out bizcochitos, hot cider, and stronger drinks to total strangers. Juniper tried never to miss it. Every holiday with her new family she forced herself to do holiday rituals, like tree decorating, present wrapping, and making homemade farolitos to line the driveway. She did all this in an effort to be happy, and to counteract the tiny arrow that lodged in her heart. The arrow was a leftover sherd from the time when all holidays had screeched to a stop—the year her sister Casey disappeared. The search for her sister was considered a "cold case"; in other words, everyone knew she was dead even though her body had never been found. The courts said ten years had to pass before they could legally declare it. Juniper agreed it was the most logical outcome—who stays away from their family for eight years? But there was a part of her heart that held out this crazy glimmer of hope. On days like today, when the blues threatened to take over and ruin things, she fought it by running. You're a big girl, she told herself. So what if your childhood basically ended at age eleven? Topher arrives today! Daddy Joe's making turkey dinner. Auntie Halle and Uncle Bart will be here, and Gran! Juniper loved Glory's mother with all her heart. She was a salty old lady who spoke her mind whether she was asked to or not. Focus on the family you have right here, she told herself.

She and Dodge crossed Paseo de Peralta to East Alameda, passing the Santa Fe River, icy this time of year. Bare cotton-wood tree branches alongside it were stark against the blue sky. The smell of mesquite and piñon fires filtered through the chilly air as she headed toward Guadalupe, where she would turn right and run through the railyard. Some dork wolf-whistled at her and she felt a small flare of anger, but didn't bother to see who it was. Santa Fe had its share of freaks just as California had, and the best thing to do was ignore them. Here she was, running with a dopey dog that would probably lick a stranger's hand. Shit. Now she was thinking of Casey again, and whoever had taken her, and now that the door was open, images flooded her mind.

The first Thanksgiving after Casey disappeared, Juniper's father had already moved out. *I can't take any more of this*, he said, and left with only one suitcase, as if his whole life fit inside it. Her mother would only sleep on the living room couch that faced the front door, because what if Casey came to the door? The TV was always on, tuned to a news channel, because what if someone found Casey, but she had amnesia and didn't know her name? Holidays didn't mean anything. Juniper tried not to bother her mom, but that last Thanksgiving she'd thought, Maybe I could cook the turkey if she told me how. *If you're hungry, make yourself a baloney sandwich*, her mother had said when she worked up the courage to ask. Then she changed the channel from CNN to local news.

A year later, her mother took an overdose of sleeping pills and Juniper figured that she went to wherever Casey was and she hoped that made her happy, if you got to be happy after you died. Juniper moved into her dad's apartment, but then one day he didn't come home. He basically left her at the curb like some ratty old couch. That was the start of being homeless, followed by foster and group homes. A frozen turkey dinner and instant mashed potatoes with something that was the color of gravy, but tasted like snot.

Then along came Glory.

What a miracle she and Daddy Joe were. "Am I ungrateful to think about these things?" she asked Dodge, who was considering chasing a squirrel that existed only in his mind—she could just tell. "Knock it off," she said, and his ears flattened in shame. She picked up the pace so he would have to concentrate.

She'd given up on finding Casey. So was it too much to ask for a little peace on the subject? The Kübler-Ross model said there were five stages of grief, but Juniper knew that was bullshit. Early in the first year Casey was missing, she realized the sorrow would last her lifetime, and what do you know, she was right. That was some hellacious backpack to carry around, but there was no law that said you had to talk about it.

She'd passed her GED at sixteen, and then Joe had pulled strings to get her into college here in New Mexico. She had a 4.0 average, volunteered twice a month at the women's shelter in Albuquerque for extra credit, and planned on graduating with the most academic bling possible. That would be a start on paying back Joe and Glory for giving her the opportunity to leave that miserable old life behind and start a new one. She forced herself to stop thinking about it by remembering how Topher kissed, which was strong and gentle at the same time, and how just being around him made her heart feel as if it had big old dragon wings, impervious to fire, scraping the sky, gathering in all the stars as if they were jewelry meant for her heart alone.

In the master bathroom with the talavera sink barely big enough to cup your hands in, Glory paused in brushing her teeth to sneeze into a tissue. She hoped she wasn't catching a cold. Obviously that would not be good for the pregnancy, but it would also ruin Thanksgiving. She wanted things to go well, because in addition to Juniper's first serious boyfriend's visit, her mother, Halle, and Bart were coming to Santa Fe for the long weekend. This would be their first stay at their house, now sufficiently remodeled to accommodate houseguests. She leaned in to turn on the shower and the baby kicked hard. Of course, as soon as she pressed her hand on her belly to feel it, she stopped. Eddie sat on the bathroom rug and looked up at her.

"Will you stop worrying about me?" she asked the Italian greyhound. From the day she first felt nauseated to the present, Eddie had followed her from room to room as if he was personally responsible for her safety. He sat on the bed while she dressed, and then preceded her into the kitchen as if she needed him to show her the way.

"Joseph?" she called out.

"In here," he said, coming out of the pantry with a box of Mexican cocoa. "I made you eggs, bacon, sausage, and Mami's torrejas."

She groaned. "That sounds so good. I'd love to eat all of that, but I think I'll just have eggs. Dr. M says I need to eat more protein. It's supposed to help with my blood pressure." Recently her blood pressure had soared into unhealthy numbers, forcing her to take early maternity leave—unpaid.

Joseph handed her a plate with two perfectly fried eggs and a side of steaming green chile from his dad's farm in Hatch. Then he set a platter of bacon and a bowl of torrejas on the table. "In case you change your mind," he said.

"Joseph, I'm turning into a blimp."

"You are not. You're gorgeous." He pushed the torrejas closer to her. "Just try one bite. I have to get the recipe perfect for the cookbook."

"All right," she said, knowing she couldn't resist the Mexican version of French toast, made with authentic piloncillos (brown sugar cones), cinnamon, cloves, and bolillos, a kind of Mexican bread roll fried in a mix of eggs and butter. "What's different about this version?"

"I used the Madagascar vanilla beans I stored in sugar for six months. I scraped out their innards and put the pods back into the sugar. I'm done with bottled extracts. Too much variation. You can't count on them. And I cut out two-thirds of the piloncillos when I made the syrup, but I cooked it nearly to the candy stage. Look at the surface where it's hardened. Perfect for cracking open with a spoon, and it keeps the syrup warm."

"I think I just gained five pounds listening to all that."

He ignored the comment. "Tell me truthfully, is it better? If I don't get the cookbook to the printers on Monday it won't be ready for Christmas."

She cut a piece with her fork and examined it. The crunchy crust was perfectly browned. The bread floated in the sea of syrup like a sleepy canoe. Once cracked open, that sea revealed a mouthwatering amber caramel beneath the surface. It was funny how pregnancy changed the taste of food. Glory had always favored sour tastes, like pickles and cabbage, but now she craved sugary foods like hot cocoa and marshmallows. The first bite made her smile. The second bite made her groan. After the third bite, she said, "You have to make this for Halle and Bart, Joe. They'll love it."

"Yes!" He pumped his fist in the air, and the wooden spoon in his hand dripped syrup, which Eddie immediately intercepted. "Excellent. Now I can finish up the cookbook."

"I'll miss tasting a new recipe every week. What ever are you going to do with yourself?"

"Oh, this is only volume one, my love. There will be others. I have to take a break from writing for a little while. Actually, I've been waiting for the opportunity to talk to you about something that happened at Candela."

Joseph was on the board of directors of the innovative women's shelter. Unlike other facilities, which offered brief sanctuary from domestic violence, Candela held classes in parenting, self-defense, and job training through the community-college outreach. "Tell me."

"I've been offered a paying position. They want me to take over running the education program. It's forty hours a week."

Which meant more like sixty, Glory figured. "Are you going to take it?"

"I'm thinking about it. Of course, I wanted to talk to you. I don't have to decide right this minute."

"Good," she said. Glory set her fork down and took a sip of cocoa. Joseph had retired with full disability from the Albuquerque Police Department, where he'd worked first as a cop and then later in the crime lab as a tech and photographer. The lawsuit on his behalf due to his injuries during a meth-lab bust had made him a wealthy man, although the injuries he suffered left him in considerable pain. The money allowed Joseph to contribute to community programs that needed support, but the shooting left him with serious back problems, and after four surgeries, he now walked with a cane. Having lived with him for five years, Glory could read the signs when he needed to rest. His face got a pinched expression, he became very quiet, and worst of all, he had this ridiculous notion that pain meant he needed to exercise even harder, so he'd lift weights or go for a strenuous walk and only make things worse. Joseph had a full life already: He was a guardian *ad litem* in custody cases in which divorcing parents couldn't agree on sharing custody, and he was on the board of directors at three different nonprofits including Candela. Lately it seemed he was at the shelter more often than the once-monthly administrative meetings.

What with the cookbook and the baby coming, their life seemed ready to burst at the seams. But his injuries had shut so many doors; this job offer had to be important to him if he was considering taking it. She cut into the torrejas, deciding to fin-ish the bowl, which she suspected was his evil plan all along. "Tell me about it," she said and took another bite.

He sat down at the table across from her. "Administrative work is one thing, and I enjoy planning the budgets, fundrais-ing, but how do I say this? The counselors they employ are all female. Nothing wrong with that, but I started to wonder what if a man—"

Glory set down her fork and smiled at her husband. The thick black hair he kept cut military short, skin the color of café au lait, and his angled cheekbones added up to one handsome man. He was so unaware of how beautiful he was that it melted her heart. "An extraordinarily *decent* man."

"Well, I like to think of myself that way, but I'm only human. I'm thinking, what does it take to help a battered woman learn to trust again? A patient man. *Estupido?*"

"On the contrary, Joe. I think it's a brilliant idea. If you want to go for it, you have my permission. Right now, though, I need you to do something very important for me."

"What?" he said, standing up from his chair and coming to her side as she turned in her chair to face him. "Oh, my gosh, was the food too much? You need me to call the doctor?"

She stood up, took his hand, and placed it on her belly. "Feel your daughter kicking? I swear she's going to play rugby."

He smiled, and then his mouth changed into an O shape and he said, "*Madre de dios!* Do you think Sears is open? We have to buy a crib immediately!"

Chapter 6

T HE BEAT-UP SUBARU Daddy Joe had bought her handled snow and ice like a champ, Juniper thought as she
neared the Plaza around lunchtime. What with the holiday
weekend, finding parking would be even more difficult than
usual. Topher's commuter van was due in at 12:45 at La Fonda.
Then came a holiday miracle. For once their parking garage
wasn't full. She found a spot right up front and pulled in. Caddy
and Dodge were in the backseat, the windows down exactly
four inches, allotted snout space. They'd been getting underfoot at home, and Daddy Joe was afraid they might cause Glory
to trip and fall. Eddie, on the other hand, seemed to take every
step Glory made as his personal business. Which left two choices
for Caddy and Dodge: go with her to pick up Topher or get
locked in the outside kennel in cold weather, where they'd
whine. Loudly. She unfolded a blanket for them to snuggle in.
"I need you guys to be very quiet," she said. "The last thing I
need is getting busted for leaving you two in the car. So behave
yourselves. Here's a bully stick for each of you." She handed out
the leathery treats that smelled like barf, and the dogs got down
to business. She locked the car and tramped through the lot to
the sidewalk that ran alongside the hotel.

She could have gone in the back way to the hotel, but it was snowing again, big fat flakes, so white and pretty. She leaned her head back and felt them land on her cheeks and nose. For more than four hundred years there had been a hotel on the corner of West San Francisco and Old Santa Fe Trail. *La Fonda Hotel*, Daddy Joe told her, was a redundant name because it translated to "the inn" or "the hotel." Santa Fe was like living life inside a history book that was still being written. J. Robert Oppenheimer had stayed at La Fonda, and so had Archbishop Lamy, the subject of Willa Cather's book *Death Comes for the Archbishop*, one of Juniper's all-time favorite novels. Dozens of famous actors, including Jimmy Stewart in the Christmas movie that made Daddy Joe get all weepy, *It's a Wonderful Life*, had stayed there, too, and even presidents. Every week the "El Mitote" column in the *Santa Fe New Mexican* reported on movie stars lunching there, or shopping the expensive boutiques in the same building. Juniper turned the corner and walked into the lobby to get warm while she waited for Topher. The one-way van ride cost twenty-seven dollars and she had paid for it. Nobody besides Topher knew she had to give him the money. So what, she told herself. This was the twenty-first century. Stuff like that didn't matter.

The lobby was decorated with strings of tiny white lights, making the cream-colored walls, turquoise molding, and painted murals look like pages in a book of fairy tales. Even on a national holiday, there were tourists. Loads of people spent Thanksgiving in Santa Fe, as mesmerized by the snow on adobe and farolitos glowing atop walls as Juniper was. It felt as if her life in California had happened decades earlier. Now she couldn't imagine living anywhere else but Santa Fe, and she considered Albuquerque only temporary. Topher's family lived on the East

Coast, a place called Long Island, which was close to New York City. He wasn't going home for Thanksgiving because he had to finish a makeup paper for Western Civ or the prof wouldn't pass him. He was also on academic probation. At first, that kind of surprised Juniper, because most of those required classes had been easy for her. Topher said the prof didn't like him.

He talked about places like Greenwich Village and Manhattan and New Haven, Connecticut, as if they were ten times more beautiful than Santa Fe could ever hope to be, which made Juniper feel a touch defensive, because to her Santa Fe was the most beautiful place she'd ever been. She didn't let on. Topher said everything on the East Coast was bigger and better: art museums, theater, the music scene, clubs. She hoped he'd invite her out for spring break to his family's condo in Florida, or to their cabin in the Adirondacks in summer. She'd Googled "Adirondacks" when he told her about spending summers there. Such a cool-sounding name had to be Native American, and it was, but what she learned kind of broke her heart. *Adirondacks* was an Anglicized version of the Mohawk word *ratirontaks*. It translated to "they eat trees," a derogatory term referencing the Algonquian Indians. When food was scarce, the Indians ate tree bark, as simple as that. Juniper understood that kind of hungry in a way most people never would, but she had never told Topher about her brief period of homelessness. She had fallen in love with the Adirondacks' lodge-style architecture, photos of canoes on huge blue lakes, and the idea of seeing a moose in the wild. Here, in Valles Caldera, she'd seen antelope, and elsewhere the usual assortment of coyotes and rabbits, but nothing bigger. With three houses, Topher's family sounded like they had a ton of money, so she often wondered why it was he was always borrowing from her. The cafeteria is always hiring, she'd told him, seeing nothing wrong with having to get a part-time job to afford college. He'd laughed and told her she was hilarious, and she played along as if that had been her intent all along, but the exchange troubled her. Juniper saved all her money from summer jobs to use during the year, and banked the crazy big checks Aunt Halle and Uncle Bart sent to her on her birthday. She planned to put every dime toward graduate school, because more and more graduate programs were doing away with tuition waivers. Shoot, her favorite prof, Dr. Carey, had only one graduate assistant this year, that annoying Chico de la Rosas Villarreal who was always saying mean things to her, and the previous year he'd had four teaching assistants. Except for loans to Topher and the burritos, Juniper was doing all right budgeting her expenses.

"Happy Thanksgiving," she told the desk clerk in the lobby.

He offered her a peppermint from the candy dish on the counter. "Can I can help you with anything, or are you meeting the shuttle?"

"The shuttle," she said. "But thanks for asking. Do you have to work all day?"

"Yeah, but I get time and a half."

"That's awesome." The guy was Navajo, she could tell, and he had a nice smile. That was another great thing about Santa Fe. People were friendly. She wandered by the display cases in the lobby and wondered who on earth could afford a beaded cowboy-hat headband for only seven hundred dollars. If she had money to burn, she'd buy something nice for Glory, like a spa day at Ten Thousand Waves. Her mom never did things for herself, and the pregnancy had exhausted her. Her dad, she'd buy him a plane ticket to Denmark where spinal surgeons were doing amazing repairs with stem cells. Otherwise she'd stash it in the bank for later on, because if anyone knew things could change in a millisecond, it was Juniper Solomon Vigil.

In the window of the fossil shop there was a four-foot-tall geode with amethyst crystals that reminded her of a cave out of a George R. R. Martin novel. It was so beautiful she almost wished it was hers, but stuff didn't give you an awesome life, experiences did. She checked her watch and wondered if the van was running late because of the snow. Was there enough time to go to Starbucks and get them each a venti latte? She hoped the dogs were behaving in the car. The run with Dodge had worn her out, with his constant pulling. She needed coffee if she wanted to make it through to dinner without a nap.

Finally the van pulled up to the curb. The driver got out to help passengers through the snow. Six people tipped him, picked up their luggage, and went into the hotel. Juniper waited, her heart in her throat, ready to be devastated if Topher didn't show. He did that sometimes, got so into his writing or jamming with friends that he forgot classes and appointments. Then the driver came around to open the cargo area and she saw a guitar case and exhaled. The driver put his arm inside the eight-seater van and shook it. There he was, hair all messy and dressed in flannel grunge and a sheepskin-lined denim jacket. The driver had to wake him up.

She bolted out the door and ran to him. He held his guitar case in one hand and with the other pulled her close. "Hey there, pretty lady," he said. "Did you miss me?"

She wanted time to stop right then, so that this moment would last forever, because it was the best feeling ever. "You know I did," she said as they stood on the corner of the sidewalk kissing while snowflakes fell down on them. Oh, my gosh, she thought, imagining in a blur their wedding at the cathedral, Joe giving her away, Glory looking happy that Juniper had found her true love. If her heart beat any faster it would leap out of her chest. "Come on. I parked in the lot. I can't wait for you to meet my parents. They're going to love you."

Topher kissed the top of her head and squeezed her hand. "Maybe I'll play some Django for your dad," he said.

"He'd love that. Me, too."

She opened the driver's door and reached over to unlock the passenger door because the lock always stuck. Caddy and Dodge went nuts and pushed their way into the front seat. "Get in the back," she scolded them, which caused them to wag their tails and push even harder.

"I didn't know you were bringing dogs," Topher said. "Are you sure my guitar will be all right?"

"Of course it will. Usually they're really good at minding. They're just excited to meet you. This is Dodge and that's Caddy."

"What's that horrible smell?"

Juniper had to think a minute. "Oh, you know, just bully sticks. Guess what they're made of?"

"I have no idea, but it smells like vomit."

She laughed. "A steer's penis."

Topher cringed. "Can you throw them out the window or something?"

She laughed and took the slobbery bully sticks from them and opened the glove box. She put them back into the plastic bag she kept them in and removed a second baggie, filled with biscuit treats. She handed it to Topher.

Dodge was being awful, bumping Topher in the head with his nose, and Caddy had that crazy border collie stare in his eye as if he was deciding whether Topher was good where he was or needed to be herded into the next county. Topher handed the bag back to her. "If these are cookies, you shouldn't make them again."

She laughed. "They're not cookies, they're dog treats."

"Why are you giving them to me?"

She handed it back to him. "If you want them to like you, it's better if you give them the treat," she said.

"All right, but they had better not bite my hand and mess up my fingering. If I can't play, how can I be famous and buy you all the things you deserve?" He laughed, so Juniper did too.

Juniper watched him hold out a biscuit for Dodge, his fingers ready to let go the minute Dodge took it. For once Dodge behaved and took it as delicately as it was offered. "See?" she said. "Now he'll adore you."

Topher held out a second biscuit for Caddy. Caddy just stared. "Come on," he said, wiggling it, "do you want it or not?"

"Go on, Caddy," Juniper urged him. "Topher's good people."

The border collie moved forward, but just as he was about to take his treat, Topher pulled the biscuit away and laughed.

"What did you do that for?" Juniper said, taking the biscuit from him.

"Big, stupid dogs like the red one are okay," he said. "But with smart ones, you have to let them know who's boss."

"This dog saved my life," Juniper said, giving Caddy the biscuit and rubbing his head, silently apologizing to her collie. "And there's nothing stupid about either one of them." She stared at Topher, wondering how she'd missed this side of him in the last three months.

"Aw," he said. "Come on, Junie. I was just kidding around."

"It's mean to tease animals," she said.

"Kiss me, and I promise to never do it again."

"That kind of crap doesn't work on me," she said, putting the key into the ignition.

Topher reached for the door handle as if he meant to leave.

"Topher?"

The silence made her stomach twist.

"Come on," she said. "Talk to me."

He looked back at her, his face sober and his blue eyes unreadable, maybe even angry. "Make up your mind. If you don't want me to stay, I can probably catch the shuttle going back if I hurry."

And who'd pay for that? she wondered. "Of course I want you to stay!"

"You're not acting like it."

She put a hand on his shoulder, then leaned in and kissed his neck. "I love you."

"I love you, too."

"You have to understand, my dogs are really important to me. I want them to love you like I do. Can we start over?"

"Sure." He turned to the dogs and gave each one a pat. "Sorry," he said, and Dodge licked his hand.

"That's better," Juniper said.

"I have to confess something," Topher said, and Juniper's heart just about stopped. Other girls stayed at the dorm over the holiday weekend. Had he cheated on her? Did he want to break up?

"I'm listening."

He sighed. "All right, then. Smart dogs make me nervous. That's the truth."

"Oh, for crying out loud," she said. "Caddy wouldn't hurt a flea. Give him time. You'll see how special he is. You'll love him as much as I do."

He gave her a grin that made her bones melt. "We're good?"

"Absolutely."

"Good. What time is dinner? I slept through breakfast. Late gig last night."

"In a couple of hours. There are tons of things to snack on," she said. "Where were you playing?"

"Church Street Café in Old Town. Speaking of which, I could use some coffee." He brushed imaginary dog hair off his flannel shirt and touched her neck, his index finger coming to rest on the bluebird tattoo. "I just finished writing a song about this tattoo," he said.

"Seriously?"

"Yep. Be extra nice to me and I'll play it for you."

Her heart soared. "Oh, my gosh. I can't wait to hear it."

Topher buckled his seat belt, tapped on her seat back, and said, "Home, James."

Juniper laughed. That was more like the Topher she loved. She backed the car out of the parking space and checked her mirrors before joining the stream of traffic. Her eyes met Caddy's. *My beautiful, brave boy,* she thought. *Imagine anyone not falling in love with you. He didn't really mean it, Caddy. He's just nervous about meeting Mom and Joe. Really, he's super nice once you get to know him. I promise.*

Glory was just filling the micaceous pottery casserole dish with stuffing to place in the oven. It was a mélange of vegetables and nuts, no bread, a recipe Juniper asked for specifically. When she heard the knock at the door, she knew it had to be Halle, Bart, and her mom. Finally! The snow had her concerned, because Californians didn't know how to drive in it. She put the stuffing down and placed the lid on top. All the way to the front door she felt herself waddle like an obese duck. There were two months to go. How could she get any bigger? She opened the door and there stood her mom, with her purple walker, and next to her Halle in the furry Tibetan lamb coat she'd bought especially for this trip. It was a soft ivory color, and perched on her recently colored hair—red—she wore a black beret. She had cinched the coat with a leopard print and rhinestone belt. Her face was thin and drawn, but she looked as if she'd stepped out of the pages of a fashion magazine.

"Welcome! It's so good to see you," Glory said, hurrying them indoors for a proper hug. "I'm sorry it's gotten so cold. How was the drive from the airport? I hope you didn't hit heavy snow. The weather forecast sure blew it on predicting this storm. Mom, you look wonderful." She bent to kiss her and felt her mother's hand go to her belly.

"Never thought I'd see the day," she said. "Bless your heart, you're as big as a barn."

Glory laughed. "I know. I can't stop eating. Halle, should I get Joseph to help Bart bring the bags in from the car?"

Halle smiled. "Actually, at the last minute Bart had to travel to Italy. There was some snafu with one of their major vineyards, and only he could solve it."

"In November? Why didn't you call me? Or go with him?"

"I figured he'd be too busy working, so I decided to come with Mom as planned. She didn't want to travel alone." She shrugged out of her coat, brushed the snow off it, and handed it to Glory to hang in the closet. "I am in love with this coat," she said.

Glory agreed. "It's stunning."

"Don't worry, I brought some wine anyway, so you don't have to go shop at the last minute."

"We always enjoy the wine Bart picks out, but we'll miss him," Glory said. "I'm just so glad to see you. Can I get you two something hot to drink?"

"Decaf, but only if you have it already made," her mother said, inching her walker across the flagstone floors toward the fireplace.

That's my mom, Glory thought. Her never-go-to-the-trouble way she had of asking for what she really needed. "Mom, sit in the wing chair. It's closest to the fire."

"Oh, that fire feels nice," Ave Smith said as she made her way to the chair. "Reminds me of your place in California."

"One of Joseph's cousins did the tile."

"The same one who did the kitchen?"

Glory laughed. "I don't know. He has so many cousins it's hard to keep them straight."

"When you marry a man, you marry his entire family," Ave said.

"Then I guess I'm lucky," Glory said.

Halle looked away.

Glory gently guided her mom into the wingback chair. She watched how Ave pulled the walker close to her, as if she didn't want it out of her sight. From phone calls and e-mail she'd known that her mom's arthritis was worsening, and she'd heard about the walker, but seeing it in person drove her deterioration uncomfortably home. She was moon-faced from prednisone, and she wore braces on each arm that extended to her palms. Her knuckles were noticeably swollen, and that had to hurt. The purple walker reminded her of a ten-speed bicycle, with hand brakes and a basket to hold her purse. "That's a very snazzy piece of equipment," Glory said.

Her mother smiled. "Just another perk of getting old."

"Your house is adorable," Halle said, walking around the living room, picking up things. She turned over a greyhound statue Joseph had found in a thrift shop and bought because it reminded him of Eddie. "Rosenthal," Halle said. "Very nice, even with the chip." She admired the flower arrangement on the dining table Glory had worked on for most of the day. "What kind of flowers are these?" she asked, pointing to the coin-sized yellow blooms.

"Button chrysanthemums," Glory said. "And I put in some branches from the tree we replaced out front. I love autumn flowers. All the earth tones."

Halle laughed. "Mums for the new mum!"

Glory smiled. "I never thought of it that way. Coffee for you, too?"

"No. After that drive I need something stronger."

Glory pointed her toward the kitchen. "Joe's in charge of mixing drinks."

"Good, because I need a triple shot of tequila." Halle kissed Glory on the cheek and walked through the arched doorway.

Glory watched her go. "Mom, she's so thin. What's going on?"

Ave Smith shook her head. "I don't want to spoil the holiday, but your sister is headed for the rapids, Glory. She needs to take hormones and go to church."

"Is Bart really in Italy?"

Ave pointed to the painting that hung over the fireplace. It was a wide blue daytime sky filled with the clouds that Santa Fe was famous for. Every day it brought sunshine into the house whether it was twenty degrees out or ninety. "Now isn't that lovely. Did one of Joseph's cousins paint it?"

"Yes, Aaron gave it to us as a housewarming present. Can you at least give me a hint of what's going on with Halle?"

Ave opened her mouth to speak, but just then Juniper and her boyfriend walked in the back door, and the dogs raced ahead into the room so they could give kisses to all the newcomers.

"Gran!" Juniper said, grinning. In her hand she held three purple balloons. "Look what we bought you. They're to tie on your walker so when you zoom through the crowd, everyone will see you coming. Gran, this is Topher."

Glory's mother laughed. Everything Juniper did was hilarious or wonderful, but if it came from Glory and Halle, they were being immature or had forgotten their manners.

"Gopher?" Ave said. "What kind of parents saddle a handsome young man like you with a terrible name like that?"

"Topher," he said, brushing his dark hair out of eyes that were so blue Glory thought he had to be wearing colored contact lenses. "It's short for Christopher, after my dad, and his dad, and the dad before that, ad infinitum. Lovely to meet you, Mrs. Smith. Happy Thanksgiving." He took her hand gently in his and pressed.

"Oh my," Ave said, looking at the boy while Juniper tied the balloons to her walker. "Be careful around this one, lovey. He's a snake charmer."

Juniper looked as if that comment had launched her over the moon. She hugged her grandmother again. "It's so great to see you. How're your bridge tournaments going? Are you rolling in nickels?"

Ave laughed. "I tell you, lately I've been on a serious winning streak. Good news for you, come Christmastime. I'll buy you an extra pair of socks. Speaking of clothes, I trust you're both planning to change for dinner? Otherwise I might think you're still wearing your Halloween costumes. Bums from the Great Depression, am I right?"

"Of course, ma'am," Topher said, patting the backpack he'd set on the floor. "I have my suit right in here."

"In a backpack?" Ave said. "Well, it's going to need ironing. Glory, set up the ironing board right here in front of me. I'm useless in most ways, but I can still press a knife-edge crease."

Everyone was seated at the dining table while Halle opened a bottle of sparkling wine. "Does anyone know what Dom Perignon said the first time he tasted champagne?" Halle asked as she expertly popped the cork without spilling a drop.

Topher leaned forward, holding out his glass. "He said, 'Come quickly, I am tasting stars.'"

"How do you know that?" Halle asked. "Are you even twenty-one?"

"My parents," he said. "All of us kids learned about wine as part of our upbringing. For example, champagne is made either by *méthode traditionelle* or *methode champenoise*. This one is the former." Halle filled his glass and he took a sip. "Citrusy, the perfect choice for Thanksgiving. And yes, I'm twenty-two."

"Juniper isn't," Joseph said, placing turkey slices on each plate. "No bubbly for her."

"Dad," Juniper said, "it's Thanksgiving! I can have a sip. I wish Uncle Bart were here instead of working. I want to learn about wines, too."

Glory was torn over who to watch: Halle, with her mouth set grimly, or Joseph, as the muscle in his jaw tensed. Glory lifted the bottle of Trader Joe's nonalcoholic sparkling cider. "You can have one glass," Glory said, "but then switch to this. It's just as festive, and kind of our family tradition."

Juniper frowned and Ave tapped her on the shoulder with

her salad fork. "That's more than I'd give to your mother when she was your age, and she was a married woman, so no pouting, young lady. Now try some of these yams. My favorite part of the holiday next to pies."

Juniper took no more than a tablespoon. "Root vegetables are really high in carbs," she said.

"Oh, come on," Halle said. "The whole point of holidays is to indulge." She set the champagne bottle down after she'd filled all their glasses, hers to the brim. "Come on, everyone. Let's toast."

"I can't," Juniper said flatly. "I'm too young to be trusted, apparently."

Ave laughed. "Watch it, sweetie. That remark might just backfire on you. Gopher, you decide what we should toast to."

"Topher," he said, laughing a little less this time.

Ave laughed again. "I'm just yanking your chain, Chris. With age come certain privileges, and teasing younger people is at the top of the list. Sounds like your parents brought you up right, so what's the toast your folks usually say?"

He lifted his glass. "'The Pilgrims made seven times more graves than huts. No Americans have been more impoverished than these who, nevertheless, set aside a day of thanksgiving.' H. U. Westermayer."

"Topher's ancestors came over on the *Mayflower*," Juniper said.

"Imagine that," Ave said.

Joseph cleared his throat. "'Give thanks for unknown blessings already on their way.' My grandmother Penny Manygoats always said that."

"Many ghosts?" Topher said.

"Goats," Joseph said, "as in farm animals."

Just then, a creaking-groaning noise that seemed to come

from the rafters cut the silence that had followed Joseph's words. Glory, Joseph, and Juniper said in unison, "Dolores, everyone's waiting for you. Go toward the light."

It wasn't only Ave who looked perplexed. Topher looked downright frightened. Halle seemed to be more concerned with refilling her glass.

"Oh," Juniper said. "I forgot to tell you that our house has a ghost. I named her Dolores."

"Did someone get murdered here or what?" Topher asked.

Glory laughed. "She came with the house. Santa Fe is filled with ghost stories, right, Joseph?" She looked at her husband's expression and knew he hadn't heard her. He was still digesting Topher's salutation. "Let's toast to Dolores, too," she said, "in hopes that one day she'll find her way home. Isn't it great to have so many traditions to choose from? Mom, will you lead us in saying grace?"

"I sure will. I'm going to say the long version for the ghost." Ave launched into the Lord's Prayer, which in Ave's version had tangents for the loved ones she'd lost in her life. She finished up with, "Lord, bless us with a new president, one who can hold to a budget, and bless the baby girl my daughter is about to bring into this world. Amen."

The baby kicked Glory hard under her ribs, as if she too had something she wanted to say. "Amen," Glory said when they were done, and everyone touched glasses, the sound of crystal ringing through the room. Every holiday Glory tried to be thankful for the bounty of her life. She smiled at Juniper, seated across the table from her boyfriend. She was relieved her mother had warmed to Topher so quickly. She hoped it made up for Joseph's chilly reception. Halle looked reasonably happy without

Bart, though she'd refilled her glass twice already. Juniper smiled at Topher and blushed, and Glory could tell that under the table, they were playing footsie.

It was time to remind Juniper of the birth-control talk.

That night, after Grandma Ave was settled in the guest room next door to hers and her mom, dad, and Aunt Halle were in the kitchen cleaning up the pile of dishes and pots and pans, Juniper walked Topher out to the casita, where he'd be sleeping. She took Dodge along with her. "Why are you bringing the dog?" Topher asked. "Scared to be alone with me?"

She laughed, but realized he wasn't far from the truth. "Dodge is kind of slipping in his training. I thought it would help to work with him while I'm home since my mom is too pregnant."

"Is it much farther? I'm freezing."

"I offered you my dad's jacket."

"And I said no for a good reason. Your dad hates me, or didn't you notice?"

Juniper didn't know how to answer. "We're almost there." Daddy Joe *was* kind of zoomed in on Topher, and not in a good way. The champagne fiasco—why had she made a stink about it? She didn't even like the taste of wine, but somehow when Topher turned out to know all these random facts and all she knew was that it came in two colors, it hit her how immature she was. Sure, Topher was a couple years older than her, but they were in the same year of college. She was smart, her GPA proved that, but she wasn't "wise in the ways of the world."

What if that was a problem that could cost her Topher?

As they made their way through the snow, Dodge picked up

a frozen tennis ball and nudged her leg. Finally she threw it back toward the house just to get rid of him. "Did you enjoy my dad's cooking?" she asked, squeezing Topher's hand.

"It was a thousand times better than commons food. Your mom is *so* pregnant. Isn't she worried about birth defects at her age?"

Juniper felt a wave of embarrassment flush her face. "Jeez, Topher. I told you, I'm adopted. She's still young enough to have a baby. And the tests came out perfect, so no worries. It's a girl."

"Won't it be weird to have a sister in diapers?"

Juniper looked up at the night sky, filled with stars and planets and who knew what else beyond the human eye's capability. The intoxicating smell of wood smoke drifted from neighborhood chimneys. She'd never told him about Casey and didn't intend to. She unlocked the door to the casita and flipped on the light switch. "The way I look at it is it will be great to have a sister of any age."

"Whoa," Topher said. "This place is *sick* awesome."

Juniper beamed. "My mom designed the whole thing. She hired one of my dad's cousins to do that diamond plaster on the walls, but I got to pick the color, so I chose orange. It's my favorite color." Juniper pointed to the wall sconces and chandelier, all dark bronze fixtures with amber mica glass inserts and shades. "I picked those out, too. The woodstove came from Santa Fe Hearthstone. It's the Tudor model, and that's real soapstone quarried from the state of Virginia. I started it up this morning so the place would be all toasty for you. You'll need to add more wood before you go to sleep, but it'll keep you warm all night."

Topher tossed his backpack on the floor and pulled off his

jacket and tie. He loosened his collar, kicked off his shoes, stretched his arms, and pulled Juniper along with him to the floor on the Persian rug. "I know what would keep me warmer. This would be the perfect place," he said.

"Perfect place for what?"

"Taking things to the next level," he said, unbuttoning the gray cashmere cardigan she wore over the dorky pleated wool skirt her grandmother had given her last Christmas. He cupped his hand around her bare shoulder, just inches from her breast.

When they had been dating a month, she'd allowed him to touch her breasts as long as he did it with a layer of clothes between them. They kissed a lot, but she'd stalled him on anything else, saying she wasn't on the pill and she didn't trust condoms. Of course at school there wasn't any way to have time alone, really private, to make things romantic. The stupid dorms didn't even allow candles. Topher had suitemates, too. The one thing he never had any of was money, like for a nice dinner out, or flowers, maybe, or a hotel room, and shouldn't the boy pay for that? They weren't in the dorm now. They were in a cozy, beautiful place that would be perfect to make love in, and what if he had been expecting this all along, misunderstanding her invitation?

He kissed her neck, right near the hollow of her throat, undoing her resolve like pulling a thread on a sweater. Until Topher, she hadn't known there were so many nerve endings there. She enjoyed the tingling sensation while mentally reviewing her anatomy and physiology: *There are four main types of nerve endings in the glabrous skin of humans: Pacinian corpuscles, Meissner's corpuscles, Merkel's discs, and what was the last one? Oh, yeah, Ruffini corpuscles.* She'd aced that course and nearly changed her major to premed. "You know," she said when the kiss ended, "if

I stay out here longer than fifteen minutes, my dad will come knocking at the door."

Topher snorted. "More like ten minutes. He was shooting daggers at me the whole time we were eating. Why? Doesn't he think I'm good enough for you?"

Juniper ran her fingers through Topher's hair. It was thick and dark, always wildly messy, but somehow that only added to his handsomeness. "He's just being protective. He probably doesn't think anyone is good enough for me. My grandmother liked you, though, and she never likes anyone."

"She's a hoot. What's the matter with her?"

"It used to be just inflammatory arthritis. Now it's treatment-refractory systemic lupus erythematosus."

"What the heck is that?"

"A much worse kind of arthritis that isn't responding to medicine. Sometimes she's really cranky, but not on purpose. It's because of the pain. Did you know that in stem-cell treatment, seven out of ten lupus patients had their pain levels drop seven to ten points?"

"Why would I know something so random as that?"

Juniper shrugged. "I don't know. I find it interesting." She tried to think of something to say to make up for sounding like a geek. "Stem-cell therapy will dominate the medical field in the next ten years. Already they're using it in Europe."

"That sounds amazing," Topher said. "I like how your grandmother rags on your aunt. She doesn't hold back, does she?"

Juniper thought for a minute while she tried to decide if that was a compliment or an insult. "All I know is she made me feel welcome from the minute I met her. She gives me fifty dollars every birthday, even though she really can't afford it."

Topher laughed. "Awesome! Coin is always welcome. What did you spend it on?"

"Nothing. I put it in the bank."

He ran his hand lower down her arm until his fingers reached her wrist. More nerve endings. "That's what makes us so great together, Junie. You're practical and you plan ahead. Me, I live in the moment." He leaned in close and kissed her again, gently prying her mouth open and poking his tongue into hers. After she'd gotten over the idea of his saliva in her mouth, it felt good, but she couldn't help wishing they'd had the chance to floss first.

"Hey," he said. "I love you."

"Me, too," she said.

She let him kiss her again, but peeked at her watch. When they stopped kissing, he was out of breath, and she knew what that meant. "Well?" he said.

"You know what I'd really like? To hear the song you wrote about my tattoo."

He sighed. "I can do that anytime. Here we are, alone together in this beautiful room, it's snowing, and so warm. Don't you want to take advantage of that?" His eyelashes were so dark and long it just wasn't fair wasting them on a guy.

"I do, honest. It's just that I'm scared—"

Topher ran his fingers up her leg. She was wearing new gray tights her mom had bought for her, and hoped he wouldn't snag them. He stopped about two inches above her knee, rubbing his thumb on the inside of her leg. More nerves she'd never paid attention to. "Scared of what? Come on, tell me. I've slept with virgins before."

She wondered how many. "Topher, I've told you before, I'm not a virgin."

He shut his eyes, smiled, and the fire crackled inside the woodstove. "Junie, you don't have to pretend with me. Trust me, I know how to be gentle."

"I'd really like to hear the song. Or maybe I should just go back to the house and see you in the morning. Want to go to the movies tomorrow?" She knew he wouldn't be able to resist playing his guitar.

"Fine." He sat up, unlatched the guitar case and unwrapped his twelve-string, tuned it, and began to play.

Juniper sat with her knees pulled close to her chest, eyes shut, listening to the voicings of the strings. Topher had explained to her that he tuned his twelve-string guitar harmonically, just like Roger McGuinn of the Byrds did. She'd Googled the term and the band and learned that McGuinn's guitar had influenced the Beatles, who her dad pretty much worshipped. To her it sounded as if each note was wearing a belly dancer's coin belt.

He sang, "On her throat there's a bright blue bird, right where I like to kiss her the most. Sometimes her heart is blue, so I kiss her there, too . . ."

Oh, my gosh, he really had written a song about her. She decided right then and there, she'd do what he wanted during this visit, make love, only just not tonight. Grandma Ave had always told her, Promise me, if you have a big decision to make, sleep on it first. She would, but she didn't think she'd change her mind. She loved Topher. He loved her. Making love was what grown-ups did, showed their feelings physically, because that was the tenderest part of love, right?

Then, wham, one of his guitar strings broke and smacked him in the cheek, leaving a huge welt. "Ow," he said, stopping. "That really hurt." He rubbed his face. "I don't get it. I changed these strings only four days ago. They're probably defective."

Juniper knew better. This smelled like the work of Dolores. She visited at the strangest times, and while usually she just messed with the lights or made that groaning noise or knocked something off the table, she occasionally did do something this blatant. It seemed almost personal, and she wanted to laugh, but held it in. *Thanks, Dolores*, she sent into the ether. *You saved me.*

Chapter 7

THE MAGAZINE SAID Española was twenty-six miles up
highway 285 from Santa Fe, the capital of the state. I'd
never been there, not even once. Seth and Aspen and I had first
arrived at the Farm at night. It was night now. I sat in the recliner the janitor had dragged in for me so I could stay by Aspen's
bed. Not that we ever celebrated Thanksgiving at the Farm, but
I felt lonely all the same. The doctor had left a pile of forms
with me that I was supposed to sign. The top one was for a spinal tap, also known as a "cisternogram." In the part of the page
where it listed "adverse outcomes," the print was tiny and went
on for a page and a half. "Cisternogram" sounded to me like a
weird kind of message. All I could think was the words inside
weren't any help. *Cistern* meant a place for storing water. There
was *star*, a word I loved for its sound and spelling, and I looked
outside to see if I could spot any, but there were too many lights
in the parking lot. A tern was a bird, like a gull, but with a much
better sound to it, and *ern* meant the same thing, but I couldn't
remember why there had to be two spellings. *Grit* was what I
got in my teeth when the wind was blowing the way it did all
summer. *Gem* was there, too, and *cat* and *tram* like there was in

Albuquerque, not that I'd ever been. But mostly the words that kept coming to me, and kept me from signing the forms, were *nor, not,* and *no.*

The doctor would be angry if I didn't sign the papers. He might even tell the people in charge to take Aspen away from me. If only I had some clean clothes and a hairbrush. Why didn't Seth come to the hospital? I couldn't even call Louella to check because she was either working at the casino or on the pueblo visiting her people and I remembered that her phone was turned off until she got more money. I leaned my head back in the recliner chair they wiped down every day with anti-septic. It was hard to sleep sitting up, but I'd slept in much worse circumstances.

Then I heard a tap at the door and there was that lady, Mrs. Clemmons.

"Hello there, Laurel," she said. She was dressed in a bright red skirt and a white sweater. "I thought you might enjoy some turkey dinner," she said, holding out a foil-wrapped plate. "I'm glad to sit with Aspen if you'd like to take a break and eat."

I looked at her, wondering why she'd interrupted her own Thanksgiving to visit me, some trashy mother and her very sick daughter. I was too tired to think about not trusting her. "Thank you," I said, my voice raspier than ever, from telling Aspen stories all day.

"You're welcome," Mrs. Clemmons said, and held out the plate.

I swallowed the tears I felt making a lump in my throat. It felt so thick I probably wouldn't be able to swallow a bite. I took the plate and walked across the hall to the family visit room. I propped the door open so I could see Aspen's room, and then I peeled back the foil: turkey, cranberry, potatoes, gravy, and stuffing. I scooped it up with my fingers and ate every bit.

When Juniper returned from getting Topher settled for the night, Glory exhaled a sigh of relief. Not for herself, but because now Joseph could finally relax. She saw the way he scrutinized their daughter as she hung up her coat and scarf. He was looking for clues as to why it had taken her forty-five minutes to turn on the lights and show Topher where the woodpile was. Glory tried to catch his eye, to send him a look that said, "Let it go. She's still got her skirt on frontwards," but Joseph wouldn't meet her eyes.

"You sure were gone a long time," he said, setting down the deck of cards he'd been using to play solitaire at the pine desk Glory had bought off Craigslist for the ridiculous price of forty dollars. "I thought maybe you two were inventing electricity or something."

"Seriously, Daddy Joe," Juniper huffed, taking a handful of almonds from the speckled blue Texasware bowl Glory used only on special occasions. While the house had the Santa Fe style structurally—vigas, latillas, built-in nichos—her own decorating touches, with vintage tablecloth curtains and hooked throw pillows, gave it a homey, comfortable feel.

Halle, sitting on the couch next to Glory, pressed the hooked throw pillow that featured an Airstream trailer over her mouth so she wouldn't laugh. Glory poked her and whispered, "Don't you dare get lipstick on that."

Halle made a face and whispered back, "This is eight-hour lipstick. You have to take it off with makeup remover."

"That sounds gross, Halle."

"It's very expensive and all the movie stars use it," she said, and stuck out her tongue.

Joe gathered up the cards and stacked them into a deck. "Well, what were you doing?"

"If you must know, we were listening to music."

He placed the cards back in their box and tucked in the flap. "Last I checked, there's no radio out there."

Juniper chewed an almond. "A *radio*? Everyone and his brother has an iPod or listens to Pandora. Besides, we weren't listening to that kind of music. He was playing the guitar for me."

"Oh, really? What was the song?"

Juniper couldn't help but smile a great big dazed-with-infatuation grin, Glory noticed. Halle poked her back and whispered, "Sounds like s-e-x to me."

Glory shushed her.

"It's called 'The Girl with the Blue Tattoo.'"

"Sounds intriguing," Glory said, wondering if he'd poached the title from that mystery book by the dead writer from Sweden.

Joseph wasn't letting it go. "Yeah? I don't know that one."

"Of course you don't, because he played it for the first time tonight. He *wrote* it. For me. And I am not humming it, so don't ask."

Halle put down the throw pillow. "Go get him. I want to hear it, too."

"Jeez, you guys!" Juniper said. "Can't I have a private life?"

"You should go to bed," Glory said. "It's been a long day."

"I have no idea how I'm ever going to fall asleep," Juniper said, and with the same dazed look she'd worn at the dining table, she wandered off toward her room.

When they all heard the door shut, Joseph said, "That nails it. I'm going to booby-trap the French doors. Glory, where do you keep the thread?"

"Thread? Why?"

"It's an old detective trick Rico taught me. You put a thread in the latch and close it. If it's not there the next time you check it, someone has opened the door."

"That's sounds so James Bond," Halle said, and giggled.

Glory leaned back against the cushions. "Joe, will you stop worrying? Juniper's a smart girl—"

"Since when have Mr. Sperm and Ms. Egg ever listened to smart? No, they meet, decide that they'd like to go dancing all night, and pretty soon there's a baby on the way."

"Like us?" Glory said.

Joseph sighed. "It's not the same thing. We're married adults. You know what? Forget the thread. I'll go have a talk with the folk singer right now." He transitioned into Spanish and Glory heard the words *honorio de hija* and she got up, stopping him before he opened the door.

"Joe, go to bed. Juniper is in hers, the boy's got a long walk through the snow to get to her, and you know the dogs will bark their heads off if anyone comes indoors. For crying out loud, Caddy *sleeps* in Juniper's bed. And hello, just last week weren't you telling me how proud you were of Juniper for making such smart choices?"

He gave her a baleful look. "When it comes to school, I trust her. Driving her car, I trust her. Boys? It's not about trusting her, it's trusting them."

Halle said, "Glory's right. Besides, it's time for some good old-fashioned sister talk. Unless you want to sit here listening to us discuss birthing options and reliving accounts of past boy-friends, you might want to turn in."

"All right. But don't you keep my wife up too late. She needs her rest for the baby." He left the great room and headed to the master bedroom, muttering to himself. Eddie pranced back and forth, torn about who needed him most—clearly upset Joseph, or Glory, the pregnant one that needed to be guarded twenty-four seven? Italian greyhounds were called "Velcro dogs" for a reason.

Glory was disappointed when Eddie stayed by her side, be-cause a little break from Italian greyhound scrutiny would have been welcome. She watched Joseph go. "I probably should go to bed, too, but I have to know what's going on, Halle. Your story about Bart having a business trip to Italy sounded as plau-sible as one of Mom's romance novels where the guy working in the car wash turns out to be a prince. Spill."

Halle said, "First I need another cup of tequila."

"Tequila, champagne, wine with dinner—you've had enough to drink already, haven't you?"

Halle's expression shifted. Out came the grim face Glory knew was hiding there all along.

"Oh, no. What happened, Hal?"

Her sister's eyes brimmed with tears. "If I don't drink more alcohol I'll lie awake all night crying, and tomorrow my eyes will look like the portrait of Dorian Gray."

"You'll also get a whomping hangover."

"Trust me, it's worth it."

"Go get the bottle," Glory said. "Listen, while you're in the kitchen, would you mind bringing me a mug of milk? Warm it in the microwave for a minute, and could you add some cin-namon and maybe some nutmeg to it?"

Halle turned and looked back at her sister. "Would you like fries with that?"

When Glory got into bed, the mattress sunk down a couple of inches under her weight. She wondered how many pounds she had gained today, and whether one day of indulgence would adversely affect her blood pressure. She saw a glint of silver and heard the clatter of beads that meant Joseph was praying his rosary. His eyes were closed and his lips barely moving. It was unusual for him, though he sometimes turned to prayer when he was dealing with difficult memories, or trying to govern his impatience with the time it took for his medication to kick in. Glory wasn't a believer in church matters, and Joseph rarely attended Mass, but maybe it was having Ave in the house that had caused this sudden shift.

A few minutes later, he murmured "Amen" and looped his rosary over the bedpost. There was another minute of silence before the dam broke. "That boy is no good, I can tell. A *vato*. What does she see in him?"

Glory smiled only because it was dark and he couldn't see her. "I'm curious. What makes him so bad? Because I must have missed it."

"Are you joking? His ancestors came over on the *Mayflower*? His ancestors *annihilated* my ancestors and stole our land, for one thing."

"So you're judging him on the sins of his ancestors?"

"Why not? It's true."

"Then let me ask you this. How would you react if someone you just met judged you on yours?"

"This is—it's New Mexico," he blustered. "He lives here; he should know the history."

"Joe, come on. He's young and he's from the East Coast. Give him time and he'll learn."

"Maybe I don't want him learning with my daughter."

Glory waited for the next part, because she knew there was more coming.

"What about him wanting to be called Topher instead of Chris? It's *femenino*, not manly. And his career plans? Majoring in *folk music*? Please. Why doesn't he walk down to the Plaza and start his career tonight? I'll give him my hat and throw in the first quarter."

Glory laughed. "I'm afraid every time I look at him I'm going to think 'Gopher.'"

"Admit it. You don't like him either."

"It's not about me liking him, Joe. Juniper's old enough to vote, to drive, to consent to—"

"Don't you say it. Do *not* say it."

Glory knew better than to utter the word *sex* because if she did, Joseph would get up, go into the kitchen and start banging pots around, wake everyone up, maybe even break something. All the while his blood pressure would crank up into unhealthy numbers. If his went up, so would hers, and Dr. Montano had been very clear on the matter: In cases like hers hypertension was a very big deal.

"She's nearly nineteen."

"But a very *young* nineteen."

She placed her hand on his arm. "Joe, I understand how you feel. You want the best for her and so do I. But Juniper is growing up. She's going to make choices you don't want her to. Some of those choices are going to be wrong ones. That's what happens when you become an adult. I saw it with the foster boys Dan and I raised. We could parent them while they were in our house and under eighteen, but after that we had to let them go into the world down the path they chose."

"Glory, she still comes home every weekend! If we let her move out of the dorm she'd be right back in her room with the posters and the stuffed animals. She's not ready to step into the adult world."

"I know, and it's our job to give her a little push in that direction, encourage her to try things, like living on campus with roommates. She has excellent grades and a good foundation. She volunteers at the shelter. She sees plenty of women who've made bad choices. I don't think you give her enough credit."

"I'm trying to."

She reached for his hand and squeezed it. "Have you forgotten how much she adores you? She calls you twice a week, takes walks with you, asks photography questions all the time. You're still the most important man in her life. She'll probably discuss Gopher with you if you'd listen instead of getting all huffy every time he says something."

"Privileged East Coast trust-fund boy, and he can't even get a good haircut?"

Glory recognized the stalemate. There was only one other card to play, so she played it. "What would Grandmother Penny say?"

Joseph groaned. "No."

"Come on, tell me."

He groaned again and she shook his arm. "Man, you never give up."

"That's right, because I'm stubborn, just like you. Story, please."

"Seriously, the only story she'd have is the story of the love flute."

Glory snuggled closer, pulling his arm over her shoulders. "So tell it to me."

"I can't. It's Lakota, not Navajo."

"What? Do you think the Lakota police are going to show up and arrest you?"

"It's too long."

"I like long stories. Come on, please?"

"Fine, I'll tell it, but the short version and no interrupting me."

"Agreed."

He let out one last huff and launched into the story. "One day this young boy went into the forest to bag his first elk. That's a big deal in Lakota. Everyone knows that Elk has love medicine. The boy waited all day in the brush. Elk watched him and waited, too. Elk was at the end of his life. He'd fathered lots of elk sons and if it wasn't this boy's arrow it would have been some white man's gun, so Elk decided it was better to give up his life so a boy could become a man instead of playing into the white hunter scenario, which, honestly, cannot be called sport. The boy aims and his arrow flies true. Elk falls. The boy thanked Elk and butchered him right there. He dragged the meat back to his village.

"On his way, he became very thirsty, so he stopped at the watering hole and aieee, he saw this winchinchala, a pretty maiden, and just like that he fell in love with her. But she wouldn't look at him, just filled her water bags and went on her way. The boy returned the elk meat to his village. They had a big fire going and everyone feasted that night.

"But the boy couldn't stop thinking about that winchinchala, so he asked his grandfather, 'What do I do to make that maiden notice me?' His grandfather laughed and told him, 'Stupid boy! You need to make a love flute. Go find a cedar tree and a branch so long, and cut it down. Hollow it out and drill holes in it, then you play a love song to the winchinchala and she'll understand what you want.'

"'Where do I find a cedar tree?' the boy asked, and the grandfather affectionately smacked him in the head.

"'Go into the forest where you found Elk. You'll know the cedar tree by its smell.'

"So the boy went off into the forest with some wasna, dried elk meat, in a bundle in case he got hungry. But all the trees looked alike and smelled the same to him. He decided to climb a mountain. At the top of the mountain he'd make a sacrifice of the elk meat and then maybe he'd be rewarded with the gift of a cedar branch. So he climbed and climbed, and man, it was a long climb. When he got to the top of the mountain he was so tired he laid down and took a nap.

"While he was sleeping, wagnuka, the red-headed woodpecker, heard his snoring and came over to investigate. The boy didn't interest him until he saw that pouch filled with wasna, and aieee! Wagnuka wanted that elk meat so bad he could taste it. The more he thought about it he had to have some. So wagnuka tap-tap-tapped the warrior boy on his head and the boy woke up. 'Aieee!' the boy said. 'What the heck are you doing? My head is not a tree!'

"Wagnuka said, 'I'm hungry. I want you to give me that wasna you got with you.'

"'You didn't kill Elk, so why should I give you any?' the boy warrior said.

"Wagnuka laughed and flapped his wings. He took off flying and landed on a cedar tree, which was out of reach of the boy. The woodpecker started singing, 'Cedar tree! Cedar tree! I know where is the cedar tree!' and he was a pretty good singer. Actually, he could make a song about anything sound so sad that it just about broke your heart.

"'Hey!' the boy said. 'Bring me a branch of that cedar tree and I'll give you a pinch of my wasna.'

"The woodpecker remained where he was. 'A pinch? I want all of it.' He started singing again.

"His song was so pretty and sad that it made the boy want that winchinchala all the more. 'Fine, you can have all of my wasna, if you bring me a branch just right for a love flute.'

"Wagnuka did just that and then he flew away with his wasna to have a feast.

"The boy tried to drill holes in the branch with an arrowhead, but he was getting nowhere fast. He was young, plus he had no patience because his father was no good, like a certain two-legged mammal I could mention. He lay down and went to sleep again. Wagnuka was enjoying his meat but he kept hearing that fool of a boy's snores. The elk meat was so good that wagnuka took pity on him, and while the boy was sleeping he hollowed out the branch and drilled the holes, and blew his song into the flute. When the boy awoke, he saw the flute and cried out, 'Thank you, wagnuka!' but the bird was nowhere to be seen. Probably he was off making deals with someone else. So the boy returned to his village to wait behind some bushes by the water hole for the winchinchala to come with her water bag to get water for her family. When she did, he popped up and played his flute, that same sad love song as the woodpecker had played for him. The end."

"Wait a minute. What did the winchinchala do?"

"She threw a turnip at him."

"After he went to all that trouble? Why?"

"To show him that she was interested. I told you, it's a Lakota tale, not a Navajo one. A Navajo would straight-up ask her to go on a date. We're not all that patient."

Glory laughed and laughed, and thought about how her husband made her smile at least once every hour, and how despite her being the size of a whale, he never failed to tell her she was beautiful, and her heart still raced whenever he walked into the room. She nestled her head into the crook of his arm. "Listen to your own story, Joe. She didn't jump into his bed, she threw a turnip at him. She was taking things slow. Juniper will, too."

He yawned. "We'll see. Anyhow, you calmed me down. Thanks. What's up with Halle and Bart? Did you get the lowdown or what?"

Glory pushed herself up in bed, then reached across to the bedpost and took Joseph's rosary down, placing it in his hands.

"That bad?"

"Yep."

"What a crazy Thanksgiving."

"Tell me about it. It feels like a bomb went off in the middle of my family."

Glory stayed awake as long as she could, but then, despite her physical discomfort, she began to drift. As worried as Joe was about Juniper and Gopher—sometimes her mom was right on target—and as worried as Glory was about Halle's issues, really, this Thanksgiving had been good.

Chapter 8

I WOKE UP this morning in the reclining chair in the hospital room and my neck hurt. My legs had pins and needles,
and my right foot was numb. For some reason the word *doctrine*
was in my mind, sounding so much like *doctor*, but not meaning
the same thing at all. Inside it there were some medical words:
doc and *crit*, a word Susie the nurse used a lot. She said the reason she was hanging up the bag of blood to flow through the
tube into Aspen's arm was because Aspen's "crit" was low. I
didn't know what it meant. Then I thought of *cord*, as in, *I cut
the cord when Aspen was born*. I really did do that. There wasn't
anybody else there to do it but me. But in *doctrine* there were
sad words, too, like *rot* and *torn*, as in *torn from your family*, or *the
skin on her neck tore like paper*, making me think this day was already bad and Aspen hadn't even had the spinal tap yet. I
watched Susie squeeze the bag to make the blood go in faster
and wondered what a crit was. What *doctrine* means is rules to
follow, or, as Seth calls them, "teachings." I had to memorize
six teachings before Seth allowed me to go out into public, and
even then, I wasn't allowed to go out alone:

Know where the exits are.

Stick to the script.

If someone asks you a personal question, ask if they know Jesus.

Cops are not your friends.

Without money or identification there is nowhere to go.

Look in the mirror. Listen to your voice. The way that you are, no one else would want you.

My first trip outside the Farm was to Walgreen's in Española on Thursday, November 11, 2004, according to the newspapers for sale in a stack by the carts. The headline read, YASSER ARA-FAT DIES IN PARIS. *A fat rat's ass, a sea raft goes aft.* Nothing good there but *safe* and I wasn't. I wondered who that was, and why did his dying make the headlines, or if anyone was sad about it. I didn't ask because newspapers were Worldly and Filled with Lies. I wasn't used to the motion of the car after so long of not being in one and it made me a little sick. Aspen was still small enough to carry in a cloth sling. We drove straight out of the farm, turned on 582. There were adobe houses and mobile homes, one with tires on the roof holding it down in case of a hurricane, I guess. That sounded interesting, having a neigh-bor, because we had just come to New Mexico and I hadn't met Louella or Billy yet. We passed Pueblo Pottery, and then I saw a forest of oak trees that reminded me so much of *Before* that my heart hurt like someone had stabbed a knife in it. Oak trees. Acorns. Leaves. Forest. *For rest, set. Roe, ore, tore, store, sore.* I made the words fill up my mind so there was no room for thoughts.

On the other side of the road it looked like another planet, all rocky and barren, no trees, nothing alive except for what grew out of rock. But nature is strong. Things can live in the most awful conditions. Sometimes they are tiny insects, ugly lizards, or beautiful butterflies. Then we turned left onto 74 and passed through the Ohkay Owingeh Pueblo with the church made of lava rock and the beautiful yellow doors with the metal hinges that look like black ferns turned on their sides. I wondered who made it. How did they get the idea? I was no good at ideas. Next to the church was the police department, but it was For Indians Only, Seth said. "There aren't any police in this town," he said, and I hadn't ever seen any so I believed he was telling the truth.

Across the street from the church was the shrine to Our Lady of Lourdes, but I didn't know who that was until I saw Frances's book of Goddesses. I saw seven cars; two of them were trucks. I saw three boys wearing puffy jackets. Two black jackets, one green. The boys all had black hair and they were playing basketball. A brown dog with a curly tail crossed in front of us and Seth honked the horn at it. She was pregnant, her belly and teats hanging low. I wanted so bad to ask Seth if I could take her home because I loved dogs and especially puppies, but sometimes when I asked for things it made him so mad he would hit me, so I didn't ask very often. The church's steeple pierced the blue winter sky like a needle and I wondered if the sky could feel it. Up to now whatever snow had fallen had melted, except for some patches in shady places. We turned right onto Highway 68 that is also the old El Camino Real, and I thought of Father Juniper Sierra mountains, or someone like that. Missions were made of adobe, right? I remembered the smell of burning candles and musty hymnals. Then it was like everything flying toward me at once, Sunshine Breakfast 89 cents at the Ohkay Owingeh Casino, Walmart, Lowe's, Chili's, Mighty Modular, Quik Wash, then Walgreen's. If only it had another L and another A, it could say *A green wall*. That sounded so peaceful.

The address of Walgreen's was 1115 N. Riverside Drive. I liked the sound of it. The glass doors opened automatically.

Above the numbers were lighted red letters that spelled *Wal-green's*. I thought of all the words hiding inside: *were, gene, wale, gal, wag, wage, near, ear, ran, slag, saw, war, law. Rag, nag.* I got tired trying to keep the list in my head. The windows had advertisements for things on sale, including paper diapers. I used cloth because it's important not to ruin the environment. Every day I bleached them in the sink and my hands got dry and cracked and sometimes bled so bad I rubbed cooking oil on them. I hung the diapers out to dry on a clothesline I put up that went from our yurt to a tree. Sometimes it got so cold that the diapers froze. They made a clean, cracking noise when I folded them.

That day everyone else who worked at the Farm had gone out to clean houses in Taos and Angel Fire for ski season. Because things don't grow so much in winter, we couldn't depend on selling vegetables like we do in summer, so we did jobs. Cleaning tourist condos was one of the ways we got money for the Farm and what Seth called his "ministry." Seth took every job that came his way, but he didn't do the work, we did. Usually he dropped the workers off and picked them up later in the van, but this time they had to take the van and the Jeep because each group had to clean seven or eight places in each location in one day. The men went but they weren't happy about it because the Bible says cleaning is women's work. I would have gone if Seth allowed me to. I am good at cleaning. When something is dirty, it makes me feel sick unless I can scrub it until it's gleaming and clean again. I would be a good janitor. I loved cleaning up after the horses and chickens because animals are so nice and I could talk to them and not feel so lonely.

But not that day.

"Laurel," Seth said that morning, "it's time to test how you do in public."

I didn't know what that meant. "Can I take Aspen with me?" I asked.

Seth said, "Yeah, but she better not cry and draw attention to us."

"She won't cry," I promised.

"Don't you start talking to anyone," Seth said. "Just because someone smiles at you doesn't mean you can trust them."

"I won't."

Seth in his Levi's, his cowboy hat, Abel's bracelet on his arm. We went to Walgreen's so Seth could fill prescriptions, even though he didn't believe in taking Western medicine. "Big pharma," he called it. Corrupt. Ruining the environment and especially the rain forests. He always said, Everything We Need Comes from Nature. So I wondered why were we getting pills? Then Frances explained to me that these prescriptions were for special pills to *sell*, not to take. It was business. One single pill could sell for one dollar per milligram, so a fifty-milligram pill of a thirty-pill prescription was fifty dollars for one and thirty pills times fifty milligrams equaled fifteen hundred dollars. Easy money, she said. Money we can use for good things. People bought them to feel high and that wasn't hurting anybody, it was a Victimless Crime. Frances, Caleb, and old St. John sold them for Seth in places like the Pueblo or Española, or Chimayo, where Frances says there's a Church of Miracles I'd have liked to see more than go to Walgreen's, but Seth was the Elder and he made the decisions.

I walked alongside him while he filled up the shopping cart with toilet paper, which we did use, chips, soda, and candy bars,

things we never ate. When he went to the pharmacy to get the
pills he had almost a full cart of things to buy and I wondered
where he was going to get the money to pay for it because lately
he was yelling a lot about not having any cash flow and how no
one ever died from eating beans and oatmeal and fasting was
good because it cleaned out the spirit. Just looking at the chips
I remembered the salty taste of nachos from *Before*, and the
bubbly sweetness of soda and how a Snickers bar got stuck in
my teeth and tasted so good all day. I hadn't had one for years.
It wasn't my birthday—Seth made everyone at the Farm take
January first as a birthday, including Aspen—but I wondered if
it was maybe my real birthday, from *Before*. How would he
know unless Abel had told him? Abel was in the desert now
and always. I couldn't ask because Seth didn't like to talk about
his brother. I didn't even remember Abel's face anymore, unless
I looked in the mirror at my neck, so I tried not to do that. But
it must have been my *Before* birthday because Seth gave me a
present of a five-dollar bill. He said, "Get something for yourself," and then he grabbed my arm hard where he always did,
just above the elbow, the bruises hidden by my sleeve. "You can
walk around the store by yourself, but don't try anything stupid
because I'll be watching," he said, low and slithery, like he was
talking snake language.

Five dollars. Abraham Lincoln. The president with the wart
on his face who wore a tall black hat and always looked sad.
Someone had killed him, but I didn't remember when or how
or who did it or why. Seth said the Outside World wasn't safe
and it was better for me to forget anything from *Before* and to
Live in the Now. I couldn't remember the last time I'd held real
money in my hands. Usually in our café I worked in the kitchen,
so I didn't handle money. Sometimes I'd find a quarter on the

floor and put it in the tip jar, but I didn't have any money that was all mine and separate. Everyone gave their money to Seth so it could be distributed equally. He paid the bills. The money felt soft in my fingers, and had a funny smell to it, not dirty, but different from anything else. I tried to imagine how many people had touched this bill and where those people lived and how their lives were going and if every single person in the Walgreen's had a five-dollar bill, then that was a lot of money and buying and spending and it made me feel kind of dizzy to add it up.

Aspen was being so good, sleepy against me, her thumb in her mouth. I looked at the store shelves filled with so many things to choose from: magazines, batteries, light bulbs, boxes of Bisquick, paper napkins, flavors of cereal, cookies in pack-ages, nail polish in all the colors, so many kinds of shampoo and conditioner, Tylenol Allergy, Tylenol PM, regular Tylenol in pills or capsules, even liquid Tylenol medicine I almost could remember the taste of—cherry? I'd forgotten that stuff existed. All kinds of toys, lotions and lip gloss, alcohol, peroxide, hair bands, jars of bubbles that came with a wand, blue, pink, black, and red flip-flop shoes, white tennis shoes, black tennis shoes, underpants, T-shirts with different sayings, Christmas lights in red, green, blue, white, purple, gold, pink, Christmas cards, or-naments, decorations—it was all there, new, wrapped up in plastic which is as bad for the environment as paper diapers but not as bad as plastic bottles which slowly leak poison into the water table and also clog landfills which are what Outsiders call dumps but it's the same thing.

When I saw the pet-food section something made me stop and look and think of the pregnant dog. There were toys and balls, chew sticks, treats, cans of food, boxes of food and dog beds and then I saw a red leash. I wanted to look away but I couldn't, because it felt like I'd forgotten to do something very important, and then something bad had happened that I could never fix. I still can't explain why it happened or what caused it, all I know is that my cheeks itched and I reached up to scratch them and felt hot tears running down my face like snot when Aspen got a bad cold that one time and I had to wipe her face all through the entire day and night. I didn't feel sad, but I was crying, just tears at first, then pretty soon this terrible noise started and I looked around to see where it was coming from and who was making it and it was coming out of me and next thing I knew Seth had me by the arm and everyone was looking.

This woman at the cash register kept saying, "Honey, are you all right? Do you need me to call the cops?" I wanted to say, "You must be as stupid as me. Don't you know there are no cops?" but I couldn't make words, only sound. Seth hauled me out to the truck and pushed me in so hard I almost fell on top of Aspen who was starting to whimper which is a noise Seth hates so I try not to let her do it. I covered her mouth with my hand.

He drove really fast and I didn't have my seat belt on which was a crime and I prayed if there were cops that one didn't stop us because that would mean a ticket and paying more money out we didn't have. Seth cursed the whole way back to the Farm. Words that offendeth the Lord that we used to believe in until we changed to believe in Our Creator because we could earn more money being Native American.

When he came to the gate at the end of our driveway, he slammed on the brakes. "Go open the G——damn gate," he said and I wondered what happened to the five-dollar bill, if I had dropped it in the store or outside the store and I knew I was going to be in big trouble either way. I opened the gate and he drove through, stopped the truck, and then he got out before I had time to shut the gate. He left the truck there with the door open and walked me to the barn so fast my feet hardly touched the ground and in the barn he slapped me so hard that I could hear the bones in my neck go pop-pop-pop in directions they weren't used to going.

After it stopped hurting, he did it again, but there was no noise that time. My neck felt hot and my face hurt and when I looked up, the world had gotten all swimmy and Aspen was crying. I tried to shush her.

Seth said, "What the *f*—— got into you?" and I really did try to stop sobbing but it was like someone else was inside my body making all those noises. "Laurel, get hold of yourself or there are going to be consequences," he said and up came his arm and I ducked but instead of hitting me again he grabbed Aspen out of the sling and held her up by one arm which made her scream and he started walking toward the door like he was going to put her in the truck and drive away without me. I knew if that happened I'd never see her again.

I remember that I clapped my hands over my mouth to stop the noise and how I calmed down really fast because I had to. Inside I was howling like the coyotes that roam outside at night smelling our chickens, but outside I was just breathing heavy through my fingers.

Who would take care of Aspen if I was gone into the desert like Abel was?

Seth wasn't her father. Abel was, but he was gone.

Frances didn't like babies.

Caleb had been arrested for hurting his own baby and old St. John said all men should get vasectomies because of overpopulation and how we were f——ing ourselves off the planet.

When Aspen was born, Abel tried to get me to give her to these people who couldn't have babies—for a lot of money—but after he and Seth thought about it for a while they changed their minds and said it wasn't safe, it would leave a trail and I could keep her. I was so happy to keep Aspen with me all the time because then I wasn't lonely.

I held out my empty arms and said, "Seth, I love you and I promise I'll never make another scene like that."

But he just held onto Aspen by her arm and I was so afraid.

"Hush, little baby," I told her, "don't you cry."

Seth said, "Is that supposed to be singing?"

I know my voice is terrible, but Aspen didn't care.

I told Seth, "Please forgive me for going crazy like that. I don't need to be Outside the Farm ever again. As long as I have Aspen, I don't need anything else."

It took a long time for him to believe me. It was very cold, but I didn't care if I got frostbite. When he gave Aspen back to me her arm was red where he held onto her and that night it turned black and blue. It stayed bruised for weeks but nothing was broken. Just before he slammed the barn door shut, I said, "Seth, I'm sorry we had to leave before you got your cart full of things," and I meant it, all those salty and sweet tastes just sitting in the cart, he must have been so disappointed.

He started laughing. "Do you even *know* how stupid you are?" he said. "I never planned to buy any of that s——, it's overpriced, processed crap idiot people are addicted to, and I only loaded up the cart so the pharmacist wouldn't think I was a drug dealer, you stupid c——."

Such a bad word. Stupid me for thinking I knew anything.

I thanked Our Creator that Seth had the prescription filled before I went nuts on him because then who knows what he might have done. Every so often he put his hand around my neck and rubbed his thumb across my scar and said, "Remember the day you got this? Remember why?"

As if I could ever forget. I didn't want to lie there and get that thing done to me that I hated and I said one word, *no*, and the broken bottle came down. I never said "no" again.

"If it wasn't for me saving you you'd be a pile of bones in a forest picked clean by buzzards. I can take Aspen away anytime I want."

I knew he was right.

"You think it's any better Outside? People act like they care but they will screw you any chance they get," he said, and then he'd whisper, "Remember what happened to Abel?"

I remembered. I tried not to ever think about it but sometimes I dreamt it. Darkness, fighting, a knife, and blood, so much blood. And *don't say a word or I'll leave you here, too.*

Then Seth must have felt sorry for me because he said, "Do you think I *like* doing this, Laurel? You *make* me do this," and he shut Aspen and me into the barn in the dark and I heard the padlock snap shut.

I was instantly grateful. I loved being in the barn, sitting on the dirt floor smelling hay smells, horse feed, gasoline, and grease. Aspen and I made a bed in the straw and cuddled. My mind kept seeing a red dog leash and black-and-white dog, so I told her the story of the Princess of Leaves to make the picture go away. Two days later he let us out. I never told him, but I loved the dark. After your eyes adjust, it is easy to find the exits. No one sees how ugly you are. Once Abel locked me into a cupboard but that was before Aspen came along. After she was born he hit me less, and then one day he wasn't here anymore and I hope Our Creator can forgive me but I was glad he was gone.

I heard Brown Horse nickering through the barn walls. If I reached around a knothole in one of the boards, I could press the automatic waterer for Brown Horse, get a handful of water, and drink it. I was still nursing Aspen. If I got hungry, I would take a handful of the sweet grain we fed Brown Horse. In the dark, you can't see the mouse turds and it tastes like granola.

So when Mrs. Clemmons came into the ICU at eight A.M. first thing I did was look for the exits. There were two, a doorway to the hall and the door to the bathroom, which had a lock but no window, so it wasn't any good as an exit, only as a hiding place, which left only one exit. It would take me four steps to get around her if she came too near me. The hall led to other ICU patients' rooms, but also to the elevator and the stairwell. There were two fire exits. The windows didn't open. Two floors down was the tiny cafeteria with the acoustic-tile ceiling and fourteen green tables and chairs and the lady behind the counter serving corn, spinach, rice, and beans. She was not a good cook like Frances, but this morning she saw me taking food out of the trash and said if I showed up when she closed, four P.M., she would give me something for free.

I could be gone before Mrs. Clemmons in her brown pants, purple shirt, and the pearls had a chance to tell anyone. I would go back to the Farm. It was only ten miles. If I stopped at the Pueblo, someone would give me a drink of water, maybe even something to eat because Indians are nice, and I could tell them I knew Louella and Billy Cata. But what was the point of escaping without Aspen? That was the part I was having trouble figuring out.

After the crashing, the doctors put a tube down Aspen's

throat to breathe for her. It went *puh-shoo-up, puh-shoo-up*, all the time, and the heart monitor had its own beep-beep sound, like a tiny horn on a tiny car that a doll might drive. They did so many tests. Spinal. Electro-encephalograph. Blood. The nurses in ICU were different from Emergency in that they only ever had two patients. They were either in the room with Aspen or in the office between the rooms where they watched televisions of their patients. Susie was our first nurse, older than the Emergency nurses, but she was nice and talked to me and Aspen, saying "Hello, darlin'" and "Let's clean you up" without telling me I was a bad mother to let her get so dirty. She said at six A.M. she had to go, but there would be another nurse to take over for her, and it was true, because a nurse named Leilah was here, and she wrote her name in red marker on the white board in Aspen's room. "Nurse: Leilah. Goals for the Day: sponge bath, normal temperature, think positive."

She wore the blue pajama-scrubs and Mrs. Clemmons wore regular clothes, so I knew she wasn't a nurse. She wasn't a doctor, either, because they wore green scrubs with white coats. Volunteer ladies, no matter how old they were, wore pink jumpers like the old ladies down in the room next to the room made of windows. They were in charge of Information, a word that had so many words inside it I got tired thinking of them.

Formation, form, on, trim, rim, am, ma, man, fort, mart, art, mint, moon; those are a few; *in for it* makes a bad story. After Aspen had her crash in the CT room, the doctors looked at me and told each other in loud voices how sad it was that malnutrition could happen in this day and age, how a mother who didn't vaccinate her child was asking for illnesses just like this, and they talked about a television show called *House*, and yelled at the nurses to do whatever they wanted right that minute, no matter what they were doing, even if it was important like cleaning a "port." Susie told me that was short for port-a-cath which was short for portable catheter which Susie said people who are bad sick have to have.

Cat, there, hate. But Mrs. Clemmons had something to do with the hospital because of her ID tag with her photo on it and the computer chip inside. "Good morning," she said and smiled. "I understand Aspen had quite a harrowing night. How are you faring?"

Harrowing? Faring? Fare or fair? I couldn't tell what she meant, but I said, "Good morning," anyway. Always be polite. "Aspen is still sleeping. They gave her medicine, but it's not enough yet or she would wake up."

Mrs. Clemmons nodded and smiled.

Already I had cracked opened the drawer on the bedside table where the Bible was. If I needed to witness to get her to leave me alone, I would start with Psalms because lots of people know the famous one, the twenty-third, and I can recite it by heart. When Seth and Abel were Christian, they talked about Psalms a lot. It doesn't mean "tree," though it sounds like it. After Seth figured out he could make more money being Native American, we stopped being Christian. Their prayers are made up right on the spot. "I'm all right," I said.

She smiled a lot. Never trust smiles from strangers. They want something. Strangers will steal from you; they will screw you every time. Aspen's ventilator made the *puh-shoo-up* noise that meant it was taking breaths for her. Every couple of hours the nurse came to suction it out and those quiet times when the machines stopped made me so nervous I thought I might throw up.

"You're very brave," she said.

"Thank you."

"It's a lovely day outside. Not too cold and the wind's stopped."

"Yes, I noticed from the window that the trees are still. Thank you."

This Ardith Clemmons had very dark brown eyes that hid her thoughts from me. She wore wire glasses that slipped down her nose like Old St. John's did. That pearl necklace with the very large pearls puzzled me. If they were real, then she was rich, so why did she have a job? If they weren't, then that meant she was attached to Worldly Things and Materialistic, which means you don't have the Compassionate Spirit and you should take a sweat and chant and fast until you do. Her teeth were so white and perfect that I was ashamed of mine. In the back where no one could see, I was missing two molars. One knocked out by Abel, one I pulled out myself so it would stop hurting.

"Mrs. Smith," she said, "would this be a good time for us to go have a cup of coffee and chat?"

"Thank you, but I have to stay with my daughter."

"We can ask the nurse to keep a special eye on her if that would make you feel better."

It wasn't a question, but she wanted me to answer. "No, thank you. I want to stay here."

That made her be quiet. After a while she said, "You don't need to thank me so often, Laurel. How would it be if I brought you a cup of coffee and perhaps a little breakfast? The family visiting room across the hall, where you had dinner? We could chat with the door open, and you'd be two steps away if Aspen needed you. You can see her room from there."

Did she count the steps like I did?

I was hungry, but Abel and Seth had taught me how to fast to make myself pure. "Coffee isn't good for you." *Thank you*, I said in my mind, but not out loud.

"Oh, I see. Is that a dietary choice, or because of your religious beliefs?"

I had to think about that. There wasn't a rule, not exactly, but Seth wouldn't let me, partly because it cost too much. "I don't care for coffee," I said, which was a lie because I drank it at Louella's all the time.

"Perhaps I could bring you some hot tea, then, or a soft drink? Do you like Coke or are you a Pepsi drinker?"

"Diet Coke Vanilla," I said. Somehow the words just came out of my mouth like they had always been there, waiting. I couldn't even think how it tasted. I was tired, and all I wanted was to shut my eyes and drift off to the sound of Aspen's machines.

"I am a Diet Cherry Coke gal myself. Tell you what. If you'll excuse me, I will go in search of some Diet Coke Vanilla and a snack and we can visit another time. Will that be all right?"

"I guess so."

"What snack foods do you like?"

"I don't have those."

"Are you going to tell Aspen more of the story I heard last night?"

"I might."

"Well, if you do, I'd love to hear it." She handed me a card with a telephone number on it, and the initials M.F.C.C.

What did that mean? Minister? Female? Compassionate? Chaplain? "I don't have a telephone."

"Just ask the nurse to page me. Good-bye for now," she said. "Aspen, feel better soon."

I said good-bye for both of us. And I remembered to not say *Thank you.*

She walked slowly down the hall to the elevator and I wondered if she was going to call the cops. Seth said there weren't
any cops in this town, but maybe a hospital had cops. Maybe
she was going to the cafeteria; they had soda machines. Frances
secretly drank Dr. Pepper soda. Some nights, when Seth had
been really mean and I was crying, she'd drag her sleeping bag
close to mine and we'd split a Dr. Pepper. She'd whisper, "You
know what, Laurel? Some Outsiders are nice. We could leave
this place, get a room somewhere, work as hotel maids." She
said that at night, but in the morning she always changed her
mind, saying once you have a prison record, no one will hire
you. I never believed her when she said we could leave, but I
listened to make her feel better. I never told Seth what she said
because then he might hurt her, too, and it was bad enough
with him hurting me.

I looked at the clock in Aspen's room and thought about how
many hours it was until four o'clock. Last night I *was* starving
hungry because I hadn't eaten at all that day. I went for a walk
to the bathroom and I watched this man eating a sandwich in
the hallway. Then he wrapped one half of it back up and set it
in the trash can by the elevator. Outside people threw perfectly
good food away all the time, even though people were starving.
Caleb and Old St. John told stories about Dumpster Diving,
which was when stores threw out perfectly good cans and let-
tuce and bananas that were brown and they went and got them.
Pick off the flies and they were good for making banana bread,
Frances said. On the Farm she froze loaves for when we had
guests like the drumming group. Right now they were probably having breakfast and eating that bread, warmed up, slathered
with butter, sunflower seeds in it, so chewy. We grew sunflowers

in the summer. I had to put nets over them to keep the birds from taking all the seeds. Once Seth took a rifle and shot a raven dead right in front of everyone. Frances said that was bad luck and Seth shot another one. I got the feeling he would have liked to aim the gun at Frances. I dug holes and buried the birds, telling them I was sorry, even though I didn't shoot the rifle. Sometimes I dream of them, too. If I could breathe life back into them, I would.

I picked up that half of a sandwich out of the trash and ate it and nothing bad happened except the cafeteria lady saw me. It was some kind of meat I didn't know, with bright orange cheese. Old St. John said the Outside World doesn't care about the homeless and hungry, but I'm not homeless. Even though I am here in this hospital with Aspen I have a home at the Farm. As soon as Aspen wakes up, we're going home. I know the gate code. Seth will be mad but he'll get over it.

One late autumn day, the princess—let's call her Leafy— insisted the guard walk with her in a different direction, on a trail that eventually led into the dark forest.

The trees out this way were so old and big that it would take ten guards with their arms outstretched joining hands around the trunk of one tree to make a circle. Their heavy branches reached clear across the road, creating places so shady that it sometimes was as dark as night in the middle of the day. Their leaves stayed green all through the seasons. They dropped pine-cones or acorns, which is a tree's way of planting seeds. An acorn is a kind of nut with a brown body and a lighter brown cap. They're smaller than a hen's egg, about the size of a grape.

I would buy you some grapes to eat if you'd wake up. *Puh-shoo-up.*

Princess Leafy wanted to take acorns with her back to the castle. She thought she might make them into doll faces. A doll would make her less lonely in the wintertime, when the leaves were gone and she couldn't go collecting.

"We mustn't go too far," the guard warned her.

"Just a little farther," the princess begged, and she sang a tune so beautiful that it made the guard remember his childhood, when there was plenty to eat, and people everywhere, other children to play with, and best of all, wild spotted horses and white ponies roaming the hills.

So they walked up a hill until they came to the edge of a cliff they'd never seen before. If the princess had been paying attention, she might have realized that someone was watching, but instead she was paying attention to the noisy river that ran below. It looked like a silver ribbon, splashing along. She imagined the rainbow fish that swam in there. Maybe she could catch a fish and bring it to the king for supper.

The water turned from silver to blue and black, then blue again. The current was swift, and the river sounded like it was laughing. Maybe it *was* laughing, at her foolishness. The princess saw five silver birds singing in the oak trees' branches. They flew around her and the guard, and then spiraled down to the river to drink. The princess asked the guard, "Have you ever seen anything so beautiful as those five silver birds?"

"Beauty surrounds us," the guard answered. "But so does danger. I implore you, Princess, collect your acorns and let us be on our way. It isn't safe to linger here."

"No one would dare to harm a princess," she said, laughing

and then bursting into song. Her singing caused the silver birds to fly so close that she could almost reach out and touch them. But birds don't wish to be caught. She reached and reached, but they knew how to stay just out of her reach. "I must have those silver birds," she told the guard.

"Birds fly south for the winter," the guard said. "They need to be warm to make nests and lay eggs for the new birds. It's not right to meddle with the ways of animals."

"Nonsense," the princess said. "I have a fireplace in my chambers. You can keep it burning. Besides, what bird wouldn't rather live indoors and have its every wish? I will place them in a golden cage so that they can sing to me when the snow falls and it's too cold to fly. Fetch them for me at once."

"Princess," the wise old guard said, "you are lovely and powerful, but things are not so simple as you might imagine. Collecting leaves that are done with their lives is one thing, but interfering with the living is unwise, and unkind. I will not do this."

"Then I will catch them myself."

The princess said things like that all the time, so the guard paid no attention. She stood at the cliff edge, her heart aching for the birds. Nothing had ever been refused her, and desire rose up and grabbed her heart. She had forgotten her search for the acorns. To cheer her up, the guard collected the best five acorns he could find. He got down on his knees and searched. Every one had the little hat with a piece of stem attached. When he turned his back to place them into the sack, a terrible thing happened. Something or someone—for he never caught a glimpse of his attacker—gave him a great shove, and off he went, tumbling over the cliffside, falling this way and that until he landed by the stream with sticks in his hair and blood on his cheeks. His bag spilled. Pages from the book were torn out, wrinkled, and flying away in the wind. He was dizzy, and he imagined that he called out for the princess. When he heard no answer, he realized he had only dreamed it. He crawled toward the water, praying she hadn't fallen in, since he did not know how to swim. In the water's reflection, he saw a great hand take hold of the princess by the arm. She gave out a single scream and then went silent, disappearing from view. The guard fainted. He was bleeding from his torn scalp, and in his leg a bone was broken. The silver birds flew around him, chirping, trying to wake him up.

But he didn't. He slept because just like you, he was so sick. I wonder sometimes if maybe he didn't wake up because he didn't want to. Sometimes, when a terrible thing happens, a person tries to forget it by going to sleep. They pretend it never happened so hard that their mind shuts off. The guard went to the place where there are no dreams. It was quiet there, with time to rest, maybe even forever. The sky turned the colors of leaves, yellow, orange, red, burgundy, and then nearly black. Darkness replaced every stitch of sunlight. Still the guard slept, while his wounds clotted and closed over with new skin. The broken bones in his arm and legs found each other and began to knit back to the way they used to be, together. He didn't wake until all five silver birds plucked at his sleeve and pecked at his face. When his eyes opened, the birds flew into the sky and took their places. You see, they weren't birds all the time. In the night they lived in the sky as stars. It was a good thing the princess hadn't taken them, or the guard wouldn't have been able to find his way to the castle.

My voice is so tired. I might take a nap.

Aspen, are you dreaming about the birds, or are you in the not-dreaming place? Rest as long as you need to. One day you'll be out in the world again, playing and singing. I'll tell you more tomorrow.

Chapter 9

T HE DAY AFTER Thanksgiving, Joseph left early for the Candela board meeting. Glory showered, dressed in maternity jeans, a long-sleeved stretchy shirt, and a fleece vest that she hadn't been able to zip for months. Juniper and Topher had made scrambled eggs and vegetarian sausages. When Glory walked into the kitchen, Halle was flipping through the newspaper inserts. "I can't believe you slept so late! It's Black Friday, we need to go shopping!" she said, even before "good morning."

Halle was dressed in taupe slacks and a black cashmere turtleneck, and she was wearing makeup and beautiful silver earrings. Since being forced to take early maternity leave from the feed store, Glory didn't bother with makeup or earrings. Just getting through the day was enough work. She noticed the bottle of Baileys Irish Cream on the table and wondered what it was doing there at nine A.M. She poured a cup of decaf and said, "You might want to dial down your expectations, Halle. Our mall has Dillard's and a JCPenney. This isn't San Francisco."

Glory's mother looked up from the crossword puzzle and said, "Amen to that. Shopping instead of dealing with your troubles doesn't cure anything, it just empties your pocketbook."

Halle shot her a look that Glory wouldn't have dared. Ave didn't flinch.

"Mom," Juniper said, "Topher and I are going to the movies. Daddy Joe said to ask what you need us to do before we go. We fed the hens and the dogs. Not that you'd know it by the way they're behaving."

All three dogs hovered under the table near Ave's chair. She was feeding them entire sausages and toast. "Mom, please don't give them people food," Glory said. "Haven't we been through this already? They get sick."

"Look at how hungry they are," Ave said. "They need more than dry food."

"As I was saying," Juniper muttered, and looked at Glory sympathetically.

"You can't go to the movies today," Halle said. "Every screaming child in the universe will be there. Besides, I thought we had this all planned. Shop, lunch, shop some more, and then manis and pedis. It's our holiday ritual, Juniper. You pick out clothes your mom won't let you wear and I buy them because I'm your favorite aunt."

Topher had just the hint of a smile on his face and Glory appreciated it. "Halle, they have to go back to school soon. Why don't you just take her sizes if you want to buy something? Or better yet, get her a gift card."

Halle shook her head and poured Baileys into her coffee. "I thought this was our tradition, Glory, girls' shopping day every Black Friday."

The truth was, it was Halle's tradition and Halle's credit cards that got swiped until her signature wore off the reverse side of the card. Glory went along just to keep her company while she shopped. But seven months pregnant was just not a great stage to be on your feet all day. "I have an idea. How about I take Mom to lunch at the Blue Corn Cafe, and you can shop at Dillard's and meet us afterwards?"

Juniper looked at Glory with the please-save-me face she'd mastered over the last several years. "Besides, the kids were already planning to see this movie," Glory continued. "You can see them tonight at dinner. We'll play Scrabble."

Ave Smith sipped her coffee and continued breaking off bits of her toast for the dogs. "I'm too gimpy to go out to lunch today," she said. "You girls want to shop, go by yourselves. I'll stay home with the dogs and read my new romance novel." Caddy licked her coffee spoon right off the table and Glory sighed. "See?" Ave said. "A dog doesn't do that unless it's hungry."

"Mom, they aren't hungry, they're mooches! For the last time, please don't feed them from your plate. They get plenty of dog food. Halle? To tell you the truth, I'm a little tired. Why don't we make turkey sandwiches for lunch, watch a movie, and visit?" She peered out the window. "Looks like it's going to snow again."

"Never mind," Halle said, excusing herself from the table with her coffee and Baileys.

"Gopher, hand me her plate," Ave said. "Looks like all she did was move things around." She began chopping the eggs into dog-sized bites.

Glory looked at Juniper and mouthed, *Please take me with you.* Juniper laughed.

"What're you laughing at?" Ave said. "Out of the way, you monsters, this bite's for skinny Freddy."

"Eddie," Glory said, and the Italian greyhound came racing around the table, his feet skidding on the floor. He reminded Glory of Kramer on *Seinfeld*, one of Juniper's favorite reruns, now that she had her own television. Seeing that Glory's lap was unavailable, he leapt into Topher's, and Topher leaned back, horrified. "Mom, if you feed him again, I'll have to break your arms. Italian greyhounds are naturally lean, and Eddie's on a special diet, remember? For his seizures?"

Her mother sighed. "Even animals deserve holiday food."

Glory took Halle's plate to the sink and dumped the contents into the disposal. "There, it's all settled. Topher, if you don't want Eddie on your lap, just say 'off' and he'll get down. Not everyone loves dogs."

Topher smiled. "I don't mind, Mrs. Vigil. I'm used to dogs."

Glory didn't miss the surprised look Juniper gave him. "Oh, does your family have dogs? Any particular breed? I prefer mutts."

"My paternal grandmother raises champion Russian wolfhounds. She shows at Westminster every year. My stepmother doesn't like dog hair, so we don't have any dogs at home."

"That's too bad," Glory said. "Borzois are such elegant creatures, but they do need space to run, and I mean a lot of space. Well, I imagine you'll have had your fill of dogs by the end of this weekend. What movie are you going to see?"

"We're still deciding. I'm up for *Twilight*, *Hellboy II*, or *The Dark Knight*, which is at the dollar theater, but Junie wants to see a chick flick."

Junie? Glory tried not to react.

"They're *not* chick flicks," Juniper said.

Topher made a face. "But *Sisterhood of the Traveling Pants*? Don't tell me that's not a chick flick."

"Well, maybe I'll go see that one on my own," Juniper said. "*Twilight* is about vampires. I hate blood. I feel sick just taking off a Band-Aid."

"I've heard good things about *Pineapple Express*," Halle said, returning to the kitchen with her empty mug. "It's about pot, though, so I don't know if your mom would be all right with that."

"Pot as in marijuana?" Ave said. "Halle, have you lost your mind?"

Halle frowned and set the coffee mug down so hard everything on the table rattled. "Yes, I have, Mom. Since I've lost my house and my husband, I decided why not just throw my mind into the abyss along with everything else? It never got me anywhere and it certainly didn't help keep my husband. Does that make you happy?"

The kitchen went silent. Glory heard a car drive by, the branches of Joseph's beloved aspen trees scraping against the kitchen window, and, under the table, Eddie pawing at her mother's leg.

Juniper broke the silence. "Aunt Halle, please come with us. We'll go see *The Secret Life of Bees*. You loved that book, right? Then you can take us to the mall and I'll show you where Hot Topic is. You're so thin now that I think you'd look great in their skinny jeans. We'll pick out a new wardrobe to go with your new life. Starting over can be a good thing. I ought to know. You sure helped me when I was so down I tried to kill myself."

Glory looked around the table in amazement. Topher: The expression on his face looked like he'd just been told folk music had been banned. Ave: Her mouth was slightly open; nothing silenced her mother as effectively as the hard truth. Halle, however, was all smiles. "Juniper, bless your heart," she said, and hugged her. "You two go on your date. When the movie's over, call my cell and I'll come meet you. We can shop at Hot Topic or wherever you want to go. I have a little something for you, so hang on while I get my purse."

When her sister hurried back to the bedroom, Glory felt her pain so deeply that her heart ached. There was nothing like the holidays for ramping up heartache. That first year without Dan she'd spent so many hours sitting in her closet crying and feeling sorry for herself that she'd considered putting up wallpaper. All her married years, Halle had lived the good life. The sprawling home in Santa Rosa, trips to Europe twice a year, designer clothes, the latest model car. Why did Bart deserve to get everything? Why not Halle, who'd made a home out of a house, thrown parties for people he worked with, and stood by him every step of the way as he worked his way up in the company? Ave had her house, free and clear; Glory had this lovely old adobe they were restoring, Joseph and Juniper, her dogs and chickens, even time off from work while she waited for the best gift of all, a new baby. There was no reason for her to feel even a tinge of longing, but there was always a moment in the day when she'd remember Dan's whistle, or the way he smelled like cedar from his woodworking shop, or how it felt to make dinner knowing that at five o'clock every evening he'd walk in the door and sing, "Hey, good-lookin', whatcha got cookin'?"

Halle was back with her Louis Vuitton purse. "Juniper," Halle said, handing her some folded bills, "show Topher how we put the Milk Duds on the popcorn. Be sure to sit in the high seats so you can kiss."

"Er, thanks, Aunt Halle," Juniper said. "Topher and I have to go or we'll miss the previews."

And zoom, just like that, there went the kids. Halle gathered up her keys. "Coming or not, Glory?" she said.

Glory knew she should go because her sister needed to talk the sorrow out. She'd been there for Glory. They both flirted with anorexia when things turned dismal in their lives, and this way she could make sure her sister ate lunch, but she was worried about her mother being alone and the dogs' digestive tracts. "Sure, I could use a bigger pair of maternity jeans," she said. "But you have to promise me we can sit and rest a lot."

"I swear," Halle said. "Mom, I've circled things you might like in the *TV Guide*. Think you can work the remote or do you need me to show you?"

Ave looked at the sisters until Glory felt as if her face should have melted. "Halle, don't spend all your money," she said. "Divorces start out with each party acting genial, but when the rubber hits the road, it's a different story."

"Merry Christmas to you, too," Halle said. "I've just decided. I think I'll spend it here in the Land of Enchantment instead of in California. How's that sound, Glory?"

Chapter 10

"A LL I NEED is one pair of jeans in size whale," Glory said. "Let's go to Target."

Halle continued tapping into her iPhone and then smiled. "Hurrah! Your Dillard's carries Eileen Fisher! Let's go there and find you something yummy to wear for the holidays."

"I can't afford that," Glory said. "I'm on leave from work. Target's right on the way to the mall. You can wait in the car. I'll just waddle in and grab them."

"You shop in that horrid place where you worked for minimum wage?"

"Hal, everyone shops at Target. Besides, it's just a pair of maternity jeans. In three months I'll give them to the thrift shop, because I'm never getting pregnant again."

Her sister set her phone down on the console. "Everyone wants nicer things. You might not think it's important, it may only be a matter of months, but looking good on the outside makes a girl feel good inside. Besides, I'm buying, so end of argument."

Although it sounded like Halle was talking about herself, Glory knew better than to argue. She couldn't help wondering about what their mother had said. And Halle without Bart—it was still hard to imagine. All Halle had said last night was, "He met someone else. You can't help who you love," and to Glory that sounded like therapist lingo, not a woman whose husband had just dumped her after twenty years.

Glory watched the road for icy patches as they drove across town. Traffic was insane, probably because it was snowing; that and Thanksgiving caused people to panic at how short a time it was until Christmas. After living her whole life in California, Glory loved how snow turned the scrubby piñon trees from a dull green to Christmas-card brilliance. They'd gotten a late start due to having to type up directions for the remote for their mom, who absolutely refused to go to lunch, but she did let Glory make her a sandwich for later, and made a solemn promise on pain of death that she would not feed so much as a crumb to the dogs. Glory saw the way Halle slipped her mom the pain medication. Ave would never come right out and say she was suffering, but when it flared, her mom's lupus took a toll. One snide comment was Mom's unfortunate tendency to be snarky with those she loved best; two meant she had a bug up her bottom and likely for a good reason; but three comments meant major uh-oh time—pain and the aforementioned folded into the mix led to hurt feelings. *It feels as if each one of my joints has the flu*, was how she described it. Maybe it had been a bad idea to ask them to travel all this way for Thanksgiving. When Glory asked Dr. Montano if it was okay for her to fly to California, her doctor had shook her head no before Glory finished her sentence. "You need a low-key holiday season," she'd said. "Your blood pressure is high normal, but if it goes any higher I'm going to have to hospitalize you." Glory knew Dr. Montano was exaggerating to get her to listen. The only person she told was Joseph. Why add to anyone else's worries?

Halle fiddled with the radio station. "I can't believe rental cars don't come with Sirius radio," she said. "See if you can find a decent station, please?"

Glory tuned in classic rock. She adjusted the volume and sat back in her seat. Twenty years of marriage, and then your husband says sorry, he can't help it, he's fallen in love with someone else? She couldn't have imagined Dan doing something like that, but what if she was being naïve? Would Joseph come home one day and say their cultures were too different? Divorce statistics made it hardly worth the trouble to take vows, but vows were supposed to be promises. Could even the most timeworn cliché be proven true, or was life simply a matter of knocking the idealism out of a person bit by bit until she waved the white flag? Glory fussed with the seat belt that pressed uncomfortably against her belly, finally placing her hand between it and her belly so it wouldn't irritate her skin. "I'm paying for lunch," she said. "It's the least I can do, you giving Juniper all that money. By the way, if you think she'll use it to buy a Christmas sweater with a sequined reindeer on it, you're delusional. She'll put it in the bank, or go to the thrift store."

"Sequined reindeer! Listen to you. I'm hoping she buys a slinky black New Year's Eve dress and dances all night." Halle looked across traffic, waiting to make her turn. "When I get home I'm turning the Volvo in and buying myself a convertible Mercedes for Christmas. Yellow. All my life I wanted a car like that. Now I'm going for it. What's your dream car, Glory?"

"Whatever I can depend on not to break down. I also appreciate air-conditioning and a working heater. Halle, I know Mom's a buttinsky, but are you sure you can afford a Mercedes?"

"No, but Bart can."

"Don't spend money for revenge."

"I'm not."

"What have you guys decided so far as your money and as-
sets?"

"Oh, sixty-forty, since I said I didn't want the house. In addition, I get ten years' alimony. Believe me, he'll feel my absence
for years to come."

"I thought California had that no-fault law?"

"Terminology," Halle said. "And if his income appreciates,
you better believe I'll take him back to court. Reassess the
whole enchilada."

"Halle, I know you're hurt—who wouldn't be? But this
sounds so calculated. Almost mercenary."

"Maybe it is. Maybe he deserves that."

Halle sang along with the radio, Elton John's "Candle in the
Wind," which always made Glory get tears and think of Princess Diana's short, unhappy marriage to the prince who essen-
tially used her as a brood mare, though no one would say that
outright.

"Halle, are you even listening to me?"

"Of course I am. That Topher is adorable, don't you think?
Are they sleeping together?"

"I doubt it. When Juniper has an important decision to
make, she usually talks to me or Joe about it."

"About sex? Glory, talk about delusional! She's not going to
tell you. Have you seen how she looks at him? You should have
a chat with her about birth control and safe sex."

"I already did," Glory said, irritated and on the verge of a
headache. If Halle made Juniper's private life her business, then
Glory had a right to Halle's. "Hal, don't be upset—"

"Do I look upset?"

"Let me finish my sentence, will you?"

"Fine. Go ahead."

"You poured Baileys into your coffee and it wasn't even nine in the morning."

"It's a holiday."

"No, yesterday was a holiday. Today is just a regular day, and nobody I know puts Baileys into their morning coffee unless they have a bad head cold or to celebrate the end of a war. It's none of my business—"

"You got that right."

"You're my sister and my best friend. I love you. Please tell me that's not becoming a habit. Hey, you drove past the turn for Target."

Halle snapped the radio off and the car went silent except for the whirring of the heater. She made a last-second lane change and right turn into the Starbucks take-out lane so abruptly that Glory had to grab the dashboard. "A venti espresso with three extra shots," Halle said into the frost-covered speaker. "My sister here would like a bucket of shut the hell up."

"Pardon me?" came the disembodied voice along with the slap of chilly air.

"A venti hot chocolate, extra whipped cream," Halle said, zapping the window closed to pull up behind the truck ahead of them in line.

"I'm worried about you," Glory said. "However things with Bart turn out—"

Halle sighed. "For crying out loud, I'm getting a divorce, not plotting world domination."

"I apologize. That came out wrong. I just—what can I do to help?"

Halle's mouth trembled. Glory could see the worry lines makeup failed to cover. "If you really want to help, rent me your guest house," she said. "I'll pay whatever the going rate is. I won't bother you and Joe, I'll live my own life. And I love Mom dearly, but in order to get through all this without killing myself, I can't be around her constant blame and dire warnings. We can hire her a home health-care companion or something. Bart will pay for it. Besides, if I stay in Santa Rosa, I just know I'll run into the tree surgeon, and that will do me in."

"What tree surgeon?"

Halle lowered the car window to pay for their drinks. "The pregnant thirty-one-year-old one that Bart's engaged to marry." She handed Glory a wad of napkins, then laughed at Glory's expression. "I know, how backwards is that? Getting engaged to someone who's already pregnant with your child before the ink on the divorce papers is even dry? Buying her a ring that I only found out about because it was on our American Express bill!"

"Why didn't you tell me that part?" Glory said.

Halle pulled the car forward. "Why do you think? Because it's so freaking humiliating! I'm forty-four. That's not all that old, but put me next to a thirty-one-year-old and suddenly I'm an infertile dried-up crone with absolutely no purpose, so toss me out with the trash."

"Jeepers, Halle, it's not your fault, it's his. How on earth did he meet a tree surgeon, let alone find time to fall in love and impregnate her?"

Halle sipped her coffee before placing it in the cup holder. "She came out to give an estimate on planting more cherry trees. You know Bart and his effing cherry trees. He wanted an entire grove planted and producing before he retired. Well, he's planted a crop, all right." When the light changed, she turned into the mall parking lot. It was about half full, crowded for Santa Fe.

"I don't know what to say," Glory said. She hadn't touched her hot chocolate.

"It gets better. Her name is Cookie and she wears a giant rodeo belt buckle that reads COWGIRLS FOR CHRIST. How ironic is that?"

"Cowgirls for Christ and she's sleeping with a married man? Oh, Halle. That's just crazy. Give me your phone."

"What for?"

"Because I'm going to ask Joe or one of his cousins to beat the crap out of that two-timing Bart. Believe me, when they're done with him, he won't be impregnating anyone."

Halle smiled as a tear ran down her face. "I'm tempted to let you."

Half of the Candela board meeting was spent reviewing the balances of various funds and predicting the budget for the fiscal New Year. Certain expenditures needed to be pushed through before December 31, but looking at the pie graphs made Joseph think about how much Christmas baking he needed to do. Theoretical budget numbers seemed a world away from actual dollars and cents. He needed to be freezing cookie dough and planning Christmas, because his family depended on him to make the sweets for the holiday.

Dr. Adame said, "Fund-raising thus far has netted only seventy-five percent of our usual target amount. That does not bode well for this coming year."

Joseph was thinking, should he make bizcochitos only? What about the Russian teacakes Juniper loved? Maybe he could sneak some arsenic into the marzipan and feed it to Gopher.

Harold Weiss was going on about the February fund-raiser,

saying that calling it the Black-and-White Ball sounded too much like "black and blue," as in domestic violence, and he wanted the name changed to something innocuous like Sweethearts Ball, and Elena Gonzales said, "Absolutely not. If we infringe on Valentine's Day, no one will attend."

Joseph didn't really care what they called it, because his back was hurting so bad he couldn't dance at either event. He pondered taking a pain pill here at the table or ducking into the restroom. "Why not just call it a fund-raiser?" he said, and was met with silence.

There was always one person on every board Joseph had served on who was adamant about *Robert's Rules of Order*, and whose voice could silence a roomful of quarrelers. On Candela's Santa Fe board, that person was Mary-Caterina Adame, a retired physician whose family had lived in Santa Fe for generations going so far back they remembered stagecoaches. In high heels she was barely five feet, and she wore her white hair twisted into a tidy chignon that would have been stylish in 1920s Paris. The gavel in Dr. Adame's small hand looked ridiculous, like she was playing with her father's tool box. Of course that got him thinking about his forthcoming daughter and genderless toys. No matter what Glory said, he was getting Baby Casey-to-be a tool set. Everyone needed to learn how to use a hammer. Once he'd caught Glory using his shoe to pound in a nail so she could hang a picture, and just the memory of it made him smile, which helped the pain a little bit, but not enough to skip the pill.

"Mr. Weiss," Dr. Adame said to one of their biggest benefactors, "kindly submit your concerns about next month's agenda via e-mail so we can get through this month's. If you have suggestions for the name change, submit them to Jamie and we'll get to it next meeting. Every person here has other places to be, and at the rate we're going, we'll be here all night."

Harold Weiss looked sufficiently chastened, and Joseph was impressed. If it had been him in charge of the board instead of Dr. Adame, Weiss would still be jabbering on due to that posturing men could not help but indulge in.

"All right. Moving along to item sixteen," Dr. Adame said. "Mr. Vigil has been offered a paying position. Should he accept it, he would begin in February, working in our Santa Fe shelter with the duties listed below. However, with his wife expecting their first child in February, he may need to delay acceptance, in which case we need to find a substitute. Nominations?"

"Congratulations, Joseph," Elena Gonzales said. Elena was Candela's Española board member, and had actually trained Joseph when he first came to volunteer three years earlier. "How is Glory doing?"

"*Muy bien,*" he said. "Just a few more months and we will have a second daughter. May God give me the necessary strength to survive another female in my household. If not for the dogs, I'd be outnumbered. "

Everyone laughed, and then Dr. Adame rapped her gavel. "We're all very excited for you, but people, we have an issue on the table. Joseph, do you have an answer for us? Or should we consider nominations for a substitute?"

"Thank you, Dr. Adame," Joseph said. "I'm still considering your very generous offer. I'm afraid I won't be able to make a decision until the baby is born. However, I am looking forward to developing our alliance with Española, so long as there's no conflict in my sitting on the board."

"I don't see a problem," Elena said.

"*Bueno.* Then may I suggest you consider Cynthia Madison

for my replacement? We've served on the school board together for the last two years."

"May I have an official nomination?" Dr. Adame said.

"Of course," Joseph said, calling for a second. Then he asked
for objections, and when none were forthcoming, the matter
was voted on, unanimously passed, and so noted in the minutes. The remainder of the meeting went well, with a few items
shelved for the January meeting. After it ended, only an hour
behind schedule, Joseph lingered behind to speak with Elena
Gonzales. "Elena," he said. "Do you have a moment?"

"Of course," she said. "What's on your mind, Joseph?"

"Do you remember that Pojoaque child-abuse case last September? The verdict must have come when I was out of town
visiting my parents."

"Oh, yes. The boyfriend went to prison."

"Good. I was wondering, did the little girl recover from her
injuries?"

Elena sighed. "Well, in a way. She recovered, but there was
some brain damage. Those shaken-baby cases are tragic."

"Where did the child end up? In the foster system? Institu-
tionalized?"

"She spent some time in Presbyterian hospital. The maternal
grandmother was awarded custody."

"And the biological mother?"

Elena sighed. "In and out of rehab. She was ordered to submit to mandatory weekly drug tests, and four hundred hours of
community service."

"Whew, that's a lot of hours."

"Yes, Judge Eloy took a special interest in this case. You're
aware of his daughter's drug problem?"

"Who isn't?" A judge's life was public, and Eloy's own

daughter had been arrested too many times to count. Despite all manner of help, the situation seemed hopeless. "It's very sad."

"The child's in a good environment and the mother, who knows? Maybe she'll accept help eventually."

"Outreach might be one way. Unfortunately, how far the arm goes depends on budgets."

"Yes, I agree. If I hear anything else about the case, I'll let you know."

"Much appreciated," Joseph said. That case had haunted him because the scenario—runaway kid, pregnant at fourteen—could have been Juniper's had Glory not taken her in. "I'll see you after the holidays. Merry Christmas to you and your family, Elena."

"To yours as well. Oh, by the way. I'd like to schedule an appointment with you to meet Ardith Clemmons. She's a psychologist at Presbyterian, looking to do some volunteer work."

"Sounds great," Joseph said. "Next week?"

"I'll get back to you."

First Joseph headed to the Candela office, where a stack of paperwork awaited him. Jamie Reed, the beating heart of Candela, was on the phone. She found openings for women where there were none and knew exactly which attorney or judge would answer the phone in the middle of the night. Joseph sat in one of the chairs recently donated from a business in town. They could never have afforded them otherwise. Money was always tight, but this year so much more so. He was grateful to live in a community that invested in the women they helped, but he worried that if the recession continued, where would the money come from?

While he waited, he looked at the print hanging on the wall, a local artist's watercolor rendering of a bird's nest with three blue robin's eggs inside. Artists took whatever opportunity they could to show their work in a town of upscale galleries. The bird was plentiful in Santa Fe, and noted for building insubstantial nests. Every year the Wildlife Center in Española took in all manner of injured birds. He wondered what percentage were robins.

He listened to the sound of children playing in the dayroom, which was partitioned off from the sleeping cots during the day. In another room, a local therapist offered massage and physical therapy. Snippets of conversations among staff members came and went and still Jamie was on the phone. Someone turned a radio to the Spanish station and not long after, someone else turned it back to classical. Out front a driver unloaded boxes from a truck that Joseph hoped were filled with donated coats and jackets.

The radio had been playing Christmas carols for a month already, and by next week the shelter would be full, because while holidays brought out the very best in most people, they brought out the worst in others. This particular building had once been an independent nursery selling sacks of fertilizer, gardening equipment, and trees. The move to a bigger location was a bonus for Candela, but sometimes he swore he could feel the ghosts of gardeners and a faint whiff of fertilizer in the air. He thought of Dolores messing up Thanksgiving dinner and smiled. Why did she stick around? What kind of unfinished business caused a soul to linger and pull pranks?

Ah, well. He picked up a pile of invoices that needed to be reviewed, initialed, and submitted to the board before payment. Protocol. That was what distanced him from helping, and the job offer was supposed to be the remedy for that. This morning when he left for Candela, he had fully intended to

accept the position offered to him, but then, as the meeting
went on, his mind wandered, impatient to get back home to his
family. It was odd, but a strange dread crept into his thoughts,
as if in taking this job he would cut himself off from another
opportunity that hadn't come along yet. Was it simply a matter
of worrying about the baby coming? Glory had child care lined
up for when her maternity leave ended. His mother was impa-
tiently waiting to be asked to move up to Santa Fe to help. *I have
been waiting to be an* abuela *for many years*, she told him in Spanish,
as if Glory didn't get how Latino families operated. What would
Dolores make of a baby crying? Maybe that would finally send
her on her way. When he worked in the Albuquerque lab,
hunches and subconscious nudges had been tools he'd used on a
daily basis. They were no match for scientific proof, but often
they pointed the way. Such hunches had rarely led him astray.

Where was this coming from?

A vivid memory came to mind of their first year in Santa Fe.
The house was undergoing serious renovations, getting new
windows, a gas line, and of course the tile setters blowing grit
everywhere. Juniper was sleeping in her room, but he and Glory
were camped out in the guesthouse until the master bathroom
was finished. She was tired of washing dishes in the bathtub and
wanted the workers out of the house. To make Glory's birthday
special, he'd driven to "the Farm," that hippie enterprise outside
Española, to purchase a prizewinning hen. In fact, the Farm was
in the next town from the shaken-baby case he and Elena had
spoken of earlier.

Nearby, on the San Juan Pueblo, the Tewa had been per-
forming the Eagle dance the day he visited, so like everyone
else he'd stopped to watch. The San Juan Pueblo was commenc-
ing restoration of their plaza, and officially reverting to their

original tribal name, the Okhay Owingeh. Butterfly Garcia and Andy Garcia were on drum; Curt Garcia and Dee Garcia were dancing. Tourists were lined up on the dirt road and the day was warm and perfect, other than there was nowhere to park a car unless, like Joseph, you had a handicapped parking sticker, which, though medically necessary, shamed him. As the dance commenced, a dark-haired woman in her forties had come running into the visitors' center, crying. *I want to file a formal complaint against Seth White Buffalo*, she said, and Joseph thought, Now there's a phony-baloney name. Tribal police had given the woman a glass of water and patiently sat with her while she told them how this Seth had taken all her money for some sweat-lodge weekend, and when she changed her mind, he wouldn't give it back. The tribal police told her, Sorry, ma'am, but we got no Seth White Buffalo enrolled here. Call the state police. Joseph had offered to call them for her. She had no apparent injuries other than monetary ones, and that was pretty much the extent of the help he could offer. He handed her a card for the women's shelter, but she didn't seem interested, and he needed to get the hen and back home in time to ice Glory's birthday cake. He wondered what brought this to mind, re-viewing his day thus far and finding nothing.

Glory's dismay at having to leave her hens behind in Califor-nia was apparent. Even though her former foster son, Gary Smith, was taking good care of them, he could tell she missed the daily interaction. The Farm claimed to breed "organically nurtured, hormone-free Wyandottes, the happiest chickens in the state." All Joseph knew was that they were a pretty breed, with lacy patterns to their plumage, and they were said to be good layers. In addition to the hens, and bilking women out of their savings, the Farm collected heirloom seeds for the national repository, something Joseph's father did with his chiles. They ran "Weekend Retreats for Spiritual Seekers," whatever that meant, and he guessed it was expensive. Their website was big on the Creator but fuzzy on particulars, with excerpts from the *Bhagavad-Gita* and the Bible side-by-side Native American quotes attributed to the Cherokee. Why did they always default to Cherokee? he wondered, Cherokee belief systems being so much more complicated than they knew, that it only made them look fake. Throw in the Buddha, haiku, and a howling coyote soundtrack, and that added up to New Age BS to the *n*th degree, but if someone wanted to pay for that, it was their business. Their policy on "freedom from government control" sounded like tax evasion to Joseph, but he'd be the first to admit that he had a suspicious mind that way. They worked the land, grew prizewinning vegetables, and raised fancy chickens, and provided jobs. What was wrong with that was exactly nothing. Their credo, "We Are All Family," struck Joseph as if some aging hippies, hangers-on after the last of the communes had closed their tent flaps, were in charge.

The drive from the Pueblo to the Farm couldn't have been more pleasant that late May day. The lilacs were in bloom, the trees all greened out, and birdsong was everywhere. Since the mid-1960s, the entire area from Dixon to Taos had been home to alternative lifestyles, including Arroyo Hondo's New Buffalo Commune. Long since abandoned, it earned a spot in New Mexico's unorthodox history not so much because it had been considered the mecca for the hippie movement, but because it had been featured in the film *Easy Rider*.

Yet what was jarring to see was so many for-sale signs along the way. Overgrown orchards, riverfront property, vacation homes in default; there was not enough employment to keep things going. Even Embudo Station's restaurant had closed, effectively canceling the opportunity for Joseph to enjoy smoked trout unless he learned to do it himself. Most New Mexico farming ventures barely broke even, and communes probably seemed like a great idea until you lived in one. One good blizzard and the back-to-the-land entrepreneurs usually hightailed it for Phoenix or L.A. Tourists bought only so many handmade beeswax candles and bars of soap featuring sprigs of lavender. Peppered all over the state were privately owned retreats promising a lifetime of spirituality packed into a weekend, and who could blame the Farm for trying to cash in on that? He wondered what their angle was. Mandala creations, and for a hefty sum a person could go away with a small bag of colored sand? River-rafting trips, or starlight ceremonies? Public sweat lodges, which, aside from pissing off Indians who considered the ritual part of their religion, could be downright dangerous?

Then, as he neared the Farm's entrance, he saw they'd opened a café. The chalkboard special that day was *calabacitas*, one of his favorite dishes: yellow crookneck and zucchini squash. He had just begun working on his cookbook, so this was educational and, if he ever published the book, he supposed he could claim a tax deduction, though that was pie-in-the-sky dreaming.

Mag's Pie Town bore more than a resemblance to the original Pie Town in Catron County, some two hundred miles south. The building had the same wooden facade, only a magpie instead of a thunderbird decorated its sign. Grandmother Penny had always said the magpie was an ally, good to have as a companion because of its ability to mimic other birds. But the magpie was also a tricky individual, a thief, like Raven, attracted to glittering things and fond of pulling pranks on humans. They also never seemed to be around when you wanted to see one.

Some folks considered their feathers to be holy, but all that
added up to a mishmash of stories to Joseph, who tried to see
every bird as living its life and thus to be respected. He drove
slowly into the Farm proper because near the Pueblo there were
so many children and dogs. He saw a three-year-old girl playing
with a brown dog that had a curly tail and swollen teats, which
meant puppies nearby. The little girl waved as he drove by, but
ran in the other direction. The dog followed his car, barking.

He thought a cup of coffee would hit the spot, and rest for
his aching back was always in order. Come to think of it, that
was the very week that he'd begun using a four-pronged cane to
get around, and he was grateful to have had it with him, because
the Farm was on a slight decline toward the river, and those surfaces were the hardest for him to negotiate. With the cane, he
could walk nearly a mile; without it, he passed for normal. Glory
and Juniper were pro-cane from the start but for the longest
time, he remained stubbornly against it. Yet it seemed as if every
month he was unable to do one more thing he loved, such as
twirling his new wife in his arms to dance music in the Plaza, or
reaching for a book on the top shelf of his library. Walking in
general took up much of his energy, but he refused to stop daily
dog outings or the photo sessions with Juniper. Oh, her shots of
the cottonwoods were stunning. She'd developed quite an aes-
thetic. Then one morning he and Glory had meandered along
Canyon Road and stopped at the Teahouse for breakfast. He got
up the steps into the café just fine, but he could not get down
them without leaning on both Glory and a Texan airplane pilot
who saw his predicament and offered his arm. Aieee, it was so
emasculating he wanted to cry remembering it, but Glory said,
Are you going to let three chunks of concrete keep you from

enjoying your life? Right then he knew he had to accept the cane or turn into a cranky old man.

He tried not to think about what concessions old age would bring. Looking at his beloved mother-in-law broke his heart. They had in common the anger at having to accept pain medication, but, he reminded himself, they also had each other, and a family accepted whatever challenges came its way. Now she had this lupus, an insidious disease, and none of the medicines improved her situation. Just looking at her he could tell she was not getting better. In fact, he wondered what next year would bring, but he'd kept his concerns from Glory.

He'd watched his wife linger over photos in *Backyard Poultry* magazine, her brow furrowing as she planned her dream flock and ways to budget for it. He'd tried to convince her that money wasn't as tight as when she lived alone, but Glory insisted on working part-time at the feed store, putting her checks into the household account. *Dios mio*, she only owned four pair of shoes, which included her flip-flops, tennis shoes, and hiking boots. When she spent money it was on Juniper, who went through blue jeans like a lumberjack eating pancakes. For herself, Glory wore jeans and T-shirts in the summer or jeans and Pendleton turtlenecks in the winter, a dress or skirt only when she had to attend a fund-raiser with him. His father adored Joseph's new wife, but the day he met her he'd taken Joseph aside and warned him in Spanish, "Be extra generous with her, because she will always put her needs second. You can take the señorita off the farm, but you can never take the farm out of the señorita."

It was advice Joseph had taken to heart. It wasn't every day a wife had a birthday, and if the wife loved hens, then the husband found the perfect hen, even if the journey to fetch it jarred his vertebrae.

To the left of the café building he remembered a spinning windmill, its gray metal blades turning atop a red tower called a nacelle. Beyond the windmill were planted fields, one pasture lying fallow, and two hoop greenhouses. The Farm was on choice acreage. There was a two-story adobe house, a scattering of yurts, and a barn in addition to the café. He parked in front of the café, next to a Jeep that had seen better days, a windowless panel truck, a newer Ford truck, and a dusty Subaru with bumper stickers all over it, including a faded FREE LEONARD PELTIER.

Now that was an oldie but a goodie—probably add a thousand to the car's worth. Even with a hundred thousand miles on it a Subaru cost you plenty. He'd been on the lookout for one to buy for Juniper, now that she'd learned to drive. He left his window down and didn't bother locking the car. Two enormous cottonwood trees to his right clattered their leaves in the breeze. The porch of the café faced the mountains. The brown mutt followed Joseph to the doorway and then lay down across the threshold so that Joseph had to step over her.

He pushed open the screen door and found himself in a sad little gift shop filled with the usual suspects: arty photographs of bees on flowers, snowcapped mountains, and startled wildlife. He admired the pieced quilts, preserves, and some rather utilitarian pottery. The floor creaked, and he wondered about the foundation. They'd managed to evoke Pie Town on what was clearly a tiny budget. Four tables were covered with red-and-white-checked oilcloth, and the ladder-back chairs had seen better days. A faint scent of lavender wafted through the window. Overhead a ceiling fan churned the air.

There were glass sugar jars with the fingernail-sized metal flap that opened when tilted, with a sticker that said, EAT ALL THE SUGAR YOU WANT, DIABETES IS YOUR CHOICE. He smiled, remembering how his mother used to smack him in the head when he put too much sugar on his oatmeal. Glory accused him of having a sweet tooth, but he dared anyone to muster the willpower to refuse her freshly baked blackberry pie. Homemade fabric curtains blew at the corners of the open windows. They had red ribbon tiebacks—clearly handmade, so there had to be a woman or two in the mix at the commune. The screens let in a nice breeze. Whoever had built this café wanted it to appear welcoming. The absence of flies suggested tidy kitchen policies, and though he didn't see a Health Department permit, he still wanted to eat there. He sat down at the table and waited.

No one came into the café. He cleared his throat, said, "Hello," and waited patiently. After a few minutes he called out in a loud voice, "Hello? I'd like to buy some lunch."

Minutes passed, with the only signs of life being Joseph's own breathing. Eventually a lanky kid with an Amish-style beard came through the door. "Café's closed," he said.

"Oh," Joseph said, wondering if it would have killed them to put up a "closed" sign. "How about the hens? I called earlier, ordered a wyandotte?"

"I can help you with that," the youth said, and Joseph followed him out the door, lunch uneaten.

The chickens had a nice patch of dirt to run in and a red painted coop. It abutted the corrugated metal barn, every window of which was shuttered, painted the same red. He saw the padlock on its door and wondered what that meant. Expensive equipment, or a pot farm? He was about to ask when the little girl came running by, calling, "Mama, Mama, my flutter by is hatching!" and she sped out of sight toward one of the yurts. "Cute kid," Joseph said, but the chicken salesman didn't bother to comment.

Jamie wound up her phone call, startling Joseph out of his thoughts. "Any chance I could prevail upon you to take this to the notary on Cerrillos?" Jamie said.

"Happy to. Anything else I can do for you?"

She grinned. "Joseph, your wife is one lucky lady. No, I'm fine here. Sorry you had to wait so long. What do you need?"

"The board-meeting notes from six months ago, if you have them. Some figures I want to compare with this month's."

"I'll e-mail them to you this afternoon."

"Great."

"I guess I'll see you in the new year. Any festivities planned?"

"Just a quiet Christmas at home with one very pregnant wife. How about you?"

Her phone rang again before Jamie could say a word. She had to answer it. Joseph initialed the invoices, paper-clipped them together, and set them into Jamie's in-box. He placed the papers for the notary into an envelope and got up to leave.

Leaning on his cane, he walked through the main shelter area. Over the years the memory of the Farm café occasionally nagged at him, like a recurring dream. He saw the Pueblo dancers in bright paint, heard the heartbeat thrum of the drums, and wondered if the woman who came to the Pueblo had ever gotten her money back. Doubtful. The only way to look at it was as an expensive life lesson. He could see that café as clearly as a still-life painting, its old-timey vibe so appealing that he wished he had gotten to try the food. But it was the padlock on the barn he could not get out of his mind. His cop's intuition had sent him a clear message: Something's not right here. Ask questions. But it had happened years ago. He mentally calculated how near the commune was to Española. There wasn't time to go today, but maybe he could phone Elena Gonzales, see if she knew anyone there, or drive up to the Farm himself after Juniper and the *vato* returned to the university, and Glory's mom and sister to California. His heart ached for Halle and what she was going through. Ending a marriage was agony, even when the love had departed. Such feelings of failure had dogged him for years. One day your life was about the two of you and the next you stood alone, wondering what to do next. Last he'd heard, his ex had moved to Michigan. He hoped she was happy.

People dropped into New Mexico with expectations of an easier life, more meaningful circumstances, but the truth was, one place was pretty much like another. Yes, a sunset at Bandelier or a view of el Pedernal did soften things, but if you wanted a life change, you had to do the work. He got into his car and drove to the notary on Cerrillos. The big box pet store was next door. Why not go inside and buy some Christmas presents for the dogs? This year Glory was going to need help getting ready for Christmas.

Chapter 11

JUNIPER SAT LOOKING out the windshield of her car, which was rapidly becoming covered with snow. It was near dusk, and she and Topher were in the theater parking lot because the movie was over. She could hardly even remember what it had been about due to the words he'd whispered in her ear just as the movie started. *After the movie, why don't we use some of the cash your aunt gave you to get a motel room at the Cactus Lodge?*

She'd had other activities in mind: Head on home and help Topher write a kick-ass Western Civ paper. A quick turn through Double Take, to see if they had any cowboy shirts that would fit Topher, because he would look so handsome in one while he was playing his gigs. Call her parents and say they were going to La Choza for red chile, her favorite, and would be home later.

The motel idea made her hot all over, although it was snowing again, and her windshield was icy. As she stood there in the wind scraping it clean, Topher had been kissing her neck, too, eventually taking the scraper out of her hand and doing the job himself when it started to hail. Santa Fe weather was crazy. Why settle for a snowstorm when you could have wind and hail to go along with it?

The Cactus Lodge was on Cerrillos, one of those places she usually drove by without even noticing. Not in a great part of town, but not the worst, either. If only they could afford La Fonda, her favorite, or the Eldorado, peacefully lit and filled with a spa-like quiet. A room with a soft bed, six pillows, linens with a thread count higher than she could count—now that was the kind of place to make love for the first time. Not in a tiny room with icky carpet and a bedspread you were afraid to sit on because you knew it had a million other people's gross skin cells and whatever on it. She and Topher had been together for three months and six days. How did a person know when the right time was to have sex? Not that it would truly be her first time, thanks to her stupidity nearly five years ago when she traded her virginity for a stupid tattoo. It would still be a really big step in their relationship. A game changer.

Her dorm suitemates all had sex with their boyfriends. They teased Juniper that she was more interested in old bones and rocks than sex. Actually, she would choose three hours in the lab with bones over sex every time. There were stories in bones, the voices of people long gone, like Casey, and insights you gleaned from the past informed your future. But sex was like the final piece to a puzzle, right? That was how adults showed their love. Her parents did it; duh, Glory was so pregnant that she looked as if she'd explode if she coughed. But shouldn't Juniper want sex as much as Topher did? Next to her, he was texting his parents. They'd called him on Thanksgiving and Juniper was surprised he hadn't called them back.

"Why don't you just call them?" Juniper asked.

"Because it's cocktail hour. The only thing worse than having to talk to them is having to talk to them when they're hammered."

That kind of broke her heart, but maybe he was exaggerating, ragging on his parents like every college student did. "So what are you telling them?" Juniper asked. If he answered, "What a great Thanksgiving I had with your family," or if he said, "That I want you to come home with me for spring break," she would say yes to the motel and that would be that.

"How terrible the cafeteria food was on Thanksgiving, and how lonely I am sitting here by myself studying my ass off in an empty dorm room."

"What? You mean they don't know you're here? With me and my folks?"

He laughed. "Of course not. They think I stayed at the dorm to finish my makeup work."

"But Topher, that's a lie."

"So? Who's going to know?"

Her, for one. "You don't know how bad lies can be. Tell one and pretty soon you have to tell five more to cover it."

"My dad went batshit when he saw my grades. If I don't pass Western Civ, he says I have to move home and get a job." He shuddered. "Believe me, that's worth lying about."

Juniper rubbed her gloved hands together, trying to get warm. "Maybe we should just go back to my house," she said. "I'll help you with your paper and then you'll pass the class just fine. That way you won't be totally lying."

"Are you kidding me?"

"If it's important enough that you lied to your folks about it then it's important enough to get the paper done right."

He turned her face to his and kissed her. Oh, if only he wasn't such a good kisser. It felt as if the kiss moved straight to her core. Bernadette and Lily, Juniper's suitemates, told stories about boys who had no clue how to kiss, how they planted sloppy wet ones on you that felt like a giant snail had walked across your mouth. When Juniper said, "Ick," they laughed so hard about it that it got them screaming. Bernadette had a very short list of boys who kissed perfectly, Topher being one of them. Evidently he'd kissed a lot of girls before Juniper. He was experienced; Juniper might as well be a virgin. Yet she had felt the pressure to have sex from the first time she met him for coffee at the Standard. Every day, every time they were alone, it was like this pulsing, amorphous entity between them that wanted to be fed and stoked and brought to life. "When are you guys going to do it?" Lily and Bernadette tag-teamed her. Topher said, "*When* we do it," as if the matter were already decided. Shoot, even Glory had hinted as much when she took her to the gynecologist for her yearly checkup. *If you want to go on the pill, just tell the doctor,* she said, *but remember, condoms are the only way to protect yourself from STDs.* Actually, Juniper was surprised Topher had waited this long. Most guys would have moved on to someone else more accommodating.

When the kiss was over, Topher looked at her with those Caribbean-blue eyes that were just plain criminal for a boy to have when hers were the color of mud with some yellow specks of pollen floating around. He rubbed her arm and touched her cheek. "What's the problem, Junie? You know I love you, right?"

"Yes." But a little voice inside her begged to differ. He never actually said the words straight out. They were always shoved in behind "You know," or sung in a song lyric that could have applied to anyone. But he'd written that song "Blue Tattoo" just for her. No other girl he knew had a bluebird tattooed on her neck. That meant something.

He kissed her again. "Is it the money? I'll pay you back for the motel room as soon as my dad transfers my allowance into my account. I just want to be with you. Don't you want to be with me?"

She nodded. There has to be a first time, she thought. So what if it isn't good? Bernadette said it was like Dance Dance Revolution; the more you practiced, the better you got. Juniper used to dread writing essays, but Daddy Joe had taught her how to write them, and now she could just *kill* on an essay test. Even a surprise, write-it-in-class-right-now essay. She loved essays. Maybe she'd love sex. She certainly loved his kisses, and the way he was running his fingertips down her cheek was unreal sick awesome tantalizing. She hadn't even liked dogs before Caddy, and now she hated to spend a moment without him.

"How about if you pay half?" she asked him, and turned the key in the ignition.

"All right!" he said. "Call your parents and tell them we're going out to dinner."

How could she lie to them after all this time of telling the truth? Years ago, when she was first living at Glory's, lying had gotten her into a terrible mess. She'd stolen money, drugs, run away, and no one outside her family knew it until she blurted it out today with Halle—she had even tried to kill herself. She was relieved Topher hadn't pressed her for details, and hoped that would be the end of it. Daddy Joe would be really disappointed if he caught her in a lie. There were a hundred reasons to say no, from the popcorn stuck in her teeth to how bad she felt about lying, but only one reason to say yes. She loved Topher and he loved her. That decided it. "All right," she said as she flipped her phone open. "But right afterwards we're going home to play progressive rummy with my grandmother."

"What the heck is that?"

"A card game."

"On the computer?"

"No, with actual playing cards. It's really fun. I'll teach you."

"Somehow I doubt that."

"Shut up," she said, and laughed. She had her home number on auto dial so all she had to do was press HOME and the call went right through. What a relief when Aunt Halle answered. "We're going out to eat. Be home soon," she said, grateful she hadn't had to lie directly to either of her parents. She drove east on Cerrillos and there it was, the ugly beige Cactus Lodge, its neon vacancy sign blinking. At least the snow softened the edges a little.

"You have to turn the lights off or I won't be able to relax," she said, looking at the stupid mirror that took up most of one wall.

Topher was already stepping out of his shoes onto that disgusting carpet. He laughed. "I can't believe how shy you are," he said. "In class you have no problem telling somebody when they're wrong, but you're scared for me to see you naked?"

"That's different. I study hard and I know things. My body is . . . different." She only knew what it wasn't, which was pretty, sexy, or in any way spectacular.

"I already love your body," he said as he pulled back the ugly bedspread. "You want to check the sheets for bedbugs?"

"Topher! Why did you have to say that? Now I'll start itching."

He got into bed and lay back against the scrawny pillows. She could see the outline of his penis through his boxer shorts. "Turn the light off."

"All right, I'm turning it off, but I can still see you."

"Then close your eyes." She waited for him to turn the light off. When he did, a flood of relief rushed through her. She quickly shucked all her clothes except her bra and underpants, making sure to lay everything on the desk/dresser so it would touch only the surfaces that got cleaned the most. She waited until she was in bed before taking off her socks, which she set on the bedside table that was bolted to the wall. On top of the table was a clock radio that blinked 12:00 in red digital numbers. She turned it around before lying down because it let off light, not that much, but enough so that Topher could see her ordinary boobs and thick waist. She ran like a maniac, counted calories, did yoga, but her waist never got even one inch smaller. How unfair was that?

Topher reached for her immediately. She pretended she was at the beach in California, that the sounds coming through the window were waves instead of the holiday weekend traffic. Salt breeze—she missed that—on her face instead of stale air forced through a baseboard heater. Some of it felt surprisingly nice, especially when he traced his fingers down her bare skin and cupped her butt in his hands. And her breasts. In his hands, they felt just the right size. Lily told her she should wear a push-up bra, but Juniper liked having small breasts. They didn't get in the way of running, for one thing, and for another, it proved Topher was more interested in all of her than just her cup size.

"Does this feel good?" he whispered into her ear while his hands traveled south. Oh, my gosh, when he touched her between her legs, it was scary how good it felt, as if her heart would pound right out of her chest. He put his leg over hers, and then he was kneeling over her, and all the while kissing her here, and touching her there. Her head spun and she never

wanted it to stop, it felt so good. No wonder Lily and Bernadette were so obsessed with sex. His body felt like one long tense
muscle as she ran her fingers around his neck and down his
back. She had no idea what she was doing, but she guessed it
made him feel good, because he made all these groaning noises
and was already fumbling with the condom wrapper, which
must have been hard to open, judging from how long the
crackling noises went on. As she lay there waiting she almost
laughed, but once the plastic tore open he got down to business, pushing her legs open, bumping against her pelvis, and
then, boom, he was inside her and it didn't hurt at all. It just felt
strangely remote, almost like at the dentist when they stuff that
roll of cotton between your gum and your cheek, after they've
shot you full of Novocain. Where was the good part?

When she and Casey were young, sent to bed and not tired
enough to sleep, they played a game where they'd draw on each
other's backs, then try to guess what animal they'd drawn. It
was easy for Juniper because Casey always drew a dog or a horse.
Casey wasn't very good at drawing, but Juniper liked how it
felt, so she'd pretend she couldn't guess, ask Casey to add more
details, drawing out the sensation as long as she could. She
wished that was what sex felt like, not all this pushing and
waiting to feel the great part taking so long. The motel room
was dark, but she closed her eyes anyway, and saw a soapy,
dishwater-filled sink, her dad at the kitchen table paying bills,
her mom ironing his shirt for the next day. It was a perfect
memory of *before* anything bad happened. But it was also a sad
memory, and it made her eyes tear up, and why was she thinking
of that when she was supposed to be having sex with the boy
she loved?

She tried to participate, rising up to meet him, and then to talk herself into feeling good. Girl, this is Topher, you love him, but it had stopped feeling nice now, and reminded her of that nasty tattoo guy, how he kept saying her name, and how she'd wished she'd lied and called herself Susan or Debbie or something. Thank goodness Topher didn't talk. He bumped against her like five more times and then he was finished. They laid there in each other's arms, and once her eyes had adjusted to the dark, she saw how ugly the light fixture was, gold metal and white glass with some dark spots that were undoubtedly dead flies. If a fly was in this motel room, it was a sure bet there were maggots within a hundred yards. The glass globe was shaped like a breast, if cyborgs had breasts with brass nipples. *Do not laugh*, she told herself. That would be bad.

"That was awesome," Topher said.

"Yeah, it was," she said, crossing her fingers as she said it.

"I told you it would be. Did you have an orgasm?"

"A little one," she said.

"That's great. I'm sorry I wasn't paying more attention—"

"Shh," she said, putting a finger to his lips.

"Next time it'll be even better, I promise," he said. He got up and went to the bathroom. She heard the toilet seat go up. Somehow the sound of him peeing was the most hilarious thing ever. She held the pillow over her mouth until she could stop laughing. Then he switched the boob light on and started getting dressed. She quickly pulled the sheet up over herself. By her watch the whole thing had lasted fourteen minutes. Forty-five dollars for fourteen minutes. That meant that every minute cost three dollars and twenty-one cents. If they'd stayed at La Fonda it would have cost them ten dollars a minute at least. If they stopped at McDonald's or Taco Bell, they could eat something, and that erased the lie a little bit. "I'm hungry," she said. "What are you in the mood for? Lotaburger, McDonald's, or La Choza? I'll buy."

Sunday morning, Halle and Glory had gotten up early so they could walk the dogs down Canyon Road.

"This place reminds me of Mykonos," Halle had said, pointing to a blue door with *clavos* studs and millwork that looked as if it had been imported from the Mediterranean. "That is the exact same color as the Aegean Sea. I wonder if I'll ever go there again."

Glory squeezed her arm. "You can go anywhere you want if you want it bad enough."

Halle tried to smile. "Yeah, by myself."

"Halle, look at me. I thought after Dan died that was it for me. Now I have Joe."

"It's just that the first step seems so steep. I don't know where to start."

"Sure you do," Glory said. "You're coming back here. As soon as you get back, we'll walk every day, and go to lunch at El Farol. We'll pretend we're rich Santa Fe ladies. We'll go in the galleries and ask questions about forty-thousand-dollar paintings."

Halle laughed. "I'm pretty sure you're going to be too pregnant to do that, but you can buy me a margarita."

"I will."

"I'm holding you to that promise." They stopped to look in a gallery window, filled with paintings and sculpture. It was too early for any of them to be open, but Glory made sure to point out which ones put out water bowls on the steps for dogs. "Santa Fe is dog-friendly," she said.

"Maybe I'll get a dog," Halle said. "Maybe Gopher's grandmother can sell me a Borzoi. Wouldn't that be the most alluring
accessory, a Russian wolfhound on the arm of a newly single
woman?"

"Men have fallen for less," Glory said. "Borzois are as inde-
pendent as cats, though, so don't expect a snuggler like Eddie.
They need room to run, and will chase prey to their own det-
riment. You might want to start with something smaller, like a
Silken Windhound. I can look for a breeder that tests for
FADS."

"Why can't I just adopt one? All the time you're telling me
to get a shelter dog."

"And I still believe that. But if you're after a certain breed,
find a breeder who tests for genetic faults. They usually have
adult dogs to adopt, already housebroken. Believe me, training
a puppy is more than you want to take on. Come on now, we
need to turn around or you'll miss your plane and Mom will go
crazy and we don't want that."

"Yeah, because she's already wacky enough."

Glory laughed. "She's just worried for you."

"Funny way of showing it," Halle said. "Just once I wish
she'd come right out and say so. All my life it's been one dire
warning after another. I guess they finally proved true."

"Halle, you just hold your head up and walk on. Lots of
people get divorced. In the long run it'll probably prove to be a
blessing. You never know what incredible thing is on its way to
you. Look at me."

"Yes," Halle said. "My larger-than-life sister who looks like
she's about to give birth to triplets."

Glory laughed. "This baby will be born wearing a size extra-large, I'm sure of it. But won't it be fun to dress her up like a little cowgirl? And not preach dire warnings to her? She's going to love her auntie Halle, that's for sure."

"And I plan to spoil her rotten, just like I have Juniper. Is it horrible for me to be jealous of you?"

Glory smiled. "I'm going to remind you of that when I'm in labor. Seriously, Hal, I'm going to need all the help you can give me. Children are a lot harder than puppies. I expect I'm going to get an education and a half."

They turned around, and just like barn sour horses, plodding on the way out and in a hurry on the way home, the dogs picked up the pace.

All Glory could think while they ate breakfast was that this was their last morning together. The days seemed to fly by and Sunday had come far too quickly. Having houseguests meant extra laundry and meals, but having her family nearby made up for it. Joseph had gone all out making Sunday breakfast. He made his broiled brown-sugar bacon, baked blueberry scones, and a perfectly browned green chile egg puff, which now sat on the kitchen table she'd found on Craigslist and oiled and waxed until it glowed. This morning she covered it with oilcloth patterned with cherries. Set on top of it, the blue calico Staffordshire dishes she'd bought at the consignment shop looked homey and striking at the same time. She planned to pass them on to Juniper one day. Maybe her daughter didn't care about such things now, but one day she would.

They shared the newspaper, which was mostly ads, while Ave did the *New York Times* crossword puzzle. For no reason

Glory could imagine, Juniper got up and took Ave's walker and raced around the house pushing it in front of her, completing one full circuit, the dogs chasing after her. Everyone was laughing. "Time to name your walker, Gran," she said, and Topher called out, "It has to be Luke, Luke Skywalker," and even Ave laughed until she was bent over from the effort. When Juniper returned to her seat, she was out of breath and smiling, and that was when it hit Glory that in a matter of hours, they'd all be gone.

"Mom, are you sure you have everything?" Halle asked as they stood in Glory's driveway, and Ave gave her a cranky look.

"What could I possibly have forgotten? Luke Skywalker is hard to miss, and my underwear and my pills fit in my purse. I'm not the one who went on a shopping spree and bought so many new clothes the airline will charge you an arm and a leg for an extra suitcase."

Halle smiled gently. "I told you, Mom. They're *winter* clothes. I'm leaving them here because I'm coming back, after we find you some home health care."

"And I told you I don't want some stranger poking around my house. I've gotten along fine without your father my whole life."

"You'll need someone to take you to the senior center, and your doctor appointments."

Ave pouted. "Maybe I'll take driving lessons, and buy a new car, too. A little yellow Mercedes twin to yours, so we can both pretend money grows on trees."

"Ave," Joseph said. "You don't want a German car. Talk about charging an arm and a leg. A hundred bucks to change your oil. Buy American."

"This coming from the man who drives a Toyota?"

"Guilty as charged," he said. "When it falls apart, my next car is going to be a Ford Escape. Those are made in Louisville, Kentucky. Hey, I have a good idea. Why don't you rent out your house and come back with Halle? We'll add on a bedroom. I have a cousin who's a contractor."

Halle gave Glory a tense look. "That's a great idea," Glory said, with as much enthusiasm as she could muster.

"And fall and break a hip in the snow? No, thank you. I grew up in New Mexico, and I don't miss their blizzards. I'm too old for change. Besides, who would feed my birds?"

"Mom, there are hungry birds in Santa Fe, too," Halle said. "We could find you a lovely place of your own if you like. There are senior centers right nearby that have bridge tournaments and outings to the casinos. Think how much fun gambling would be."

Ave waved her hand. "Not doing it, so stop your babbling."

"Look how nice a day this turned out to be," Glory said, quickly changing the subject. The sun was out and the sky was blue, but the temperature was as cold as if they stood on a mountaintop in Angel Fire. Glory scanned the sky as if doing so would make their drive to the airport and flight home smooth and quick. Hopefully, Ave would fall asleep on the way home. Juniper and Topher came out of the house hauling swollen backpacks and grocery bags filled with leftovers. Topher had the micaceous pot Juniper was taking back to the dorm under his arm, wrapped in bubble wrap. He seemed to warm up the last few days, playing cards with Ave, helping Joseph carry in firewood, clearing the dishes from the table, helping Juniper load the dishwasher. Glory was suspicious of all that help. No guy lifted a finger like that unless he was feeling guilty about something. She planned to bring it up to Joseph in a few days, to get his assessment of the situation.

"Thanks for your hospitality, Mrs. Vigil," he said. "I had a great time."

Joseph shook his hand. "Keep playing that guitar, man," he said, as if Topher was the next Eric Clapton. Glory read the subtext of the conversation as clear as if it were skywriting. *Adios* and good riddance, you lazy, ambitionless *vato.* Any day now my daughter will realize she can do much better and dump your *Mayflower* jackass.

"Daddy, we have to go," Juniper said.

"You have a full tank of gas?"

"Yes, and I changed the oil last week, and I don't need any cash. Bye, Gran. Bye, Aunt Halle." She grinned. "Or I guess I should say, see you later?" She gave Joseph a hug, then turned to Glory. "Take care of yourself, Mom," she said. "If you need me to come home for anything, just text me, okay? I can be here in fifty-nine minutes."

"You know how I feel about speeding," Joseph said.

Glory laughed. "Honey, I'll be fine. You study hard and be safe, and we'll see you at Christmas," she said, looking at Juniper and noticing a definite change. She leaned in for a kiss and whispered in her ear, "You'd tell me if something was bothering you, right?"

"Of course I would," Juniper mumbled. "You know. It's just the holidays."

Glory knew. Given the chance, memories of Casey, her mom dying, and her dad deserting her moved right in like bossy tenants. Maybe it would always be like that, but Glory was trying her best to make new traditions and good memories for the girl she'd come to love. She had a fleeting moment of insight that maybe they should name the baby something else, that hearing Casey's name for the rest of her life might do Juniper more harm than good. She needed to start thinking about other names.

"Will somebody help me with this dad-blasted seat belt?" Ave said, and Topher stepped forward.

Once Ave was settled, Topher folded Luke Skywalker into the trunk. He slid his guitar case into Juniper's car and turned to wave good-bye. Glory held up her hand and felt Joseph at her side. "Safe travels," he said, just as he always did, and Juniper said just as *she* always did, "Dad, Albuquerque's only one hour away."

After the two cars drove off, he and Glory turned to walk toward the house. To her eyes it looked impossibly big and lonely. Not even the Christmas farolitos Juniper and Topher had put up could help that.

"I think somebody has a case of the post-holiday blues," Joseph said.

"It's probably hormones," she answered. "I can't help but worry."

"About what? Our daughter is earning a 4.0, your sister is coming to stay, and your mom has a superhero for a walker. I imagine we can talk her into moving eventually. Especially once our little bambina arrives. Did I mention you're gorgeous?"

"I'm fat," Glory said, and kissed her husband, but the unease remained. I ate too much at breakfast, she thought. I've got to get back to watching my diet.

Two days later, Joseph went to visit Fidela, Rico's widow, and her two boys who had recently moved up to La Cieneguilla on the other side of town. Fidela needed help putting together bunk beds for the boys and a million other tiny fixes a husband could take care of, if only Rico hadn't died in the accident that injured Joseph.

"I'll be back in time to make you dinner," he told Glory. "Promise me you'll take a nap?"

"You don't have to talk me into it," Glory said, and right after he left, she did lie down on the bed and shut her eyes.

But there was no peace in it. She thought of how she still had a nursery to put together. The crib was still in pieces in its box. A can of low VOC apple-green paint needed to go up on the walls, but Glory couldn't manage a paintbrush, even though she wanted to. Five yards of pink-and-purple cotton fabric— was that enough for crib bumper pads and curtains? The pattern was there, but the fabric hadn't even been cut. There were diapers to stockpile, bottles to buy and baby lotion and wipes, but somehow Glory couldn't summon the energy to do any of it. Halle would help when she arrived, right? Maybe she'd throw her a baby shower, help put things in their places. Right now, with an empty house and a few hours to herself, this was the only opportunity to grab a nap before she had to do something else. She thought of her hens roosting in their warm coop in the snowy weather, the dogs in their flannel beds by the fire, and Eddie glued to her side. She was nearly asleep when the weird metallic groaning started up.

Ahhhwwwooooaaawww. Then silence. Dolores, or plumbing?

Glory remembered her first night's sleep in the new house, around two A.M., when the same low groaning made everyone sit up straight in bed and call out, "You okay?" Eventually they gathered in the kitchen with mugs of warm milk.

"Daddy Joe," Juniper said. "Find a reasonable explanation for that, please?"

Glory said, "Jenny warned me when she first showed me the property that any house this old had a ghost or two, but I thought she was kidding."

"There're no such thing as ghosts," Joseph insisted.

"Really?" Juniper said. "Come on. If there are no such things as ghosts, then why are there like nine million ghost stories in Santa Fe? La Fonda's gambling salesman, the headless horseman of Alto Street, Casa Real Health Center, La Residencia Senior Center—man, would Gran love that—the Grant Corner Inn, and what about the Mission San Miguel? That whole block is supposed to be haunted."

"You listen to me, arbolita. It's easier to be superstitious than it is to replace plumbing," Joseph answered. "Whatever that noise was, it was mechanical. When we have the money I'll call my cousin Pedro the plumber. He can figure it out in no time."

As if the ghost had waited for him to get high up on his horse, the groaning came again. Glory watched Joseph's face turn pale. "I hope it's not the boiler." He got up to fetch his toolbox and began muttering in Spanish.

Glory and Juniper sat where they were, laughing, and then Juniper said, "Our ghost deserves a name. Since she's such a pain in the butt, how about we call her Dolores?" and that was that. They said good-night to Dolores, went to bed, and slept through the night.

The Vigils grew used to the noise the same way they did to the out-of-plumb doorways and the guest room always being chilly. Just when Glory was sure they'd heard the last of Dolores, it would happen again. She seemed to be fondest of the dinner hour, especially when they had guests, or the early-morning hours, but Glory remembered the one time she had the chimney man over to sweep out the living-room fireplace. He was sitting at the kitchen table going over the estimate, and Dolores let loose with one of her howls. "What the heck was that?" the man said, and Glory laughed. "My husband thinks it's the plumbing, but I'm pretty sure we have a ghost." The chimney sweep got up from the table and walked out the door without another word. They ended up having to find another company to do the work.

Much to Joseph's dismay, a peek into the plumbing and heating system didn't reveal any explanation for the periodic groaning. Dolores wasn't predictable, and of course she never groaned when they wanted her to. Glory had a theory that Dolores only visited 103 Colibri Road part-time, and when the house was quiet, she was out haunting other homes, sort of like a spirit time share.

Glory had no fear of ghosts, but the dogs had other ideas. Two seconds after the groan, here they were, as always, butted up against Glory in a king-size bed that now felt more like a twin. Dodge was shaking and even Caddy seemed upset. Glory suspected it was more digestive fallout from Ave's endless treats suddenly coming to a halt than the ghost, and Juniper and Gopher's fault, too, for getting them accustomed to long afternoon walks that Glory suspected the kids took for the opportunity to kiss rather than exercise the dogs. Cadillac kept nosing her in the side with a tennis ball, and now Dodge was trying to get Eddie to play, leaping about on the mattress, sprawling his front legs in a pose that always reminded Glory of yoga, barking the supersonic cattle-dog bark that made Dolores's groaning theme song sound like a lullaby.

"Off the bed," she said, but they were having none of that. She tried pushing them away, but they were heavy and hunkered down. Eddie ignored Dodge's overtures for a while, but even an Italian greyhound couch potato had his limits. Suddenly he leapt off the bed, clearing Glory's belly by a hair. That did it. She sat up. "You guys need a walk," she said, and began getting out harnesses and coats. The dogs went berserk, yipping and jumping at the good fortune of two walks in one day, because little did she know that Joseph had walked them early this morning while she slept in.

It had been months since she'd worked with them, and when training stopped, bad behaviors returned. When Halle got here, Glory would make a list of things she was too pregnant to do, and dog walking would be number one on that list.

Glory found her gloves and scarf, pulled on her down coat that barely reached her sides, thanks to her belly, and tucked her hair inside a knit cap. Getting her boots on took some effort, but finally she managed, though she gave up on zipping them. She held Dodge and Caddy's leashes in her right hand, hoping that Caddy would keep Dodge in line. Eddie's leash was in her left hand, not a balanced walk, but the best she could manage under the circumstances. They went out the door, turned into the alley that connected them to Canyon Road, and walked through the newly fallen snow, dog breath steaming in front of them like smoke. Glory never got used to how beautiful winter could be here: Chimneys puffed out smoke, snow dusted adobe walls decorated with farolitos, both old style with candles in paper bags and the modern electric kind, illuminating the streets at dusk with an old-world charm. They reminded her of votive candles in the red glass holders that Joseph sometimes stopped in to light at the cathedral when he was sending up special prayers. The scent of burning piñon wood made her feel a little drunk. Bare cottonwood branches starkly contrasted with the blue sky, and while cottonwoods were lovely, they weren't Solomon's Oak, her beloved old tree in California, under which the modern-day druids worshiped, couples married, and photographers, like her Joe, loved to photograph.

So many memories: Dan cutting firewood. Piper and Cricket nickering on cold days when she fixed them a hot bran mash they could apparently smell coming before she walked out back to the barn. She wished she could have brought the horses with her, but they were growing old and used to their life at Solomon's Oak. Trailering across two states would have been rough on them, not to mention the altitude and climate change. She would have had to board them out, and that was no life for them at their age. Gary was good about e-mailing pictures every week. Soon after he took over Solomon's Oak, he and Robynn had married, and she was pregnant with twins, due in spring. Glory thought of her dearest friends, Lorna and Juan, the way they decorated the Butterfly Creek General Store with lights at Christmas time, the big party they always threw, complete with a rocking band and more food than anyone could eat. She'd first danced with Joseph there, and felt the first stirrings of love in her broken heart. She and Lorna had shared countless heart-to-heart conversations alongside the riverbank. In Santa Fe Glory was friends with Rico's widow, Fidela, and had a cup of tea every week with her neighbor, Margaret Yearwood, but it wasn't the same as being home in a place she'd lived her whole life. Every Christmas she and Joseph sent Lorna and Juan a box filled with homemade jam, jars of green chile, lime pistachios, and sage bundles. As soon as it was safe to travel with the baby, Glory was going to visit with little Casey, or whatever her name turned out to be.

She stopped to catch her breath, surprised how the slight incline of Canyon Road felt strenuous. It had to be lugging around the baby weight. And darn it, Glory felt a headache coming on. She wasn't allowed to take her migraine medicine while she was pregnant. Not even a Tylenol. She had planned to walk longer, but felt so tired she made herself turn toward home. Then Dodge spied a child with a sled and barked, lunging forward to play, yanking the leash in her hand so hard that she stumbled in her unzipped boot. "Dodge!" she called out, but it was too late. He'd already pulled the leash in her hand, tipping her off balance, and she had turned her ankle. She took a breath, thankful she hadn't fallen. The dog went wackadoo in the snow and considered every child playing outside an invitation for him to join in. When she hauled the leash back in, Caddy startled and tried to pull away, so the effort to contain both dogs required all her strength. Just as she cried out, "Enough!" she felt a twinge in her belly, like pulling a muscle. Dodge had forgotten all his manners, Caddy didn't understand why he was being punished, and Eddie, meanwhile, trotted along like he was above it all, oblivious. She caught her breath, gathered the leashes, and although it made her arms ache, kept everyone on a short rein the rest of the way home.

They crossed Acequia Madre and arrived back at the house a lot later than she'd thought. Her belly felt tender where she'd pulled that muscle. Her ankle ached a little, but not enough to warrant an X-ray. I won't tell Joseph, she thought, as she unleashed the dogs and sat down hard on the couch, too tired to pull off her boots. She had to catch her breath again, something

that had been bothering her of late, as the baby pressed against
her diaphragm. When she felt a strange pull across her belly, she
placed a hand there, trying to understand what it was. It didn't
feel like a kick. When it stopped, she managed to toe off her
boots. She lay down against the throw pillows and dozed while
the dogs stretched out in front of the fire. The next twinge
woke her up. Surely it couldn't be a contraction. She looked at
her watch, marked the time, and when another one came fifteen minutes later, felt her heart fill up with dread. Seven months
was too early to give birth safely. She picked up the phone and
called Dr. Montano's office. Surely the doctor would say it was
nothing, Braxton Hicks, or some other pregnancy phenome-
non explained in the books she'd been meaning to read. She told
the receptionist what happened, and as expected, Dr. M was
busy with a patient. "She'll call you back," the woman promised,
and Glory hung up. Not even a minute passed before the phone
rang.

"Glory," she said, "I hear you're having some discomfort.
Tell me exactly what happened."

"It's probably nothing. I walked the dogs and I think I pulled
a muscle in my belly."

"How much does the dog weigh?"

"Sixty pounds or so. I had my collie on that side, too, but he
only weighs forty pounds at the most. I didn't fall or anything,
but I did stumble, sprained my ankle a little, and there was a
sensation, I don't know. It just felt like a pull. I lay down right
away. About a half hour later, I felt it again, just a twinge, then
another one, fifteen minutes after that. Three times so far."

"Describe the pain."

"It isn't pain, it's more like pulling. Like someone is yanking
me into a corset. I'm sorry to bother you when you're busy with

other patients, it's just that I figured better safe than sorry." She
forced a laugh.

"No, you did the right thing. Is Joseph home?"

"Not yet. I expect him in a couple of hours."

"Call him."

"All right, but—"

"Can you ask a neighbor to drive you to the ER?"

Glory's neighbor, Margaret Yearwood, had recently been
diagnosed with MS and didn't drive. The neighbors on the
other side were snowbirds and had left for the winter. "Dr. M,
I'm fine, I can drive myself to your office."

"I'd rather you not. I'm calling you a cab right now. I'll meet
you at St. Vincent's in fifteen minutes."

"Do I really have to go to the hospital?"

"If it turns out to be nothing, what's the harm? But if it's a
problem, given your age, we need to be extra careful."

Here we go again, Glory thought. I'm old, my hair looks like
Medusa's, and any minute I'm going to break out in warts, but
worst of all, I endangered my baby to walk dogs. "All right," she
said.

"Call Joseph. Tell him to meet us there."

Glory tried Joseph's cell phone, but it went straight to voicemail. Coverage in La Cieneguilla was spotty. She left a message,
wrote him a note, and taped it to the microwave door, their
official message center. She found her purse and a poncho that
fit better than the coat, but when it came to putting her snow
boots on again, she couldn't muster the energy. She slid into a
pair of slippers and waited by the door, watching for the cab
from the window. Only when it arrived did she allow herself to
feel frightened. The cab driver came to the door. He was a sweet
old man, insisting on helping her into the cab and covering her

with a blanket after he latched an extension on her seat belt. "Thank you," she said. "I need to go to St. Vincent's ER."

"Yes, I know." He crossed himself and removed the rosary that was hanging on his rearview mirror and placed it in her hands. "We'll pray to the Holy Mother together," he said. "No one carries a prayer to the Lord better than Our Blessed Mother. Now try to relax, ma'am. I'm a very good driver and we'll be at the hospital before you know it."

When the next pang came, she was trying not to cry, but the headache behind her eye was now so fierce that she thought one tear might split her head open. What a time for a migraine, she thought; I wonder how bad it will get. At the ER entrance someone was waiting with a wheelchair, silly when she could walk by herself, but she sat down, grateful for the ride. All she had to do was hand over her insurance card and ID. She was whisked into a room straightaway, and transferred to a gurney with the help of a burly male nurse. He took her blood pressure and gasped. "Whoa," he said. "Doctor wants you to lie down on your left side."

"Can't I lie on my right side instead? That's the side I sleep on."

He looked at her as if assessing whether or not it was really necessary to explain, then launched into an explanation. "The human heart isn't the best design. Your inferior vena cava is on the right side, which means if you lie down on that side, your heart is forced to pump harder. This automatically elevates your blood pressure." He paused a moment, and then said, "Your blood pressure is already, shall we say, elevated?"

"How elevated?"

"It's better if we wait for your physician. Try to relax."

Why was this happening? Just because she was older? Dodge

hadn't pulled that hard. For the first time ever she wished Do-lores would just pack up her crap and move on. This wouldn't have happened if she'd been able to take her nap. And how ri-diculous was it to lie here fuming at a so-called ghost? Not to mention her pounding head.

Dr. Montano pulled the curtain aside and smiled. "Hey there, Glory." The male nurse pointed to the BP monitor. "Holy Mother of God," Dr. Montano said. "Get a monitor around her belly, raise her legs above her heart, and call CT."

The nurse nodded. "Her gums are tacky," he said. "Dehy-drated."

Not one word of that made sense to Glory. "Speaking of dehydrated, I'm really thirsty. Could I have a drink of water?"

The male nurse and Dr. M. answered at the same time, an emphatic "No."

"Run her IV wide open," the doctor said.

"Will do," the male nurse said.

"The IV will get you hydrated soon enough, Glory. Later we can try some ice chips, but not right now."

"What about my headache?" Glory said. "Isn't there some-thing you can give me?"

"I'm afraid not." Dr. Montano listened to her heart and lungs.

"Am I in labor?"

Her doctor smiled while she moved the stethoscope onto her belly. "I don't think so, but we're going to watch you care-fully."

"Then after the IV, I can go home?"

"Not just yet. I'm going to give you some methyldopa to get your blood pressure down. I'll need a urine sample to check for albumin."

"Egg white?"

Her no-nonsense doctor exhaled. "Look, I'm not going to mince words. I'm concerned you're heading into pre-eclampsia, and toxemia usually follows. That worries me much more than a few contractions. Try to relax."

Everyone kept saying that, as if she had the power to turn serenity on like a light switch. And those little pulling sensations—how could that be a contraction? "So the baby's all right?"

"I think so, but let's see how the next couple of hours go."

"Can I at least sit up?"

"Sorry, Glory, but I hope you're comfortable in this position, because you're going to be on bed rest for a while, maybe even the remainder of the pregnancy."

What? How could a couple of twinges deliver her to this state? "Do I have to use a bedpan for the urine sample?"

Dr. Montano smiled and looked at the nurse. They both chuckled. "First thing every patient asks. No one ever died from using a bedpan. Juan here is going to help you do some relaxation exercises and deep breathing. Work with me, all right? Our goal is total relaxation."

"I'm trying," Glory said, aching with tears she was determined not to shed.

"Good. Breathe in." She looked up at the monitors and the cuff around her arm inflated. "Breathe out. Where's Joseph?"

"I tried his phone but it went to voicemail. He's over in La Cieneguilla, helping a friend of ours move. Cell coverage there isn't great."

"Breathe. I seem to recall you saying he used to be a cop here in Santa Fe, is that right?"

"No, it was Albuquerque. But that was a long time ago."

"That is not a deep breath. You can do better. All the way

in. Fill up your lungs. Cops have this lifelong bond when it comes to helping each other out. Write down the address for me and we'll get someone from the police force to drive out there and fetch him. Shut your eyes. Keep up the breathing. He'll be here before you know it."

Dr. Montano left. The blood pressure cuff did its thing. Glory could hear another doctor talking in a low voice to the male nurse. The bedpan arrived via a female nurse, and thanks to all the liquid in the IV, peeing was not a problem, but it still was disgusting to have to perch there like some whale trying to fit into a sardine can. And she was still thirsty. An hour went by with the breathing. The twinges had stopped, but Glory was afraid if she moved they'd start again. When the male nurse came to give her the medicine, he said, "How's the headache?"

"Oh, you know. Horrible."

"You're doing great on the breathing. I'll be right back." He returned with an iPod and headphones. "Listen to some quiet music, it'll make you relax and help the time pass."

"Thank you," she said, and as R. Carlos Nakai's flute drifted into her ears, Glory thought, Juniper would totally make fun of this music. She was dreaming of California, the pull and sweep of the ocean waves, humpback whales blowing air as they surfaced before another deep dive, when Joseph showed up. He pulled a chair close to her gurney. "Shh," he said when she tried to talk. He straightened her headphones, kissed her hand, and smiled at her like everything was all right. Anyone who'd been a cop for five minutes knew tricks to keep his face impassive, but the rattle of the rosary beads he carried in his pocket said otherwise. She tried to think of it as a kind of backbeat to the flute music, and not for the first time did she wish she could believe in God the way her mother did. When she tried, it was like sitting in the dark by herself, nothing there. She felt the baby turn inside her, but it wasn't like the twinges, more like getting comfortable because probably she hated lying on her left side, too. The IV dripped into her arm, and her headache was a little bit better now that Joseph was here. I'm right where I'm supposed to be, she told herself, and tried to sleep.

Chapter 12

"YOU'LL BE PERFECTLY safe," Mrs. Clemmons told me when she arrived with a bag of presents this morning, and a box of doughnuts. *Ugh, dough, oh, ho, hug, hut.* It couldn't be my birthday from *Before*, not for this many days in a row. Inside the bag were clothes. New ones, store-bought: three pairs of Jockey underpants in plastic. Plastic was so bad for the environment but did the Outside World care? No. Socks on a plastic sock-sized coat hanger. Where would you hang it? In a dollhouse? Aspen and I built a doll log cabin once, using sticks we gathered and flour-and-paste glue. Seth got mad and threw it in the fire. He said, *All that time you spent fooling around with that you should have been cleaning the kitchen. Clean, lean, lace, ace.* The sticks caught fire quickly, and Aspen cried while they burned. I put my hand over her mouth and hugged her. *We'll make another one,* I whispered that night while we tried to go to sleep. *This time we'll hide it and he won't ever find it.*

In the bag was a shirt that buttoned instead of my turtleneck that covered my scar. The clothes had that new, bad smell of chemicals that Frances says are slowly killing the earth. There was a brown-and-orange box with shoes called Merrell Jungle Mocs. I don't know why anyone would need shoes meant for the jungle if you didn't live in a jungle. The only word I could find inside *jungle* was *gun* and I hated guns. It was a crazy lot of presents, but no one ever gives you something for nothing. I lifted out a packet of six pink razors. "Disposable," the label read. Now there was a word: *Pose, pods, seal, sable, plea.* No one asked the earth if it minded plastic. Next a new blue hairbrush, with no other hair in it. A purple toothbrush in a wrapper like the razors. A box with toothpaste inside; we used baking soda at the Farm. Suave hair shampoo called Waterfall Mist. *Waterfall* sounded just like it was in real life, lovely, with a season in there, too, if you capitalized the F in *fall.* We used bar soap at the Farm. Suave conditioner also called Waterfall Mist. I didn't remember what conditioner did. The label read, *Bring out the natural beauty of your hair with the gentle cleansers and conditioners in the revitalizing scent of clean ocean air! Hypoallergenic. New formula has longer lasting fragrance. Compare to Bath and Body Works.* I had never heard of them.

Clean Ocean Air. *Lean, cone, rail. Ace, cane, real.* That made me remember the ocean. Blue water white foam brown sand seagulls. Where was the ocean? *Can, no, on.* Such a big blue roaring.

Once that came into my mind, I couldn't read the label anymore. For some reason, it seemed selfish to think of the ocean and have presents while Aspen had a machine breathing for her and needles poking her for blood tests and what did all this stuff cost? *Nothing is ever free. Ever. People will screw you.* It looked expensive. Inside the Jungle box were brown suede shoes. *Suede, sued, used, dues.* Suede was animal skin, which meant an animal died for it, which was wrong wrong wrong, but the shoes in my hand were the softest things I ever held besides Aspen when she was born, and they were size 7, my size. How did Mrs. Clemmons know? Could she read my mind like Seth could? *Do*

the right thing, even if it's the hardest thing. I held the bag out for
Mrs. Clemmons in her black pants and white blouse and that
same pearl necklace she wore every day so far. "I'm sorry but I
can't take these."

"Oh? Why is that?" she asked, her silver hair cut short like a
man's, not allowed at the Farm but in the Outside World women
are vain, behave like men, don't know their place, put on a skirt.

"Because I don't have any money to pay you back."

"I wasn't expecting you to," she said.

When she didn't take the bag I felt panic in my stomach.
"Seth doesn't allow it."

"I see," Mrs. Clemmons said. "You don't want to go against
Seth. It sounds as if his opinion is very important to you."

"He's the Elder. We love him. I love him."

She smiled like she understood. I wanted to say, How can
you smile? Who is your leader? What consequences do *you* get
when you don't follow the rules? Do you get shut into a closet
with no place to go to the bathroom? Do you have to fast for
three days? Take a stupid sweat? The rocks come alive in there.
They turn into people and they know all your sins. I was feeling mean because I was tired. Sleeping sitting up in a chair was
hard and the constant beeping of machines made me want to
scream sometimes.

"Here's another idea, Laurel. Let me know what you think.
Perhaps you could borrow the clothes for as long as you're here
at the hospital with Aspen. Would that be allowed?"

Row, borrow, rob. "I'd have to ask Seth."

Mrs. Clemmons reached into her pocket and brought out a
cell phone that she put on Aspen's table. "Am I correct in remembering that you told me Seth has a cell phone?"

Had I told her that? I couldn't remember. All the days here

seemed like one long day, and sometimes I answered questions and sometimes I might have imagined she asked them. "Only for emergencies."

"Wouldn't Aspen being in the hospital Intensive Care Unit be considered an emergency?"

I thought about it. "No, I don't think so. Seth says the only medicine children need is sleep."

"I see. Tell me something, Laurel. Are you concerned that Seth might be angry if you called?"

Oh, he would be angry, all right. I had defied his orders, stolen money, and then I hadn't come home to do my chores. "I'm sure of it," I said.

"What if I called him and explained the situation? Or what if a doctor called him?"

I shook my head. "That would make him very angry."

"Sometimes life delivers what I call extenuating circum-stances," Mrs. Clemmons said. "Do you know what I mean?"

Tent, taunt, exit. Add an *r* and you could spell *nature*, which is beautiful and free and always there to make you feel better. "Not really."

"Thank you for telling me that. I'll try to explain myself dif-ferently so I'm clearer. Aspen getting so sick, you had to make a decision for her well-being by bringing her here so the doctors could try a different kind of medicine to help her. When a per-son ignores the rules to help someone, that's called bravery. God understands."

"Oh, we don't believe in God," I told her. "We used to, but now we're Native American."

She frowned at me. "Seth might be relieved to hear what is happening with Aspen, and with you. After all, you've told me that the Farm believes everyone who lives there is part of a family. So wouldn't it be a good thing to let him know how you both are so he can tell the others? What do you think?"

One minute we were talking about the clothes and then the phone and now being brave, but she didn't know I had stolen ten dollars. *Thou shalt not steal.* I couldn't work it out in my mind. "I left and he didn't know and I went to Big Pharma and the Outside World and he would be so angry he might put me out. Then where would I go?"

"I can help you find a place."

"I don't have any money."

"There are places to stay that don't require money."

Nothing is free. Ever. People will screw you. "But even though Aspen came out of my body she is everyone's daughter because that's how the Farm works."

"What if—"

"Please," I said. My head hurt and my stomach was growling so loud she could hear it. "No more. Put the phone away. Take the clothes back."

Some time went by while she didn't say anything and I didn't say anything and Aspen's machines made their whooshes and clicks and beeps. *Puh-shoo-up.* I wanted to slap that machine, just to make it shut up. Aspen looked like she would wake up any minute. Like all I had to do was wait. Like if I left the room, she'd wake up, and not see me there, and then she would do the crashing again, or worse.

Then Mrs. Clemmons said, "Tell you what. I'll leave the phone here with you so that you can make the decision without any pressure. I believe I have come up with a solution that covers all the bases. Laurel, how about this? Just for today, you take the clothes and toiletries. You shower and change into the clean clothes. I'll take your own things home with me and wash them, and return them to you tomorrow. If you still feel that you can't keep the clothes, you can switch them out for the clean overalls and turtleneck and you never have to see the new clothes again. How does that sound?"

The overalls were just for doing chores. After that I put on the skirt and that was how women were supposed to dress. "We're supposed to wear skirts."

"I didn't know that, but I'm sure I can find one for you. What about pants temporarily?"

Temporary. *Air, pore, liar, temp* as in high temperature like Aspen's. I was so tired. "Fine. Call him," I said, and told her the number.

I didn't know if it was okay or if I was just so tired and a shower sounded so good. Maybe a part of me had already turned Worldly in my heart because the minute I saw those clothes I wanted them. So much so that I wanted to say burn these old clothes, I never want to see them again. But if Seth heard that, he would tear the clothes off me, lock me into the barn, and take Aspen away forever. But he wasn't here. Aspen was asleep in a coma. Already I could feel the new clothes on me, changing me, because I was born with Sin and filled with Sin and Unrepentant and just plain bad. I said yes to the clothes. I had no intention of giving them back, not now, not tomorrow, not ever. Mrs. Clemmons stayed with Aspen and I went to the nurses' locker room to take a shower.

I stood in front of the shower stall in the nurses' quarters where there were lockers and mirrors and, thanks to Mrs. Clemmons, no one but me. Then I couldn't remember if I'd locked the door, so I had to go check it. Mrs. Clemmons promised no one could come in while I was here. I tried the door again. Me doing the locking—that was a first. I went back to the shower stall and it was so different from at the Farm—some kind of metal, not the stone walls Frances had built by hand with rocks she collected. It might be a trick like Seth said they did to people in Germany during World War II, not showers with water, but execution by gas you couldn't even smell. He knew everything. I tapped the metal shower walls in a lot of different places. Nothing there seemed different, or tricky, no trapdoors. I turned the faucet on and touched the water with my fingers, and then I smelled them. Water, unless there was a secret ingredient or germs. How would they allow germs in a hospital? Now that I was standing here, the steam rising, I really wanted to take that shower.

Warm water. Soft bar soap that made my skin feel so smooth. I washed my hair twice, and left the conditioner on while I just stood there feeling warm water on my back. When I drew the razor up my legs I felt as if I were a snake shedding its ugly old skin that would wash down the drain forever. I couldn't remember the last time I'd done shaving, but once I put the razor in my hand, it knew what to do, so I must've done it *Before*.

Wasting water is wrong, but the truth is, I never wanted that shower to end. I rinsed my hair and shut the faucet off and just stood there with the steam in the air and the water dripping off me, peeking out of the shower in case someone had come in but no one had come in because remember the door? Locked. Dummy. Stupid. Ugly. *Locked.* I placed one towel down on the bench and sat on it, facing the door just in case. I used another towel to dry myself off and rubbed my hair. It felt so soft it seemed like it was someone else's, Aspen's, when she started to grow hair, corn-silk soft and so white-blonde like Abel's. I opened the package of underpants and chose the blue ones. I never had blue ones unless it was *Before*. The bra felt very strange but I finally got it figured out from the picture on the package and pulled up the straps tighter and there I was wearing a bra, and I liked how it felt and I didn't want to take it off. The jeans felt sinful against my legs, tight, showing off my body instead of hiding it. *A woman's body is sinful*, Seth said. *Beware of wicked women; Eve diverted Adam's obedience from God; women must not wear men's clothing.* I got to wear the overalls while I cleaned but then I was supposed to wear the skirt. Did that matter anymore?

Just before I left for the shower I let Mrs. Clemmons dial Seth's cell-phone number for me to talk to him, not her, just so he'd know where I was. A message came on that said the number was no longer in service. "Does that concern you?" she asked.

Con, corn, nor, core. "He does that sometimes," I told her. "He buys the kind of phone that you use and throw away. Frances said it isn't ecological. He told her that sometimes it's better to be safe than ecological."

"Safe from what?" Mrs. Clemmons asked.

I didn't know how to answer so I didn't say anything.

After my shower I put my dirty clothes into the bag Mrs. Clemmons had given me, and when I slid the shoes on it was as if someone was holding my feet, wishing them long walks and warm toes always. I couldn't stop looking at them, touching the suede, brushing it one way and then the other, forgetting the animal they came from. I brushed my hair free of tangles, and then when I looked in the mirror I saw my scar. Everything I felt about the clothes being new and beautiful and mine went away. The truth was that no amount of conditioner (*diet, tide, roe* is fish eggs) or clothes was going to make me look like someone that anyone wanted. Or sound like it. Seth was right. I was ugly and the scar was hideous and my voice was terrible and it was my fault that Sin was in my blood and who else would want me? No one. If not for Aspen, what good was I to the world? If she crashed again and didn't come back, where would I go? Maybe the place Mrs. Clemmons knew of, but why would I bother if Aspen was gone? I buttoned the shirt to the very top button. When I turned the collar up, it itched, but it hid most of my scar. Much better. Now I could walk back to Aspen's room without everyone giving me a dirty look.

On the way, it dawned on me that I could just walk right out of this hospital, go into a store, use a telephone, learn to drive a car. Be Worldly. Why not, since I was Sinful already? But Seth needed me the way Abel had—*God wants you to be with me because you keep me from hurting other girls*, he said, all those times he hurt me on purpose.

I accidentally pushed 1 instead of 2 and the elevator stopped on the first floor instead of the second, and I thought maybe if I could just see that tall ceilinged room of windows one more time, I would feel more like a person with doors right there instead of trapped inside with nowhere to go. I walked out of the elevator and down the hall toward that room and there was something I didn't know was there, called a Gift Shop. In the window three plastic plugged-in aquariums each featured a different scene. One had a roll of brightly colored fish swimming that flashed with light whenever the fish swam by. I knew it wasn't real but it was like a dream in that it felt almost real. The second one had butterflies flying, all kinds, and all colors. I knew they weren't real, either, but they were beautiful all the same, and all I could think was how much Aspen loved butterflies and how she would love one of the electric butterfly aquariums but I had left my purse in her room but wait I didn't have a purse and I had no more money. Maybe I could steal one. Old St. John said stealing was easy if you knew how. If she would just wake up, I would, I would take one and give it to her and they could add it to the bill for her being here.

The third one had big smiling gray fish and the word *purpose* came into my mind and then a second later, *dolphin. Pin, lop, hop.* Just looking at them I remembered something from *Before* and I hadn't done that in years. Another place, another time, I had seen real dolphins, swimming and jumping, for real. There was cold water splashing on me and people screaming happy screaming, and there was ice cream and carrying a black-and-white stuffed animal and someone big holding my hand. It was such a fun day I thought maybe it was a birthday, not January first like for everyone, and I wanted to be there again so badly I almost had to sit down.

A lady who worked in the gift shop came over to me and said, "Dear, can I help you with something? Are you lost?" and I wanted to tell her yes, I need help to remember the dolphin day but that would sound crazy so I shook my head no and hard as it was I walked away from the aquariums and didn't go in the tall window room, just headed to the elevator and pressed 2.

Inside my body it felt like I was filled with broken glass. Every step I took hurt. What was the matter with me? Was I getting sick? All the way back to Aspen's room I had tears that would not stop. New clothes didn't help. Scars never went away. Somewhere there were real dolphins and I had seen them but I couldn't even remember them all the way because I was so stupid. I thought how I could leave the hospital and go looking for the dolphins, but when I got back to Aspen's room the doctors were in the hallway, talking to Mrs. Clemmons. They had mad looks on their faces that could not mean anything good.

"What happened?" I said in my ugly voice that made them look at me like I was worse than dirty or sick or stupid.

"The doctors are concerned that Aspen is losing weight," Mrs. Clemmons said, and took my arm and pulled me into Aspen's room, past the doctors. "It doesn't mean she is sicker." She put both her arms around me while I cried about a fish I couldn't even remember and the weight I couldn't make my daughter gain. "All of this is taking quite a toll on you," she said, and I wondered how she could see my thoughts the way Seth could. Was it something people were born with, or a trick? She couldn't be like Seth, though, because every time she came to visit, she brought me presents, clothing, or a sandwich, or Diet Coke Vanilla in cans that were 100 percent recycled, she promised. She didn't want to hurt me. She knew about Waterfall Mist conditioner and razors and my Jungle shoe size. She didn't call the cops or a social worker because she was a psychologist, a word I couldn't even spell unless I looked at her card. She didn't trick me to tell her about Seth. Mrs. Clemmons listened when I told the Princess of Leaves story and she said I was good at stories, that I could be a writer if I wanted to. She talked and she tried to make me feel better. It was kind of like having a friend or even a mom, and the minute I thought about having a mom, more tears came hot and painful down my face burning like acid and I wanted to scratch my eyes out, anything to make it stop hurting.

She helped me sit down in the chair I slept in and held my hand. "Laurel, you take all the time you need to get yourself together," she said. "I'll go outside for a while to give you some privacy, but I'll be back. You don't have to talk to the doctors right this minute. Here, let me take your dirty clothes."

While she was gone, I thought about the Princess, lost in the dark woods. The monster that had taken her from the guard had zapped her with a bolt of lightning, and her legs wouldn't work. She tried to speak, but the words came out jumbled. Later, he forced her to drink a bitter tea. He wanted her to eat food, too, but she refused until one day the hunger was so strong that she would have eaten acorns raw, poison, but she didn't do that because she wanted to see the king and the queen again. Eating is the first step to finding my way back, she told herself. Cold oats or beans, I can't escape if I'm weak. "You should eat," I whispered to Aspen. "You have to wake up and eat or else the princess will be stuck with the monster forever."

When the nurse came in later that night, Carolyn, one I hadn't met before, she said, "I'm supposed to put in Aspen's feeding tube."

"I thought Susie was our nurse today."

"She's at dinner," Carolyn said. "It won't take a minute. I've done a million of these." She gloved up and unwrapped a plastic package with tubing.

"What is that?" I asked.

"It's a flexible tube that goes into her nose and down into her stomach."

"Will it hurt?"

She snorted. "Your daughter's in a coma. She can't feel anything."

"Will a feeding tube make her wake up?" I asked.

"Your guess is as good as mine," she said. It didn't take very long. Now Aspen had four tubes total, breathing, pee, IV, and feeding.

Five days ago she was playing in the snow. Catching snow-flakes. Our dog Curly ran beside her trying to bite them. That had made her laugh so hard. She stayed outdoors until I dragged her in, and then she didn't want dinner, only to sleep. She shivered like she couldn't get warm. Then her nose ran, she got a fever, then the seizure, and no more waking up. Coming to the hospital was a blur to me, rocking chairs, numbers, ice baths, CT crashing; now I had to add to that list bad blood counts and losing weight and the feeding tube. Every day I prayed to Our Creator to make things better, but it wasn't helping. Seth always said, *Believe in good things and good things will happen*, but I knew it wasn't true, it was a saying to make Frances and Caleb and Old St. John stay through the winter and work harder. If you go you can't come back, he said, and that made them stay because where else would they go in the winter? Old St. John sometimes went into town and came back with a bottle and drank until he was as stupid as me. That made Seth laugh, but if Frances had done it, he wouldn't have laughed, and he would have yelled at her, maybe hit her, and for sure made her fast and do a sweat.

I hated sweats. Not the darkness, the heat. Smelling poisons coming from other people's bodies. Being naked, trying to stand the heat longer than I wanted to. If you got too hot and had to go outside of the sweat lodge you were supposed to yell, "All my relations!" to make your ancestors and relatives send you the strength to go back in. Seth said that was the Way, and We Were All Family, but I knew that was a lie. My people from *Before* were dead and I only had one relation, Aspen. Today's shower had felt so good. I was clean and dressed in new clothes, but tomorrow they would be dirty, and then what? Wash them in the bathroom sink? The restroom is for patients only.

Later, Susie the nurse came in with a big shot and this creamy-colored stuff inside. "Hello, darlin'," she said to Aspen.

"Is that medicine?" I asked.

"No, sweetie, this is nutrition. I'm going to put it in her NG tube. Come watch. I'll show you how and then you can do it."

Susie was the nice nurse. For two days we had her, and then it was Leilah, not as nice. Carolyn in between when the nurses were on breaks. I watched Susie press the plunger on the shot and the creamy nutrition disappeared down the tube. "How long until she gains weight?" I asked.

Susie smiled at me. "Everything takes time, Laurel. Why don't you go get something to eat yourself?"

"I already ate today," I said, remembering the doughnuts. Also, it wasn't even three thirty, which meant I had to wait until the cafeteria closed at four.

"You need to keep your strength up so you don't end up in the bed next to Aspen," Susie said.

That was another saying, because there wasn't any bed next to Aspen's. If there had been, I would have lain down in it and watched her forever. I always remembered to smile at Susie. "Thank you, Susie," I said.

"You're welcome. Don't you look nice today?" she said, as she gathered up her supplies and left. "That shirt is a good color for you."

"Thank you," I said. When she left the room I looked at myself in the mirror in the bathroom I wasn't allowed to use. Blue plaid, soft cotton, size small, brand of Levi's. Yes, the shirt was pretty.

Not me.

All day my thoughts were hiking up and down so many ideas. *Is, as, said, sad, die.* I couldn't shut them off. If I started to fall asleep, I'd startle myself awake from some strange kind of dream place, where dolphins leapt and people with no faces were laughing. When I tried to put the pictures together in my mind, I got angry that I couldn't. Anger scared me so bad, because what good ever came of anger? None. Only *rage* and *age* and *nag* inside that word. I remembered those times Abel got so mad at me costing money or me crying because I was lonely. Early on when we were in the California forest, I wasn't as good at shutting up as I am now. It took me a while to learn how to stop thinking, to go into a quiet place in my mind and stay there until things were safe again. But in the hospital, there was no one to be quiet for and my mind kind of went wherever it wanted.

Years ago, I'd hear Abel yelling at Seth about the Outside World, or how he'd gotten ripped off by someone he sold drugs to. He'd stomp around our camp, throw things, break things, make this roaring sound that meant he was so mad that he had to take it out on something or someone and eventually that someone was me. He'd slap me until I was curled up into a ball with my hands over my face, and then he'd pull me to my feet and throw me against the shack wall or onto the shack floor. Hands around my neck, squeezing. Knees on my legs, opening. Afterwards, when he was calm, almost sleepy, I'd whisper, "May I go home now?"

He'd laugh the same way Seth does now. He'd say, "I'm going to explain this to you one more time, so you had better listen. By staying with me you keep me from hurting other girls. That's your purpose on Earth. God chose you for me. God put you in my path. God wants you to stay."

I'd cry and sleep. Cry and sleep. Pretty soon I just stopped asking. When I stopped asking, I thought he would be nicer to me. But that didn't happen until I was pregnant, and even then I knew if he wasn't hurting me, he was Outside of camp, finding another girl to hurt until I wasn't pregnant anymore.

Every day that Seth didn't come to the hospital I felt better in one way and worse in another. What if Aspen died? Where would I go after they took her body away? What purpose did I have if I wasn't a mother? Should I ask Seth if he would give me another baby? No, that wouldn't help, because the baby would be someone else, not Aspen. I told her new parts of the Princess of Leaves story because I had so much time to think and I hated thinking. The day she was born, when I had to push her out and cut the cord myself, that was when the story began. That was the day I knew that the reason people told stories was because stories made things standable, or whatever the right word was; Mrs. Clemmons would know. The princess was lost and hurting, but eventually, if I told the whole story, she would find her way back.

"Wake up, Aspen," I whispered to my little girl. "Without you, there isn't any reason for the princess to try."

The doctors knew a lot, and I tried to believe they could make her better, but what if they didn't know everything? They said Aspen couldn't hear a word I said, she was in a coma. Maybe she would hear me deep in her sleeping and when she woke up, she'd tell me, so I went on with the story. Not too long after, I noticed Mrs. Clemmons standing in the doorway, listening. We didn't look at each other, but I knew she was there.

Days after the monster had knocked out the good soldier and taken the princess, the monster did a terrible thing. He took out his weapon and stole the princess's voice so she couldn't call for help. He didn't care about her singing voice, not one bit, and the cut he made stole her voice. Then he took her to his horse and put her across the horse's back as if she was a saddle blanket. He made her drink another bitter cup of tea, which she knew now was a sleeping potion, and when the princess woke up, she was in a forest of the tallest trees she'd ever seen. The trees were a beautiful red color, and so tall she couldn't see the tops of them. Instead of leaves they had needles and lace, a whole new kind of pretty to look at, but so different from trees with leaves she didn't like them at first. This was the monster's lair. One day the princess woke to see that the monster was no longer alone. He had a twin brother. They were building a castle to keep her in. "Where are the turrets and windows?" the princess asked in what was left of her voice, which was low and raspy, like when the wind pushes a tree branch against a window, *skree, skree,* a terrible, scraping sound. Inside scraping is *crap* and *pain* and *raping,* so that makes sense.

"Keep your mouth shut," the monster who had taken her said, but the princess couldn't have said anything more if she tried. The cut on her neck was long and ragged, not deep enough to kill her, but deep enough to take away her songs forever. She had to hold her skin together, because when she tried to speak, it started bleeding again. Already she understood her singing was in his knife. She knew she had to get it back, but how? Two monsters against one princess is not an easy fight. She told her-self, a princess without a voice isn't the worst thing. You must concentrate on staying in the world, so you can find your way back to the king and queen, to let them know you're all right and that you love them. But the princess knew if she were to ever get to that day, there were going to be many tasks she had to complete, none of them easy. That day, if it was coming, was a

long, long way off. So she shut her eyes and she tried to sleep, and
when the monsters came and woke her, she pretended she was
sitting by the fire in her castle room. The first monster liked to
tie her up and do terrible things to her, things she didn't even
know could be done to a person. After a couple of days of that,
the monster's brother went away, and when he came back, he
had a potion that he used to glue her skin back together. He
wrapped the cut with white fabric spun from a thousand silk-
worms, and he told her not to speak, and she obeyed, not in
her heart, not really, but in her deeds. That's because sometimes
you have to pledge yourself to a bad king in order to save the
good one.

"Laurel," Mrs. Clemmons said. "The doctors tell me that
Aspen's spiked a fever. They want to switch her antibiotic. Is
that all right with you?"

I looked at her and said, "There was nothing the king and
queen wouldn't give for their daughter to be safely returned to
them. They would live like paupers to have their daughter safe
at home where she belonged. Their hearts would be broken."

Mrs. Clemmons nodded.

"The question Aspen always asks at this point is, 'But a heart
can't break, can it, Mommy?'"

"What do you tell her?" Mrs. Clemmons asked.

"I tell her the truth. Everyone has a broken heart at one time
or another. You know why? Because without the cracks, how
else can love find its way in? I'm sorry, but it's better to know
the truth. When a heart breaks, it does hurt. Not the way a
bone does when it needs a cast. Mostly it aches. When something aches all the time, it can grow so sore that it feels as if the
parts that make everything work have come apart. That's what
happens. That's what my heart will do if Aspen leaves me. She

has to get well. I don't care what medicine the doctors give her. Just make her wake up."

"I'll tell them," Mrs. Clemmons said.

As he hobbled his way toward the castle, the guard went over what he might say when he returned without the princess. He knew he had to make up a story or be hanged. As he limped back to the castle, these are a few of the stories he concocted:

The princess demanded to go into the forest to collect acorns from the tallest tree with branches stretching out over the cliff-side. I held her by the shoulders to keep her safe. I kept my weapon nearby, but the princess spied the river flowing down the ravine, and once she saw the silvery water, she demanded to climb down to it and gather the leaves floating on the surface. I told her just as you instructed me to do, "One day we'll go, but today is not that day," but she leaped into the water and the current carried her away. Look at me, my clothing wet, my face scratched, I have a broken leg and my ankle cannot support me. Though I cannot swim, I waded into the water and searched, but found no sight of her. I accept whatever punishment you deem appropriate.

Or perhaps this story: Sire, I regret to tell you that a man I've not seen before stole your daughter. He took my weapon, my chain mail, and beat me until I was down. Then he took the princess. But do not fear, for it was a case of love at first sight. Once the stranger heard her singing, he became a man possessed. He swept her up onto the back of the blackest horse I've ever seen. He spurred his horse and away they galloped, his silver horseshoes sparking, in the direction of the darkest forest. I'm certain he was a prince.

———

Mrs. Clemmons brought me another dinner. Pizza, salad in a Styrofoam container (ruining the earth, not biodegradable), and two bottles of orange juice that tasted too sweet so I didn't drink them.

"Would it be all right if I ate my dinner with you?" she asked before she took out her containers (look for the number 1 on the bottom, that means recyclable) or even sat down.

I could have said a lot of things, such as "Be my guest" or "It's a free country" or "Your guess is as good as mine," but I said, "All right." I liked her sitting there beside me, eating.

I can't be mean to someone who brings me food when I'm hungry. That's what Seth did a lot of the time. He didn't make me have the kind of sex Abel did, all pushing and shoving and slapping if I cried, or cuts and hands tied or hands around the neck, squeezing. Seth used to comfort me after Abel was mean. He brought me water and he carried away the bucket I had to use because there was no bathroom. But it turned out he still wanted the same thing Abel did, only in a way where I didn't cry or fight. All I had to do was lie there, he said. Afterwards, when it was finally over, he would say, "There. That wasn't so bad, was it?"

"Laurel, are you crying because you're worried about Aspen's fever?" Mrs. Clemmons asked me. "The doctors are on top of this. The new drugs will help."

If I looked at her I would make the sound, I just knew it. "That's part of why," I said. "Sometimes the story is sad and it makes it hard to tell."

"Isn't that true of most things in life?" she said. "If you leave out the sad parts, then the happy parts aren't quite as happy, are they?"

"I guess not."

"You know, sometimes I think a person just has to have a good cry. And sometimes they just need to vent. Do you know what I mean by that?"

"Like a volcano has to steam or else it blows everything up?"

"Exactly. You're so insightful, Laurel. If you would ever like to vent, I'll be happy to listen and keep whatever you say between us. Otherwise, I won't press. Your life is your own, Laurel. You get to make the choices."

I looked at her then. Was she making fun of me? The room was dim because all along it had been getting dark, and I couldn't see Mrs. Clemmons's face, just the outline of it, with her short hair and her big body and the pearls shining at her neck where I had a red scar. By the light of Aspen's machines and monitors, Mrs. Clemmons reminded me of this picture Frances had shown to me a long time ago, in one of her books about Gods and Goddesses. She said it was the oldest stone carving of a woman ever, as old as woolly mammoths and dinosaurs, which I didn't believe entirely. I couldn't remember the name. The Venus of Willingness?

Something like that.

Chapter 13

THE SUBJECT OF Juniper's eight A.M. class was the last-minute details for the trip to the Pueblos, the capstone of their quarter's study of pottery. Dr. Carey was in Washington, D.C., for a conference, so they were stuck with his TA, Chico de la Rosas Villarreal. Chico was extra hard on Juniper because he didn't think she belonged in a 600-level class. He'd said so right to her face. "You should be in high school, not taking up a space that should go to a grad student." He was such a freak. She was paying her own way. So what if she was younger than everyone else? She passed all the prereqs. She got A grades.

A year or so back, she'd met Chico for the first time. She went to Dr. Carey's office hours, eager to show him some blue-and-white pottery sherds. One of Daddy Joe's cousins was re-doing the shower stall in the master bedroom. He had to dig down several feet to put in new plumbing. When his shovel uncovered something white, he stopped and called Daddy Joe to take a look. Juniper followed. She picked carefully through the soil and found nine white pottery sherds with a blue pattern on them. No way they were Indian—they looked like porcelain. Chico looked annoyed when she walked into the office.

"Dr. Carey's not here," he said. "What do you want?" Then he looked back down at his pile of work papers.

She'd almost turned and gone, certain that Chico not only wouldn't be interested, but also that he wouldn't know the first thing about dating pottery. But he'd made her so mad. "Look," she said. "I found these in Santa Fe one block from Acequia Madre. It's probably nothing, but I was hoping Dr. Carey could take a quick look at these, maybe give me a direction so I could date them."

Chico sighed, set his papers down, and held out his hand. She carefully transferred the sherds, making certain not to touch Chico and catch his cooties. He pushed his glasses up his forehead and stared at the pieces, his brow furrowing. Then he set them down carefully and began pulling books from Dr. Carey's shelf. An hour went by, their heads together, flipping pages, consulting the computer, and in the end they had dated the pieces back to the year 1700 C.E. "They're Asian import, obviously," Chico said. "They probably belonged to a wealthy family. May I keep them for a few days? I'd love a chance to photograph and catalogue them, but I don't have a camera with me."

Juniper said, "That's okay. I have my camera with me," and brought out her old 35mm Pentax.

It should have been a bonding moment, but after that Chico seemed to avoid her in the lab. When he subbed for Dr. Carey and saw her name on the roll, he seemed to give her a much harder time than anyone else. The sherds had their own shelf in her desk in her room in Santa Fe and were among her most treasured possessions. She'd gotten an A last quarter, and she was currently getting an A. If there had been a higher grade than A, she would have gone after that, too. Maybe Dr. Carey *had* made an exception allowing her to take the upper-division course, but she deserved to be there, and that was what mattered in the end. Didn't she always make sure she was in her seat fifteen minutes early? Didn't she know the material frontwards and backwards? Whenever Chico asked a question, wasn't hers the first hand up?

"Where's Anna?" Chico asked as he took roll and students began pairing up. Anna Decker was forty, a mother of two kids, back in school to finish her degree, and she was Juniper's lab partner. They made a kind of odd couple, but Anna didn't make a big deal of Juniper's being the same age as Anna's oldest daughter, and Juniper didn't say anything about Anna being old enough to be her mother.

"I have no idea," Juniper said. Most likely Anna was sleeping in, or one of her kids was sick. It was freezing cold out and Juniper wished she were in her own bed at home in Santa Fe, with Cadillac keeping her feet warm and a fire in the kiva.

After finishing roll, Chico said once he'd checked everyone's reports they were free to head on out to the assigned Pueblos. Juniper opened her project folder for him to check and waited. She took out her cell phone and checked her text messages. Nine from Topher. She sighed. Her going to the Pueblo for three days and two nights did not sit well with him. *I'm playing a gig at the college pub, and everyone knows that a real girlfriend always shows up to support the band.*

She'd tried to explain to him. *This field trip counts for half my grade. I knew it was coming up long before you got your gig.*

Apparently he was pouting because the text messages were stacked up and whiny: *You better come home tonight! Drive back!* She didn't want to read any more texts for fear that he was breaking up with her. She shut her phone and set it on her desk.

Juniper and Anna had been assigned the Ohkay Owingeh Pueblo the first week of the quarter. Until 2005, when the tribe took back their original name, it had been called the San Juan. She remembered when Governor Richardson had announced the name change and ordered it to be put into use immediately, and Daddy Joe had said, Wow, that's going to keep some sign maker busy. All Juniper could think was that anthro texts would have to update their editions, and then they'd cost even more than they already did, which was a fortune. She spent far too much time already trying to find used textbooks online so her parents wouldn't go broke.

Juniper was bummed that the pottery she and Anna would be studying was so plain. She wished she'd gotten the Hopi or San Ildefonso, but then so did everyone else in the class. Dr. Carey always said, If you do your research, there's something astonishing to discover in the plainest pot. Juniper put on a brave face, figuring she'd never get anywhere without paying her dues.

Instead of the usual conversations and kidding around, today there were only murmurs in the anthro lab. Everyone took this assignment seriously because it was the culmination of the entire quarter's work, and prep for next quarter's seminar. Chico made his way around the room like the stork he was, and Juniper studied him as clinically as an artifact. He had this dorky way of walking, and even skinny-leg jeans were baggy on him. Topher was rock-star thin, but Chico looked like he was starving. He wore hiking boots that made his feet look huge, but to be fair, they were Danner Mountain Lights, awesome boots, much superior to her Big Five clearance specials. And he always showed up in a herringbone-tweed sport jacket so unfortunately ill-fitting that she couldn't believe anyone could look in the mirror and not see how ridiculous it looked. The sleeves were too short, but he did fold them back. It was a sort of umber color that reminded her of picking up after the dogs. All he needed was a safari hat and people would start calling him Dr. Livingston.

She straightened her pages and listened as he told Betsy and Eduardo they needed to go back to the library and get more background before they headed out. He fawned all over Hugo and Ricardo about how they had done such a spectacular job, and Juniper thought, Duh, they got San Ildefonso—of course, it's freaking amazing pottery. It wasn't her fault the Ohkay Owingeh favored simpler designs. At least they used micaceous clay. It photographed like it was filled with ground-up stars, and she had taken total advantage of that, using her 35mm camera to take the pictures. Digital was great, but the camera she wanted was out of her reach, financially. Daddy Joe had helped her with the f-stops and had even come all the way down to Albuquerque to introduce her to the curator at the museum, another relative on his banyan of a family tree. She'd put her photos and scans up against Hugo and Ricardo's any day of the week. Her mom had proofread the essay for her, and not one comma was out of place. It was a slam dunk, except for Anna being absent.

When Chico arrived at her table, he sat down in Anna's chair and clicked his ballpoint pen so he could jot notes on his grade book or whatever. Why he didn't just use a laptop, standard use for TAs as well as profs, she couldn't imagine. A lock of greasy black hair fell over his eyebrow and the sides were shaggy, covering the tops of his ears. Juniper wanted to tell him to get a decent haircut, for crying out loud; they were only thirteen dollars at Supercuts. Or grow it out. The in-between thing made him look like a vagrant. From time to time, she imagined him with a long black braid. That would work, so long as he ditched the tweed jacket. Skinny guys like him should wear long-sleeved T-shirts, earth tones, and a beaded belt. If he gained forty pounds, he could pass for Benicio del Toro, because he had the forehead-wrinkling frown down pat. His eyebrows were bushy, his eyes black and piercing.

Chico cleared his throat and said, "I suppose you're stuck with me as your partner today. Bring me up to date on your project."

Juniper separated the parts of the report, laying them out in stacks. "This is our factual background and research. These are the interview questions. And these are the photos."

"Nice pictures," Chico said, flipping pages of her report until he came to her bibliography. "But come on, Juniper? Failure to cite your sources is an automatic fail. That's something every lower-division college student is expected to know."

She was *not* a lower-division student; she was a year from graduating with her B.S., but she let him finish, ignoring the ire that rose inside her chest and made her whole body heat up. She planned out everything she was going to say. Daddy Joe had taught her that speaking respectfully and calmly went a long way in cases like this. When Chico was all done trashing her bib, she took a breath and then began. "Thank you for reminding me about that essential information, Chico. You're absolutely right. Ordinarily, no one without a bachelor's degree should be sitting in a 600-level class, but then again, I'm not your ordinary student. I'm here by Dr. Carey's invitation, and I think we both agree he's brilliant and hasn't made any mistakes to make us think otherwise. Nevertheless, a mistake like not citing sources does deserve to fail. It's vital to get the details right. I actually learned that before I even went to college, and what a valuable lesson it was. The reason I didn't cite the photographic images or attain permission to use them is because it just so happens that the photos are mine. I took them. I thought I'd wait and ask you how to properly cite them so that I didn't make a mistake before I turned the project in to be graded."

He was Spanish, dark-skinned like Daddy Joe, but she could see a definite color change in his face as he realized he was the one who had stepped in the pile of manure, not her. Then he said, "Really," as if he could not believe she knew how to use a camera. Had he forgotten the sherds? He looked through the photos and back up at her. "Some of these older pots look like museum pieces."

"That's because they are."

"I hope you didn't use a flash."

"I didn't."

"So how did you get them? Take them when the guard was out of the room?"

Oh, wait for it, she thought. "Actually, I asked the curator's permission."

He had absolutely no reaction to that comment. He flipped through each photo, matching the text in the report to the pot as if he were looking for mistakes now. "They're quality," he said, as if it were C work.

When he set down the photos she picked up one he'd missed. "This pot happens to belong to my parents. It won a blue ribbon at the Taos County Fair. I bought it at Indian Market and the potter is Louella Cata, one of the best in the Ohkay Owingeh nation. I made an appointment to talk to her at her studio. If it's all right with her, I thought I'd make a podcast of our interview. Post it on the school's website. And I plan to seek print publication of my interview, with the potter's permission, of course."

He didn't say anything for a while. He frowned that frown he was so good at. So close to Benicio and yet so far, she thought. "I see what you're saying," he said, "and I applaud the idea, but not if it's at the expense of your project. You don't think a commercial market might edit your work into blandness?"

"What if it does? The podcast reflects well on the department; even an edited print publication benefits the potter and delivers information in a way more general readers will be exposed to."

Was he deliberately trying to make her nervous?

"Here's my concern," he said, putting down his pen and grade book. "This assignment was a collaboration. Without Anna's input, this could turn into your project. Is it fair to have such commercial goals for something you did together?"

Juniper was going to kill Anna for bailing out at the eleventh hour. She took a breath. "You're familiar with J. J. Brody's seminal essay, right? Anna began with that text's approach as our structural blueprint. My contribution was analysis of Stephen Trimble's photos in *Talking with the Clay*. Half the articles we studied were all about the 'respect of tradition, the joy of innovation'—not my words, I'm paraphrasing an article from the *New York Times*—but that's ignoring the story behind each potter's life. In the end it comes down to a human story, Louella Cata's story. I'm taping everything today, so Anna can look at it and we'll finalize the project together."

Oh, for crying out loud, why wasn't Dr. Carey here today? She was reciting a bunch of stupid tangents, not how it all came together. She cleared her throat. "Ohkay Owingeh pottery is more about function, day-to-day use, and utility than it is art. Theories can overlap, right? When they become polythetic instead of deconstructed, there's like this whole other realm to examine. So the interview is actually the most important part of the project. Yes, it's more work for me because Anna isn't here today, but since the interview will shift everything, it doesn't really doom the project if I do this part by myself since Anna and I will finalize it together."

Chico frowned again.

He was probably jealous that Juniper thought of publishing it before he did, because this interview was going to be totally publishable. She was planning on sending it to Wolf Schneider, who was editing next summer's two-hundred-page Indian Market magazine. When she graduated she planned to wear so much academic bling around her neck that she'd need a chiropractor.

He took his time reading over the interview questions she and Anna had created. He hadn't taken that much time with anyone else's. "I still see a problem when I'm supposed to grade your joint efforts."

"Maybe," Juniper said, "you could look at it this way. If Anna were here, and we went to do the interview and then suddenly she was called away because of an emergency, I'd finish by myself. I'm sure if Anna had to miss this trip it was due to something serious. She did half the background report and she edited my photos. We wrote the questions together, so it hardly matters who asks them so long as we both do equal work on the rewrite of the paper. In the end it will demonstrate totally equal effort and therefore be easy to grade."

Chico looked at her without saying anything for so long it was starting to freak her out. Finally, she said, "What is so fascinating about my face? Do I have egg on it or what?" Then it hit her, he was staring at her tattoo. "You know, Mr. Villarreal, lots of people have tattoos and not all of them are bikers and criminals. It's practically the same thing as wearing a necklace."

"Sorry," he said, looking away. "I didn't mean to stare. Sometimes when I have a problem to work out I stare into the middle distance. Actually, I was just thinking about the breadth of your effort. I have no problem with that. The problem with you going alone is that you're not going to have an observer, just an interviewer. Observation is nearly as important. And you're young, and I don't think it's wise to send you off alone. I'll accompany you today. That means I'll need to rearrange a few things. So excuse me, please. Where's your car?"

Seriously? She was going to have to spend three days with Chico? "My car's in the parking lot." Duh, she wanted to say, but refrained.

"Color?"

"Primer-gray-and-silver Subaru Outback. There's an Obama sticker on the bumper."

"Okay. I'll meet you there in ten minutes. Don't leave without me." He got up and walked away.

Great, Juniper thought. Just great. She picked up her phone and sent Anna a text. OMG, where R U? I'm dying here.

The morning after her emergency-room visit, Dr. Montano released Glory with orders that she stay in bed. After a week of total bed rest, she'd see her in the office and they'd reevaluate, but chances were she'd be on her left side until she delivered. Joseph could tell it was quite a blow to her, what with Halle arriving any day now and all the work in the nursery to be done. The contractions had stopped once she was hydrated, and her headache was gone, but Dr. Montano stressed that Glory needed to take and record her blood pressure throughout the day, push fluids, eat more protein, and work on having no tension or stress whatsoever.

"Try telling that to the dogs," Glory had said, and Joseph knew she was right.

"Hire a dog walker or send them to dog day care," the doctor said.

"Caddy and Dodge might go for that, but not Eddie," she said. "He looks too much like a dog toy to handle other dogs. He'd spend the day running and hiding, and probably have a seizure from the stress."

"I bet our neighbor Mrs. Yearwood would be happy to dog-sit," Joseph assured the doctor.

Glory had slept, but Joseph was wiped out, unable to rest due to the hospital noise and lights and, though he'd never let on, fear that the baby would come early. When they got home, he put some eggs on to hard-boil and plotted out high-protein snacks to purchase at the market. Then he made a phone call to Elena Gonzales. She'd set up a meeting with Ardith Clemmons, a psychologist on staff at Española's Presbyterian hospital, who was interested in doing some pro bono work for Candela. He hated to have to reschedule, but there was no way he was rested enough to drive to Española.

"Elena," he said when she answered her phone. "I'm afraid I can't leave my wife alone just now," and he explained Glory's situation. "Any chance you can meet with Mrs. Clemmons alone, or can we postpone the meeting until next week?"

The moment he said the words, it occurred to him that in two and a half weeks, it was going to be Christmas, and he hadn't even put in his order for a fresh turkey.

"I'll get in touch with her and call you back," Elena said. "Shall I call you at Candela or at home?"

He gave her his cell-phone number. "Probably best to call me here. I don't want Glory disturbed by the phone."

"Give her my best," Elena said. "I'm sure everything will turn out all right, but I'll add her name to my prayers."

"Always appreciated. Thanks, Elena."

He opened cans, and the dogs, having missed dinner last night, went nuts, nails scrabbling against the floor as he measured out dry food and remembered to add Eddie's phenobarbital. Once the bowls were distributed and everyone was eating, he listened to the messages on their answering machine, and it seemed as if everyone they knew had decided to call last night. Ave, who wanted to complain about Halle. Halle, who wanted to let them know Las Vegas was her new favorite city. The cable TV people wanted to make sure the upgrade package served all his needs, because for forty-nine dollars a month more . . . He deleted that message before it played out and wasted any more of his time. Credit-card companies were deeply concerned that he hadn't applied for all manner of new available interest rates. So much for donotcall.gov, he thought. The only person they hadn't heard from was Juniper, and since Thanksgiving he'd been worried about her and the trip to the Pueblo, if she'd be safe throwing her sleeping bag down on a total stranger's floor for three days. When he confided this to Glory, she asked him, "If you're that freaked out about a nearly nineteen-year-old, what is a baby girl going to do to you?"

He didn't have an answer for that. And the truth was, he didn't like to think about how overprotective a father he was going to be. He'd become an uncle to Rico's boys, but they were practically as tall as he was, and besides, boys were different, tougher, and they could not get pregnant. What Glory did not know (and if he had his way, would never find out) was that when he'd taken the trash out to the curb the week after Thanksgiving, he'd found two troubling items: an empty package of Zig-Zag wrapping papers and a torn condom wrapper.

He'd tried not thinking about it, but sitting in the ER all night with Glory, it was either that or her toxemia and preeclampsia, and whether she would carry the baby to term or end up in the PICU with tough decisions facing both of them. He tidied up the kitchen, washed the dog's bowls with scalding-hot water and soap, set the eggs to cool, and went outside to feed the hens, all the while wishing he could have gone to the meeting in Española. Maybe he should take the job at Candela—it was close to home, and work kept a person occupied. He'd call Juniper later, see how things were going at the Pueblo. Though he wanted to fall into bed and sleep for twelve hours, he decided to walk the dogs first. They needed to burn energy and Glory needed the quiet. Already he could tell it was killing her to be idle. He went to the bookshelves and chose some novels for her to read.

Glory looked up as he piled the books next to the bed. She'd changed into clean sweats and fuzzy socks, and her hair was damp from the shower, which meant she'd gone ahead and taken one when the doctor had said full bed rest immediately. "I can't help but think of all the things I could be doing," she said.

He unplugged the laptop computer from the dresser and put it next to her on the bed. "You're from California, go surfing. Promise me you won't get up the second I leave the house."

"I won't," she said. "I may give birth to a daughter who's got a flat head on one side, but I will stay in bed, if you promise to take a nap."

"After I walk *los perros*. Look at them; they're bouncing off the walls. I'll find someone to help with them, too."

They were racing in and out of the bedroom, doing laps, or as Juniper called it, "the zoomies."

Glory agreed. "Tomorrow will you go to the library and get me some movies?"

"No need. I upgraded our cable so you can watch movies all day long. New releases like *Hellboy* and what was the other one, *Girls in Pants Who Travel*?" He waited for her to laugh and wasn't disappointed.

"I love you, Joseph."

"I love you, too. But I bet you secretly wish my name was Gopher."

"Actually, I think 'Ferret' suits you better."

"You're a cold woman, Mrs. Vigil."

She laughed. "Sorry. Gotta call them like I see them."

The dogs looked up expectantly, because if something was funny, they wanted in on it. There were a thousand words for "walk," and all of them started with happy voices.

Joseph changed into boots while the dogs paced back and forth. Eddie used the interval to gather his favorite toys; the stuffed rabbit that looked alarmingly real, the canvas veterinarian that no longer had a head, and various wounded stuffed toys leaking filling. One by one, he brought them to Glory and wagged his tail before setting them down on her pillow.

"Thank you so much!" Glory said enthusiastically each time he placed one on her pillow.

"Why are you saying thank you to an animal that doesn't speak English?"

She looked up at Joe. "This is a huge honor in the dog world," she said. "He's bringing prey to me for the kill."

Joseph smiled and fell in love with her all over again. "Of course he is. Without you, a stuffed rabbit means *nada*."

Glory scratched Eddie's head. "I love this dog. Do I smell coffee brewing?"

"Decaf. I'll bring you a cup. I thought I'd take the dogs before it starts snowing again."

"Be careful, it's icy out there. I thought I heard a message from Halle on the phone."

"You did." Joseph went to the kitchen and filled a cup with *crema* and a little sugar. He poured the coffee in and stirred, then brought it to Glory. "She said she was in love with Sin City."

"Las Vegas?"

"That's right. She said she'd be here in a day or two, depending on her luck."

"And my mom?"

"She wanted us to know that Halle was gambling away her settlement money and that she needed hormones and religion, not necessarily in that order."

Glory laughed. "Nothing new there. I hope Halle's all right."

"Sounded to me like she's having the time of her life."

"Joseph? Don't forget Eddie's coat." At the sound of the word, Eddie immediately darted under the bed.

"I won't. You relax."

She clicked the television remote. "Daytime television makes me remember why I never got one," she called out to Joseph.

"No one's forcing you to watch it," he answered. "Don't forget to take your blood pressure."

He harnessed the big dogs and chased Eddie around the house. The Italian greyhound despised the fleece coat he needed to wear when the temperature dropped lower than fifty, but he did enjoy walks, so the poor little guy lived in a state of indecision. When

Joseph finally caught him, he Velcroed the garment around the dog's chest and gathered up the leashes. It wasn't that ridiculous so far as dog clothing went. Glory had managed to find one in a tasteful Burberry plaid, which was perfect for walks around the upscale shops in the Plaza. While Joseph was locking the door, Dolores let out one of her groans, and he told her, just as he always did, "Everyone's waiting, go toward the light." It had become such an automatic response, he rarely thought of it.

Out they went into a Santa Fe winter morning that already seemed as if it was turning dark. Tired and grateful, Joseph settled into the pace and passed the homes of his neighbors, admiring trees in winter, trees in general, remembering how not so many years ago he'd created that photo album of the giant trees of California, the fulfillment of a lifelong dream inspired by Solomon's Oak. Imagine, a childhood desire led him to his wife and daughters and into this astonishing life that had seemed forever out of his reach. *Thank you*, he whispered.

Glory couldn't find a movie worth craning her neck to watch, and how uncomfortable could it be to read a book lying sideways? Unbelievably uncomfortable, it turned out. She pulled open her bedside table to see what was in there, lamenting her inability to keep the drawer neat. Inside were a broken book lamp, its cord in tangles; three nearly empty ChapSticks; a glove designed for wearing to bed to soften rough skin, but not its mate; forty-eight cents (one of the dimes was a Mercury head, silver); Moon Drops, some kind of herbal mints designed to ease an insomniac into the land of Nod that she'd been talked into by a sales clerk at Herbs, Etc. and that didn't work; a cherry cough drop still in its wrapper; crumpled tissues she was too lazy to put in the trash; and, would you look at that: There it was. The blue ribbon from the pot Juniper had bought for them on their anniversary.

The day she found it would forever be etched in her mind, because it was a trifecta of life-changing events: Indian Market, her birthday, and the day she'd discovered she was pregnant.

Chapter 14

G LORY HELD THE blue ribbon in her hand, remembering the moment she and Joe discovered it inside the pot.
Stamped in gold onto the satin indigo background were the
words FIRST PREMIUM, TAOS COUNTY FAIR and the New Mexico
state seal dated 1912. All micaceous pots required seasoning before their first use, an arduous process of rubbing the clay with
olive oil and even heating it to condition the clay before cooking in it. Joseph picked up the pot, inverted it, and out fell the
ribbon. They had marveled at the surprise, and then Joseph had
put his hand inside the pot to check for anything else. "Uh-oh,"
he said, and looked at her. "I hope Juniper didn't pay a lot of
money for this."

"Why? It seemed like a nice piece."

"Oh, I'm not saying it's ugly, just that it isn't authentic, Indian
made."

Joseph held the pot out for Glory to put her hand inside.

"Feel the ridges? How even they are?"

"Yes, what about them?"

"That means it was thrown on a potter's wheel, not built by
hand. Indians use the coil building method."

"Don't say anything to Juniper," Glory urged. "She was so proud of buying it for us."

"No worries, my lips are sealed," he said. "Besides, I can still cook in it." He continued with the oiling and Glory sat down at the counter, playing with the ribbon. Suspended from the ribbon was a gold thread with a white entry tag from the fair, No. 9278. It read:

ARTIST: Louella Cata
        Ohkay Owingeh Pueblo
LOT: II
CLASS: Hand-molded
ENTRY: Bean pot

The area for the phone number and address was torn and had clearly suffered water damage at some point. But when Joseph had looked at the bottom of the pot, the maker's incised signature definitely read "Laurel," followed by something that started with the letter S—they couldn't make out the surname, but it didn't look like Cata. They decided the judge must have put the ribbon in the wrong pot, and chuckled a little at the surprise of that. Later they told Juniper about the ribbon, but not about the pot's dubious background. She rarely cooked anything beyond microwave popcorn, so they assumed she'd never notice, but, as Glory remembered now, flat on her side and unable to do anything about it, at Thanksgiving Juniper had taken that pot back to school with her, intending to connect with the potter on the Pueblo she was assigned to study. Well, the matter was out of their hands now. No stress, she reminded herself.

Glory had intended to track down the owner and send back the ribbon, but autumn was the busiest time of year at the feed store. People were stocking up for winter, and her pregnancy nausea pretty much drained her energy for anything else. But stuck in bed, this was the perfect opportunity to remedy that. Maybe it was a small matter, winning a first-place ribbon, but Glory would have been proud if it were hers. To her way of thinking, an award like that belonged in a family album, even if the pot was long gone. It had the potential for such a great family story—remember when Auntie Laurel won the County Fair in 2006?

Now that she was stuck in bed, Glory could find the address and mail it back. Joseph's laptop was sitting right there. She opened it, and typed into the search engine: "Taos County Fair, 2006, Arts & Crafts, blue ribbon, Laurel S." Everything that came up was about the upcoming year's fair, which category to enter, deadlines and forms to fill in.

She tried the County Fair website. There was a cute newspaper story about a 4-H girl's prize pig getting loose and how it took fifteen minutes to catch it. There were a couple shots of prizewinning floral displays, but not much else. Maybe they hadn't posted the results online, but a first-place winner? Surely that was in a newspaper archive, or something. For an hour she narrowed her terms and searched, but didn't find anything. She returned to the upcoming fair site and downloaded the pdf file for categories. There it was: Traditional Arts/Native American, and four categories for pottery. She tried searching the artist's name, Louella Cata. Immediately up came Pueblo Pottery, Ms. Cata's studio, an address and the artist's résumé, and, along with her e-mail, a phone number. Maybe she would know how the mix-up happened, and if not, at least she'd have her blue ribbon back. It was kind of unsettling to find such personal information that quickly. Glory wondered what would happen if she searched Juniper's name. A click of the keys and there were links to Juniper's MySpace page, her student ID at UNM, and then a dozen pop-ups claiming to be able to erase such information for a fee. Who falls for that, Glory wondered. It isn't even logical. The Internet was creepy. She had to admit it worked both ways; she'd found the potter's name and phone number. She dialed it on her phone, but a recording came on, saying the number had been disconnected.

I'll put it in the good old U.S. Mail that's struggling so hard to stay alive in our digital age, she thought. If it comes back, there's nothing lost. She looked for a pen to write the address down, but of course there wasn't one nearby, and she couldn't write with ChapStick. She settled for typing it into an e-mail she sent to herself, and then wanted to face-palm herself for being so dense. Send an e-mail to Louella Cata! Her address is right there. She typed, pressed send, and of course the computer beeped, giving her a low-battery warning, and the plug-in cord was all the way across the room. Suddenly exhausted, she shut it off and decided to take a nap. At least she had vivid dreams to look forward to, another side effect of pregnancy.

When Chico got into Juniper's Subaru his knees were up around his face. "Let's go," he said.

"Get out," Juniper said. "Let me move the stuff in the cargo area around so you can push the seat back. How tall are you?"

"Six foot five and three-quarter inches," he said.

"Wow. You might be the tallest person I know. I suppose people make cracks all day, like 'How's the weather up there?' and 'Why aren't you playing NBA basketball,' right?"

"Unfortunately. And I've never been good at sports."

This all felt so strange. She wasn't used to anyone in that seat besides Topher, who was normal height, or her suitemates when they needed a ride to the store. She and Anna had had this whole day planned out. In the back of the car Juniper had her photography equipment, latex gloves in case they were allowed to inspect antique pots, her laundry basket, embarrassingly full of dirty clothes (which Anna might not have minded, being a mother and all), cross-country skis Topher had talked her into renting from the student union (they were planning a trip as soon as the quarter ended that involved him teaching her how to ski, and staying at a motel she was paying for), a pile of library books, her project, the pot she gave her parents wrapped in bubble wrap, a case of Diet Coke Vanilla, twenty bags of beef jerky from Trader Joe's, a bag of McIntosh apples (they stayed fresher in the car than in her dorm room), a five-pound container of almonds from Costco, and a brick of cheddar cheese. And dog hair. Lots of dog hair. There were blankets covered with dog hair, and her sleeping bag and backpack, which always bore a fine coat of border collie and cattle-dog hair. It stuck to everything. She was convinced it was barbed.

She could feel Chico's eyes boring into everything. Anthropologists were trained to look at artifacts, to use inductive reasoning, to build a culture from specific objects left behind. Well, she hated to think what he made of her car. She shoved everything except the pot to the driver's side of the cargo area and moved Chico's seat all the way back. "There," she said, handing him the pot. "You can hold this in your lap, because if anything happens to it my dad will freak. It's like his favorite cooking pot."

"Looks like you wrapped it up well enough to make it through nuclear war."

"Ha ha," she said. He was pathetic in the social-skills department. Had he ever gone on a date? Kissed a girl? She imagined
him twenty years down the line, his black hair turning silver,
that same stupid sport jacket, or by then would it be one with
suede elbow patches? He'd wear thicker glasses by then, wire-
frame glasses with Coke-bottle lenses, and he'd look like a
great grey owl standing there in front of the classroom telling
someone else their project was "decent." Finally, an hour after
her planned departure time, they were on their way. Juniper
was driving the speed limit and Chico was looking out the
window, saying nothing.

"Mind if I turn the radio on?" she asked.

"Let me do it," he said. "NPR or classical? Or how about a
CD?"

Classical? That didn't surprise her. "Of course," she said. "Why,
did you bring some music?"

"Even better," he said, smiling with that geeky set of super-
white teeth that seemed too big for his mouth. To be fair, she
did have to concede he had Benicio's smile. He reached over
the pot and opened the backpack at his feet. Soon he held up an
audio CD, *Before the Dawn: Recovering Our Lost Ancestors.*

Juniper's jaw dropped.

His smile wilted. "I should have known you'd already read
it. I also have *Guns, Germs, and Steel.* It's really good. Unless—
you've probably read that, too."

She laughed. "*Before the Dawn* is on my Christmas list. I
haven't read it. But I have read *Guns, Germs, and Steel,* twice, and
I'd read it again if we weren't in the middle of finals. I can't believe you picked those books. That is freaking awesome."

"One of the perks of being Dr. Carey's TA is that he gives
me all the stuff publishers send him that he doesn't have time to

read or review. I have a fairly extensive library. You're welcome to borrow anything."

"Wow," Juniper said. "I'll take you up on that since I drive to Santa Fe just about every weekend. Listen, I have some apples and cheese in the grocery bag behind my seat if you're hungry."

"Thanks. I'll take an apple. I didn't have anything in the fridge for breakfast. This time of year I'm kind of broke."

"I thought TAs got a free ride and get paid a stipend."

He laughed. "They do, which allows you to exist at the poverty level. Every dime goes to rent, and my utility bill is way up there in winter. I could've had free housing on campus, but I'm over sharing bathrooms and listening to roommates party at three A.M. I eat a lot of Top Ramen."

"Top Ramen is great except for the noodles," she said. "Too many carbs. You should try some of my dad's menudo. He makes it by the gallon for me. I have some in my freezer."

"Stop," he said. "You're making me homesick."

"Thank goodness it's almost holiday break."

"Actually, I can't afford to go home for the holiday break."

"That's too bad. Where's home?"

"Chicago."

"Wow, that's kind of far away. Why didn't you go to graduate school there, or on the East Coast?"

"I went to Yale for my undergrad. Then I wanted to study with Dr. Carey. And my great-grandmother's family came from Pojoaque. They spelled their name V-i-l-l-i-r-e-a-l back then. They were one of the original land-grant families in the 1930s. My dad was born there."

"What made your parents move to the Midwest?"

He peeled the organic sticker off his apple. "It wasn't their choice. They died when I was still a kid, so I got sent to live with the nearest relative, my auntie Isa in Chicago. It was a big change for me, but everyone treated me right. So should we listen to *Before the Dawn*, or will that spoil your Christmas?"

He had told her more in ten minutes than in the three years she'd been at UNM. Maybe he was human after all. "No way. When I like a book, I read it over and over. I love reading, don't you?"

"Sure. So long as it's not term papers or essays written by—"

Juniper held up a hand. "You should probably stop right there, it being thirty-five degrees out and me having to kick you out of the car if you diss my work."

He smiled. "I was going to say 'freshmen.' Your essays are really good. You have tremendous insight."

Normally he would have added, "for someone so young," but she could tell he was trying to act human. "Stop it," she said. "Aren't I the one who's supposed to be buttering you up for a good grade? You're probably immune to that."

"Mostly," he said. "But it never hurts to try."

Whatever that meant, the conversation stalled. They listened to the CD and drove for an hour and a half in silence. Just before they arrived in Pojoaque, Juniper turned to Chico. "Want to stop for a minute?"

"What for? We're almost there."

"To stretch out. Plus, I'd really like to see where your family's from."

"Okay," he said. "That's really thoughtful of you."

"Yeah, I'm pretty great like that," she said, and laughed when he looked at her so puzzled. She bet he'd never had this long of a conversation with anyone alive. How sad was that?

She exited the freeway. They made a U-turn and pulled off the road. It felt good to get out of the car, and Juniper turned her neck back and forth until the knotted muscles gave. Chico walked around the car, coming to a stop at the edge of the road. He looked west, then north, and finally stopped, shrugging. "Things have really changed here," he said. "I don't know where I used to live, but I'm pretty sure it was that way." He pointed to a trailer park, and suddenly Juniper, remembering her parents' mobile home, liked him a little bit more.

"I know how you feel. The same thing happened where I grew up," Juniper said, stretching her arms above her head, amazed at how quickly the time had gone by. "Developers cleared out my entire neighborhood to build luxury homes by the lake. Never seemed to get around to building them, though. Man, it's really cold, isn't it?"

Chico returned to the car and got his thermos out of his backpack. He unscrewed the top, poured a cup, and then handed it to her. "Coffee from the Standard. My only luxury. Want some?"

"Thanks, I love their coffee," she said. "I go there a lot."

"I know. I've seen you there plenty of times."

"Seriously? Were you in camouflage or something? I never saw you."

"You're always with that rich kid who looks like Jakob Dylan."

She was instantly embarrassed. He must have thought that her not saying hello meant she was being a snob. No wonder he was horrid to her in class. She wanted to tell him that yeah, Topher-Jakob was so rich he still owed her money from the Cactus Lodge, plus twenty dollars this week so he could buy new strings for his guitar. "I'm sorry I didn't see you. If I had, I would've said hi. You could have said hi to me, though. Why didn't you?"

"You guys always look pretty focused on each other. I didn't want to interrupt."

She thought a moment. "Is this a teacher-student thing? Are you required by university law to keep your distance outside of class?"

"There's no rule about saying hello to students in public places. I used to go drinking with my professors at Yale. I even roomed with a graduate assistant my last semester there. His name was Ahmed and he taught me seven different ways to make Top Ramen, including curried."

She laughed. "It's the universal food of college students everywhere."

"You're shivering," he said. "Let's get back in the car."

They did. "I usually give the noodles to my roommates and just drink the broth part," she said. "You know, too many refined carbs and all. I avoid any food that's white."

"Really? Are you on a diet? You don't look like you need one."

"It's just a healthier way to eat. You should read *Dr. Gundry's Diet Evolution*. I'll lend it to you. Listen," Juniper said. "So next time you see me, say hi. I can't drink beer with you, though."

"Because of carbs?"

"I'm not old enough to drink alcohol yet. But I can drink coffee."

"What about Jakob Dylan?"

She snorted. "Believe me, you wouldn't be interrupting anything all that interesting unless you're obsessed with writing the next timeless folk song."

"Is that so?"

She was looking straight ahead, studying traffic, but she caught a peripheral glance when he turned to look at her. She saw how his eyes were the color of coffee, and his caterpillar eyebrows actually had a nice arch to them. Maybe he was cuter than she originally thought, but then he wasn't walking around at the moment like a stork that had dislocated both knees—he was sitting in her car and they were talking about things they were both interested in. "Trust me. I'd way rather discuss coprolites than Eric Clapton's amazing fingering on 'Layla.'"

He chuckled.

She took her right hand from the wheel, waving it to try to deflect how badly that sentence came out—fingering? He must think I'm sex-obsessed. "I mean, you know, music is great and I do love classic rock. Who doesn't? 'Layla' is awesome, but Eric Clapton stole George Harrison's wife and then wrote a song about her, which is pretty awful, and really, I'd much rather hear about your classes at Yale. Who did you study with? Were there all kinds of brilliant visiting professors? Do they let you pick an area or do they make you study everything? How many anatomy classes did you take? I loved Anatomy and Physiology. I swear, after I took it, I thought about being a doctor for like ten minutes, but in the end I decided against it."

"You get to choose a major coursework. Up to three cognates."

She had no idea what that meant but she'd look it up later. "Sounds great."

"I've never studied harder than I did there, let me tell you." He paused a moment, then said, "It's none of my business, but you're way too good for that guy."

"I am?"

He nodded, and she saw the way he was looking at her. For once it wasn't about how she was too young to be in his class, it was something else entirely and it was making her feel a little faint. She rolled her window down an inch, grateful for the cold air. "Will you stop staring at my tattoo?" she asked.

He smiled. "You're wearing a turtleneck. I didn't know you had one until you mentioned it this morning. Where is it?"

She pulled the neckline of her turtleneck down for a brief flash. "It was a moment of madness. Now you need to forget about it," she said. "That was great coffee. Just what I needed to perk me up."

"Then the next time I see you at the Standard, I'll buy you a cup."

"And I'll bring you some of my dad's menudo so you don't starve to death over Christmas. Speaking of Christmas, do you have any plans?"

"No."

"You could come to Santa Fe. My dad cooks so much food you wouldn't believe it. Really, think about it, okay?"

"Sure," he said, but she could tell he didn't mean it.

As soon as they entered Española there were all these old-timey shop fronts on either side of the road. "Look at this place," Juniper said. "It's as if the town stopped in 1952. I bet if we walked into that shop"—she pointed at a Western-wear shop with a sign in the window advertising Carhartts—"there'd be cowboys in there playing checkers, dusty old miners weighing their gold, and dance-hall girls trying to get them to buy them a drink."

Chico laughed. "Visual anthropology is becoming a popular field. Does your mind always work that way?"

"I guess. Doesn't yours?"

"Something similar."

"Does that surprise you?"

"Not at all. What made you want to study anthropology? Family vacations to the Petrified Forest? Did you see dinosaur bones in a museum, or watch some TV special about Olduvai Gorge?"

"Nothing like that," she said, and hesitated. If she told Chico about Casey, he might just feel sorry for her. She'd been burned before, and up until this moment, hadn't told anyone in New Mexico. She took a breath. "When I lived in California, this girl went missing. Some years later, a dog uncovered some human bones way out in the middle of nowhere, and for a while, they thought the bones might be hers. It would explain what had happened to her, and her family would have something to bury, you know?"

"Did they?"

"No. They were the bones of a much younger girl. This professor at UC Santa Cruz dated them, and suddenly this local ghost story kids used to scare each other with turned into a true story." In a way, Juniper almost understood the way anyone she told couldn't keep it a secret. The story was so dramatic that they had to tell someone. But that person would look at her differently from then on, and changing her name, all her hard work to become Juniper Vigil, would be for nothing.

"Then what?"

Juniper took a breath and let it out slowly. Just the idea of Casey made her want to stop the car, jump out, and run ten miles. "To be honest, I don't really like talking about it. But my dad used to work in the Albuquerque crime lab, which, by the way, he says is in no way like that TV show. He said they were always scraping the coffers for equipment. Anyway, he knew this professor was a forensic anthropologist. It blew me away how much information the professor was able to tell about the bones, how old they were, what gender, how they fit into history, what had happened to them. Up until then I thought anthropology was like archeology, some poor guy sitting out in the hot sun all day using a paintbrush to remove specks of dirt from a pottery sherd while courting melanoma. As soon as I saw those bones, it was like something inside me came to life. I didn't care if it meant I had to go to school for a thousand years, I knew that I wanted to be that guy, who can look at bones and tell their story."

When he didn't say anything, she thought, great, I sound like the geek of all time. Like my idea of perfume is formaldehyde! Like I grew up believing Indiana Jones movies were documentaries.

Chico looked at his watch. "We should probably talk about the interview."

"You're right," Juniper said, her face bright red from embarrassment. Her stupid mouth did not know when to shut, but she couldn't think of anything educational to say. "There's the turnoff," she said, and put on her blinker.

It was only a short way over the Rio Grande and down a couple streets before they arrived at the Ohkay Owingeh Cultural Center. They knocked, but no one was there and the doors were locked. "What the heck?"

"Did you call to confirm?" Chico asked.

"Of course I did, yesterday, as a matter of fact," Juniper said. She peered in the window and knocked on the glass. Nothing. Nobody was in there.

"Some Pueblos operate on Indian time," Chico said. "Let's leave a note and head out to the pottery studio."

"But we're an hour early."

"So? What's the worst-case scenario? She's not there, and we leave her a note, drive back into 1952-land, and find a coffee shop. If you want to do forensics, you have to learn to be patient."

"You sound just like my dad. I don't get it." She thought of Casey, that endless wait. "I'm probably the most patient person on earth, actually."

Chico laughed.

"What's so funny?"

"Forget it," he said. "There it is."

Juniper pulled over at the white mobile home with the sign PUEBLO POTTERY. Its roof was weighted down with tires, and the trailer coach could've used a coat of paint. Behind the mobile home there was a rickety corral and a small barn. The unfinished wooden steps creaked as they went up them, and she thought of Dolores, how their ghost had taught her to pay attention to sound. No one answered this door, either.

"Great," she said. "This day is just going from bad to worse. Maybe Anna knew something, not showing up. Or I should've had my tarot cards read or thrown the I-Ching or something. Are you going to fail me because my appointments didn't show?"

"Did you even hear what I said about patience? Let's sit in the car for a while and talk about the interview. Maybe Louella Cata is out riding her horse. Besides, we're going to be here for three days."

"How do you know for sure she has a horse? And if she does, why would she go riding in weather this cold? That doesn't make sense. Maybe she got called into work or something. Although there is a pickup truck next to the barn, but it doesn't have a trailer hitch."

"Juniper, just get into the car already."

"I will when you promise not to fail me."

Chico held up a gloved hand. "I solemnly swear I won't fail you for this course. Now will you get in the car? I'm freezing."

They got back into the car and Juniper turned on the heater, hoping it wouldn't run her battery down. She fetched her sleeping bag and unzipped it, pulling it over them like a blanket. "You have to admit you agree with me that she wouldn't be out riding a horse. What's the temperature? Twenty? Who rides a horse in the snow? How do you know she even has a horse?"

Chico pointed. "What do you see around the corner of the barn?"

"The same thing you do, a falling-down corral devoid of horses."

"Currently devoid. Do you need glasses?"

"No. Why?"

"Because if you look at the far edge of the corral, there're some green hay bits on the snow."

"Where? I don't see them."

Chico put his arm around her shoulder and leaned her forward and sideways and it freaked her out, him touching her. "Behold, open corral gate. Note pile of manure that looks like horse droppings. Either I have more skilled powers of observation, or I'm the reincarnation of Saint Anthony of Padua. Which do you think?"

"I think you have this unfortunately mistaken belief that you're funny, like Patton Oswalt," she said. "Trust me, you're not." WTH did I say that for, she thought. Her grade-point average was never going to recover.

Chapter 15

W HEN I CAME out of the bathroom down the hall marked FAMILY RESTROOM (though there was no place to rest), the doctor posse was there again, standing outside Aspen's room, talking in low voices. I started to run. "What happened?" I said before I even got to them.

"Mrs. Smith," the oldest doctor said, the one who was always snotty to me.

His nametag said Morris J. Armstrong, M.D., and he had white hair but a bright red mustache. His face was long and his teeth reminded me of Brown Horse, and I realized I hadn't thought about her, or my dog, Curly, and I was scared that maybe no one had taken over my chores, and the chickens, what about them? Chickens could live for a long time without food, but not water. I hoped that some of the snow had melted because then they could drink that. "Tell me what's wrong," I said. "Tell me right now."

Dr. Armstrong said, "We've been reviewing your daughter's case. The consensus is it's time to disconnect the ventilator. We were just waiting for your permission to move ahead."

"You mean stop the breathing machine? No." I turned to

Mrs. Clemmons, who was always on my side. "Can you make them go away? Could we get another doctor?"

She looked at me the way she did some days, like her mind was working on something else and her being in the room, talking to me, was only a small part of a much bigger thing going on. "Laurel, calm down and take a breath. Let's listen to what Dr. Armstrong has to say. Nothing's going to happen without your permission."

Right there in the hallway with its shiny polished floor and that tart smell of medicine coating everything from Aspen's blankets to the air molecules, the walls closed in until it felt like I was in the back of the van the day the Brothers Grimm took me. Even though that was many years ago, I still remembered it as though it had just happened to me. Later Frances told me the name for the machine was Taser, but I always thought of it as a bolt of lightning, like bright white cracks across the sky before storms. I thought I was going to faint the same way I had back then. I had peed myself and the bones in my legs didn't work, so I couldn't fight back. I just had to let them put me in the van. But this time I had to fight back, because Aspen's life depended on it. Hot tears came into my eyes. "Can't you see how hard she's working to get well? Sleeping so much? She's trying to get better! Why give up on her now?"

Mrs. Clemmons took hold of my shoulders. "Laurel, the doctors want Aspen to recover just as much as you do," Mrs. Clemmons said. "That's why they became doctors. Let's listen to what they have to say."

I crossed my arms in front of myself, and the top button of the shirt came unbuttoned. Mrs. Clemmons looked right at it, and I saw the way she looked at me, like I was disgusting and dirty the way that would never wash off. My neck was all hard muscle, the way it used to get when Abel yelled at me and I would crawl under the table to avoid what might happen next, and which usually happened anyway. He wasn't as big as Seth, but he was stronger and meaner. "I thought you were Aspen's friend," I said. "I don't believe you anymore."

Mrs. Clemmons's face went slack, like I had disappointed her after the nice clothes and food, but she wasn't Aspen's mother. I was. I am.

"Intensive care is expensive," Dr. Armstrong said. He took the finger pincher off Aspen's first finger and my heart beat faster while one of the lines on the machines went flat. "Aspen is stable enough for transport. We're all in agreement. It's time to disconnect these machines. We'll transfer her to a long-term facility, where she'll receive passive physical therapy. In order to do that we need to try to wean her off the machines."

"Or you could just keep on giving her the medicine," I said, hot panic filling my chest. "She never had medicine before, so maybe it's just taking her longer to get better than other people."

The doctors looked at each other and then they looked at Aspen. Not me. This wasn't a good thing, not good at all.

"There's a long-term facility in Roswell that's a perfect environment for Aspen. They can do things for her there that we can't."

"Why not? You're doctors! You're supposed to make people better."

"Aspen *is* better," he said. "Every day she's on the ventilator will make it that much harder for her to live without it. Her illness has subsided. That fever spike resolved as soon as we changed antibiotics. We've been monitoring her blood gases and values. If you'd just listen—"

"Where is this Roswell?" I said. "How much more does it

cost to stay here? I could get a job. I know how to clean houses. I could pay for the extra care and the breathing machine. Roswell—could I walk there every day? Because there are animals on the Farm I have to feed because it's my job and no one else's and I can't just let them die. Isn't that what you're doing to Aspen? Taking away her breathing machine and then seeing if she dies? How much money are we talking about?"

The doctors just looked at me.

"What?" I said. "Why won't you answer me?"

Mrs. Clemmons—how did she stay calm like that—placed her hand on my arm. "Money isn't the central issue here," she said. "There are programs Aspen would qualify for, so don't give that another thought. As soon as we're done talking here, I'll be happy to drive you to the Farm myself to check on your animals. Roswell is in the southern part of the state. You can't walk there, but there are other ways to get there, and if you decide that's where to go, I'm sure we can find someone to look after your animals here. Everyone here can see how much you love Aspen. You're a good mother. I don't think you heard what the doctor said. Aspen *is* better. She's well enough to be moved. Everyone in this room wants to see Aspen get well. Won't you listen to the doctors for a few minutes? I promise you, nothing will change until we're all in agreement as to Aspen's best interests."

That was the most amount of words Mrs. Clemmons had ever said to me, and I was having trouble working them out, separating them into categories, finding the stories in them. All I could remember was her last sentence. *Set. Rest. Trees.* "What do you mean, 'best interests'?"

Dr. Armstrong made a noise. I couldn't tell if he was clearing his throat or being disgusted, the way Seth got whenever I said more than a sentence.

Mrs. Clemmons looked at him the same way Abel used to look at me. She said, "Dr. Armstrong, I think now would be a good time to continue your rounds so that Mrs. Smith and I can talk this over."

"Ardith," he said, taking a step toward her and making his voice all nice. "I don't understand what the problem is here. Her stats are within normal range. Her heart rate is normal, except for the murmur, and that can be handled with medication. The pneumonia is gone, she's responding to stimuli; this is the protocol. Disconnecting the vent is a long process and carefully monitored every step of the way. Clearly if the mother can't grasp what we're saying perhaps there are competency issues—" he said, but she interrupted him again.

"Mrs. Smith and I will talk *privately* and get right back to you."

Dr. Armstrong didn't like that, I could tell, because his jaw flexed the same way Seth's did when he was going to lock me in the barn, or back in California, in the shack. Already I knew Mrs. Clemmons was smart, but now I saw she was also powerful, because the doctors left the room. Power was something I'd never had. Abel and Seth made all the decisions for me. The Brothers Grimm.

We went into Aspen's room that felt like home to me now, the way everything was the same every day. The whiteboard that said the name of her nurse in red marker, Susie or Phyllis or Carolyn or Ana or Leilah. The white blinds kept the light from bothering Aspen's eyes, and gave me a place to look out of so I didn't feel locked up. The clean restroom she'd never used yet and I wasn't allowed to use because I wasn't the patient. The janitor cleaned it every day anyway. Aspen was in the bed, still breathing from the machines that beeped fast when something was wrong and beeped more slowly when nothing was wrong. *Puh-shoo-up.* The feeding tube went down her nose feeding her. Cream-colored nutrition. She hadn't had it long enough to gain any weight, but she hadn't lost any either. I stroked her hair and wished I could wash it in the Waterfall Mist shampoo and conditioner. We only ever used bar soap on it at the Farm. *So, sop, sap.* Washing her hair would make her feel like the princess in my story. *Leaves, save, leave.* "In a little while, I'll tell you more of the story," I whispered to her. Then I asked Mrs. Clemmons, "Are you the Elder of this hospital? Do the doctors have to mind what you say or receive consequences when they don't?"

She looked out the window and then back at me. "I'm not sure I understand what you're asking me, Laurel. I work here," she said, "but I'm not in charge of anyone. We're part of a team. You know how I explained 'best interests' to you? I wonder if you could explain to me what you mean by 'receive consequences'?"

I petted Aspen's arms and legs and she twitched and frowned around her tubes. All she had to do was wake up and then we could go home. Wake up wake up wake up. "You know, receiving punishment or extra chores. Sometimes staying in the barn overnight, other times cleaning the already clean floor. Sometimes hitting."

"That doesn't sound pleasant or fair."

"It wasn't bad. In the barn I could hear Brown Horse making noises right outside, and after Aspen was born, she'd be there with me."

"What about the hitting, and the chores?"

"Chores don't bother me. Hitting only hurts for a while."

"I see," she said in a voice that reminded me of mine, raspy, choking, like she was trying not to yell and I wondered how I had made her mad at me. "Is that how you got the scar on your neck?"

My hand went right to it. No need to cover it now. "It doesn't hurt anymore. It's just ugly, and that's why no one else would want me."

"Seth told you that?"

I nodded.

"May I ask what you did while you were in the barn? Did you sleep?"

"Sometimes," I said, "unless Seth wanted—mostly I told her the story."

"Yes, the Princess of Leaves story. You have a vivid imagination, Laurel. I think you could be a writer."

"I'm not very good at writing things down."

"Is that because you didn't finish school?"

"Um. Yes."

"Who would lock you into the barn? Was it Seth?"

"Of course. He's the Elder. You know, in charge of everyone, especially me."

"Why you, 'especially'?"

I didn't know how to answer her. "Before Seth, it was Abel and Seth, then when Abel wasn't there anymore, it had to be Seth." I started to say more, then decided that wasn't safe because what if he heard? "Seth is in charge of everyone at the Farm. Most people are Sinful and Wayward. Seth helps them find their way if they're spiritually lost. Consequences are teachings."

"Someday I hope you'll trust me enough to tell me about the scar on your neck. I'm assuming it was the result of punishment."

The faintness came back, like when Curly got too playful and jumped at the back of my knees. "Please don't ask me."

"Why not? Will Seth punish you for telling?"

"He would kill me," I whispered, but she heard me all the same.

She turned around and looked at me. "Laurel, I'm going to ask you something difficult, and I want you to try to answer. I know you don't like to talk about it, but I think it's important, all right?"

I was sweating in the new clothes, and they itched so bad I wanted to rip them off. "All right."

"Is Laurel Smith your real name?"

The ocean, I remembered it. It roared in my ears. Waves on top of waves. Coming at me one-two-three, too fast to get my breath before I went under. Not dolphins: whales, big and gray and crowding me. My heart thudded so hard I thought I might need Aspen's breathing machine. My voice came out of me in stops and starts. "Whu-whu-why do you want to know that?"

"Because I've become quite fond of you and your little girl. I want to help you. You're a wonderful mother, and I am impressed with the things you've told me."

"You're going to call the cops or a social worker, aren't you? Please don't. Please, just forget about me and Aspen. We're not important. Thank you for your help and the clothes and food. I'll pay you back and we'll be even."

"Calling the police hadn't even crossed my mind. Is there a reason I should call the police?"

"No. Everything will be fine when Aspen wakes up. We'll go home to the Farm. I'll do extra chores. I don't mind sleeping in the barn, really."

"It's snowing out."

"I know how to keep Aspen warm. Don't worry about us."

Mrs. Clemmons turned and looked out the window. When

she turned back, she said, "Let's put all that aside for now. I know you don't want to hear this, but I think the doctors know best on this ventilator issue. I've seen it done before. The weaning process may look frightening, but what if it means Aspen could breathe on her own, and get strong again?"

"That would be good." But inside me I was thinking, What if she can't?

"There you go. We have some common ground here, Laurel. Understand, the doctors will reconnect her immediately if she can't breathe on her own. Laurel, is Seth Aspen's biological father?"

My mind had always felt like a shut curtain, as if I could only be in one part of it at a time. I liked it that way, because it meant I only had to think from here to there and I could stop thinking before it got too hard. I made words smaller so that I could see their stories in the same way. Safety: *safe, tea, say.* Silence was safety's partner. Together they had a bigger story, one in which I could *sail, listen,* or *flee.* But now Mrs. Clemmons was putting a knife through the curtain, and I couldn't duck quick enough for it to miss my neck. I knew about knives and broken bottles and bleeding and feeling like you couldn't breathe and holding your hands over the tear to stop the bleeding. But it was hard to find the tear here. "Seth is a good Elder," I said. "He found me. He allowed me to choose my own name."

"I see," she said. "Thank you for sharing this information with me. I can tell that you trust me, and that makes me happy."

Always be polite. "You're welcome."

A few minutes later, she said, "I have another question, but again, if it's too private you don't have to answer. What was your real name before it was Laurel? The name you were born with. Before you met Seth and Abel."

Hot tears. Ears roaring. I felt like I did on that bad, bad day when Abel got his knife out and said I wasn't worth keeping anymore. Soon the sound would come, and Seth would hear and he would kill the animals and make me watch. Then he'd kill Aspen, and then he'd kill me and there would be nothing, but maybe that was Our Creator's plan, and all these days I'd lived already were His Grace or Mother Earth's wish? I got up from Aspen's bed and tried to walk but my legs wouldn't work and I nearly fell down until Mrs. Clemmons caught me. She helped me sit down in the chair where I spent most of my time. Orange chair. Smelling of antiseptic. I slept there.

Then she knelt down in front of me and placed her hands on my shoulders so that we were close enough to feel each other's breath. I shut my eyes but the hot tears kept coming. "What is it, Laurel? What has you so upset?"

My eyes itched and I opened them to rub away the itch. It was hard to look at her but I did. "I'm sorry, Mrs. Clemmons. That is one thing I can't tell you. I promised a long time ago that I wouldn't say it out loud ever again."

She nodded. "What about writing it down? Could you do that?"

She had a pen and a notebook in her pocket, and before I could answer, she offered them to me. Blank paper. Nothing on it unless I wrote something, and if I did it, that something would change everything. "Seth killed my parents," I whispered. "He promised he would kill everything I love if I ever told," I whispered. "I've seen him kill things."

Mrs. Clemmons's nostrils flared and I wondered if she ever felt such hot tears. Did anything ever make her so sad that she'd make the sound? Probably not, she was smart and knew how to

talk and I was stupid and worthless and nobody wanted me except for Aspen who would not wake up. "Laurel, I can assure
you, Seth will not get anywhere near you."

"Aspen."

"He won't get near her, either. I promise."

"But Mrs. Clemmons," I whispered. "The animals. He could
hurt the animals. He might have already. He did it before."

She put her hand over her mouth and then I did see the hot
tears. I didn't want her to feel so sad because I felt sad enough
for both of us. "Seth made me a place. But he's got the devil in
him like everyone does. He can be mean and it's my fault.
When he hurts an animal he does it to show me how angry he
can get and what will happen if I don't follow the script."

Mrs. Clemmons still had tears coming from her eyes. This
was all my fault, Aspen being so much trouble, and me with
filthy clothes and her having to buy me things she probably
couldn't afford and her job was so hard, especially if she had to
work with people like me and those doctors who were supposed to heal people but couldn't, not always. She tried to help
me. She had tried so hard I had to give her something in return.
So I took the paper and pen from her and I printed my old
name:

CASEY T. MCGUIRE

I handed it to her and then I sat back in the chair to wait for
the bad things to happen, one-two-three, forever. Sometimes
Seth told lies, For the Greater Good, but the one true thing I
never doubted was that Seth promised that no matter where I
was, or who I was with, if I told, he would find me. First he'd kill
everything I loved, including Aspen, and then he would kill me.
Inside *Kill* is only *Ill*. No other words, no story. I prayed for the

animals. "Brown Horse, I'm sorry," I said. "Please forgive me, and Curly the dog and the chickens. I will dig your graves and put stones on top. I won't ever forget you. I'll bury you myself and pray for you always."

Chapter 16

JUNIPER'S BUTT WAS frozen and her hands felt stiff; all that would have been tolerable if Chico wasn't sitting so close to her that she could hear his breathing. If they fell asleep, could someone say they had "slept together"? Topher wouldn't be happy about that. He'd sent her five more texts but she hadn't read any of them. It was bad enough that she'd have to tell him she and Chico had done the interview together. Maybe they should go back to town, get some coffee, come back in an hour. A quick look at her watch made that plan seem pointless. By the time they drove to Española and back, they'd be late for the interview.

"Sorry," she finally said to Chico, who looked quite content covered up by her sleeping bag. "I can't sit here another minute. I'm going for a walk to get my blood moving."

"I'll come with you."

"Suit yourself." She reached into the cargo area for some beef jerky and tucked an apple into her pocket. Maybe eating would warm her up. She opened the almond can to grab a handful, and then from behind, Chico touched her shoulder. She shrieked. "What are you doing?"

He held up his hands and stepped back. "Are you always so

jumpy? I was trying to fix your scarf before it falls off you. I know how you get all lost in thought. How many scarves have you lost this winter?"

"Not that many. Why?"

"Because every time you come to class you have on a different one." He tucked the scarf ends in and stepped back.

"Thanks. Sorry I freaked out a little there. I just wasn't expecting it."

"Forget it. Which way do you want to walk?"

They heard a horse whinny, and Juniper pointed in the direction where the sound had come from. "I love horses. Besides, we've already seen that way, so let's go this way."

Ahead of them, a paved two-lane road stretched into the distance, frost-heaved in places and rutted in others. New Mexico in winter was various shades of brown and bare branches. The evergreen piñon trees stood short and stubby compared to California's redwoods. To Juniper, their severe beauty was always a challenge. The left side of the road revealed the rocky, harsh beauty of Ghost Ranch, yet the right side, near the river, was like an entirely different ecosystem. She imagined it in summer, with corn growing everywhere and farm stands selling fruit and heirloom tomatoes. "In New Mexico, everything comes down to water, doesn't it?" she said to Chico.

"How do you mean?"

"Who has it, who sells it, what they do with it. My grandparents are farmers. What do yours do?"

Chico put his gloved hands into his pockets. "They're retired. My grandpa was a mailman. My grandma taught school, but now she has dementia. They live in an assisted-living facility near my auntie. It's a terrible disease," he said. "I hope it never happens to anyone you love."

"Thank you for saying that. I'm sorry you have to go through it."

He shrugged. "What can you do? You have to honor your grandparents."

They walked for a while, the snow crunching beneath their boots. Every now and then a flake hit her in the face, but it was barely snowing. The wind picked up, chapping her cheeks, and she pulled her scarf up over her nose. Then ahead of them, they saw a for-sale sign advertising "14 acres, well/water rights, established orchards/greenhouses." All that was behind a metal gate with a keypad entry.

"Seems kind of weird for out here in the sticks, don't you think?" she said.

"Some people want privacy. Cool mailbox."

The old coffee can serving for a mailbox was painted New Mexico's famous sun-bleached indigo blue, a color you'd never find in a paint store. Stenciled in white on the side were two words, THE FARM. The fence all around was chain link instead of coyote fencing, which was a kind of New Mexico tradition.

"This place sort of creeps me out," Juniper said to Chico.

Just after she spoke they heard the horse whinny, the sound now coming from the opposite direction. "Sounds like the horse is loose," Juniper said. "We'd better catch it before it gets hit by a car."

"Look over there," Chico said, pointing to the two-story adobe house. "The front door's wide open. That can't be on purpose, not on a day this cold."

Juniper peered over the fence. There were no cars, no people, just a two-story adobe house with an open door and a yurt with a giant tear in its side. To their right a wooden building was boarded up, but according to the bleached sign, it had once been a café. It reminded her of a bad dream, and she wished they'd stayed in the car and fallen asleep no matter what Topher might think. "Chico, I think something is wrong in there."

He nodded. "I'm getting the same feeling. We should call the cops."

Juniper looked at him. "Seriously? Do you know how long it would take a cop to drive here? What if this is Pueblo land? They won't come at all. I think we should find that horse and see if someone's hurt or needs help."

"The gate's locked. How are we supposed to get in?"

"You can boost me over the fence."

"Juniper, there is no way I'm doing that. Let's go back to town and stop at the Pueblo police department. They'll investigate or call the cops. I'm sure we passed it on the drive in."

But Juniper's mind was on the horse, and she was already on the fence, climbing up the chain link like it was made for exactly that purpose. "Anyone home?" she called out when she hit the ground on the other side. "Hello? Your front door's open."

The horse whinnied again, and she cocked her head, trying to tell where the sound was coming from. A barking dog appeared, rib-showing thin, no particular breed, like the brown res dogs New Mexico was famous for. This one wagged her curly tail as soon as Juniper extended her hand.

"I wouldn't do that if I were you," Chico said. "What if she has rabies?"

"Oh, for crying out loud, Chico. She doesn't have rabies." Juniper took some beef jerky out of her pocket and handed it to the dog. She sniffed, then took the jerky gladly, snarfing it down. She whined when no more was forthcoming. Then the dog lay down and showed her belly for a rub the same way that

Caddy did. "Look at her, Chico. She's someone's pet, and she's starving. Climb over and help me."

"I hate to think what you'd be doing had I not come along today," Chico said as he placed the toes of his boots in the chain link.

"I'd be asking Anna to climb the fence is what I'd be doing. This dog's being neglected and one thing you might not know about me? I've called campus police three times for people leaving their dogs locked in cars. I'll get between a three-hundred-pound gangster and his pit bull if he's abusing it. I have the SPCA on my speed dial. I loathe cruelty to animals. If there isn't anyone here to take care of this dog, I'm bringing her home with me."

"The dorm won't allow dogs."

"Eff the dorm. I'll take her to my parents' house."

Chico jumped down to the ground beside her. "We're taking a quick look and then we're calling the cops."

Juniper was already halfway to the house. The two of them called out, "Hello?" over and over. Aside from the dog thinking that was an invitation to play, there wasn't any response. When they neared the front door, Chico took her hand, and she had to force herself not to say anything, because he was being protective of her, that's all, the same way her dad would, and the truth was, she felt a little afraid. The dog refused to go indoors. All Juniper could think was there's something horrible in there. There's something not even the dog wants to see.

The entry of the house was a long hallway with plastered white walls, a basket of magazines, among them *Wellspring* and those free newspapers you could find at Whole Foods. The light switch didn't work. There were pictures on the walls of Buddha, Jesus, and several of those Hindu gods with all the arms. To the left was a room with a big wooden table and six chairs, three of them knocked over. On top of the table were brochures advertising spiritual retreats. The large kiva-style fireplace was full of ashes. A stack of yoga mats and cushions sat on the floor.

The kitchen reminded Juniper of those books of unexplained mysteries she'd loved when she was a kid. Stories of ships abandoned at sea, tables set, a meal in progress, and no one could explain what became of the missing crew or why. She wondered if there had been something similar going on here, because draped over one chair was a down jacket, and on the plates at the table there were the remains of a breakfast. A round loaf of bread looked chewed on one end. If the dog hadn't gotten to it, mice had. And where were the people?

"Hello!" she called. "Anybody home?"

Out the sliding glass door behind the house was a canvas-covered dome-like structure, and when Chico saw it, he said, "Sweat lodge. This is one of those New Age places. You know what I mean, like a spa, but for meditations and retreats. Probably they went broke, put it up for sale, and some realtor showing the property left the door open."

Juniper said, "I'd believe that if the indoors wasn't in such a mess. Who puts their house on the market and leaves dirty dishes on the table? Maybe somebody homeless came in here and camped. Let's go check the bedrooms."

Chico stopped her in the kitchen. "I'll check them. You go back outside to find the horse."

"Shouldn't we stay together?"

"You'll be fine."

He reminded her of her dad right then, being all protective. If Daddy Joe knew where she was and what she was doing, he'd blow a gasket. Back outside, she hoped the property was abandoned, not some kind of mass-suicide scene with dead bodies that had Kool-Aid stains on their mouths. What if some madman sneaked up on her with a knife? Or strangled her with a piece of piano wire? Listen to yourself, she said. Where in the heck is someone going to get a piano wire out here? Stop watching *The Sopranos*. Her heart hammered. She made the kiss-kiss noise she used to make in California when she wanted the horses to come to the fence. No more whinnying at all. The dog stuck by her, happy-go-lucky, her curly tail in the air, as if now that Juniper was here she'd be getting regular meals again. "Don't worry," she told her as they walked toward two hoop greenhouses that hadn't been visible from the road. "I won't leave you here."

The hoop houses were amazingly tall. Even Chico would feel small in here. There was a heating system, lines for drip irrigation, and a worktable covered with envelopes, vermiculite, and spilled seeds. She'd made sure to call "Hello?" before she opened the door, but once she was inside, she had to stop and look around. There were so many plants that it couldn't just be some hippie family's greenhouse. This was a professional setup, designed to grow vegetables through the winter. Maybe at one time they'd sold crops at farmer's markets, or to restaurants, but not now. Everything—winter root vegetables, forced carrots, tomato plants—was dead, blackened from freezing and starved for water. The best temperature-regulation and watering systems weren't any good if they were turned off. Someone had shut things off and then left, in a hurry. She half-expected to find a marijuana crop, but if there had been one, they'd taken it with them. She exited the hoop house and went to the barn. A torn sack of spilled feed lay on its side, probably the dog's attempt to feed herself, but there were green bales of hay stacked high, and horse tack. Just no horse.

Chico made sure to warn her when he came walking her way, "It's only me, don't panic. The bedrooms were empty, but they're set up like hotel rooms. Maybe this place was a B and B."

Then Juniper shushed him. "Listen," she said. "I'm positive I heard a horse. If we follow the sound, maybe we can find him."

"It might be easier to just follow the tracks," Chico said, and pointed. The corral gate was open, and right there in the snow were hoof prints leading back toward Pueblo Pottery. Two sets, two horses. They set off following, the brown dog by their side. Eventually they caught sight of the horses ahead of them. A woman was riding one, ponying the other horse alongside.

"Hello?" Juniper called.

The woman rider stopped. The bay she was riding turned around as she faced them. The chestnut horse whinnied. "Hey," she said. "Who are you and what are you doing with Laurel's dog?"

"Saving her from starvation," Juniper said. "What are you doing with that horse?"

"Juniper," Chico said. "Calm down." He smiled at the woman on horseback. "Are you Louella Cata?" Chico said.

"What if I am?"

"We're the UNM students who made the appointment to interview you. We arrived a little early and you weren't home, so we took a walk. We saw the front door open and thought maybe someone needed help, so we climbed over the fence."

Meanwhile, Juniper had caught up to the horses and when she saw the ribs showing on the chestnut horse, she got mad all over again. "There's hay in the barn," she said. "Why isn't anyone feeding these animals?"

The woman on horseback waited for Juniper to finish being angry. "Yes, I'm Louella. The horse I'm riding is mine. The chestnut belongs to freaks that live at the Farm. A bunch of selfish assholes, if you ask me, because it looks like they cleared out and left the animals behind to die. It doesn't make any sense. Laurel wouldn't have left her dog behind for anything. I've spent half the morning moving the surviving hens to my barn. A couple of them won't make it, but the others stand a good chance."

"Who's Laurel?" Chico asked.

Louella Cata looked down at him. "Well, she used to live there. A week or so ago her daughter got real sick and my brother gave her a ride into town. I don't get it, because Laurel took great care of the animals. She'd feed my horse whenever I had to be away. She loves Brown Horse as much as she does her daughter. After three nights of listening to that mare whinny all night and Curly howling, I thought I better go check on things, you know? When I saw how it was, I decided I'd put the horse in my barn until Laurel or Seth or one of the freaks return. Listen, I don't know about you two, but I'm freezing my tits off out here. Does one of you want to ride the mare back to my barn? Becoming a human Popsicle wasn't on my day planner. "

Though it had been a couple of years since Juniper had ridden, she climbed right up onto the mare's bare back. She took the halter rope from Louella, quickly fashioned it into a rein, and then she reached down to scratch the mare's neck. "Hey, little brown horse. You're all right," she soothed. "I'll buck those hay bales over here as soon as we get you settled. You'll be all right."

She didn't even think of how insane all this might look to Chico. The feeling of a warm animal beneath her and the tart smell of horse sweat had transported her back in time to riding with Glory through the oak groves in California. Until then, she hadn't understood what it meant to love a horse, to actually consider its needs more than its existing for your entertainment.

"You guys go on ahead," Chico said. "I'll catch up."

Louella and Juniper cued the horses into a trot, and Juniper felt her face break into a smile. The feel of the warm body beneath her was familiar and a painful reminder that she hadn't ridden a horse since moving to New Mexico. At some point she was going to have to find a place to ride.

Once they got to the barn, the women quickly dismounted and took the horses into the barn. Louella flaked off a large portion of hay and divided it between the horses. When she reached a scoop into a bag of grain, Juniper said, "Careful. If she eats too much too quickly, she could colic or founder."

Louella looked at her sideways. "You some kind of horse whisperer like Laurel?"

"Not at all. When I lived in California, my mom had horses. I don't know a lot else, but I do know how to feed a horse, and what will make them sick."

"Well, isn't that a relief," Louella said.

Up close, Juniper could see that the woman wasn't all that much older than she was. "Why?"

"Because most people pretend they know everything about horses, and when you put them on one, they break their neck. Come on, let's go inside where it's warmer. I'll make some coffee. I hope your boyfriend doesn't freeze to death."

"He's not my boyfriend."

Louella laughed. "Are you sure about that? Looks like he wants to be."

Juniper dismissed the comment without a word. What was the point? This Louella hadn't seen Chico in the classroom. Not for the first time did she imagine him in the *Little House on the Prairie* days; he would have been the male equivalent of a strict schoolmaster, his lunch consisting of a cold potato and a dipperful of river water. What did you do when you were born two hundred years too late? You taught at a university.

They walked through the back door of the mobile home, and once inside, Juniper felt like Alice through the looking glass. Though the outside of the home looked totally ghetto and in need of repair, the inside was surprisingly orderly, with worn furniture and threadbare rugs. Every surface was immaculate. One side of the mobile home was a pottery studio, with shelves of equipment and clay stains on the floorboards. On another set of shelves were probably fifty micaceous pots of varying size. The other side of the trailer was the living area. In the center of the room was a kitchen with ancient stovepipe running up the wall and outward, linoleum so old it had no recognizable pattern anymore, and a rickety old metal table that looked like it was once used for holding merchandise at a craft fair. Around it stood four mismatched chairs with vinyl upholstery, most of them ripped and leaking stuffing, but Juniper would bet on it they were clean enough to eat off.

"It's not the Ritz," Louella said, and went to the sink to fill an aluminum kettle. "Sit down wherever you like."

Near the front door was the head of a massive elk, its triumphant rack two feet across, with marble-glass eyes that were stilled for all time. The only thing that saved it from being the saddest thing Juniper had seen in quite some time was the turquoise-and-silver squash-blossom necklace draped over one antler and the pink cowboy hat on the other.

Chico came indoors, knocking the snow from his boots before stepping in. He gestured to the front door. "Juniper, give me your keys and I'll bring the equipment in."

"See what I mean?" Louella said, and laughed.

Juniper's face burned as she turned to Louella and gave her a frown that said back off. "I'll help you, Chico. It's stuff for your interview, Louella. Be right back."

When they opened the front door, there sat the dog, tail wagging, as if to say, Did you forget about me? "Can I let the dog in?" Juniper asked.

Louella laughed. "Sure. I'll get her a bowl of water. When Laurel comes over to throw pots, Curly always comes along. Go on, Curly, you know where the dog bed is."

The dog barked once at the elk head, then trotted across the room for a stack of old horse blankets. "She always does that," Louella said, getting cups down from the cupboard. "Curly lets you know what's on her mind."

Chico insisted on carrying in the photography equipment and the recording stuff. Juniper grabbed both their backpacks. At the last minute, she decided to bring in the bag of food she'd brought. After the strange introduction, it was a friendly gesture. Maybe it would patch up any leftover weirdness. She nestled the bubble-wrapped pot in her right arm and waited for Chico to set down the equipment before opening the door for her. No way was she going to drop that pot. "Thanks," she said.

"You're welcome."

"Look at all this food," Louella said. "Thank you for bringing it to me. I like this brand of almonds. Not too much salt on them. I have to watch my salt and my sugar both."

Juniper thought, Oh well. I can go shopping later. They ate at the table, Louella filling their cups with coffee every time they drank more than an inch. After they were finished, Chico cleared the plates and Juniper set up her equipment. She tested the microphone, shot some test footage, played it back to make sure everything was working. After a million little adjustments, she pulled out a conventional notebook and two mechanical pencils, because Dr. Carey had told them never to rely on technical equipment. Besides, there'll always be something the tape missed, some word or phrase you meant to write down later, but you'll forget it. Daddy Joe had told her that crime scenes were like that, too, that the smallest thing could sometimes make the difference between a case that got solved and one that went cold. For a moment, she thought of Casey, the cops and FBI and jillions of people who'd looked but failed to find one good lead.

"So what do you want to talk to me about?" Louella said.

Though she'd been preparing for this interview all quarter, Juniper was sick-to-her-stomach nervous. She'd gone over it in her head hundreds of times and had her interview questions memorized so she wouldn't sound like an idiot reading a script. Of course, she'd planned to be armed with the cultural center's information, too, but so far this day had turned out entirely wrong. She was afraid that her voice would come out strangled or that she'd develop instantaneous laryngitis. She cleared her throat. "Thank you for agreeing to allow me, I mean us, to interview you. I've spent the last quarter studying Pueblo pottery, and meeting you will bring it all to life in a way textbooks can't."

Louella looked at her, waiting.

"Okay," Juniper said. "I guess my first question is about your mentors, or your inspirations? Where did they come from? What made you want to be a potter?"

Louella smiled at her. "Why are you so nervous?"

"I'm not nervous."

Louella laughed. "Yeah, you are. I have a suggestion. Why don't you throw those prepared questions out the window and let's just talk some woman talk, all right?"

Juniper didn't dare look at Chico. He was either sitting there racking up the points to subtract from her project, or he was arming himself with reasons why Dr. Carey should refuse her admission to any more grad-level classes. "Sure," she said, though she was anything but. "That sounds good."

Louella laughed again. "What a day, huh? Chickens, horses, and now you two. Those idiots on the Farm, now there's a story. I could tell you a lot about them that ought to be in a police file, but I know you want to talk to me, so maybe later." She got up and walked to the other side of the room, picked through the finished pots until she found the one she was looking for, and then came back and set it on the table, a lopsided bowl that had obvious flaws. "This is the pot," she said.

"Which pot is that?"

"My first. The one my grandma taught me to make. I used to go stay with her when my mom couldn't be there. I was always jumping on the backs of my grandpa's draft horses, riding them without bridles, and man, that used to be so much fun. Then I fell off and broke my ankle, and imagine a wild kid not even being able to go outside. You ever break a bone?"

"Yes." Juniper thought of her own broken ankle, four years ago, when she'd tried to kill herself. The bones had to be surgically pinned, and there were casts for weeks and months of physical therapy. If Aunt Halle hadn't sat with her most days, she would have lost her mind. Of course, Caddy had gone missing, too, and looking for her it wasn't just the knowledge that it was Juniper's fault that destroyed her, it was missing the dog that'd become her best friend. She tamped the memory down as far as she could, but it was like opening a jar of marshmallow spread in high-altitude Santa Fe, increasing in volume faster than you could contain it.

"So one day Grandma is at the end of her rope with me, and she hands me some red clay, and says, 'Here, make something other than noise for a change.' She showed me how to coil, stack, and pinch. Pretty soon I didn't want to do anything but the clay. So that spring, Grandma said if I wanted to do things right, I had to learn it from the ground up. By that I mean she showed me where to dig out the clay, and how to process it. It's a spiritual act, you know. We thank Mother Earth for letting us have some of her precious self."

"I've watched Felipe Ortega's videos," Juniper said. "He says digging up the clay is kind of a sexual act, but holy."

Louella laughed. "You're pretty brave for a white girl, aren't you? Nobody outside the tribe ever wants to talk about that."

"I don't mind," Juniper said. "I think it makes sense if you cherish the earth."

Louella placed the pot in Juniper's hands. "What do you feel when you're holding it?"

"Well, it feels cool, I guess, and round. Not smooth but not rough, either. It feels important to me."

"Why?"

"Because you told me it's your first pot." In the background she heard Chico cross his legs, and the dog scratching. "What's it feel like to you?"

Louella took it back. "I don't feel any of those things. I feel my grandma's hands on mine, and remember how her house smelled like masa all the time, because she made her own tortillas. And I hear the TV. She kept it on morning to bedtime. 'It's nice to have company,' she always said, like TV was the one thing keeping her from being lonely."

"But if you were there, too," Juniper said, "how could she be lonely?"

Louella cocked her head sideways, the same way she had looked at Juniper in the barn with the horses. "Man, here you are in college and you don't get how she was lonesome? Stop thinking with your brain, girl. What's your heart tell you?"

Juniper swallowed. She wished Chico would disappear, because this so-called interview was getting uncomfortable. She had no idea how she was going to write it up. "Maybe she was lonely for adult conversation, or wished she had a job, or a better life?"

Louella took a drink of her coffee, and then looked inside as she swished the remaining liquid around before drinking it. "Maybe she was lonely because my mom was an alcoholic who'd go off on a tear and forget about me for weeks at a time. Maybe Grandma wasn't sure how to fill that hole in my heart, so she handed me clay."

"I'm sorry," Juniper said. "That sounds difficult."

"Hell, yeah, it was difficult. She thought she was done raising daughters, and she knew she couldn't do nothing for my mom. Lost cause, she used to say."

"Did your mom ever get sober?"

"A week before she died in the hospital down the road there. Indian Health Services contracts with Presbyterian hospital. She died in a clean room, but nobody was with her. Grandma didn't think I was old enough to see something like that, but I was. If you don't get to say good-bye, it haunts you."

Juniper didn't know what to say. All quarter they'd talked about interview methodology, anthropological approaches, the use of proper terminology; they'd even had a journalism professor come and speak to the class. All that studying, and everything came down to Casey and the good-bye she hadn't gotten to say. She was on the verge of tears and couldn't speak a word. She heard Chico scoot his chair closer.

"Thank you for sharing that, Louella," he said. "Maybe we should take a break and check on those horses. What do you think?"

"Good idea," Louella said. She'd left the kettle simmering on the stove, and got a hot pad to carry it out to the barn. "Gonna make them a bran mash," she said, "it being so cold."

"I know how to make that," Juniper said, thrilled to have a task to do. "I can do it if you like."

Louella pointed with her chin to the cupboard. Juniper opened it and took out a big yellow bowl. "The bran's in the fridge," Louella said. "Otherwise mice get into it."

"We had that problem in California. Mostly in the barn."

"Yeah, well, I bet you didn't have packrats. Big-eyed mothers, babies clinging to their back like possums. I left my rubber boots in the barn all summer, and the first time I went to use them, them rats had made a nest in my boot. They find a waterproof house, they're gonna move in."

They worked together until they'd made a steamy porridge for the horses, and then Chico opened the door so they could all go out to the barn. The curly-tailed dog came along. Chico opened the barn door, and they could hear the horses "whicker-ing," a sound Juniper used to hear in California when she and Glory fed them a mash, or a handful of sweet feed. The smell and quiet of the barn brought it all back to her, like a fist clasping around her heart. She wondered if that particular noise was part of a horse's language, and wished she could translate it. Louella poured half the mixture into a green bucket and handed the bowl to Juniper. "You feed Brown Horse. She's Laurel's horse.

I'll do Lil Sweetheart. That's my horse, and yes, I named her when I was twelve years old."

Juniper felt the heaviness of the mare's head as she dove into the mash, all the while making that happy noise. The horse reminded her of Dodge, who would lick his dinner bowl clean, then flip it over and lick the underside as if he expected there might be another dinner waiting for him. Behind her, she heard the sound of Chico taking pictures with her camera, and she didn't even mind.

After they were done, Louella let the horses wander out into the corral. She led Chico and Juniper to a stall with the door shut and pointed over the gate. "I put the hens in here," she said, and scraped the last of the bran mash into their feed. The hens went berserk, and Juniper noticed they were the same kind that Glory had, that wyandotte breed her dad had driven all the way up to buy—then it hit her—here. He'd bought Glory's hen from this place she'd found abandoned, the Farm. New Mexico was a small-town kind of state. Daddy Joe always said, "Six degrees of separation was invented here in New Mexico."

On their walk back to the trailer, it occurred to her that Louella was showing her the way with the interview. This was the paradigm for the "open-ended interview," where you let the answer determine what to say or ask next. All she needed to do was establish a context, and they could pick up right where they'd left off. Once they were seated, this time in the living-room furniture, she cleared her throat and went for it. "My mom died when I was twelve. She wasn't an alcoholic, but she abused prescription drugs. Actually, she overdosed on purpose, so I guess you'd say she committed suicide. I didn't get to say good-bye either."

"Now I'm the one who's sorry," Louella said. "Maybe I was giving you a hard time there. So can I ask you something?"

"Sure."

"What did you fill the hole in your heart with?"

Juniper turned to Chico. He had his professor face on, the slight frown, his lips pursed. But in his eyes she saw kindness, so she forged ahead. "Drugs, boys, getting a tattoo, whatever made the hurt stop. I guess what finally filled it for me was my parents who adopted me. My adopted mom taught me to ride a horse. My adopted dad taught me how to make Indian spaghetti sauce. He also home-schooled me until I learned that the beauty of education is that you can never learn enough." She swallowed hard. "I've lost a lot in my life, my sister and my real parents, but it's pretty full right now. And I love pottery. When my parents were redoing the plumbing in their Santa Fe house, we found so many pot sherds under the foundation I couldn't believe it. It felt to me like holding the past in my hand. That probably sounds silly."

"What part of Santa Fe?"

"On the edge of the historic district. Colibri Road."

"I know that road," Louella said. "My great-grandma worked for a rich family near there. Housekeeper."

"We don't have a housekeeper," Juniper said. "My parents both work, but my mom's about to have a baby."

Louella smiled. "Girl, you don't need to feel guilty for having an easier life. Have you ever made a pot?"

Juniper shook her head no.

Louella stood up. "Come on. Let's go make a pot. You, too, Mr. Silent over there in the corner." She walked across the room into the other half of her spare home, a place where art was born. Juniper watched Louella reach for the clay wrapped in plastic and get out her tools. She could imagine Louella's grandmother, trying to keep a motherless child busy while living her life around the grief of losing her own daughter by degrees. Juniper felt like she had learned more in the last hour than she had in all her college classes. She could not wait to see what happened next.

Chapter 17

GLORY WOKE UP to Halle calling her name and the dogs' barking. From the bedroom doorway, her sister looked as if she'd stepped out of one of the seven circles of hell, the one with free drinks, hours at the slots, and very little sleep. "You can't even sit up to say hello to me? You leave your front door unlocked? Some crazed art collector could have strayed off Canyon Road and come into your house by mistake and—"

"And what?" Glory asked, yawning. "Steal the one decent painting we have on our mantel? I'd call Aaron up and ask for a new one. For your information, I'm stuck in bed here due to my blood pressure, so don't pick a fight with me." She sniffed and waved her hand. "How was Vegas other than cigarette-smoky?"

"I swear that town runs on Adderall," Halle said, sitting down on the edge of the bed. "I probably slept a total of two hours. I did see that Cirque du whatever thing on the Beatles' music. It made me cry like a baby."

"Why?"

"Glory! Because it was the Beatles. Because they wrote the best love songs ever but never will again. Sitting there by my-self all I could think about was John murdered by that crazed fan and George dead from brain cancer—what kind of god gives a man with that much genius cancer? I ask you."

"At least their music is forever," Glory said. "I feel sad about it, too, but you should take the theological questions up with Mom."

"I'd rather not hear another lecture from her. She already thinks I'm headed for hell. Where's Joseph?"

"Out buying food because I have to lie here forever."

Halle sat down on the bed and opened her purse. "Stop whining. I brought you a present."

"I'm not whining," Glory said. "What did you get me?"

"Open it and find out."

Glory tore away the tissue paper and there was a baby onesie with FUTURE SHOWGIRL silk-screened on the front in glittering red letters. "This is the tackiest thing I've ever seen," Glory said. "I love it."

"Actually, I have something even tackier," Halle said. "Doggie nephews," she said in a high voice that got all their tails wagging, "Auntie Halle couldn't leave Las Vegas without bringing you presents. Behold." Out of her silver oversized purse she took a rubber pork chop with LAS VEGAS stenciled on it, a set of squeaky red dice, and for Eddie, an Elvis jacket made of ivory-and-gold pleather. "Take note this is the *skinny* Elvis model," Halle said. "They have a fat one, too."

Eddie took one look at it and hightailed it under the bed.

Glory was laughing so hard she got tears. Halle laughed along with her, and the two big dogs jumped and jigged around the bedroom, knocking over Halle's purse and the stack of books on the floor, whacking their tails into the television screen, certain all this excitement indicated some kind of holiday. Eddie squeezed out from under the bed and ran out to the great room. "He's looking for his Christmas stocking," Glory said, and laughed all over again. "How long have you been gone, Hal? Because it feels like a thousand years since Thanksgiving. I am so glad to see you."

Halle gave her a kiss on the cheek, hugged her as best she could, and when Joseph walked into the house an hour later, they were still on the bed laughing.

"What did I miss?" he asked, his hands full of grocery bags.

Glory held up the onesie.

"Aieee!" he said. "No way my daughter is wearing that horrible thing." He stepped forward to grab it.

Glory tucked it under her belly and Halle held up the Elvis jacket. "How about this?"

"Just to make sure I'm in the correct universe," he said, "I'm going to step outside and try coming back in again."

"What are you making for dinner?" Halle asked. "Whatever it is, put lots of alcohol in it."

If their laughter hadn't drowned him out, they would have heard him muttering to himself in Spanish about *hermanas locas* and several other things.

Juniper carefully unwrapped the micaceous pot layer by layer until it sat on Louella's table. She was hoping that Louella would remember making it, would be so thrilled that Juniper had bought one of her pots; that the story she'd tell about this particular one would be so meaningful that it would not only impress Chico but *make* her paper skyrocket into the A-plus category. Louella smiled, picked it up, and turned it over and over in her hands. Juniper watched, jotting in her notebook, *can't stop touching. Does a sold pot still feel like hers? She's smiling and shaking her head. What's up—does she see flaws I miss?* Chico was across the room, taking photographs of Louella's other pots, and sneaking in a few of the deer head when Juniper wasn't looking.

Finally Louella said, "Girl, I'm sorry to bust your bubble, but this ain't my pot. But I do know who made it."

"What do you mean?" Juniper said. "There was a blue ribbon inside it for the Taos County fair. It had your name on it and everything."

"That's another reason it has to be a mix-up," Louella said. "I'd never sell one of my prize-winning pots. Those are in the case over there," she said, pointing to what Juniper had mistaken for a bookshelf. A Storm-pattern red-and-black woven blanket covered most of its contents until she moved it out of the way. "Let me get that pot out and show you."

The case was locked, and Louella moved back several other pots to reach the one she was talking about.

"See the difference?" she said to Juniper. "This pot is handmade. Like I showed you, the clay goes into the puki, coil by coil. I build it up layer by layer, stopping every four coils to scrape it smooth and to add water and so forth. Couldn't you tell this one here is wheel thrown?"

"No. I assumed it was handmade."

Chico set the camera down on the table to look.

Juniper was mortified. How could she be in his class and not recognize the difference between a hand-built pot and a wheel-thrown one? The telltale signs now seemed so obvious as Louella pointed them out.

"You said you knew who made it," Chico said. "Can you tell us her name?"

Louella laughed. "Laurel. She made that pot a year ago sitting right there at the potter's wheel. Wasn't all that great of a day, as I remember. That freak Seth had given her a black eye and I was trying to talk her into going to the cops, but she wouldn't go. She said it was her fault for making him angry. I damn near called them cops myself. She wouldn't hear one bad word about her 'Elder.' "

Juniper listened closely, imagining this Laurel who made pots, who loved horses and dogs but abandoned them to starve with bales of hay just out of reach. Why let any man whale on you? How could it ever be a woman's fault enough to deserve a black eye? Candela taught her that much.

Chico said, "Juniper?"

"What," she said flatly.

"If you think about it, this angle doesn't take away from your project, it adds to it. Plenty of top-rate museums have been duped into buying fakes. Sometimes they're so well made it's hard to tell the difference. Especially if you can track this Laurel down and interview her."

"Why would I do that? She's not Indian."

"Does that matter so much?" Louella said. "I have some white in me. Does that mean my pots aren't important?"

Juniper was near tears, she was so embarrassed and angry. "You're right, Chico. I'd *really* like to interview Laurel." What she didn't say was, And ask for a refund of my three hundred freaking dollars. "But somehow I don't think she'll be back to the Farm."

"Go by the Urgent Care," Louella said. "Maybe even the hospital. Can't hurt to try. Her last name's Smith and her daughter's name is Aspen. If she's not there, maybe they'll have a forwarding address. And listen, if you find her, ask her what I'm supposed to do with fifteen chickens and her horse. The hay's not going to last forever."

"Thank you so much for your time and for showing us how you create pots," Chico said. "Juniper will send you a copy of the finished interview. Would you consider allowing it to be published?"

"Heck, yeah," Louella said. "Make sure you put my website in there. I love making traditional pots, but damn, I'd like to sell a few, you know? I work nights at the casino and pick up odd jobs when I can."

"We'll make sure your website's prominently noted," Chico said. "Thanks for allowing us this time."

"It's me who should be thanking you, for all that food. It'll keep me going until my next paycheck. My grandmother was right. It's nice to have company." She stood up to see them out.

Juniper slapped her hand against her thigh, the same way she called Caddy. "Come on, Curly," she said. "I'm taking you home with me."

"Hey, that's nice of you. I'm sure Laurel will be grateful."

Laurel. The name kept popping up like a jack-in-the-box, Juniper thought. The mere sound of it annoyed her. The day was wrecked. She wanted to go home to her parents' house, grab Caddy, and sleep for twelve hours, hoping to wake up and discover that this whole experience had been a dream.

The brown dog had no qualms about jumping into her car. She hopped over the console to the cargo area as if she did it every day. Juniper had tossed her unzipped sleeping bag there before she and Chico went for their walk. Curly made a nest and put her head on her paws. Instead of groceries, she now had a dog to feed, walk, and water, a definite complication, but the only one that made sense of the day.

They drove back toward the Pueblo in uncomfortable silence. Sooner or later, she was going to have to talk to Chico, but right now there was something more important that she needed to do. When she didn't stop at the Cultural Center, Chico said, "I thought that was where we were spending the night?"

"Every third word out of Louella's mouth was Laurel this and Laurel that," she said. "I'm going to the hospital to find her lying ass and ask for my money back. I paid three hundred dollars for that pot! That's like a whole month of work for me. Not to mention giving my parents a fake. My dad is Navajo, Jicarilla, and Spanish. I'll bet he knew it all along and didn't say anything because he didn't want to hurt my feelings."

Chico put his hand on her shoulder and she roughly shrugged it off. "Juniper, Louella said her kid was sick. Are you sure you want to get in the middle of something like that? It seems kind of mean to me."

Her anger had tempered itself into steel. It was as if she saw this straight-ahead road with a bull's-eye at the end of it. She was armed, aimed, and not going to miss. "I'm sorry her child is ill. I hope she gets better. But she can spare me fifteen minutes while I explain to her the ramifications of selling a pot under false pretenses. It's against the freaking law to pawn off something as Native-made when it isn't. Not to mention really bad karma."

Chico sighed. "I think you should cool down first."

"I'm cool."

"No, you're not. Louella got you talking about your biological mom," he said. "Even a doofus like me could see it ripped off a pretty big scab. I think that was probably the bravest thing I've ever witnessed. Let's go get some coffee. You don't have to talk to me about it, but I think you need a little time."

"You want more coffee? Jeepers, could I be any more jacked up than I am already? Louella's blood must freaking percolate the way she downed the stuff. I have coffee grounds in my molars. You know me better than that. I won't be mean, I'll be honest."

He rubbed his face. "Juniper, I never suggested you were mean. Far from it. But trust me, this isn't a good idea."

"Chico, I am doing this. You can sit in the car with the dog."

"I'm not letting you go in there alone. We can leave the dog in the car for fifteen minutes."

"No way, a dog can—"

"It's winter!" he said. "For crying out loud, the dog was living outside and eating horse feed. I think she'll survive if we leave all the windows down a few inches. I'm coming with you, and that's that."

Before today, the most ever people in Aspen's room I counted was four—her nurse, me, a doctor, and Mrs. Clemmons. Not today. Today there were five—Dr. Armstrong, two nurses, a respiratory therapist, and a pharmacist. Dr. Armstrong wouldn't let me go in the room, and there wasn't any space for me. I watched from the doorway. Mrs. Clemmons stood next to me, her hands pressing down on my shoulders like if she let go I might float away. Anything that happened next—me growing wings and flying out the window—wouldn't have surprised me one bit. Because after I wrote my name down, my mind was dizzy with remembering things. Oh, my goodness, it hurt so bad to let the memories inside. It felt like I had a cloud of bats in there, flapping their razor-sharp wings into my organs. I tried not to cry, I always tried, but this time I couldn't make myself calm down even when I held my hands over my mouth. When I started making the sound, Mrs. Clemmons had another doctor come and listen to my breathing and my heart. She wanted to give me a shot, but

I panicked because what if it was like Abel and Seth gave me, knock-out medicine in disguise? Most of the time I never saw it coming. Things would just be going along, and then Abel would grab me and the next thing I knew, I was waking up with him inside of me and I wouldn't even know where I was or how I got there. How do you tell someone from Outside that's how things happened and why you need to keep control?

Mrs. Clemmons sat with me and held my hand while the doctor examined me. She explained how sometimes a person can get so upset that the best thing a doctor can do is give you medicine to relax. "No lightning," I kept saying, "no knocking me out. I have to stay awake for Aspen."

The other doctor explained that I'd feel a pinprick, but that the medicine would work fast, and it would help me. Mrs. Clemmons said, "I won't allow anyone to hurt you. Just like with Aspen's doctors, no one will do anything without your permission. All right?"

"All right." It was just like the doctor said, one moment of bee sting and then a feeling of peacefulness, like after Abel died and Seth threw his body out in the desert. Once he was gone, my world got so much better.

"I'm going to have the security guard stand outside Aspen's room," Mrs. Clemmons said, and this big man in a black suit stood in front of me. "Henry," she said. "Can you explain to Mrs. Smith what your job is?"

"Happy to, ma'am. I make sure no one goes into or out of this room."

"You're a cop," I said, though it was hard to talk with the shot inside me, slowing things down.

"Henry is not a policeman," Mrs. Clemmons said. "He isn't even carrying a gun, are you, Henry?"

"No, ma'am."

"What about lightning?"

"Pardon me?" Henry said.

"She's referring to a stun gun. A Taser. Do you have one of those?"

"No, ma'am. No weapons whatsoever. I have a radio," he said, and smiled. "Not the kind that plays music."

My brain felt heavy in my head. My eyes wanted to close, but I wouldn't let them.

"Henry will make sure no one goes into Aspen's room without your permission."

"You don't know Seth," I said. "He always finds a way." Whenever I said his name I could see her getting a little bit mad, but not at me.

"That may have been so in the past," she said, "but in order to get to you or Aspen, he'd have to go through Henry and me. There is something I want you to start thinking about, Casey."

My name. My real name. She kept saying it. It was out there, she knew and pretty soon other people would know. Seth would wait until I least expected it. Then he would move through the dark, cutting, hitting, lighting things on fire.

"When you're feeling better, you're going to have to speak with the police."

"Why?"

"Because what Seth did to you was a crime. He has to be stopped before he does it to some other girl. The police will need your help and they'll have lots of questions. Do you understand?"

I wanted to understand. Just as much, though, I wanted not to think of Seth or Abel ever again, the same way I hadn't thought of my life *Before*, when I was Casey for real. *Say. Easy, case, yes.* The memories came too fast to make any sense. "I'll try," I said, "but could we wait until Aspen is better first?"

"I'm sorry, but not this time," she said. "The police need to know as soon as possible." She patted my arm. "I'll stay with you the entire time, and if you need to take a break, I'll make sure that happens. The police in California will want to talk to you, too, and they'll help us find your family."

"I don't have a family anymore."

"Why would you say that?"

"Abel said they didn't want me back after he, you know." I pointed to my throat. "He said he and Seth went back at night and they killed them and my sister."

Mrs. Clemmons squeezed my shoulder. "If that were so, don't you think that would have been a national news story?"

"I don't know."

"I'll check, but you've got to start sorting out what they told you and what's the truth. Abel and Seth told you lies in order to control you."

I didn't believe her. "They're gone. Killed. Abel told me how he did it. Seth won't talk about it. Aspen's my only real family." I thought about Caleb, Old St. John, and Frances, how angry they would be at me for telling and ruining all the progress of the Farm. "Please, Mrs. Clemmons," I said. "I'm worried about my animals."

"I'll send someone to check on them. Try to let your mind drift, Casey. That will help bring things to the surface. California was a long time ago. Everyone will understand that you did what you had to in order to survive."

California. Such a big word, so much inside it. *Calf, can, nail. Fail, nor, naa, no.* When I shut my eyes I saw oak trees rushing water sunshine ocean waves seals a trailer horses blue jays birth-day cakes Christmas trees spaghetti and meatballs a pillowcase toothpaste a rubber ducky a closet filled with clothes pouring rain new shoes Easter baskets a smiling woman and a smiling man and a sister who always got me in trouble a dog. Abel and Seth's voice crept into every memory, staining it, like an old sweater with the silver buttons turned into tin, telling me don't you dare say a word don't even breathe anytime we want we can strangle you cut your throat deeper this time then what will you do when you can't scream anymore and do you know how long it takes to bleed to death from that less than a minute your heart beat will pump your blood out in four seconds but you'll live long enough to know you're dying and then who's going to take care of the brat? We are. You know what we'll do as soon as she's old enough? Or maybe we'll strangle you, that will last longer and to be sure to listen for the click of bones when we fracture your larynx one little crack and then no matter how you try to breathe there is no fixing it good-bye. I thought about the times Abel did strangle me, how much it hurt for days and days. The one time with the broken bottle when he shoved and Seth pulled me away so that all I had was the long cut but it bled and bled until Seth glued the skin together and of course it pulled apart and he had to do it over and over again every day while Abel said this is all your fault you could try keeping your mouth shut which I guess I did because here I am alive and he's not, desert stars lightning take his silver bracelet wipe off the blood, we can sell it.

I wanted to know my dog Curly was all right, and Brown Horse and the chickens, but even thinking about my dog made me cry because of things Seth had done before. If you need to love something so bad, try loving me, he used to say. If you can't find it in your spirit to be thankful for everything I do for you, then maybe you don't deserve animals. Aw, look what you made me do, Laurel. Look hard. Take a sweat. Pray for forgiveness. Look at yourself, how ugly you are inside and out. You'll never be able to sing that brat a lullaby. Who'd want you now? The answer is no one. No one. No one. Think about that, Laurel.

But I was Casey now.

Mrs. Clemmons talked on her phone. The doctors were discussing steps in the procedure. *Proceed, prod, cord, cure.* The student doctors wanted to watch everything, and for me to step aside and let them because they had to know how to be doctors someday. "No," I said. I wished I could say, "Stand behind me or go away. I'm not moving," but I was too tired to make words.

The one thing I knew for sure was that I never wanted to be called Laurel Smith again. Laurel Smith was someone whose skin I put on because my real skin was buried deep inside me, like when a tree dies from the inside out. Daphne turned into a laurel tree to escape Apollo; I turned into Laurel but couldn't escape. *Pace. Peas. Sea.* That day it all happened was right there inside me. I shook my head no. Mrs. Clemmons with her pearl necklace and matching earrings, her wire glasses and her brown eyes; everything about Mrs. Clemmons was a smile. "Your name is Casey McGuire," she said, and she took hold of my hands. "You never have to be Laurel Smith again."

The first thing the doctors did was unhook the breathing tube from the breathing machine, just to try it, they said, like when Susie the nurse had to clean the tubes. They talked to each other in the secret language that only they understood, but I made myself listen and store the words in a list inside my head.

"Hemoglobin eight," and "Suction, please," and "What is the patient's ABG," and "What is her PAo2," and "Administer bronchodilators." I watched and listened and inside my heart I thought how weird it was that here I was, praying for real, and whatever Seth thought of that didn't really matter. The shot doctor came back to wait with us. She said, "Would you like me to explain what the doctors are doing?"

I nodded.

"Aspen has been under sedation since her seizure and cardiac-arrest episode," she said.

"You mean the crashing?"

"Yes. That medicine is what helped her to lie still while the ventilator breathed for her. The doctors are titrating that medicine down to see if Aspen will take a breath on her own. If she does, then they'll slowly decrease the mandatory breaths coming from the machine, and let her fill in the gaps with her own breaths. Right now she's at twenty breaths. Next, they'll decrease it to eighteen and see if she breathes two breaths on her own. This could take a long time, maybe all day."

"If her body forgot how to do the breaths, how do they make it remember?"

"Casey, I want you to take a look at all the people in her room. Two doctors, one nurse, one respiratory therapist, and the pharmacist. He's in charge of the medicine. Each of them is doing one step. The respiratory therapist is making sure she starts to remember how to breathe."

"What if she doesn't?"

"Then they hook the machines back up."

"And if she remembers?"

She smiled at me. "Now you're thinking positive. Once Aspen is breathing on her own, they'll extubate, which means that they'll take out the tube that goes down her throat and into her lungs. It's a critical moment."

"What if she forgets again? Can they put the tube back in time? What about the feeding tube?"

"That's why they do this in steps. If she doesn't breathe on her own, they'll hook her back up until she seems stronger, and they'll try again a little later. The feeding tube will come out once she starts eating on her own. "

Big pharma, Seth would say. Treating people like lab animals. Like he had room to talk. If it worked, I wondered how to explain to Aspen that we weren't going back to the Farm. Then it hit me, where would we go? One week after they took me, after Abel had raped me three times in a row, I asked if I could go home now. Abel laughed. I asked if I could at least have my clothes. He lit a cigarette and blew smoke in my face. Please let me go, I begged, back to my family, and he said, Do you honestly think they'd want you back now?

I said maybe since it wasn't my fault they would want me back.

"Too late. Seth and I went back last night and killed your parents," he said.

"Not my sister," I said. "She's still in elementary school."

"And that is supposed to matter to me? Maybe I took her, too. Maybe I've got her tied up in the van."

"Please don't hurt her," I said. "She's still little."

Abel took hold of my neck and I shut my eyes. He whispered into my ear, "If you want me to be nice to you, then you'd better start being nicer to me." Then he tied my hands up behind my back and left, locking the door. Shutting out the light. I had to do deep breaths to not panic at being closed in, in the dark at first. I cried that night, but by morning I realized he was telling me the truth about one thing; I had to be nicer. It wasn't until much later on that I accepted that he'd never tell me the truth, but that never stopped me from hoping. Probably my family didn't want me back. But they deserved to live. They worked hard and took care of me, made all those dinners and bought me new clothes for school. They weren't stupid, like me, to think running away would change anything. I couldn't really see their faces in my mind. Just flashes of things: my mom's silver bracelet with the moon face. The hairs on my dad's wrist that went under the face of his watch and then came back out the other side. My sister was only a set of braids in my mind. She ruined my clothes, touched my things. Maybe sometimes my mom wasn't as nice as I wanted her to be, but after Abel and Seth took me, I would have rather been beaten every day of my life and on restriction forever than go through what Abel, and later Seth, did to me. When Aspen was born I thought that meant I had to marry Abel. That we'd become a family and then Aspen would go to school and I would have to make the dinner and vacuum the floors. Things wouldn't be great, but it would be a different way, something I could learn to do so he didn't get angry and hurt me. There was so much I didn't want to think about, that I had to forget about my *Before* life.

Instead, it was like living a new life in the camp with the redwood trees. It was our life until the cops started coming around, and then it turned into something different on that car ride from California to the Farm. The first night we stopped in the desert to go to the bathroom at this rest stop. They wanted me to sleep, and gave me pills, but they made me sick to my stomach and I threw them up, so eventually they stopped trying and told me I could stay awake, but they'd better not hear one peep out of me or they'd leave me in the middle of nowhere. They both took drugs back then, smoked things, and sometimes like during the drive, Abel said they needed to get "jacked up" so they could drive all night. I pretended to be sleeping when they got into the terrible fight, but that was one thing I remembered. It was so real in my mind it could have happened yesterday.

The tube was unhooked now, and the doctors were talking in louder voices, asking, "What are her SATS?" and "What's her PEEP?" And "tidal volume," as if Aspen had been under the ocean all this time, waiting for us to pull her to the surface. Mrs. Clemmons and the shot doctor talked on the phone to other people and whispered to each other. I kept my eyes on Henry without a gun. Sometimes he smiled. Once he even winked. I wondered what had happened to him that he could stand there that long, not saying a word. Had he known someone like Abel? Was he secretly a cop, with a gun hidden somewhere in his uniform? Maybe I could get his kind of job in the Outside World because I could go without talking for the longest time, too. Even after my neck healed I could be silent. Not Abel, though. All "jacked up" he talked nonstop about things that made no sense like alien abductions and radio frequencies and secret underground radioactive government shelters in case of nuclear war. Five times during that drive Seth told him to shut up, but he wouldn't.

When they stopped at the rest stop, Seth took me into the pit toilet so I could pee. When we came out, Abel was smoking a cigarette of Seth's, and that did it. Seth yelled and Abel yelled back and Abel took out his knife and Seth grabbed it, cutting his hand and it must have hurt really bad because he made the noise, and then he turned the knife around, and it happened so quickly, I didn't have time to scream. Seth cut Abel's neck the way Abel cut mine, but deeper, and he was right, it was only four seconds before he stopped being alive.

Seth put Abel in the backseat and told me to get in the front or I would be next. "This is your fault," he said. "I'm tired of taking care of you. Now that you have the brat you're even more expensive. What the f—— am I supposed to do with you?"

I said, "You could let us go." It was the wrong answer. "Hit me," I said, "not Aspen," and he did.

Abel took drugs he was only supposed to sell. He'd get himself all "wired," his pupils huge, and he did stupid things like call attention to himself, which was why cops came, and we had to leave. Just get in the car and go.

Was I lonely and afraid? Yes, but after Aspen I could stand it. Before, when Abel and Seth were arguing, I used to wish they would hit each other so hard they would both fall down and die. If that couldn't happen, I wished they'd hurt each other so bad they would need my help. I would help. I'd show them how to be a nice person. I'd help them go back into the Outside World. But after Abel died, we drove around for hours until Seth found a place to leave his body. Take his bracelet. That's worth money. After that, I just wanted the car ride to be over, for us to be at the next place we were going to, so I could change Aspen's diaper and then I could go to sleep.

The pharmacist explained to the nurse how much less of a drug to give Aspen so she would wake up. Dr. Armstrong was arguing that it was more important that Aspen wake up on her own time, not to stress her. A student doctor in blue pajamas was telling another one how exciting it was to watch this play out, like it was a skit they were putting on. I got tears. Mrs. Clemmons said, "Children are resilient, Casey. Dr. Armstrong is a huffy old guy, but he's the best at what he does. If my little girl was sick, he's who I'd want taking care of her. I wouldn't exactly like to go to dinner with him, but he's very accomplished at his job, Casey. Focus on that."

Mrs. Clemmons had a little girl?

I saw Aspen's neck when the doctors moved out of the way, a pale pink half circle that reminded me of a baby bird that hasn't got its feathers. Aspen and I used to try to save the robins that fell out of the nest at the Farm. Better than anybody, I knew how a person's neck is the strongest and the most vulnerable part of the body. I was never going to allow anyone to do to Aspen what had been done to me, and I was imagining how to explain all that to the police without making the sound when I heard a different sound, the best sound I ever heard, which was Aspen coughing. "Ready to extubate," Dr. Armstrong said, and the other doctor said, "Wait. We need to suction again, please." Susie the nurse was standing close to Aspen and the respiratory doctor held onto a blue round ball connected to a clear plastic face mask. The student doctor told the other one, "Whether you're intubating or extubating, hold your breath. It's the perfect test of time. If you need to take a breath, so does your patient."

"This is my first extubation," the other doctor said, as if Aspen was going through all this just for him to learn it.

The shot doctor got a page and told me she had to go, but she'd check back with me soon, but I kind of hoped she was busy enough with other problems that she wouldn't come back. "I'm tired of talking to people," I told Mrs. Clemmons. She found me a chair to sit in, but when I sat down I couldn't see anything, so I stood back up.

Dr. Armstrong let the other doctor pull the tube out of Aspen's throat, and everyone was holding their breath, not just me. He pulled kind of slowly but maybe that was how things like that had to be done. After it came all the way out, everyone sighed, and the nurse put the ball/breathing mask thing on Aspen's face and squeezed. Then she took it away, and after a few times, back and forth, we could all hear the sound of Aspen coughing. The student doctors clapped. I heard Mrs. Clemmons say, "Thank God," very quietly, like she didn't want anyone to know. Another nurse came out of the room to get me. She was smiling, and she hardly ever smiled. "She'll be disoriented," she told me. "Now that she's off the paralytics, she might have some jerking muscle spasms, but that doesn't mean it's a seizure. Don't expect her to start talking all at once."

Dr. Armstrong called Aspen's name, but she didn't answer him. He rubbed her chest with his knuckles, and she whined. It was the first sound she made since the cough and I held my breath. He pressed a pen against her fingertip and she whined again, and moved away from him all on her own and I was so proud of her for being that little and to know to move when someone was trying to hurt you. That was a lesson it took me a long time to learn, but I never stopped trying to teach her how to do it. "GCS?" Dr. Armstrong said, and the respiratory therapist said, "Nine." I whispered to Mrs. Clemmons, "What does that mean?"

"The Glasgow Coma Scale. Aspen's score right now is a nine, but you watch, it'll rise as time goes by. The higher the number, the better it is."

Then she went into the room to watch Dr. Armstrong put a different kind of oxygen mask up Aspen's nose. The clear tubes went around her ears. He told the nurse, "Any drop in SATS, I expect to be paged immediately." People started to leave the room, and when I turned to give them space, I noticed Mrs.

Clemmons wasn't there. Had she told me she was going somewhere, and I forgot? Or was this going to be my life now, on
my own? When Dr. Armstrong left the room, he told me, "I
told you she was ready."

"I'm sorry I didn't believe you," I said. "Thank you from my
heart."

His face got that flushed color and he said, "Go sit with your
little girl," and then he went next door to the nurses' room, and
it was just Aspen and me and Aspen blinked at me. I held her
hand.

Between every patient room there was an office where the
nurse watched a television of her patient. Dr. Armstrong went
in there and started talking on the phone. Him behind the glass
like that reminded me of the gift shop and the aquariums, and
how once I had a job I could take my own money in there and
buy one for Aspen.

"You're too upset," Chico said. "Go in the gift shop and buy
the girl a present." He went to the information desk by himself.
"We're looking for a friend," he told the volunteers at the Information desk. "Laurel Smith? Her daughter, Aspen, is a patient?"

Juniper chose the first thing she saw, a fake plastic aquarium
with dolphins swimming by on a lighted roll. Ten bucks, and
tacky, but what kid wouldn't want one of those? Chico was
right. At first she'd been seething, just ridiculously angry. It
wasn't a part of her she liked to admit was there. She thought
she'd left all that anger behind in California, and she tried to
calm herself down, mentally reviewing the periodic table of
elements. Hydrogen, helium, beryllium, boron, carbon . . .
suppose this Laurel person sold the micaceous pot because she

needed the money? After all, she had a sick kid. Louella had made it clear that she thought the Farm people were freaks, at least this Seth person. But would that get her three hundred dollars back? Was that even what she wanted?

"Shall I wrap this for you?" the clerk asked.

"No need, but could we have a pink balloon?" Chico said, placing his hand on the small of Juniper's back. The gift-shop clerk untied one from a bunch near the register, handed it over, and Juniper paid. "The elevator is this way," Chico said. "The daughter's in ICU, so we might not even get to see her, but a nurse will let Laurel know we're here, and then she can probably meet us in the family visiting area."

When the elevator door opened, Juniper looked down the long hallway and saw a security guard and several people dressed in street clothes outside a room, and she wondered if that was Laurel's daughter's room. Did all those people mean bad news? Seeing them, thinking about a kid so sick she had to be in ICU kind of made her hate herself. In the scale of life, three hundred dollars was nothing. Then she recognized a face among the crowd, Daddy Joe's friend Elena Gonzales. She'd met her twice, at fund-raisers for Candela. Before Chico could stop her, she walked up to her and touched her shoulder, interrupting her conversation with another woman. "Mrs. Gonzales? I don't know if you remember me, but you know my dad, Joseph Vigil," Juniper said when Elena turned to her.

"*Hijole!*" Elena said. "You're Juniper, aren't you?"

"Yes, ma'am."

"Joseph talks about you all the time." She stared, open-mouthed.

"Is something wrong, Mrs. Gonzales?"

She patted Juniper's arm. "Forgive me, I'm just surprised you got here so quickly. We only just called your dad on his cell phone but there was no answer. Juniper, this is Mrs. Clemmons, the psychologist on her case. I know you're anxious to see her, but we're going to have to follow her cues. We don't want to overwhelm her. After all, it's been seven years."

Juniper looked at the women and frowned. "Excuse me, but I have no idea what you're talking about. Chico and I—he's my TA—we just wanted a moment with Laurel Smith if it's convenient."

"Well, of course you do!" Mrs. Gonzales put her arm around Juniper's shoulder. "*Dios mio*, I know it's hard to believe. It's a miracle. You have all the time in the world, now."

Juniper extracted herself from the hug as carefully as she could. "I have no idea what you're talking about or what you said to my dad. I'm just here to speak with Laurel Smith. If it's not a good time, I can wait."

"And you brought a present for Aspen!" Mrs. Gonzales gushed. "Isn't that just like a sister—an aunt."

Juniper felt a shudder pass through her. Too much coffee, too much emotion in this day, and now one of her dad's friends stood before her crying and making no kind of sense, calling her an aunt.

Chico caught up. "Mrs. Gonzales? I'm Juniper's friend. Would you mind backing up a little?" he said. "We're not following you."

Elena frowned. "Yes, I see," she said, and turned to the older woman in the pearls and pantsuit. "Juniper, this is Mrs. Clemmons. Ardith, this is Juniper. How would you like to proceed? Should we go sit down in the family visiting room? How much should I tell her? Or should we wait for Joseph Vigil?"

Mrs. Clemmons had one hand on her pearl necklace, and

with the other she touched Juniper's arm. "My goodness, it's wonderful to meet you, Juniper. Now, I'm sure this is going to come as a shock—"

"What is?" Juniper said. "Take the present for the kid. Tell Laurel Smith when she has a moment, I need to talk to her about a pottery bowl I—"

The words died in her mouth. The woman who walked out of the hospital room stood rooted before her. Juniper saw a thin, blonde girl not much older than herself, with a terrible scar on her neck, but there was something else about her. Her cheekbones, her eyes, the way she lifted her hand to cover her mouth because she'd needed braces but her parents couldn't afford them. "No," Juniper said. "This cannot be happening."

Chico took her arm. "What's wrong?"

Juniper couldn't speak. All she could do was point, and the woman seemed to be having a similar reaction to seeing her. "What's your name?" she asked. "Are you Laurel Smith?"

"For a long time I was," the woman said in a voice so raspy it hurt to hear it. "But now I'm who I was before. I'm Casey McGuire again. Who are you? Oh, gosh. Si, site, rite, tire, sire, sir, it, I, ire, resist, sis, *sister?*" she babbled as if she only had a loose hold on language. "Is that who you are? Are you my sister?"

Juniper felt her knees go out from under her as if the muscles had been cut. Only Chico holding on to her kept her from falling to the floor. She tried to speak, but no words would come. She couldn't take her eyes off the girl.

"Mrs. Clemmons believed you were still alive," Casey said. "Not me, though. She said if you were alive she would find you. How did you come here from California so fast? Did you fly in a plane?"

One minute Juniper was on her knees and the next this per-

son, Casey, was kneeling in front of her, arms around her, making the same noise Juniper had made the day she came home
from school to find her mother on the couch, facing the door
the way she always did, because until her dying day she believed
Casey would come home. Nobody else believed that, but she
did, and now it was too late to tell her she'd been right. Juniper
could feel the chill of her mother's skin, and see the amber plastic pill container on the coffee table, the lid off, the bottle
empty.

The present fell from her hands, and Chico intercepted it
before it hit the floor. Juniper thought, If keening is the highest
form of grief, and hard to listen to, this sound is one notch
above all that. The sisters held on to each other and sobbed, and
Elena Gonzales and Ardith Clemmons shooed the staring
nurses out of the way, making a protective circle around them.
Chico picked up Juniper's purse, because it had fallen off her
shoulder. He looked inside and took Juniper's cell phone out.

"Where were you?" Juniper said. "We looked for you everywhere."

"I would've come back if I could," Casey told her. "These
men took me. They hurt me. I have a daughter."

"A daughter?" Her voice was so awful. "Casey," Juniper said.
"My God." Her sister started to pull away, but she clung to her
fiercely. "Don't let go. Please, even if this isn't real, let me pretend it is. Don't let go just yet. Please."

"I won't, Juniper. I promise. I'm not going anywhere ever
again."

Chico scrolled through Juniper's stored phone numbers, by-
passing "Topher" and "Aunt Halle" and the number for the
pizza delivery that would come to the dorms. He found HOME
on her speed dial and he called the number. He turned away

and waited for her father to answer. When he did, saying "Joseph Vigil," Chico cleared his throat.

"Mr. Vigil, you don't know me, but I'm the teaching assistant in Juniper's Cultural Anthropology class."

"*Dios.* Has something happened?"

"Yes, actually, sir. Something has happened." He swallowed hard around the lump in his throat. "Sir, Juniper and I are at Presbyterian hospital in Española. She's not hurt, I promise, but you need to get up here right away. You have to see this."

"Son, I don't know what you're talking about," Joseph said. "Slow down and start at the beginning, *por favor.*"

"Sir, does Juniper have a sister named Casey?"

"She did," Joseph said. "I'm afraid Casey disappeared years ago. What does she have to do with this?"

"That's what I'm trying to tell you, sir. Casey is here. Honestly, she's standing five feet in front of me. Juniper is with her. They're hysterical. Fossils, I can deal with, other cultures, even other languages. Women crying, not so much."

Joseph tried to exhale, but all that came out was a sob. "Please," he said. "If you could just stay there with her until I get there, I will be eternally in your debt."

"Of course. I won't let either of them out of my sight. Oh, there's a Mrs. Gonzales here who says she knows you. Would you like to speak with her?"

"*Absolutamente.* Put her on. Thank you, son. Thank you."

Joseph stood there listening to Elena Gonzales, his friend of many years, his trusted colleague, tell him a story he simply could not imagine was true. Over and over, sure he was mishearing her, he asked her to please repeat it. Her voice in his ear was like Grandma Penny's when he was a child, telling him a story to help him go to sleep. After a minute, they said good-bye and he hung up the phone. He stood in the kitchen looking around at the beautiful tiles Glory had selected, the copper pots hanging on the wall, the stack of mail on the counter waiting for him to separate it into recycling and bills to pay. He gave his family the nicest things he could. He planned for their future and made investments. His goal was to give them the best life he could, opportunities he'd never had for himself, and this house was proof of his success. But the stove, the refrigerator full of food he'd just unpacked, the dishes and decorations, even the walls could fall down, blow away in a moment and he would pitch a tent in the backyard. The most important thing was that Casey was alive, Juniper was there with her. A sick child. And the psychologist he'd had an appointment with only days earlier, an appointment he'd canceled because he didn't want to leave Glory alone after the ER scare, was at the heart of it. Joseph knew his roles—husband, board member, former crime-lab photographer, and expecting father. His life was one of simple choices: Paper or plastic? Cash or credit? Chicken or fish? But what was happening at this moment was so far out of his league he was stunned into silence. The words of photographer Wynn Bullock came to him, though he'd never met the man and had never heard his voice. *When I photograph, what I'm really doing is seeking the answers to things.* And Joseph knew exactly what to do next. He picked up his keys, and like he always did, twirled the silver concho key fob Glory had given him for their anniversary, and he headed out.

From the shelf in the great room where he kept his lenses and camera bodies, he fetched his Leica-M, the finest camera he owned, and one he rarely used since the advent of digital photography. But the Leica took black-and-white photographs like no other camera. The photos somehow had another dimension to them, or perhaps it was the grain, the photographic particles that gave a photograph its foundation. He loaded it with film, shot two pictures with the lens cap on, and opened up his camera case.

He packed his 50mm lens. It was his favorite when he was in the crime lab, helping to solve crimes by noticing, capturing, allowing intuition to choose the detail in the shots and reason to figure them out later. No color to distract. He stood for a moment in the great room of his home, feeling the cool flagstone underfoot, hearing the soft sounds of his wife and sister-in-law talking in the bedroom, the click of a dog's nails as Dodge or Caddy went through the dog door to bark at the hens or to do their business. He was struck by the notion that over the centuries, others had stood in this very spot in this house as well, allowing monumental news to sink in. It was too bad there wasn't a book somewhere recording all that, helping whoever lived there next to avoid mistakes. But of course that was dreaming. Then he took a step, fully intent on speaking to Glory and Halle, and to change life as they knew it forever. Before he got there, however, he stopped and took his cell phone out of his pocket to call Elena.

"*Bueno*?" she said.

"Elena, it's Joseph Vigil again. I have to ask you one thing. Casey, did she live on that place called the Farm?"

"Hold on, Joseph," she said, and he could hear her whispering to Mrs. Clemmons. She returned to the phone. "I've no idea how you knew that, but yes, she did."

His heart sank. "I'll explain it to you later. I'm leaving now. *Gracias*," he said, hung up, and went into the bedroom. Halle was sitting on the floor watching some talk show in which a group of women were arguing, but Glory wasn't. She was holding on to the blue ribbon and thinking about the potter, he could tell. "My love," he said. "Halle, turn off the television, please. Something wonderful has happened and I need your full attention."

In the momentary silence that followed, that single breath of time, Joseph noticed for the first time how much the two sisters looked alike, and how alike their souls were, so connected beyond the superficial differences. Had she been in search of a new life, Glory would drive past the glitter and show of Las Vegas, saving her quarters for gas money. Halle would stop at the buffets, throw quarters into the slots, spend whatever money she won on silly presents for those she loved. They were sisters who'd each lost a father and a husband, yet the trials they had endured had brought them together every time. Soon a child would bind them closer. Casey and Juniper were also sisters. Casey had a child already. He pictured that little girl on the Farm, singing about a butterfly.

"Everything about our simple life is about to change," he said. "I must drive to Española immediately. Casey's been found. She's alive, and Juniper is with her. Please, just wait here and try to remain calm. I'll call you as soon as I know more. I love you both, and I would stay and explain, but I must go." He turned and walked out of the room even though they were calling after him. If he turned, if he let their expressions get to him, he'd be in no shape to drive.

Chapter 18

A SPEN WAITED FOR her aunt Juniper to come into the room before she began to wake up in earnest. Juniper sat next to Casey, holding her hand, watching her niece; that skinny little girl in the hospital bed, dwarfed by medical equipment, was her niece. "Mama, I'm thirsty," were her first words, and though she was given a small drink, two minutes later, she said, "Hi, Mama. Where were you? I'm thirsty," and ten minutes after that, she said nearly the same thing, only with sass. "I wish *somebody* around here would get me a glass of water."

"The doctors said it would be like this," Casey said. "We just have to wait and be patient. Juniper?"

"Yes?"

"I don't know how to ask this."

"Just say it."

"How did you get away from Seth and Abel? Do you hate me that they killed our parents?"

"What are you talking about, Casey?"

"Seth told me he killed them, and you. How did you escape?"

Juniper steeled herself. "A lot happened while you were gone,

Casey. Maybe we should wait until my—" what did she call him? Daddy Joe, her other dad, the one who didn't abandon her? She had no idea how to bridge that chasm. When Chico came into the room with her purse and a sack, she welcomed the interruption.

"I brought you two sandwiches, one ham and cheese, the other a BLT. I know, carbs and all that, but if you're hungry."

Juniper let go of Casey's hand and stood up. "It's fine, Chico, thanks."

He looked at Casey and then at Juniper. "You look alike, you really do. What do I say? 'Glad to meet you' doesn't really cover it, does it?"

Casey smiled. "Thank you for taking care of my sister. Are you her boyfriend?"

Chico sidestepped the question. "We have a present for Aspen. I don't know if now is the right time—is it?" He took the plastic aquarium out of Juniper's purse and set it on Casey's lap.

Aspen tried to sit up. "Mama? Is that for me?"

Casey went to her daughter and opened the present for her. "Those are dolphins," she said, pointing to the roll inside the plastic aquarium. "I think this toy needs batteries."

"Already put them in," Chico said. "Click the red switch on the bottom and you're good to go."

Juniper watched her sister showing the toy to her niece. "A long time ago, your mom and I went to Sea World Aquarium and petted real dolphins. When you're all better, we'll plan a trip."

Aspen clutched the toy aquarium close, and wouldn't let go. "This is mine," she said.

"That's not going anywhere, honey," Casey said. "It's yours."

"Or maybe we'll go to the ocean," Juniper said. "March is whale-watching season."

"What's an ocean?" Aspen asked.

Juniper looked at Chico. How did you explain something like that to a child who'd never been more than a few feet out of a yard?

Chico said, "It's like a lake, only busier."

Juniper took his arm and squeezed it. "We'll be right back."

Out in the hallway, she asked him, "What time is it?"

He looked at his watch. "A little after four. Should I drive your car back to school, and catch up with you in a few days? I feel like I'm in the way here."

A nurse walked past them and then turned into a patient's room. "I kind of don't want you to go. Would you stay for a while?"

"Sure," he said. "As long as you need me."

"Thank you," she said. "I know this day is beyond weird. It's just that I'm not sure what to say."

"Just say what's in your heart."

Juniper bit her lip. "I know Dr. Carey doesn't believe in Incompletes, but I really hope you can talk him into giving me one."

"Are you serious? Juniper, all you have to do is write up the story of this day and you'll have your A."

"She's my sister," Juniper said. "We all thought she was dead."

"That's why your mom killed herself, isn't it?"

Juniper nodded.

"I called your dad. He's on his way."

"Dad?" Casey said, peeking her head out of the room. "Is Mom coming, too? They're alive?"

Juniper looked at Chico, then back at her sister. "Casey,

where did Mrs. Clemmons go? Let's ask her to sit with us while we talk."

Glory lay on the couch, staring at the silver aluminum Christmas tree Halle had bought at Ace Hardware. Her sister was decorating with purple, hot-pink, and lime-green ornaments only. If Glory had the energy, she might have told Halle that she preferred a traditional tree, trimmed with cranberry and popcorn strings, but she couldn't muster the strength. After her subtle and monochromatic previous life, gray being the foundation color, this new Halle was all over the spectrum. How did she find pink pinecones? Glory wondered. How strange it felt to let go of a ritual as fundamental as decorating your Christmas tree, but if anyone needed to be in charge of something, it was Halle. Besides, all Glory could do was lie there and try not to get too emotional.

This might just be the most horrible thing I've ever heard, she'd said a couple of days ago, crying silently into the phone while she listened to Juniper tell her the story of Casey's last seven years with the Grimm Brothers. One was dead and the other missing. When Joseph got home later that night, he had told Glory and Halle that in order to help Casey ease back into any kind of life, they all had to behave as if Seth would be caught. Halle had said, "I'll go find the bastard myself."

Now her husband was outside on the portal, where they were breaking ground for a room addition. The contractor, whose last name, unsurprisingly, was Vigil, said it would take less than four weeks to get the room habitable. The middle of winter and they were cutting a doorway into the oldest wall in the house, one that dated back at least to the 1800s but probably older, the contractor said. It reminded Glory of her first visit with the realtor four years ago, and the unloved state her home-to-be was in. Contractors had descended then, and in retrospect, it seemed like the remodel had taken only a few weeks.

Crunch. The sound of crumbling stucco rained down, making a mess on the portal. The clunk-clunk-clunk of hammer taps, looking for support studs. Soon they'd stop for lunch and that would take them two hours at least. Joseph had promised they would nail up plywood over the exposed walls every night, and sweep up the mess as they went along. It struck Glory that there had to be some kind of primal urge in men to tear things down, to look inside, to understand how things were built and imagine they could do it better this time. All she could think was how crabby she'd be when that fine coating of plaster dust covered every surface.

Four weeks was thinking positively.

Oh, well. In her last phone call with her mom, Ave had said, "Pish-posh. With a newborn, the more noise the better. The last thing you want is everyone tippy-toeing around a baby. She needs to learn to sleep through racket or you'll never have your life back. Now, what names have you come up with? I've always liked the name Mabel, myself. Or how about Myrtle? Or Wilma? Those are good, old-fashioned names that stand the test of time."

Mabel Vigil? A somber-faced portrait from the Palace of the Governor's archives came to mind, some naïve East Coast wife who followed her husband across the prairie and found herself living in a shack with a dirt floor, waking every morning to the braying of donkeys. Glory placed one hand on her swollen belly. Your name will come the minute I see you, she promised her daughter. Eddie, the Italian greyhound, snuggled next to her on the couch. Every time the baby kicked, he growled at being disturbed from his sleep. More tapping, more stucco/ adobe falling. The house wasn't the only place running out of space. Sometimes she could make out the length of the baby's arm or leg against her flesh. So crowded in there. Another month, Dr. Montano said. The time will fly by.

On the wings of a tortoise, Glory thought, and as she heard another chunk of wall drop, she shut her eyes.

Halle came in through the front door with two grocery totes filled with green chile peppers. "I bought out Whole Foods," she said, and dumped them out on the coffee table in front of the couch.

Eddie grabbed one, and Glory took it from him without moving an inch. "Explain to me why we need a thousand chiles?"

"To string them for the tree, of course."

"What happened to tinsel?"

"Not New Mexican enough. Think of the green against the silver tree, the purple lights, and all these ornaments. It's going to be stunning. I'll ask Joseph to take pictures, make a brochure, put them in the hotels and restaurants, and start a business decorating for the holidays. I have great taste." She took out a spool of thread and a pack of needles.

Glory wished she had a camera, because someone needed to capture on film Halle threading a needle, otherwise no one would ever believe it. When she lived in California, Halle hired an interior designer to decorate her house for the holidays, a different theme every year, paired with wines Bart saved for the parties they threw, or exotic drinks they served, like that one year, "Sand in Your Shorts." "Sounds like a wonderful idea," Glory told her, thinking Halle was in for another disappointment. "Be sure you don't rub your eyes."

"Jeepers, Glory," Halle said. "Just because I had a cleaning lady doesn't mean I can't learn a few domestic tasks. Why don't you help me? It's not like lifting your arms will send you into labor."

"It's more fun watching you do all the work."

"You always were the lazy sister," Halle said, and without missing a beat, Glory answered, "I see you've taken up bald-faced lying."

Halle laughed. "How much do you weigh? Next to you, that poor dog looks like a stick."

The little greyhound was sleeping on his back, leaning against her belly, cockroaching. Glory patted Eddie's chest, and he groaned happily. "He's helping me rest up for the big day."

"The other day I was reading about those water births. It's supposed to be easier on the baby."

"Joseph would have apoplexy. I'll have the baby the old-fashioned way, in a hospital with an epidural and my cheering section. Did I tell you Juniper decided she wants to be there?"

Halle squinted at the eye of the needle. "That's the best advertisement for birth control and safe sex ever."

"No sex is safe," Glory said. "Look at me."

"You do look a bit like that whale Captain Ahab was always chasing."

"A hungry whale. Why don't you take a break from the chiles and make me a snack? I'm feeling like red grapes. Peeled. And some sliced cheddar. That Dubliner cheese you bought at Trader Joe's."

Halle made a disgusted sound. "I'm not your slave."

Glory laughed. Halle indignant with her sister was a recovering Halle. She still broke down in tears a couple of times a week, trying to puzzle out how her marriage had died. Glory listened and said things would get better, that mourning takes time. Halle's response was always the same, How long, dammit? Glory had no answer for that, but Halle's heartbreak was certainly getting things done around the house. She had painted the baby's room, assembled the crib and changing table, stockpiled diapers that would last little No-name until her teenage years, and already bought the baby book. There was the sound of another crash, and Glory groaned. "I don't suppose you'd go see what is happening out there?"

"How about I put on some Christmas music to drown out the noise?"

"Nothing overly jolly, okay?" Glory watched her sister fiddle with the iPod system Juniper had set up. She had no idea how it worked and didn't really care. The purple twinkle lights blinked from the tree and the smell of chiles in the air reminded her of the roasters that sprang up in the fall in one parking lot or another around town. Tomorrow Casey and Aspen would arrive. They'd bunk with Juniper in her room, where a trundle bed had been installed until the addition was finished.

Halle fiddled with the volume, and the air was filled with Vivaldi's violin concerto in A minor. Halle returned to her chile stringing and Glory felt the music soar through her heart.

"Ladies," Joseph said, tracking dust into the great room, "take a look at what Clemente and I uncovered."

Cupped in his hand was what looked like a bird's nest, or a mummy's wrappings, the cloth was so disintegrated. Inside was a four-inch-by-four-inch retablo, the paint faded and crackled over time to a matte finish. The painting of a madonna was unmistakable, with a golden halo and a blue cape—the Virgin Mary's colors. Beneath it were the words, "*Nuestra señora de los Dolores.*"

"What's that mean?" Halle said.

"Our Lady of the Sorrows," Joseph translated. "Dolores."

"Juniper is going to love that," Glory said.

"Where is my arbolita?" Joseph asked. "I wanted to show it to her right away."

"Out having coffee with Chico. So where did you find it? In between wall studs? Was there anything else?"

Joseph frowned. "It was in a nicho. Clemente said we had to tread carefully, this part of the house being so old and the structural beams in who knew what shape. This nicho had been stuffed with newspaper and plastered over, just barely. I guess the rags kept it intact."

"Are you going to take it to the museum?" Glory said.

"No," Joseph said. "The museum has retablos coming out their ears. This one wants to stay here, where it's lived for two hundred years. We're going to move the doorway over a couple of feet in order to keep the nicho intact."

Glory smiled. "I think that will make our Dolores happy. Who knows? Maybe she'll decide it's time to move on."

"I doubt that very much," Halle said. "Dolores is not going to abandon Colibri Road just because you found some old relic. We're her reason for being. Her audience."

"You're probably right," Joseph said. "Anything I can get for you?"

Glory smiled. "Right after you sweep up the dirt you tracked indoors you should call Juniper."

"Sorry about the dirt. You know, I was thinking we could take Casey to visit my dad's farm. We could all go, even the dogs, get out of your hair for a few days."

Glory reached over and tugged on his jeans. "No way. I like you in my hair."

"Eww, stop," Halle said. "None of that double-entendre mushy business while I'm in the room." She added another pepper and Glory could hear the squeak of the needle going through the jalapeño's flesh. The smell was making her hungry, but then, what wasn't?

Joseph said, "*Hermana*, if that sounds suggestive to you, maybe you're the one with the dirty mind."

"Right," Halle said. "Takes one to know one."

"I'm going to get the broom before this discussion goes out of control," Joseph said.

Glory was ashamed of herself, complaining about a little bit of dirt, considering how full the house would be once Casey and Aspen arrived—and their dog. Such was life, handing you a new complication just when you thought your plate couldn't hold any more. Somehow you found the room. Besides, there was nothing she could do other than lie here, waiting. For Aspen to be released, for Casey to arrive; Halle, for her divorce papers; and, lest anyone forgot, the baby who was still without a name. They hadn't even gotten to Christmas.

Then she heard a shriek and saw that Halle was pressing her palms over her eyes and wailing. "I told you not to touch your eyes," Glory said. "Joseph," she called out, "there's eyewash in the master bathroom. Can you fetch it for my sister?"

"Right away," he said.

"Does he have to be so freaking optimistic?" Halle said,

splashing water from her drinking glass onto her eyes, ruining the careful makeup she plastered on every morning.

"Unfortunately," Glory said. "That's just the way he is."

Juniper met Chico at the Plaza Starbucks. She walked in the door, looked around, and there he was, seated at the table near the front window, two coffees in front of him.

"Hi," Juniper said. "I can't believe you'd voluntarily drive up in this weather."

"I got you a latte, hope that's okay."

"They're only my favorite," she said. In her pocket, she felt her cell phone buzz. It was probably another text from Topher, and she didn't feel like answering it. After all she and Chico had been through, Topher's coffeehouse gigs and declarations of love seemed unimportant. Since the day they found Casey, Chico had called her every day, asking about her sister, how Aspen was doing, and what she was reading or listening to or just thinking about.

"The coffee's pretty good here," Chico said.

"Not as good as the Standard's, but it's decent."

Juniper's phone buzzed and vibrated. She took it out of her purse, frowned at it, and set it on the table between them.

"I heard from Louella," Chico said.

"What did she say? I hope she liked my paper."

"She loved the photos."

"And the rest of it?"

"Well," he said, "she said it was kind of 'long.'"

Juniper laughed. "It is. But it turned out to be a complicated story."

"Speaking of stories, she had one to add to it. That's why I wanted to meet you."

The cell phone buzzed again.

"Jakob Dylan?" Chico said.

She nodded. Fifteen texts this morning alone.

Why weren't you at my gig?

I thought you were going to help me proof my essay?

Where were you last night?

"At some point you're going to have to respond," Chico said. He was dressed in a red-and-black buffalo-check wool shirt over a crisp white T-shirt, and one of those Elmer Fudd caps with ear flaps, and thank goodness, because they were so near the door that every time someone opened it to go in or out, it felt like a blast from the Arctic.

"I'm deciding what to say," Juniper said.

"I bet I can help you with that."

She handed him the phone. "Go for it."

Chico turned it sideways and started typing. Juniper thought, Look at us, we're not even thirty years old, but we're all heading toward trigger-joint surgery. I should become an orthopedic surgeon. Too bad I hate blood. After a minute, he handed it back to her without having pressed SEND.

She read what he'd written and smiled. Then, looking up at him, making and without breaking eye contact, she pressed SEND. She turned the phone off and put it in her purse.

"I can't believe you did that," he said.

"Why not? You pretty much said everything I was trying to say."

"Do you want to go have lunch?" he asked. "My treat."

"I'm not really hungry."

"What about a refill on your coffee?"

She held up her hands, which were trembling. "I'm already flying on the caffeine express," she said. "Tell me what Louella said."

"Remember her saying one of her grandmothers worked for a white lady on Colibri Road?"

"Did she find any photos?"

He shook his head no. "Isn't it enough to discover that you guys are connected in another way besides Casey?"

Juniper sipped her latte. "I guess I'm addicted to sherds and bones, stuff I can hold in my hands. Was that it?"

"She said the lady she worked for took care of injured hummingbirds. Her garden was full of them."

"We get a lot in the summertime," Juniper said.

"I thought we might go to the Palace of the Governors's archives," Chico said.

"Why would we do that?"

"Because if there are any photos or stories, that would be where to start looking for them."

"Right now?"

"Why not?"

"Is this a date, or an anthropology thing?"

"Would that make a difference?"

She set her coffee down. "Let's go before you change your mind."

"Don't forget your scarf."

They stepped over the guitar player and his dog sitting outside Starbucks, and walked down San Francisco Street, passing holiday shoppers, women wearing Indian-blanket coats in patterns as old as time, couples headed for lunch at La Fonda. Even on the coldest day of the year Indians sat in the eaves of the Palace of the

Governors, jewelry laid out to sell. One vendor had a cache of antique postcards, and they stopped to look at them. "That's Acequia Madre," Chico said. "Colibri Road is less than a block away. This photo probably dates to 1900, 1910."

"If only there was a postcard of our street back then," Juniper said. "Wouldn't that make the perfect Christmas present for my mom and dad?" She held up another card. "Look at that poor burro. He's got to be carrying an entire bale of hay."

"Or you could think of it this way, he's packed his own lunch."

She laughed and bought all ten postcards, thinking someday Aspen might like to see what old-time Santa Fe looked like. They walked down the sidewalk to the side entrance of the museum gift shop.

"They have the most popular photos for sale in the gift shop," Chico said. "You can order anything from the digital archives."

The computer in the gift shop provided instant access. While they browsed, the clerk chatted on the phone with some book vendor.

"No Colibri Road anywhere," Juniper said, after trying all kinds of search options and coming up with the same result: *Your search has produced 0 records.*

"Why does it have to be that exact road?" Chico said.

"Duh. Because we live there?"

"Think about it," Chico said. "That's like saying only the turquoise mined in the state is worth making into jewelry. It all comes from the same earth. Try Acequia Madre, Canyon Road, and the Plaza."

In a sepia-toned photo entitled "Acequia Madre near Manhattan Street," they studied a mill built of adobe bricks and stone. In another photo, dated 1910, a little girl with a bowl haircut stood in the road next to a dog that reminded Juniper of Curly, Casey's dog. That photo lifted Juniper's heart and at the same time broke it, because while it was a cliché that pictures could be worth a thousand words, it meant nothing if you didn't speak the same language. They tried to puzzle out a surviving page of a newspaper handwritten in a spidery, thin script.

"The handwriting is gorgeous," Juniper said, "but I can't read a word of it."

"There's actually a computer program that deciphers cursive," Chico said.

"You're such a geek."

"Takes one to know one."

Juniper smiled. Chico leaned in so close to her that she could smell the soap he'd used to wash his face. They scrolled though photos of a fire at the men's club just off the Plaza, the smoke clouds reminding her of Casey's pot, the object that had taken Juniper from pride to anger to an unthinkable reunion. There was an article on a flood that had been traced back to the 1600s, decipherable by the absence of trash in a layer of strata, and there were so many portraits of white men with mustaches that a stranger might think there were no other ethnicities in early Santa Fe. "Rich men, outlaws, and criminals," Juniper said. "Where are the ordinary people?"

"They're the ones behind the camera," Chico said.

Juniper looked through every photo in the store, finally settling on the Acequia Madre photo of the girl and the dog. "If only this dog was a hummingbird," she said. "Then it would be a great Christmas present."

Chico opened the door for her. "This date isn't over yet. Follow me."

"Where are we going?"

"To the Frank Howell gallery. We're going to find you a hummingbird."

A few minutes later they stood in front of a print of Frank Howell's painting *Reunion*. A woman was front and center, the subject of the painting. Her eyes were closed, her arms lifted, palms facing upward. She wore some kind of deer-hide garment, and her long hair was streaked with silver, like a grandmother's. Surrounding her were twenty hummingbirds in flight. "Oh, my gosh, Chico," Juniper said. "How did you ever find this?"

"School," Chico said. "In Howell's biography, he said, 'The painting is a wonderful kind of inner mirror, and reflects the inner you, not your external appearance.'"

"I'm impressed. How do you know so much about art?"

He shrugged. "A long time ago, I wanted to be a painter. I was never much good at it, but occasionally I dabble."

"Are you kidding me?" Juniper said. "Can I see your paintings?"

"Let me think about it," he said, and Juniper felt the distance between them return to TA and student.

She looked at the price tag. "Too bad this print costs more than my car," she said.

"This isn't the only painting he did with hummingbirds," Chico said. "Excuse me, where are your posters?" he asked the clerk. The man pointed toward a bin near the window. Chico began paging through them.

"There's something I've been wanting to say to you," Juniper said.

Chico didn't look up. "Is this about your grade again?"

"It's not about school. There's something I want to tell you, but I'm nervous."

He pulled three posters out and leaned them against the wall. "None of these is over forty bucks. My personal favorite is *White Hummingbird,* but *Two Sisters* might be the most appropriate choice."

"You're such a damn stork," she said.

"A stork? What did I do now?"

"Maybe you should be asking yourself what you didn't do. Did you even hear what I said?"

He looked at his watch. "I should get going before it gets dark," he said. "One of my headlights is out."

"Yeah, no kidding."

He looked back at her. "What did I do wrong?"

"Haven't you ever had a girlfriend?"

"Not since grade school. Harriet Wilkinson. I gave her my St. Christopher medal and she threw it in the dirt. I've kind of given girls a wide berth since then."

"That's a good reason to retreat from the female gender."

"It made sense to me."

She reached out her hand and took his. "What a load of bullshit. You've liked me since the day I brought those pottery sherds into Dr. Carey's office."

"I won't deny it."

"Why didn't you say something?"

"For a brilliant student of anthropology, you are a very slow girl," he said, and smiled at her. In fact, he couldn't seem to stop smiling. He squeezed her hand, got brave enough that he put his arm around her, and kissed her forehead. In the background, they heard the clerk clear his throat and they broke apart. Juniper could feel the ghost of his lips against her cold face.

"So we're buying the albino hummingbird and the *Two Sisters*," he said to the clerk. "Can you put on a ribbon or gift wrap?"

"Happy to," the man said, and wrapped each print in butcher paper, applying a purple stick-on bow. "Thanks for shopping local, and happy holidays. After the first of the year we'll be relocating to Canyon Road."

"Thanks," Juniper said.

Posters in hand, they walked out onto the sidewalk, into the street, at the corner of Washington and Palace of the Governors, chained off from through traffic. They stepped carefully around icy patches, passing shoppers toting bags and gifts. A snowflake or two whirred through the air. A hotel van pulled to the curb of the Inn of the Anasazi, unloading passengers, and that was when Chico finally got up the nerve to kiss her. Topher had been an accomplished kisser with all the right moves, easy for her to follow. Chico was learning as he went along, and Juniper knew that what she would remember about this moment was that. Chico being so tall she had to stand on her tiptoes, and still he had to duck his head to reach her. It occurred to her that the more they kissed, the better he was doing. When they broke apart, they looked at each other and neither said a word. They began walking toward his car as if it had been the plan all along. Juniper tried to memorize every detail so she could relive the moment later: the sidewalk cold under their feet, the store windows lit up and decorated for Christmas, how the snow appeared blue in the shadows. The wind chapped her face and she didn't care how red her cheeks were, or that she wasn't wearing makeup, or had coffee breath, or any of those things. Chico's walk relaxed, in tune with her step for step, and she thought, *I could spend the rest of my life with this guy. Out of all the people on the planet, how is it possible we found each other?*

A crowded house on Christmas Eve was nothing out of the ordinary to Glory. In California, there were always foster sons passing through, or Lorna and Juan's Christmas party, and if it wasn't that, she was preparing for an upcoming wedding, or taking care of a lame horse, or worrying how she was going to pay the mortgage. Since moving to New Mexico, there had been none of that, but this Christmas her house was filled up in a different way. Halle was in the kitchen making peppermint-candy cupcakes. Casey and Aspen sat by the Christmas tree, their first one ever. Whenever Aspen reached for a bulb, Casey gently took hold of her hand. "No, that's where the ornaments live," she explained, and by the time she finished the sentence, Aspen was already on to the next new adventure. Glory wondered what next Christmas would be like, when her own little girl was here. Poor Joseph, surrounded by women, except for the dogs.

Curly was trying to win Eddie over, but Eddie remained unconvinced. No dog has ever worked so hard to fit in, she thought, while Eddie "tested" Curly by stealing all the dog toys and sitting on them. Curly wagged her tail, ever hopeful. Caddy lay by the fire, near enough for Casey to reach out and touch him. Glory wondered, did he remember the day Casey disappeared? Was it Casey's DNA that informed him that this was Juniper's sister? Did the sight of him remind her of the terrible night she was taken?

Since their arrival a few days ago, Aspen had been exploring the house, opening closets and drawers and emptying them of their contents, whether it was pots and pans or winter coats or file cabinets. Juniper patiently allowed her to dress up in her clothes, then reminded her, "Now, those aren't your things. You can play with them, but you'll need to put them back. Here's your dresser. Most of the drawers are empty, but after Christmas they'll be filled to the brim with new things that are all yours."

Not one word had been uttered about Topher, but there was plenty of talk about Chico. Glory noticed how Juniper jumped every time her cell phone rang. She'd take the calls privately, and after she hung up she walked around the house humming, offering to vacuum or chop firewood. When she asked if Chico could come for Christmas, Joseph said, "Your mom has a full house," and Glory interrupted to say, "What's one more person? But he'll have to sleep on the floor." Juniper assured her he was the most flexible person ever, and he'd be fine with that, and thanked them so profusely that Glory and Joseph exchanged a knowing glance. The day after Casey was found, Joseph had formally declined the Candela job. He was busy organizing an animal-therapy program, recruiting volunteers to staff it, and arranging training.

At the center of things, watching her family's massive life changes, Glory lay waiting and wondering, watching Aspen in particular. There was something about the little girl that seemed odd, and Glory wondered if it had to do with the scarring on her heart. It left her with premature ventricular tachycardia; Glory could always tell when her heartbeat was out of rhythm, because the girl would cough. Not that it seemed to inhibit her activities, far from it. Here she was, one week out of a coma yet running around a strange house, eating everything that was offered to her, and chattering as if she had grown up around these people forever. Glory envied her the ability to move on, and was grateful that the task of mothering kept Casey busy. Nearing seven, Aspen still entertained imaginary friends— perfectly understandable, Ardith Clemmons said, given her seclusion. And oftentimes she sat by herself telling that story Casey had entertained her with over the years. *One day the princess stopped sleeping and got up and walked away from the bad man and came to Santa Fe, New Mexico, because the Christmas tree needed her help and so she made cupcakes for it and remembered to feed the birds because it was winter and the flowers were all asleep . . .*

Every day, Juniper and Aspen filled up the bird feeder and put out fresh water. Aspen stood at the window naming the birds: wren, woodpecker, scrub jay, raven, sparrow, first by their common names, and then in Latin. Joseph had given her a bird book, and now she carried it everywhere she went. "That little girl is very smart," he said, marveling at how quickly she learned. She seemed particularly enamored with the sparrows, of which there were several varieties she seemed determined to master. "Chipping sparrow, rufous sparrow," she called out, and every time she spotted one, she ran to Glory and patted her belly. When she laid her little hand on Glory's stomach, she would say, "Hello, Sparrow," and then run off to look out the French doors, or to watch the feeder. She had no fear of Glory's chickens, she was at ease with the dogs—Dodge especially seemed to realize she needed him to be calm—and while that made sense, it still seemed extraordinary for a dog who'd been out of control only a few weeks earlier. The first time the house ghost groaned, Aspen looked up at the ceiling and said, "Shh, Dolores, time to be quiet."

Had Juniper told her about the ghost? Glory wondered. Had Joseph? The retablo had been moved to the fireplace mantel, above the Christmas stockings, beeswax candles, and garland of pine. Halle said she hadn't told her, and how did a person explain a ghost to a child who was just learning about Santa, anyway? Yes, she was odd, but bless her heart, with everything she'd been through, wasn't that the least of her problems? Glory no longer complained about the drywall dust, what with flour flying through the air and more of the sprinkles going into Aspen's mouth than on the cookies, but what the dog didn't lick up the broom would take care of, and Glory found herself missing housework, just a little, something to make her feel a part of the crowd versus lying idle at the center of things.

Halle surprised Glory. She let the little girl play with her makeup, pester her from breakfast to dinnertime, played Candyland until even Glory never wanted to hear the word again. Ardith Clemmons had driven down from Española and come to their house to engage the family in therapy, so while they got used to each other, Casey would still be able to count on her to feel safe. Seth White Buffalo hadn't been found—yet, Joseph said. But all those years she'd been captive, thinking her parents and sister were dead, and then finding out her mother had committed suicide had taken a toll. Casey had nightmares, so she slept with Juniper and Aspen. Some nights Glory woke up and could hear them talking.

"Things will improve," Ardith Clemmons said. "They already have."

Christmas Eve, everyone went on the Canyon Road walk except for Glory. She hadn't felt well all day, so she went to bed early, a little cranky. If you could call this sleep, she said, when she woke up to pee what seemed like every ten minutes. At three A.M. the house was quiet as she made her way to the bathroom for what she hoped was the last trip until morning. But when she stood up, she felt a trickle between her legs, and knew at once it was her water breaking. She cleaned up, changed into dry clothes, and checked her overnight bag. She went to the great room to look at the Christmas tree until she had her first contraction, figuring she might as well let Joseph sleep, because who knew how long labor would last?

But when she walked into the great room, there was Aspen, lying on her stomach, staring at the Christmas tree. "Hello there," Glory said. "What are you doing up?"

Aspen, adorable in Snoopy footed pajamas, looked at her with big eyes. "Waiting for Sparrow."

Glory smiled. "I think you mean Santa."

"No," Aspen said, her little voice a trill. "Santa comes tomorrow. Sparrow is coming tonight," she said, and she stood up and placed both her hands on Glory's belly.

Glory felt a contraction then, not as painful as she'd imagined, but not exactly comfortable, either. "How did you know that?" Glory asked, taking Aspen's tiny hands and giving her a squeeze.

Aspen hugged her back, and said, "Dolores told me."

Outside, the snow was falling all around them.

ACKNOWLEDGMENTS

It would take hundreds of pages for me to properly thank the folks who help me along the way in writing a book. To my agent, Deborah Schneider, your wisdom, guidance, and belief in my writing all these years have kept me going, and I am so grateful for your friendship. Likewise, it is my great good fortune to work with Nancy Miller at Bloomsbury, the editor who has made writing these last two books the most rewarding experience of my career. I'm blessed to have writer friends from whom I derive solace, inspiration, and strength: Anne Caston, Rich Chiappone, Earlene Fowler, Judi Hendricks, Nicky Leach, Caroline Leavitt, Jodi Picoult, Wolf Schneider, Sherry Simpson, David Stevenson, Candelora Versace, and Carolyn Turgeon (especially for her feedback and suggestions). There are two vices that keep me going, Coca-Cola Cherry Zero, and Old Gringo boots (thank you, Amy Fairchild and Ernie, for finding my green-and-purple Takas, which made my author photo). For thirty-eight years my husband Stewart has been my touchstone, my rock, and the light of my life, along with our dog posse both here and in heaven. To my son Jack, newly college-graduated, newly single, your future is bright and filled with rewards you can't see right now, but trust me when I say that the good parts are coming and will provide a foundation to build on and remember. Writing books has always been my dream and brings me great joy, and every day I am thankful for the opportunity, but Jack, you are and always will be my one true masterpiece.

A NOTE ON THE AUTHOR

Jo-Ann Mapson is the author of ten previous novels, including
the beloved *Hank & Chloe*, *Blue Rodeo* (also a CBS TV movie),
and the *Los Angeles Times* bestsellers *The Wilder Sisters* and *Bad
Girl Creek*, a book-club favorite. She lives in Santa Fe, New
Mexico, with her husband and their three dogs.

www.joannmapson.com